Canaletto

and the Case of Westminster Bridge

Janet Laurence is also the author of the successful series of culinary mysteries featuring Darina Lisle, the most recent *Death à la Provencale*, *Diet for Death* and *Appetite for Death*.

Janet began her career as a cookery writer, producing a weekly column for the *Daily Telegraph*. She has written four cookery books, contributed articles to a number of publications, including a series on historical cooking for *Country Life*, and is the author of *The Craft of Food and Cookery Writing*. Under a pseudonym she also writes contemporary women's fiction.

Canaletto and the Case of Westminster Bridge is her tenth novel.

Janet Laurence

Canaletto

AND THE CASE OF
WESTMINSTER BRIDGE

PAN BOOKS

First published 1997 by Macmillan

This edition published 1998 by Pan Books
an imprint of Macmillan Publishers Ltd
25 Eccleston Place, London SW1W 9NF
and Basingstoke

Associated companies throughout the world

ISBN 0 330 36982 2

1 3 5 7 9 8 6 4 2

A CIP catalogue record for this book is available from
the British Library.

Phototypeset by Intype London Limited
Printed and bound in Great Britain by
Mackays of Chatham PLC, Chatham, Kent

This is for my darling husband, Keith,
with many thanks for everything he does
to make my writing possible

Acknowledgements

I have consulted too many sources to list them all but my greatest debt for information on Canaletto has been various books by J.G. Links. My attention was first drawn to Canaletto's time in England by the *Canaletto & England* exhibition mounted by the Birmingham Museums & Art Gallery in 1993 in association with Merrell Holberton Publishers, London, and sponsored by British Gas. I also have to thank David Bomford of the National Gallery, London, for much valuable information, and Rosemary Baird, Curator at Goodwood House, for showing me the paintings by Canaletto owned by the Duke of Richmond and Gordon. The full, fascinating story of the building of Westminster Bridge is told in *Old Westminster Bridge, The Bridge of Fools* by R.J.B. Walker (David & Charles, 1979). The staff of the London Library have provided much help and information. However, any errors in this story are mine and mine alone.

Finally, I am deeply grateful to Tessa, Shelley and Maggie, known as The Group, for their invaluable help and advice during the writing of this book. Any merit it has is in large measure due to them.

Prologue

There was no moon. Only stars studded a clear but ominously dark sky.

Footsteps stumbled along a rough path and a voice cursed, slurring the words 'Devil take it, where's the lantern, you damned knave?'

'Keep to the path, man.' A lantern was swung forward, hanging from a hawthorn stick, its light unsteady and inadequate.

Another stumble, another curse. 'Fairbrass, where the devil are you? You said you'd help me home.'

'Here, Scallion, put your arm around my shoulders. Don't foul the lantern, you fool!'

The hawthorn stick was knocked from Fairbrass's hand and its light extinguished amongst the scrub edging the stony path.

As Fairbrass cursed and bent for the stricken lantern, Scallion picked up the stone he'd marked beside the path and brought it crashing down on the other's head.

The aim was true; Fairbrass fell without a sound.

With a small grunt of satisfaction, Scallion removed a dagger from the scabbard he wore inside his breeches and tested its edge. Working by starlight, he turned the unconscious body over and drew the knife across its throat in a deep slit from ear to ear. A ghastly gurgle issued from the dying man's windpipe and in the darkness Scallion smiled. There was no trace now of the unsteadiness he had shown blundering along the path.

He wiped the bloody blade on a clump of grass and returned it to its scabbard. He found the lantern, took out his tinderbox and relit it. Holding the light high, he searched out the copse of scrubby trees he knew was a little way ahead, off the path, on the edge of the quarry. With a piece of twine from his breeches' pocket, he tied the lantern to a convenient overhanging branch. That would mark the copse.

Back he went to the dead man. For a moment he stared down at the body, thinking. If he dragged it by the heels, it could leave tracks, a trail to its resting place. On the other hand, if he threw the body over his shoulder like a sack of grain, his clothes would be stained with blood.

Then Scallion laughed. A fox, attracted by the smell of death, lifted a paw as it listened, then slunk away, chilled by the sound.

Rapidly Scallion stripped off shirt and breeches. Mother-naked, he bent and flung the dead man's body over his right shoulder then staggered towards the copse and into the trees, ignoring the whippy branches that scratched and tugged at his flesh.

In the little wood, his eyes accustomed to the dark, he concealed the body amongst the undergrowth as best he could.

There were those who could cavil at the way the deed had been done but, damn the world to hell, its execution had been good enough.

He emerged from the wood, pulled up a bunch of

fresh grass, wiped the stickiness from his ribs and shoulder blade, then dressed himself again.

His mission was complete. The job had been tedious but not difficult.

Scallion checked his knife and his purse. His next commission involved travel abroad. It promised to be even easier and more lucrative than this one.

Chapter One

If only his stomach hadn't been so uneasy, Canaletto might have enjoyed his first sight of London on a fine May morning in 1746. As it was, interest fought with nausea and lost.

It had to have been last night's salt pork. The end of the victuals laid in for the voyage from Venice and no doubt wormridden. *Dio*, what wouldn't he give for a dish of rice soup! Made to old Maria's receipt.

Face as cratered as Vesuvius, taciturn and ancient as the hills, she had been efficient, parsimonious and a marvellous cook. Would he find anyone as suitable as Maria to look after him in London? And just what would English food do to his Italian digestion?

Well, at least this interminable voyage was now almost over. The anchor had splashed down into the dirty waters, sails were being furled and his fellow passengers were gathering eagerly along the boat's sides.

He knew he should join them but now that they were here, his courage failed. Suddenly he felt again all the reservations that had rushed upon him with the first pitch and yaw of this infernal vessel as it met the Adriatic swell.

They'd not been a day out of Venice before a fellow passenger, a merchant trading in silks, had insisted on

4

dragging out his details, and then given a silent whistle, his inquisitive brown eyes popping out. '*The* Antonio Canal, the topographical artist Canaletto? The one who paints all the famous views of Venice for visiting aristos?'

What exquisite delight to hear himself spoken of with such admiration! Canaletto had shrugged deprecatingly. 'I paint Venice, yes,' he'd said modestly. Then couldn't resist adding, 'I have some fame for my views, it is true.'

The merchant had looked at him quizzically, 'Deserting your homeland, are you? The English wanting views of London? A Canaletto of their grand dwellings?' Was there a hint of scepticism there? A suggestion that the possibility of this was remote? No, it couldn't be.

'There is a new bridge across the Thames,' he'd said with some of the excitement he'd felt on first learning of this. 'At Westminster. Everyone talks of it, says it should now be open.'

'And, cunning fellow that you are, you're going to paint it for the mad English, eh?'

Canaletto had given a slight smile and, never one to open up to strangers, said no more.

The merchant had hardly noticed. 'You are no doubt sensible of the situation. We all go to London to get rich,' he'd added expansively. 'You should see the building that is going on, the shops that are opening. The clink of coins is everywhere.'

'You would invest money in London?' Canaletto had asked cautiously, remembering the heavy leather satchel that reposed below decks.

'Invest? Why, sir, I invest every trip. No better

return, no safer market.' Then he'd rather spoilt the impression of careful conservatism he'd given by adding, 'Today London is the home of opportunity. In London there is hardly a man but is looking to make his fortune. In London a man can buy himself position and everything needed to enjoy it. London in fact, my dear sir, is the place to be.' With an airy wave of his hand, the merchant had gone off to talk to another passenger.

Canaletto had been left torn between confidence and suspicion. To someone accustomed to the rigid social strata of Venice, London sounded dangerously volatile. Especially for a man of fifty.

A mean-featured fellow who'd come aboard at Le Havre and announced his name as Jack Scallion now moved towards him.

Scallion reminded Canaletto of the worst rogues of Venice, a species the painter knew well. He had a darting shiftiness of eye, a knowing twist to his mouth and an ingratiating grin that suggested the wisdom of counting your fingers after shaking hands with him – if you were the sort of fool who'd allow him to get that close. For a finishing detail, Scallion sported a single ornate earring, a golden snake coiled through one of a pair of ears that stuck out like gargoyles on a church.

Picking up his heavy leather satchel, the painter moved hastily to the other side of the boat, his stomach rebelling dangerously against the sudden activity.

He found a convenient coil of rope and sat himself down, hoping his guts would settle. Then was flung roughly to the deck as a sailor pushed him rudely aside and grabbed the rope.

Canaletto exploded in a torrent of imprecations,

tried to rise, groaned, clutched his mouth, then, somehow managing to retain his grasp on his satchel, pushed his way through to a railing and emptied his stomach into the gently moving waters of the Pool of London. *Mama mia*, what an arrival!

He wiped cold sweat from his forehead, pulled a small flask from a pocket in the capacious skirt of his second-best coat and rinsed his mouth with the last of his brandy. Then he adjusted the set of his wig, itchy after the freedom of a bare head for the voyage, and looked at last on London.

What he saw was not reassuring.

A jumbled collection of paltry buildings, nothing of substance among the lot of them. Had he undertaken the perils of this long, unpleasant voyage, brought himself to the very frontier of Europe, the last outpost of civilization before the vast ocean and the savage Americas, for *this*?

A fellow passenger spat into the water and voiced an equally disappointed opinion of their destination. Which, perversely, made Canaletto shrug his shoulders and point out that it was, after all, only the port of London, an industrial quarter. The actual city would surely offer grand buildings and majestic prospects. He almost believed it.

A lighter arrived to take those who would ashore. ''Ere, mate, sling that this way!' A hand reached out to aid Canaletto with his heavy satchel.

He pretended he couldn't understand English and obstinately retained his grip on the heavy bag, stumbling into the boat and scrambling over the planked seating. He had a sour satisfaction in noting Scallion uncomfortably hemmed in between the stout silk merchant and an equally corpulent trader in spices.

Their craft full, the two oarsmen rowed through an army of small wherry boats that darted around the anchored seagoing vessels like fleas round sleepy cats.

The lighter bumped into the wharf, another hand secured the boat to a bollard then offered help to the passengers. But Canaletto, hefting his heavy bag, his face perspiring with effort, clambered ashore on his own.

Wet, slippery stones swayed beneath his buckled shoes with all the unpredictability of the sea. Curse it, why couldn't the ground remain firm, as ground should?

Canaletto's attempts to maintain his equilibrium were not helped by the hubbub around him. The Pool of London might have been a scene from the Inferno. Cargo appeared to be dumped anywhere. Porters shouted. Metal rang on hard stone as the heavy iron circling barrels and securing containers crashed unmusically on the unevenly quarried surface of the quay. Sacks thumped down in a way that threatened to split their hessian; boxes clattered to the ground equally recklessly. Worst of all, the air rang not with the liquidity of Italian but the ugly, jarring accents of English. Until now, Canaletto had never realized how much he loved his native language.

He stood on the quayside with people jostling him from all directions. His sole contact in England was an Irishman he hadn't seen for many years, Owen McSwiney. Could he possibly know when Canaletto's boat would arrive? A doubtful but faint hope that he might come kept the painter scanning faces. Even after so long a time, he would recognize the other man

8

instantly. Canaletto never forgot a face, or any other visual detail.

After a while of being buffeted and jostled, Canaletto accepted that McSwiney had not come to meet his boat. Which meant he would have to try and sort out his boxes and the customs himself.

Canaletto put down his bag. In one of his pockets he had a paper with McSwiney's direction. The sooner he sent for the Irishman, the sooner he'd be provided with a decent glass of wine, something appetizing to eat and, pray heaven, a comfortable bed. Followed by a stimulating talk of patrons and commissions.

Before, though, he had tried more than one pocket for McSwiney's last letter, Canaletto realized the crowds surging around him made this just the sort of situation to suit a sneak thief. On board he'd been incredibly confident about the safety of his property; after all, where could a thief disappear to on a boat? As long as the locks were untampered with, as long as he kept it beside him when they were in port, he'd been happy. Such security was worth the possibility of their ship being taken by a French privateer. Now uneasiness crept up on him like a beggar on the Rialto.

Canaletto found a quiet section of the quay, placed his precious bag between his legs and relished the feeling of its solidity against his calves. He found the letter, then, as he drew it out, his attention was caught by the busy port scene.

Half-furled sails sagged like badly hung sheets on washing lines, sailors lined spars, securing billowing canvas with neat ties, and everywhere masts caught the uncertain sun, graceful geometry against a sky that was dimmed with dirty grey clouds, no clarity of Italian blue here.

Canaletto's fingers itched for pen and paper. The lines those spars made against the jumble of buildings, the impertinence of the little boats that scampered about the water! Lost in the scene, memorizing its effect, he was oblivious to all around him.

He failed to see a mean-faced figure with an ornate gold earring approach. He failed to notice a heavy gantry start to move or to hear someone shout a warning.

Suddenly a figure cannoned into him with stunning force. As he fell, he sensed something whistling through the air above his head. His letter blown from his fingers, he rolled over the slippery stone towards the edge of water-soaked wooden piers and the depths of the Pool of London.

Chapter Two

Green slime slipped beneath Canaletto's fingers as he clawed and scraped for a hold. His feet scrabbled against a bollard and the murk of the river rose up in gut-churning, foetid blasts.

Just before he joined the waves slapping against the wharf, Canaletto's fingers found an iron ring; he clutched at it and swung helplessly just above the Stygian depths of the water.

He shouted for help, looked up and saw a lethally heavy iron gantry hook cutting through the air with vicious force, the centre of its swishing arc at the exact point which his head had occupied the moment before he had been sent careering towards the water.

Canaletto clung to the iron ring, his feet uselessly attempting to gain a purchase on the scum-lined dock wall, and wondered how long he could hold on. Then help arrived. Hands grabbed his arms and hauled him back on to the wet stones. He lay like a beached whale, gasping for breath, fear leaking from every pore. On his back, in foreshortened perspective, he could see the gantry, square-angled like a heavy-duty gibbet, the pendulum motion of its terrible swinging hook gradually slowing against the drear sky. There was no sign of the person who had set it in motion.

'God in heaven, what an idiot! Just standing there waiting for death! Haven't you got ears?' A person in skirts stood over him, breathless and angry. The skirts, he realized, were muddied and torn as though she, too, had slid over the rough-stoned surface of the dock.

Groaning, every muscle in his body aching, Canaletto managed to sit up. Now he could view his rescuer.

She was perhaps nineteen or twenty, hands busy with the hopeless task of trying to straighten her ruined cotton dress.

Angered and frightened in equal measure, he shouted at her, the English words coming fluently, 'Drown me, would you?'

'Huh!' she shouted back at him. 'Prefer to have your head knocked off, would you?'

She was one of the plainest girls he'd ever seen. Not ugly, none of her features was pronounced enough for that. Just plain, with forehead too deep, a nose that was snubbed, face a scintilla too long, mouth a morsel too wide, and a freckled skin. But her hazel eyes had merit, anger made them sparkle and they were set nicely apart. And her hair was the colour of bright copper. Her body, though, lacked curves and there was nothing to tempt a hand to slide round her waist or fingers to toy with the white fichu that decorated the neck of her dress.

But she could have been a Venus come to earth and Canaletto would not have been moved. Twice in his life he had lain his heart before a woman he'd thought as warm and generous in her character as she was beautiful in her person. Each time his worship had been played with as cruelly as a cat plays with a mouse. After the first time, it had taken thirty years before he could trust enough to give himself wholeheartedly again. Only to find himself betrayed once more. Now he assessed women as clinically as he did the buildings he painted.

Around the girl gathered a small but curious crowd debating excitedly exactly what had happened as the hook slowed its homicidal swing.

Then Canaletto saw that his bag was gone.

Panic and rage filled him. He scrambled to his feet, grabbed the girl and shook her, searching for the English he needed. 'My bag, it is took! You do it! Now, you tell me, your accomplice, who he is?'

The hazel eyes first widened then narrowed. A flush coloured the pale face and made her almost pretty.

'That's him!' A grubby youth pointed towards the customs house. Canaletto saw Scallion carrying away his precious satchel.

'That my bag! Stop!'

The figure gave a quick look behind him, heaved the satchel under his arm and broke into a run.

As one the crowd followed, hallooing, crying and whistling as they ran amongst the bales and barrels stacked all around the quay.

Flying in front of them all went the girl, bunching up her skirts as she ran, her small feet carrying her lightly across the uneven ground.

The thief stumbled over an iron bar lying in his path, nearly fell but regained his balance and continued.

Age tells. Too soon Canaletto could run no more. Fighting for breath, anxious beyond belief, he climbed on to an abandoned dray, its carters part of the pursuit, the horses standing patiently. For a moment, the cart bed swayed beneath his feet, creaking and shifting like a boat, then he managed to stand erect and found he could see above the heads of the running crowd. The thief was nearing a collection of crude buildings and narrow passages that stood back from the quay. Canaletto groaned, if he made it there, the thief would lose his pursuers and the bag would be gone forever.

But then the girl was at his heels, swinging her reticule by its cords. The little bag looked too flimsy to do more than swat a fly but somehow it tangled with the villain's legs and brought him down.

With a loud howl, the crowd swooped upon him.

Canaletto scrambled down from his perch and thrust his way through them. He used his elbows and ignored resentful cries until he'd worked his way to where the thief had his arms securely held by a couple of stout watermen, his face distorted with rage and fear.

The girl sat on the bag. She was bent over, panting and holding her side as though nursing a stitch.

As he came through the crowd, she looked up, her eyes sparkling with achievement. 'Signor Canal, all is safe!'

His relief at the bag's recovery was shattered. How did she know his name? And his real name, too, not the diminutive by which he was commonly known.

He hauled the girl off the satchel and knelt down, his legs now trembling so much they could hardly have held him upright had he wanted to remain standing.

He inspected the lock; it wasn't even scratched. The leather, too, appeared to have suffered no more than the expected amount of wear and tear.

Canaletto gave a great sigh of relief. Then he realized that a rumble of resentment was running through the crowd. He gathered his wits. Where was his wig? No doubt in the dock. For the first time he felt the fresh breeze that blew around his naked head with its stubble of hair. Never mind, he could still make a deep and gracious bow, the right leg elegantly displayed. He ignored the dreadful green and brown stains that disfigured the white silk stockings, pushed to the back of his mind the knowledge that his second-best coat and breeches were ruined and summoned his most fluent English. 'Signorina, you have my most profound thanks. First you save my life, then you rescue my poor possessions. Anything within my humble power is yours to command.'

The girl rose, picked up her mob cap and stuffed her copper curls back inside it. 'Not lost your manners with your wits, then, Signor Canal?' She placed her small hands at either side of her waist and looked at him, her head on one side, a town sparrow considering a possible morsel, then broke into a grin. 'Eh, but you're a sight!'

If there was one thing Canaletto hated, it was being made a figure of fun. He, the grand painter, the man of the world, the sophisticate with the manners for every occasion to be the butt of anyone's wit was too much. He took a deep breath, then, suddenly, had to put out a hand to grab the nearest shoulder as profound weakness flooded through him.

Through the mists that threatened to close over his head, he felt himself being lowered on to a barrel. 'Get his head between his knees . . . it's the shock . . . poor gentleman . . . a brandy, who's got a brandy?'

'Hey, watch him!' shouted the girl.

Canaletto heard a roar from the crowd and raised his head in time to see Scallion slip like a well-greased wrestler from the hands that had restrained him. In

15

a moment he'd evaporated into the dark and narrow passages.

Canaletto groaned and sank his head into his hands. How was he to find out the truth of what had happened now?

'Don't 'e fret, sir. Us'll 'ave the watch on him!'

'Aye,' agreed another of the crowd. 'Tell us where you're staying and we'll let you know when he's caught, then you can lodge a complaint with the justices.'

Canaletto reached inside his coat then realized he'd lost the paper with McSwiney's address. What was he to do now?

Chapter Three

Canaletto turned to the man who had asked for his direction, his smart green coat and brilliant red breeches suggesting some position of authority. 'Please do you know a lodging house, respectable, comfortable?'

Details were hurled at him by members of the now helpful crowd. 'You can find him care of Edward Rooker, at the sign of the copper plate in Fleet Street,' said the girl firmly. 'This is Signor Antonio Canal, the famous artist, newly arrived from Venice.' The crowd, already dispersing, were not interested in this piece of information.

'You know McSwiney?' Canaletto asked, trying to get a grasp on the situation.

'McSwiney? No, I know nothing of him. I'm Fanny Rooker, Edward's sister.' The girl bent down and slipped a hand through his right arm. 'Can you manage to walk?'

Carefully Canaletto got himself to his feet.

'Lean on me,' Fanny urged.

She was small but her shoulders seemed sturdy and he felt ludicrously decrepit.

Also furious at his loss of dignity. 'Signorina, Canaletto is not yet senile,' he hissed. Using every ounce of his considerable will-power, he picked up the heavy bag and staggered towards that part of the quay where they were unloading the baggage.

Fanny followed with a sigh that said all men were idiots and this man worse than most.

Before Canaletto had gone more than a few steps, reaction set in and his legs refused to carry him further. He set the bag on the ground, leant over, hands on thighs, and fought to remain on his feet.

The girl was beside him in a second. 'It's a wonder you can walk at all, sir!' she said in a way that made it possible for him to accept help. In a moment she'd got the satchel in one hand with her other arm around him. 'Sit on this bollard and get your breath back. Your bag's here.' She placed it at his feet. 'I'll see to everything else.'

In what seemed a moment Fanny Rooker had found his wig, brushed off the worst of the debris, and settled it back on his head. Then she proceeded to sort out his baggage with remarkable efficiency.

Caneletto sat fighting gratitude with suspicion. Her appearance on the scene was too pat. How did she know who he was? Who had told her he would arrive this morning? Could he trust her? And Edward Rooker, who was he? Weariness soaked through to his bones. But he couldn't stop wondering about Scallion. Was the man a common opportunist? Or something more sinister?

Canaletto thought back. The fellow had come on board at Le Havre. Dressed in rough kersey, a simple holdall slung over one shoulder, he'd sidled up to Canaletto as the painter had stood watching the French port recede, wondering just how rough this last stretch of passage was likely to be. 'Scallion's the name, sir, Jack Scallion. Be interested in a game of cards, would you?'

All the English were mad, the painter had been told in Venice. This fellow certainly was if he thought he could take in one of Canaletto's experience. He'd turned a disobliging shoulder to him. '*Non capisco*,' he spat out.

But the fellow had repeated the question in halting Italian and the painter had had to tell him vividly and idiomatically to be gone.

Which he had. But whichever part of the boat Canaletto went to after that, there was Scallion.

Obviously he had been marked the moment the rogue came on board, then he had grabbed his opportunity on the quay.

The question was, why had Scallion selected him? Canaletto stretched his strengthening legs and contemplated the silver buckles on his shoes. Was it they that had marked him out? But the silk merchant had looked equally prosperous. Could the ruffian have been sent by someone who knew what the painter would be carrying?

But no one had known, had they?

Canaletto thought back. There was one person he'd told, but that was many months ago, when he'd thought they would share life together and it had been natural to discuss his possible plans to come to London. They'd lost touch a long time since. And any plan would have to have involved knowledge of the boat he was coming on. Who had known that? McSwiney, of course, and one or two Italians in London, but they would not have been interested in having him waylaid, surely?

Another oddity was this girl, this Fanny Rooker. How had she known he'd be here this morning? Was she an accomplice of Scallion's playing a deep game or a saviour to whom Canaletto owed an inestimable debt of gratitude? Canaletto looked at the neat figure disputing with a wherryman. Did he have any option but to trust her? He couldn't remember a single one of the lodging house names that had been shouted at him. Even if he could, would it prove any safer than placing himself in this girl's hands, at least until he'd somehow discovered Owen McSwiney?

'Come sir, I've hired a wherry to take us up river.' Fanny was back with a pleased smile. Oh, to have her youth again; to be able to throw off the effects of a headlong dash after a bruising fall with such ease!

With fatalistic calm, Canaletto allowed her to assist him into the small boat where his boxes were already stowed. He huddled beside her in the stern as strong, economical oarstrokes moved them out into the river.

'That's the Tower of London,' Fanny said companionably, indicating a massive turreted square. 'One of the oldest and most historic of our buildings.'

'London has many such fine edifices?' Canaletto asked. He was not, in fact, impressed. The admittedly picturesque pile of dark grey stone had no classical lines, no gracious proportions. Then he told himself not to be so crabby. He'd made masterpieces from material far less promising.

Fanny laughed, a sound somewhere between a chuckle and a ripple that was immediately infectious. Despite his suspicions, Canaletto felt his spirits start to rise as she said, 'Why, London's the finest city in the world, sir. Just look about you!'

He looked but the Tower was the only building with real size and solidity. True, London appeared a large city. Buildings jostled for room beside each other, threatening to tumble into the river. Here and there scaffolding marked new developments and Canaletto remembered that the merchant had called it a booming city. But there was nothing grand, nothing spacious, nothing to match the great palazzos and piazzas of Venice. Canaletto thought of the brushes and pigments stowed in the iron-bound box that now rested in the wherry with his other belongings and felt something approaching despair.

'We are so excited at your arrival, Signor Canal,' Fanny exclaimed, her small hands held neatly relaxed in her lap, her back straight. 'For you to leave Venice and come here! Oh, how our own artists are going to have to look to their laurels! Look, sir, that's the Monument, what they put up after the dreadful fire eighty or so year ago.'

Canaletto looked at the mighty pillar she pointed out. Stray shafts of sun were now breaking through the grey clouds, one caught the gilded, brush-like top and for a moment he could imagine it was on fire.

A cautious optimism began to grow within him. This city was not Venice but it did breathe a life of its own. There, on the river bank, was an octagonal tower that must be part of the water system for the city. It held the eye with a curious charm, and was oddly impressive.

But where was the new bridge? Surely it couldn't be the one they were now approaching, loaded along its length with a great burden of shops and houses that looked as though they had been there for centuries.

'Nay, sir,' replied Fanny to his query. 'That be London Bridge. Westminster Bridge is further upriver.' She clutched at the side of the boat as it rocked against the whirling and eddying of the waters against the great piers. The wherrymen pulled harder at their oars and for a moment it seemed the force would be too strong to allow them beneath the bridge. Canaletto felt again the treacherous movement of his stomach.

'The wherrymen offered us to alight afore the bridge, so we could walk along and then re-embark afterwards,' Fanny said, watching him anxiously. 'But I thought you would not like being parted from your baggage.'

Indeed, he would not!

Then, suddenly, they were through and into a stretch of water as calm as a lake.

And on the limpid surface sat an ornate barge with raised cabin at the bow, its gold and red paint blazing, some twenty oars on each side flashing silvery water as they dipped and feathered.

'What craft is that?'

Fanny screwed up her eyes against strengthening shafts of sun. 'A livery barge, sir. The Goldsmiths', I think.'

'There are many such?'

'More than several, sir. In October the new Lord Mayor has a procession. Quite a sight it is, barges and craft of all sorts.'

This was more promising! Canaletto closed his ears to Fanny's cheerful chatter of London celebrations and turned his attention again to the buildings. On the northern bank there was a veritable forest of spires rising above the ragged roof line. How many churches must there be in this heretic London? Was it, after all, a godly city?

The wherrymen started pulling for the shore and Fanny broke off an account of spectacular pleasure gardens further upriver at some place called Vauxhall to say, 'Here we nearly are.'

'But the new bridge,' Canaletto insisted. 'I must see Westminster Bridge.' He looked ahead but a wide bend in the river cut off his viewpoint. 'It is far?'

'Nay, but I have only contracted with the ferrymen for Whitefriars Stairs,' protested Fanny, her forehead frowning.

Canaletto's normal care over his hard-won money was overcome by his urge to see the sight that had brought him all this way. 'Offer more,' he said grandly, felt in his pocket for some silver and held it out.

Fanny snatched up the coins before the wherrymen had a chance. 'Too much,' she snapped. 'There is a fine view only just round that bend.' She proceeded to bargain with the boatmen and soon reached an accommodation.

The boat continued upriver with Canaletto straining for a first glimpse of this famous bridge, grateful that his eyes seemed not to suffer from age in the same way as his bones. They had not lost any of their legendary keenness.

And quite soon he could make out a series of graceful arches built in a stone so white it almost sparkled.

'Nearer, nearer,' he urged the boatmen.

Excited at last, he imagined the waters populated by elaborate barges, their glistening paintwork backed by that pristine stone, its smooth whiteness set off by a brilliant blue sky (he discounted the smudged grey above them), the whole underpinned by the sparkling river. What a pageant!

Then he looked more closely at the bridge. 'Why, it is not yet finished!' Wooden scaffolding could be seen supporting arches on the southern bank and it was patently clear that considerably more work was needed on the superstructure.

'And danged thing never will be,' one of the wherrymen declared. 'More 'n eight year they been workin' on it.'

It seemed a long time to Canaletto, even for what was obviously a major construction project.

'You have seen enough, sir?' asked Fanny with a trace of worry in her voice.

Canaletto realized that a longer view would cost more money. He nodded to her. 'Is fine,' he said.

The disappointed wherrymen turned their craft and started to row back downriver.

Canaletto now realized that in this part of the river, the two banks offered a dramatic contrast. Around London Bridge the southern bank had been crowded with buildings. Here, though, it held but a narrow band of houses, wharves and boat yards. Beyond were trees and open fields. Yet on the opposite bank were large houses with impressive terraces (nothing compared with Venetian palazzos but they did have a certain dignity and were obviously owned by men of substance), and behind were spires and rooflines stretching far, far back in a rich tapestry of an affluent society. A country cousin looked across the river at city riches that must appear so near and yet so far.

Unlike the canals of Venice that provided a network of links offering easy access, this great water road seemed to divide the city, denying the riches of one part to its so-near neighbour.

The wherrymen brought the boat to shore on the city bank at Whitefriars Steps, well below the new bridge. All around them were timber yards, eloquent testimony to rapid urban growth but equipped with a plethora of wooden gantries that reminded him forcibly of his all too recent escape from death. Climbing a hill ahead of them was a jumble of rickety buildings that looked as though they could house any number of assassins.

Taking firm hold of his satchel, Canaletto disembarked nervously behind Fanny. He was unable to banish a sense of profound apprehension as he stepped from water on to land.

Chapter Four

Safely ashore, Canaletto waited while Fanny organized the carriage of his boxes. Then he followed her up step after step, through a series of narrow and mean passages reeking of the nastier aspects of human existence. Eyes skinned for a reappearance of Scallion or any other rogue, Canaletto fought for breath, shifting his bag from one hand to the other. Once Fanny looked back. 'Doing all right, sir? Not far now, I promise you. Shall I carry your bag?'

He shook his head. He couldn't have spoken, not if the Doge of Venice himself had commanded. Fanny raised an eyebrow, grinned in a way that expressed exactly what she thought of his obstinacy, then continued upwards with enviable speed.

Just when he was about to beg her to stop for a moment, they passed between two tall houses and came out into a wide and busy street. The air rang with the sound of carriage wheels, horses' hooves, the barking of dogs and hawkers' shouts. Children darted dangerously between the vehicles, their shrill cries adding to the cacophony. Down the road tramped a small company of military, followed by a couple of ironic cheers.

Fanny led a confident way through the mayhem hailed by several pedestrians; a large, handsome fellow in a leather jerkin and moleskin breeches gave her a hearty kiss and received a poke in the ribs in exchange. 'Now, Sam Wood, you keep those for Mary.' Fanny's eyes laughed at him. 'And tell her I'll be over tomorrow to start capturing a likeness of your baby as I promised.' Her quick steps crossed the street, evading carriages and sedan chairs. They passed several shops with customers coming and going. At one point an eruption of scaffolding round a new building of brick forced them dangerously off the sidewalk. And Canaletto had to move quickly to avoid being trampled by a horse's hooves. What a contrast to Venice!

There was such a sense of urgency about London. Here was a city developing by the minute. Things happened here. What was it the merchant had said? That this was a place where all came to get rich?

Fanny stopped in front of a shop whose window displayed a large print. Above, a copper plate hanging from iron brackets proclaimed: 'Edward Rooker, Engraver.' She pushed open the door and a bell rang with a musical note.

Very unmusical was the argument inside the shop.

Behind the counter stood what had to be Fanny's brother, Edward Rooker; his open-featured face was a male replica of hers and his eyes were an identical hazel. Even their anger matched that of her own as she had first confronted Canaletto.

'My charges! You complain of my charges! Try finding cheaper! You won't, not for quality work!'

The customer thrust his large, snub-nosed face across the counter. 'You engravers, you're all a bunch of crooks! Parasites on the backs of painters. Well, you can't cheat me! I'm making my own plates and you can give *that* for my business!' A thumb was clicked across two fat fingers under Rooker's nose, then the customer whirled around and stumped out of the shop, pushing past Fanny and Canaletto without apology and slamming the door behind him, leaving behind a quick impression of a bulging forehead, heavy jowls and a personality that had set the air vibrating.

'Oh, Ned! What did you say to Mr Hogarth?' asked a dismayed Fanny.

Edward Rooker picked up a large copper plate and flung it petulantly on the bench behind him. 'I only quoted him a fair price.'

'I told you to make it keen not fair! When I think what engraving his new series could have done for your reputation! You've got little enough . . .' she broke off, bit her lip, took a deep breath and turned to Canaletto.

'Meet my brother, Ned, Signor. One of the best engravers in London.'

Could her appearance at the dock be explained so simply?

It was as if she hadn't spoken. 'What a penny pincher! Can you believe it, first he imports engravers from Paris and now he's going to engrave his works himself!'

'He won't be the first artist to do so,' she said impatiently. 'Ned, here's Signor Canal.'

But Ned had snatched up a jacket from the bench. 'I can't stay here after that.'

For the second time Canaletto was forced to step aside to allow an angry man out of the small shop.

For the briefest of moments Fanny's shoulders slumped then her chin came up. 'I'm sorry, sir, but, as you can see, Ned's really upset.'

'Mr 'Ogarth, he is important painter?'

She blinked at him from a moment. 'Oh,' she said easily, 'he has his following, for those who like the satirical approach. He's not a landscape artist, though. Now, where are those men with your cases?' She darted out of the street door only to be back within the second, organizing the stowing of his luggage and the paying of the porters.

Canaletto brought out his purse but she pushed it away. 'First a bite to eat. You'll be hungry?'

Yes, by God, he was! Canaletto was suddenly aware of the gaping void in his stomach.

'Are all English young ladies like yourself, Signorina Fanny?' he asked, following her up the narrow stairs to a room the size of the shop with a window overlooking the street.

'How like me?'

'So practical, so competent, so in authority?'

At that she chuckled, the delightful gurgle that had attracted him on the boat. 'When Ned reappears I'll ask you to repeat that. He believes his little sister is good for almost nothing.'

She offered him a chair and disappeared.

Canaletto lowered his bag carefully to the floor.

The room was scantily furnished: three chairs, a gateleg table which bore a recent, not very skilful repair to one of the movable legs, a small corner cupboard and a side table. The polished floor was half covered with a faded and worn rag rug. The unlit grate held a dented pewter jug with an arrangement of dried flowers. Everything was dust free and well polished.

Canaletto surveyed everything carefully and decided

that here was a hardworking, respectable household short on income.

On the wall hung a framed print, a topographical view of the Thames at London; that very stretch, in fact, they'd just come up. Originally painted by one Samuel Scott, engraved by Edward Rooker.

Canaletto considered the work of both men carefully. Scott was undoubtedly talented and the engraving had been skilfully done. Edward Rooker might not be the finest engraver in London but he was certainly more than competent.

The patronage of an artist of Canaletto's standing would undoubtedly be of enormous benefit to a struggling engraver. Edward Rooker was in need of benefit, judging by the encounter with the English painter they'd interrupted and Signorina Fanny's reaction.

Was that why the sister had come down to the docks to meet him? But how had she known his boat? And how had she recognized him? Could he be certain she had no connection with Jack Scallion, the thief who had so nearly made away with his precious satchel?

As soon as she reappeared, he needed to question Signorina Fanny closely. In the meantime it would pay him to look again at Samuel Scott's work. Here was an English painter of *vedute*. Someone who could perhaps be considered a rival?

Once Canaletto would have dismissed the very idea as ridiculous, this man by no means approached his own genius. But the days were gone when Canaletto could for all intents and purposes name his own price for a view of the Grand Canal or the Rialto.

He ignored the engraving and strolled restlessly around the small room. Was it just the war, that plaguy dispute between princes over who should succeed to the throne of Austria, that had driven away the flow of rich English, the principal purchasers of his paintings?

So thought Joseph Smith, Englishman and major merchant in Venice, now the consul and for so many years Canaletto's main patron and conduit of orders from English aristocrats.

But during his long voyage, Canaletto had tried to calculate the number of Venetian scenes he'd painted. He'd mentally added up the different views of the Piazza San Marco, then those of the Molo and of the Grand Canal, then all the other vistas, the *vedute*, that his brush had produced. It had soon become too much and he'd abandoned the exercise. Perhaps it was no wonder that commissions had dried up, every English Milord must have at least one of his pictures, several he knew had more.

At that thought he cheered up. If these rich English aristocrats had wanted more than one view of Venice from his brush, surely they would want some of London? And, of course, of their own properties. What other artist was so skilled in distilling the essence of architecture?

A sense of renewed confidence flowed back to Canaletto. After all, Joseph Smith had given him letters of introduction to several of the aristocracy who had ordered from him in the past. But he needed to locate Owen McSwiney. That ebullient Irishman knew his way around society. There must be some way of finding the man. Perhaps the Rookers could help; they were, after all, on the fringes of the artistic world.

And then McSwiney would handle the introductions and negotiate the commissions, for a fee, of course.

Even so, Canaletto should soon be in receipt of sums exceeding even the best of his Venetian income.

The glittering prospect was soothing and Canaletto wandered over to one of the chairs to rest his legs, now aching from his fall. But his attention was caught by the sight of Miss Fanny's reticule sitting on the side table. To his painterly eye the material bulged oddly.

Canaletto went over and picked it up. The weight of the little bag surprised him. After hefting it in his hand for a moment, he gently pulled apart its strings and inspected the contents.

What he saw renewed all his suspicions and added yet another question to the list that had to be asked of Miss Fanny Rooker.

Chapter Five

Fanny closed the door of the Rooker parlour behind her with hands that trembled. For a moment the stresses and strains of the morning threatened to overtake her. But she hadn't come this far to let the situation slip through her fingers now.

She shouted for her sister-in-law.

Lucy did not appear.

Fanny went down the stairs fuming. Since Lucy had married Ned, life in the Fleet Street house had become a misery. Where once Fanny had been mistress, Lucy now ruled; ruled but still expected Fanny to do the work.

And as for Ned, how dared he make such a salma-gundi of this morning, then disappear like that?

Fanny gave another yell for Lucy then locked the street door and went to prepare a tray for their guest. Quickly, efficiently, she assembled food; but, despite all the luggage now immovably placed in the back passage, she had a nasty feeling Signor Canal could evaporate from that upper room like mist off the river.

What a curious fellow he was. Nothing to him, really. Smaller and slimmer than most men she'd met. But with style. My, what style, even with his stained and torn clothes and naked head.

And what eyes the man had! Brilliant grey, they lit

up his thin face. And how he used them. The way he'd studied everything as they came up the river. He'd looked at the water tower as though his eyes were compass points, measuring until every angle must have been noted.

Fanny's uneasiness increased and she stood quite still, her hands arrested in the act of cutting a chunk of cheese. This was a man it would not be easy to fool. Then she told herself robustly that they meant him no harm, had indeed already done him service, and forced herself to get on with the business of collecting food for a hungry man.

Carrying the laden tray upstairs, she pushed open the door of the parlour with her heart beating fast. But Canaletto was still there, his wig askew, the muddy patches on his clothes beginning to give off a curious odour, his long fingers beating a restless tattoo on the arm of the chair.

Fanny placed the tray on the side table, pushing her reticule out of the way. Then she arranged the gateleg table beside her guest, being careful how she placed the damaged leg, and spread a clean cloth. 'Here's small ale, cold mutton, best Cheddar cheese, bread and some butter,' she said as she put down each together with a plate and a knife. Then she poured some of the ale into a pewter mug and handed it to him.

Canaletto looked at the drink doubtfully. 'Is not wine?' he asked. But he polished off the mug quickly enough after Fanny had shaken her head and she refilled it as he hacked off a slice of mutton and chewed at it eagerly.

'Ah, Fanny, at last you're back!'

In came Lucy, looking as though she'd give birth on the best rug at any minute.

'Signor, may I present Mrs Edward Rooker? Lucy, this is Signor Canal.'

Lucy simpered as the artist rose and gave her a small bow, then walked heavily across the room and sat in the chair by the window, easing her back with both hands. 'Where *is* Ned?' Her voice whined, a fit match for her face. In the year since she'd captivated Ned her blue eyes and pink mouth had lost their smiles and the chubby features had developed a permanent scowl. 'Down the tavern,' Lucy answered her own question. 'That's where. No thought to my condition.' She stopped arching herself and collapsed against the back of the chair.

'And can you wonder when you make his life so unpleasant? What with complaints over your lot and nagging at his work, is it any surprise Ned slips out now and again?'

'Now and again! He lives there!' Lucy wrinkled her nose and looked around the room. 'Fat mutton! You know I cannot stand the smell of fat mutton now!'

'Signora, forgive me.' Canaletto picked up the dish of meat and handed it to Fanny.

She put it back beside him. 'Lucy likes to fuss, sir, she doesn't mean anything.'

The truth of this was immediately obvious as Lucy forgot her complaint and gazed curiously at the guest. 'So you're the famous painter there's been all the fuss over; even my brother, Alderman Fowler, has heard of you!' Her mouth lifted in a shadow of the flirtatious smile that had captured Ned. 'No doubt I should welcome you to London but I expect Fanny has already done that.'

'Look after Signor Canal, Lucy.' Fanny whipped out of the room and raced down the stairs.

She found Ned in the third tavern she tried.

If he'd been sitting disconsolate in a corner, maybe she could have forgiven him. But he was laughing with two or three others, waving his beer mug as though he had no business to run, no wife and almost-born child to provide for.

Fanny took a deep breath. 'Ned!'

'Oh ho, it's the wife!' said one of the others.

Ned looked down at her, 'Worse, chum, it's the sister. The wife I can deal with any day.' He gave her a scowl and with a sinking of her heart she knew the tavern had been preceded by a stop at a gin shop.

Fanny stamped her foot. 'Ned, I won't stand for this, come back at once. Do you think Signor Canal is going to wait for you all day?'

Ned's upper lip curled. 'He'll only jerk the finger at me, just the way Hogarth did. I'm better off here.'

Oh, Fanny could have hit him! How dare he stand there drinking ale like that, letting his business go to ruin after all she had done for him?

But as fast as it had arisen, Fanny's anger disappeared. Poor, dear Ned, wife-nagged and sister-pecked. He'd been such a hard-working love until he'd had the misfortune to marry that Lucy and business had turned sour. 'Come on, Ned,' she said gently. 'Signor Canal is in my debt, he's offered me anything within his power. All you have to do is show him what an excellent engraver and thoroughly reliable fellow you are.' With a swift movement she removed the beer tankard from his hand and led the way out of the tavern.

She turned in the doorway and saw him hesitate. 'Ned!' she shouted at him.

'Holds the pot while you piss in it, does she?' asked one of the other men.

Ned turned red. 'I'll sort her out,' he said grimly.

'You take too much upon yourself,' he said when they were outside.

'If I did not, your business would collapse.' Fanny walked swiftly towards the shop, pushing her way through the other pedestrians.

He grabbed her arm and pulled her round, his face tight and mulish. 'Nay, I'll take no more of this. I'm not some sort of ball for you and Lucy to bat between you. My life is my own.'

Fanny stared at him. This wasn't the beloved brother she'd worked for and looked after ever since their parents and three siblings had died of a fever four year ago, leaving them to comfort each other.

They had had to part while Ned completed his apprenticeship as an engraver. Fanny had been taken in by a neighbouring household and worked for her board and lodging. Two years ago, just turned seventeen, she had joined her brother in the house left them by their father and Ned had begun to show her the tedious preparation of the plates and the ordering of the workshop.

For a little time all had been delight for Fanny as she worked for Ned and kept house for them both.

Then Lucy had entered their lives.

'You would turn out your sister?' Fanny stood

squarely on the road before Ned, her face a mixture of bewilderment and outrage.

Ned groaned and clutched both hands to his head. 'Did I say that?'

'Something very like.' Fanny placed her hands either side of her waist and stared him down.

Ned spun round in frustration, knocking into a ragamuffin urchin selling laces. The long pole with its roughly tied burden almost poked Fanny's eye out. The boy gave her a cheeky grin then dashed across the road to avoid a cuff round the ear.

'Ned!' Fanny took hold of his arm. 'You must come home. Arguments over Lucy can wait. I've left her entertaining Signor Canal and if we are to make capital from my aid to him this morning, you should not delay in paying your respects.'

'Canaletto!' Ned exploded and swung round to face Fanny again. 'He can go to the devil as far as I'm concerned. 'Twas your idea and a poor one at that. Why should a painter of his reputation waste time on an engraver such as me?'

Fanny was torn between outrage and sorrow. 'Ned, you know your worth! There's not an engraver in London with more talent. If you can only leave the drinking and concentrate on your work!'

'There you go again, hounding me and nagging me. A man should have liberty to take an ale with his mates.'

Ned swayed slightly on his feet. Fanny studied his truculent face and knew it would be hopeless trying to reason with him further. None was so obstinate as Ned when he'd got some idea in his head.

'Signor Canal is a painter of genius,' she said shortly, 'and we cannot afford to ignore this opportunity.' She started to push her way through the crowds back towards their shop and home.

'Only a painter of viewpoints,' she heard Ned throw after her but she knew he was following and, for the moment, that was enough. When Ned had sobered down, he'd see matters her way. Skilled engraver though her brother was, Fanny was the one with vision, with ideas, with ambition and Ned was the first to acknowledge this. At least, he had been.

It was only as Fanny hurried up the narrow stairs that it occurred to her it might not have been one of her better notions to suggest Lucy entertain their guest.

Chapter Six

Fanny opened the door into the first-floor room in time to hear Lucy say, 'My husband's sister has no thought for my feelings, sir. I am not mistress in my house, Ned looks to Fanny rather than me. My best petticoat has disappeared, it cost ever so much, a present from my brother, Alderman Fowler, who I will have you know has influence, but does Fanny care?'

Fanny despaired. That stupid, careless girl! The lost petticoat was just typical of Lucy's pretensions, looping her skirt to her waist to show it off until her pregnancy was so advanced even she could see how ridiculous it looked.

Fanny caught an expression of deep weariness on Canaletto's face; she saw the sardonic look in his eyes and her heart sank.

Ned stood speechless in the doorway like a lummox. Fanny kicked him sharply on the ankle and he stumbled towards the Italian. 'Signor Canal,' he said, 'we are honoured to have you in our humble house.' Then he hiccuped.

Canaletto surveyed the young man for a long moment. 'And what plan have you for me? After the pantomime from Miss Fanny?'

Ned looked bewildered. 'Fanny? What happened?'

Fanny's ready temper rose, 'Next time you're threatened with death, I'll not interfere.'

'So there will be another time?' The detached tone was loaded with innuendo.

'I think you might have a greeting for your wife, Ned,' Lucy broke in.

'Lucy, do you realize how important Signor Canal's presence here is?'

'Please, Signorina Fanny, explain, I would be most grateful,' Canaletto hissed softly.

Fanny stared at him pugnaciously.

'Ow did you know I was to arrive?'

Ned took a little step nearer, steadier on his feet now. 'Signor Canal, your friend Jacopo Amigoni wrote to my old master, to whom I was apprenticed, with details of your arrival. He let me know and sent an engraving of your portrait. Either Fanny or myself has gone to the docks for the last three days, hoping to meet your boat.'

'Ah, Signor Amigoni!' Canaletto said slowly. 'Yes, my good friend had a most prosperous time painting in England.'

'Edward is a most skilful engraver,' Fanny rushed in. 'We thought that maybe an engraving of one of your works could advertise your arrival. Nobody could do it better than Ned.' She believed that.

Canaletto rose, drawing his slim body to its full height. 'I have foremost reputation amongst landscape artists. I have introductions to leading English patrons, all nobili. What need have I of engraver half drunk before the morning is over, his hand too much in shakes to hold the burin?'

For once Fanny could think of nothing to say.

Lucy looked at the painter, her blue eyes wide and ingenuous. 'I heard you were Italian, Mr Canal?'

He swung towards her, startled, then nodded.

'And yet you speak English quite like a native,' she marvelled.

Canaletto unbent just a little, 'Thank you, signora. I deal for many years with English nobili in Venice. It has paid me to learn the language.'

'My!' Lucy lapsed into silence.

Fanny took a deep breath. A few hours ago this ingrate had promised to give her anything in his power. 'Working in Venice is not the same as working in London,' she said, rather more sharply than was perhaps wise.

Canaletto gave a small, scornful laugh. He walked over and tapped the print on the wall with a disdainful finger. 'This Samuel Scott paints a pretty ship but his buildings leave much to be desired. He lacks my vision, my skills.'

'Indeed, signor, that is why Ned and I want to help you,' Fanny said hastily. 'Why I came to meet you.'

'Why you nearly killed me?' The voice with its lilting Italian accent dropped the words like icicles on a frozen pavement.

For a moment Fanny thought he'd muddled his English. 'You mean, why I saved you?'

His expression grew even more scornful. 'Miss Rooker, you save me only so you can – how do you say it – you set me up? Yes, that is it, you set me up so you can knock me down.'

Fanny had never been more astonished in her life. 'Believe that and the devil may take you. As for that bag,' she pointed at the leather satchel leaning against his chair, 'anyone can walk off with that as far as I'm concerned. Just tell me what makes you think I gulled you.'

'Gulled?'

'Tricked,' she said impatiently. 'Set you up.'

He pounced like a hawk on a shrew, 'Then I am right.'

'No! I just want to know why you should think I did.'

Canaletto swiftly crossed the room.

He held up the reticule by its strings. 'You are not innocent, English signorina. I ask myself how this little bag that look no weapon, can fell villain. I look inside and, see!' With the sleight of hand of a conjurer he produced two heavy copper plates from the bag. 'I do not think innocent English signorina carry such things.'

Fanny laughed, relieved. 'Lud, yes! With the cheek of the lads we got round here you need a bit of an advantage.'

"'Tis true, sir!' Lucy leaned forward as much as her pregnant bulk would allow. 'Fanny gave me the same – and taught me how to aim and swing. London's a rough and ready city for a pretty girl, even for a plain one.' She threw Fanny a glance full of spite.

Canaletto returned the plates to the bag and swung it experimentally. 'But the hook, just at that moment?'

Fanny shrugged. 'As to that, you must ask elsewhere. I didn't see who worked the gantry, just the way it moved and you, standing there as though waiting to be felled. Signor, I swear on my honour, I was only at the docks to meet you. But for Mr Hogarth wanting to talk business, it would have been Ned.'

Canaletto continued to gaze sternly at her.

Fanny began to falter. Everything had seemed so

simple when she and her brother had discussed the idea. If they could persuade Canaletto to offer Ned the chance to engrave one of his paintings, Ned would be made. Now, faced with this sophisticated, suspicious Italian, nothing seemed simple at all. She had one card left to play. 'When you said you'd grant me anything in your power in thanks for saving your bag, I thought, maybe . . .' she allowed her words to trail away.

Canaletto drew up his slight figure. 'An Italian's word is sacred.' He made a grandiloquent gesture, 'I have no plans for an engraving but perhaps at some time there will be favour I can perform for your brother or yourself.'

'Oh, ay,' said Ned bitterly. 'We all know we can trust foreigners! You just take your things and remove yourself from my premises, *signor*.'

All the difficulties Fanny had endured in this house over the past year rose up before her. Lucy's whines and bad temper, Ned's sulks and the insults he'd paid her just this morning.

She looked Canaletto straight in the eye and summoned all her courage, 'Why not take me as your apprentice? That would be ample repayment for saving your life.'

Chapter Seven

For a moment Canaletto's English deserted him, so astonished was he by her effrontery.

Before he could react, Mistress Lucy rose in wrath. 'Fanny, how dare you imagine that you could become a painter! 'Tis Ned who will be the artist while you manage the engraving.'

This seemed to unnerve the little Fanny.

'Ned? A painter?' She swung round on him sounding bewildered. 'You have commissions?'

He shuffled his weight from one foot to the other and with grim amusement Canaletto watched him caught between the two women. He could almost feel sorry for this foolish fellow.

'Well, Lucy's brother John has given me a commission for a watercolour of his guild's new hall.'

'See, soon he won't need to engrave any more.' Lucy leant forward, her body awkward but her face for once vibrant with eagerness. 'He'll be a proper artist.'

'One watercolour doesn't make a business, Lucy. And Ned is as skilled a craftsman as any painter.'

Canaletto liked the way she stood up for her brother.

'But Fanny, I would so like to be known as a painter. Lucy thinks . . .'

'Lucy thinks! What does Lucy know?' Fanny swung

back to Canaletto. 'Come, signor, can you not take me as an apprentice?'

'Can you afford the premium, signorina?'

She looked stunned. 'The premium?'

So, he'd been right. She expected him to take her on without a payment.

A faint flush warmed the plain face, the freckled nose shone brightly. 'How ... how much would the premium be?'

Canaletto had enquired into just this point before leaving Venice. An apprentice or two could not only assist him should the commissions flow in as quickly as he hoped, but their fees would help his expenses until he received the first payments for his work.

'A single payment of fifty guineas or a yearly sum of ten.'

Fanny gasped. 'Signor, I couldn't raise near such a sum.' She took a deep breath, 'But I could be valuable to you in ways a regular apprentice would be unable. I can cook for you, look after your clothes, watch that you don't get cheated by suppliers. You will need materials, pigments, canvases, supporters, brushes. I know the market, I can look after your interests.'

Canaletto sighed and squashed a moment's brief sympathy with this eager girl. 'Signorina Rooker, please. Are you acquainted with the grinding of pigments for work in oils? With the choice of mediums?'

Fanny blinked.

'With the preparation of canvases? Do you have knowledge of the correct varnishes?'

Fanny opened her mouth then closed it again.

'As apprentice I need an artist who can mix my colours, arrange my studio, organize my work. Who will, after some tuition, assist with the painting of minor detail.'

'Oh, I am skilful with the brush, signor.' Fanny took out a sketchbook from a drawer in the gateleg table. 'See!'

Canaletto found himself unable to resist leafing through the contents. The girl had talent, no doubt of that. There were sketches of street characters such as Canaletto had seen on their way to this unfortunate house and of the street itself, houses leaning crazily over pavement and road. But these were the early attempts of an untrained eye with no use of colour wash to fill out and shade the drawings. Yes, maybe this girl could one day be of use to him but only after a long period of tuition.

Meantime she would be too, too *organizing*!

'Of course,' said Lucy slowly, 'if Fanny were to become your apprentice, Mr Canaletto, then Ned and I could have this house to ourselves. Fanny has let so many of the rooms I hardly know which is still ours! My brother, the alderman, says it's no house to bring a baby into.'

'Signora, to make use of space is of benefit to any family. My family is citizens of Venice but my parents let out rooms and so safeguard food for us.' His stomach gave a lurch, no doubt the fat mutton.

'Have you premium, signorina?' he repeated.

'Of course she hasn't,' Lucy said with asperity. 'Neither Fanny nor Ned has enough to buy me a decent petticoat. And I wouldn't be surprised if it isn't Fanny herself who has made off with my best one.'

'Lucy, be quiet!' Fanny said impatiently. 'This is no business of yours.'

'But it is of mine.' Ned's open face was sullen and aggrieved. 'You're *my* apprentice, Fanny. You are supposed to assist *me* in my work. How am I to manage without you?'

'Why, do what Signor Canal says he must,' Lucy commented waspishly. 'Take someone who can pay a premium. Two apprentices would more than compensate for turning out the riff raff we have in this house. And enable you to spend time on your painting.'

'Fanny knows my ways,' Ned muttered. 'Can you never understand what I need, Lucy?'

'Signor,' Fanny reached out a hand in painful supplication. 'Did you not say you were in my debt?'

The tensions in the room flew around Canaletto and made his head ache.

'Stop!' he cried. 'No more! I cannot trust any of the family Rooker. Understand? I leave now.' He picked up the heavy leather satchel and made for the door.

'But, signor, you can't!' Fanny set her small figure in front of the door, her arms akimbo.

Canaletto pushed her aside. 'I go now,' he repeated.

'Let the ungrateful bastard leave.' Ned grabbed at his sister's arm.

'But, signor, your baggage,' wailed Fanny.

'I send for it!'

Canaletto grappled with the key for several minutes before he could open the shop door, then he was out on the street. He found a kerchief in a pocket and wiped his face with relief.

He had no idea where to go but at least his life was his own again. Even his stomach seemed to have settled. He hefted the satchel, tried not to mind its weight, and started walking.

People jostled him on all sides, banging at his bag, making him anxious for its safety. A white-clad baker pushed past with a tray of pastries on his head, a slatternly maid with a dirty kerchief hardly veiling thrusting breasts stood in his path while she dallied with a lascivious rogue, who stole from her basket of food with one hand while he paddled in her bosom with the other. A leather-aproned tapster staggered under a barrel of ale perilously close to Canaletto, then two carpenters carrying long planks of wood forced him to leap out of their path, into the way of a group of drunken layabouts laughing as they lurched along the road, pushing respectable folk into the paths of chairs, carts and carriages. And the noise! Itinerant hawkers' shouts mingled with the jingle of harnesses, the creak of wheels, the cries of friends and acquaintances. As if all this was not enough, beggars pulled at Canaletto's sleeve and skirt, demanding money. He brushed them away and looked around, desperate for some sort of conveyance that could take him out of this rabble.

'Cab, sir?' called a coachman perched up behind a carriage pulled by a gaunt and bony horse. With sure skill he guided it between two carts and a sedan chair towards the side of the road, scattering some of the mobbing beggars.

'Yes!' Canaletto eagerly pushed his way through to the vehicle, opened the door and sank into the seat with a sigh of relief. Safe at last!

'Where to, sir?' asked the driver, opening the little door in the roof.

'Just drive!' shouted the hard-pressed Canaletto, unable to think of anything but the need to reach some more salubrious place.

The driver cracked his whip. Slowly the cab began to move and the couple of beggars who'd kept banging at the window fell behind.

Canaletto drew another sigh of relief. Then rubbed at the window as the cab turned into a dark and narrow lane.

What was this? Where was he being taken? Alarmed, Canaletto drew down the window and attempted to shout up at his driver. 'No, no! Not here!'

There was no reaction, the horse didn't falter. Canaletto struggled with the door. For the second time that morning he appeared to have been kidnapped! Then the cab stopped alongside the entrance to an even narrower alley.

'Here we are, squire,' shouted the driver. 'I've brought him just as instructed.'

The cab door was yanked open and a long arm pulled Canaletto out, dislodging his wig into the mud.

Panic filled the painter as he recognized Scallion. He gave a strangled shout as he saw the man raise a knife. The sound echoed in the empty alley as the knife was brought down in an evil swing that drove the blade through his waistcoat and into his ribs.

For a moment Canaletto felt nothing but incomprehension. How had this fellow found him? What was his foul purpose? Then overpowering weakness and exquisite pain flooded through him. He fell to his knees in the filth and mud of the alley and his unprotected head banged against a projecting stone on the corner of the building. His sorely tried bowels gave up any attempt at control and he sank into a darkness deeper and blacker than the waters outside Venice.

Chapter Eight

'I tell you I won't do it!' the Viscount Purbeck said petulantly. He leaned towards the mirror on his dressing table and carefully pressed a small black patch on to his chin over a pustule. He was in his shirt sleeves. At the back of the room was his great four poster bed, its covers dishevelled.

'Come now, Richard, is this gallant? To rail against the prospect of a rich wife? One who is comely to boot?' James Bennett leaned easily against the wall, his sober black suit a nice contrast to the young lord's cream breeches and richly embroidered waistcoat.

'Oh, it's fine for one such as you,' Richard sneered. 'You now have all you desire. No longer my tutor, now secretary to my father, the noble Marquess of Brecon. No doubt you see yourself holding some rich sinecure within the twelvemonth!' The hand securing the patch trembled slightly and the minute circle fell to the floor. Richard swore and reached for another from the little glass stand that held a selection.

James Bennett's eyes narrowed but he kept his tone light. 'After bear leading you, my Lord, through Europe for nigh on twenty-four months, not to mention rescuing you from matters we will not talk about, a person of any charity would consider I deserve my fortune.' Then, despite his care, a note of bitterness crept into his voice. 'If, indeed, fortune it is. Your father is a hard taskmaster.'

But Richard heard only the first part of the speech. He stretched out his arms and sighed luxuriously, arching his slim back. 'Lord, but we had fine times on the continent! Don't you wish we still were there?' His eyes sought James's through the mirror's reflection.

'It was not the best time for a Grand Tour and I am happy to have brought you home without falling foul of fighting armies, marauding highwaymen or politicking Venetians,' James said austerely.

Richard's full mouth puckered in pique. With a swift, sudden movement, he picked up his breakfast cup and flung it against the panelled wall. Chocolate sprayed over polished wood and porcelain shards decorated the Aubusson carpet. 'You said you'd never mention Venice!' he screeched and his eyes looked wildly at the secretary.

James felt his entrails tighten. He'd thought Richard so much better, so much more balanced. God in heaven, he thought, what if he loses control now? Now, when everything is so nearly in place?

'Richard, that is all in the past. There is no need for you to panic whenever the name is uttered.'

Richard's gaze dropped uneasily. 'I heard a rumour yesterday,' he muttered.

James could guess immediately which rumour that would be. 'That Signor Canal comes to England?'

The protuberant blue eyes flickered towards him. 'What if . . .?' Richard left the unspoken question hanging in the charged air between them.

James stood behind the young man and laid his hands gently on his shoulders, feeling the thin bones through the embroidered material of the waistcoat. 'No need to worry about Signor Canal,' he said softly.

Richard's gaze locked with his in the mirror. 'Lord, James, but you can look sinister at times,' he whispered and James felt the bones shiver. 'What have you done?'

'I? I have done nothing, why should you suggest there is anything to be done?' James smiled, feeling the stiffness of his lips. 'We don't know if the painter comes and, if he does, why should you fear anything?'

'Oh, that we had never gone to that place!' He buried his face in his hands.

'Hush,' James pressed the shoulders reassuringly. 'I tell you, you have no need to worry.'

Richard raised his head, gazed up into the secretary's eyes then gave a nervous, high-pitched laugh. 'Why do I trust you so?'

'Because I look after you,' James said calmly. He studied their silvered reflections. Not more than four years between them but so different in appearance. There was his face, control in every line of the high cheekbones, the firm chin, the well-shaped mouth, the steady grey eyes. It was a face of distinction and how much more suited it was to the position of heir to the Marquess of Brecon than the other, that of a wayward youth whose shaved head shone eerily above the bulging eyes, beaky nose, overfull mouth and chin that sloped too quickly down to an unattractively prominent Adam's apple. How fickle fortune was that the better man should have been born to an insignificant lawyer from Bristol instead of to a noble lord!

James closed his mind to the thought. 'Now, you agreed, did you not,' he continued calmly, 'that marriage to Charlotte More was your only option?'

53

After a moment Richard reached towards the dressing table, picked up a small knife and pared a ragged fingernail, bitten at some stage in the night. Then he exchanged knife for file and neatened off the shape. The expression in his eyes was hidden by his lowered lids as he concentrated on his task. 'Marriage to Charlotte More is independence from my father,' he said as if repeating a lesson.

'There you have it,' James exclaimed encouragingly. He released the young man's shoulders and wandered round the room. 'You know what depends upon this match. We have worked, your father and I, long and hard to bring it about.' That conjunction of his name with the marquess's pleased him, suggesting as it did a closeness that in reality he was still working towards. 'Miss More's marriage settlement is to save your family's fortunes.' He flicked absentmindedly at the rumpled folds of the bed's silk coverlet. 'Any hint of reluctance on your part could be the ruination of all our hopes.' As soon as the words were out of his mouth, James knew he had made a mistake.

Richard flung down the little file in renewed petulance. 'You suggest a city miss without a hint of breeding to her name expects me to play the lovelorn swain?'

James laughed lightly. 'Hardly that, Richard. Common civility is all that's called for.'

'And you dare to suggest my manners require correction?' The blue eyes, bright as freshly opened cornflowers, glinted dangerously.

James felt a surge of deep irritation. All this young whippersnapper had to commend him was a lineage that could be traced back to the time of the Conqueror. None of his own intelligence, understanding, education or manners. Then his glance met Richard's and he recognized the unhappiness and insecurity that lay behind the belligerence.

'Softly, Richard,' James said gently.

Richard glanced away. 'My lord, my father, should have offered for Miss More himself,' he said sulkily. 'He is marquess, not I.' Then he glanced up and gave another high-pitched giggle. 'Foolish creature I am, he is too far involved with another.'

James heard the sibilant intake of his own breath as if it belonged to another. 'You mean?' he asked as casually as he could bring himself to.

'Why, Anne Montesqui, idiot that you are!'

'Mademoiselle Montesqui?' repeated James as stupidly as ever Richard could sound.

Richard swung round in his chair to look at his erstwhile tutor. 'Come, James, you must have known my dearly beloved father has been paying court to the beauteous Anne ever since I introduced them.'

'I, that is to say, my lord has not – ' he took swift command of himself. 'Has my lord himself told you this?'

Another high-pitched giggle. 'Lord save us, you know my father never makes me acquainted with his actions. No, 'twas the coachman, Peter, who has formed an attachment with the lovely Anne's maid. Rose tells him there's scarcely a day passes but my father isn't there to pay court.' Richard leaned forward and stroked a light coating of salve on his mouth.

'But,' stammered James, still unable to credit what he was hearing, 'Mademoiselle Montesqui has been out of town for the last two weeks.'

Richard's finger stilled as he stared at James through

the mirror. 'So,' he said softly. 'Is that the way the land lies? Tut, tut, James, you should have told me.'

'Nothing to tell. I merely called once or twice on Mademoiselle Montesqui. After our acquaintance in Venice, you understand?'

Richard wagged a remonstrating finger, 'Out of your league, James.'

James felt hot resentment spill through him and was almost grateful for it. At least it held at bay the searing jealousy that was threatening to choke him. 'You read too much into the situation, Richard.'

'Then how you will enjoy working for my father after she has become my step-mama!'

James held his body rigid. 'What's this? The fantasy of some maid?'

Richard shrugged. 'Maybe. But you know my father!'

Indeed James did. 'Rash, intemperate, possessed of more muscle than brain,' the marquess's mother had once described her son. 'He will bring the family to ruin before he's forty.' The old marchioness had died before she could see the truth of her words made plain.

Richard's mouth pouted sulkily. 'He should still marry Miss More and then keep Anne as a light o'love.'

Fury replaced resentment in James but he forced his voice to remain light. 'Can you think Miss More would prefer an older man when given the choice of one such as you?'

'I dare say,' said Richard with one of his rare flashes of intelligence, 'it is her father who decides who she will accept. Though what fixes his interest on our ruined fortunes, it is hard to understand.'

James looked around the richly furnished room. 'Building this house may have depleted the family coffers but it is by far the grandest mansion in Piccadilly. Then there is the family seat with all your acres in Gloucestershire. There are not many available titles can offer such an impressive land holding for a city merchant's grandchildren to inherit.'

'But we, Miss More and I, are to have our own town house, are we not?' Richard grasped at the one saving factor of this proposed match.

James managed a reassuring smile. 'Indeed, that is part of the marriage contract. Come, sir, why this hesitation? You have met Miss More, did you not say she is a pretty young thing? Think you cannot manage her?'

Richard's gaze flickered uneasily. He picked up a silver-mounted rabbit's foot and brushed a smidgeon more rouge on to his pale cheeks, then pencilled the angled eyebrows a deeper shade of black. He gave his reflection a brilliant smile. 'I'm a pretty young thing, too, am I not?' he said, giving a sideways glance at the secretary.

James rose. 'Indeed, Richard, you are. Now, come, your coat.' The valet had been dismissed as soon as James had entered the chamber so the secretary picked up the full-skirted silk coat, its cuffs richly embroidered to match the waistcoat, its colour a deep rose red that matched the heels of Lord Richard's silver-buckled shoes, and held it out. 'No girl could ask for a more handsome swain.'

Richard gave another giggle. 'I'll come to you for lessons in flattery, James.' He slipped his arms into the sleeves, shrugged the coat into place, then picked up his tie wig, dressed at the back with a large black bow, and arranged it on his head. 'Should I call William for more powder, do you think?'

James Bennett surveyed the stiffly curled confection and shook his head. 'It looks superb, my lord.'

Richard gave him a quick dig in the ribs. 'Oh, you! Well, come, let's not keep my lord waiting.' He clicked his fingers at a small pile of curly brown and white hair that lay on the coverlet. A spaniel with a frisky tail and eyes that bulged even more protuberantly than its master's leapt off the bed and ran eagerly towards the door.

Richard picked up a silver snuff box, flicked it open and offered James a pinch. The secretary shook his head. Richard dipped in a thin finger and thumb, raised the snuff to his nose with an elegant gesture and, closing his eyes, inhaled deeply. Then he slipped the box into a convenient pocket and headed for the door. His hand on the brass doorknob, he hesitated, looking back under his eyelashes. 'But trade, James, trade!'

'Richard, the East India Company can hardly be compared with shopkeeping! And Balthasar More's wealth is worthy of respect.' James controlled the exasperation in his voice with difficulty. He followed Richard out of the room with a sense of foreboding. It would be a miracle if this morning's ceremony went through without a hitch.

And what was he going to say when he had to address the marquess? His new knowledge burnt in him.

Chapter Nine

Down in the library two sets of lawyers went carefully through sheaves of papers.

Seated on one of the largest chairs the room offered was Lord Richard's prospective father-in-law, Balthasar More, in an old-fashioned, full-bottomed wig, bulky coat and riding boots. His left hand rested on a stout, silver-mounted stick and shrewd eyes set close either side of a slightly hooked nose surveyed the bright colours of the Savonnerie carpet underneath his feet with moody satisfaction. The marquess had not yet arrived.

As Richard and James entered, Balthasar More looked up. 'Ah, the bridegroom!' he said in a voice that rattled like gravel. He made no attempt to rise.

Lord Richard made an elegant leg but the bow he gave was almost non-existent. 'Sir, your servant,' he said in bored tones, then strolled towards the window and stood looking at a model of the new Westminster Bridge that was displayed on a side table.

Balthasar More flushed deep red.

James hurried forward, noting with dismay that no refreshment had been brought to the room. 'Mr More, the marquess will be here directly. I am sure after your journey you will welcome some Madeira.' He pulled the bell rope. 'Is Miss More not to be with us today?'

The merchant's face slowly returned to its more normal colour. 'Aye, I'd like wine,' he acknowledged shortly. 'As for my daughter, she will arrive with Mrs More presently. I came on ahead. It is more seemly we discuss any remaining settlement details without her presence.'

'Of course, Mr More. As always, you think of everything.'

Balthasar More shot him a penetrating glance and remained sitting at attention.

A servant arrived and James ordered wine and ratafia biscuits to be brought to the library. 'I trust the ladies enjoy the best of health?' he enquired courteously as the man left the room.

The merchant grunted. 'Mrs More has a recurrence of her old trouble. She will miss Charlotte's ministrations, no one knows better how to settle her nerves.'

James went over to the table where Richard stood still studying the model. 'Hear that, Lord Richard? A fine thing to have a wife who knows how to settle nerves!' In an undertone he hissed in his ear, 'Talk to Mr More. Remember, the contract is yet to be signed.' He gave an encouraging press to Richard's shoulder, then approached the table where the lawyers were still organizing their papers, picked up the settlement document and pretended to scan its well-rehearsed paragraphs.

'Sir, you will have noted the progress on the new bridge?' enquired Lord Richard a trifle sulkily, approaching where the merchant sat.

'Damned pernicious construction,' Balthasar More rattled out bitterly. 'It'll be the ruination of the City's wealth, as your father well knows, being as how he is one of the Commissioners.'

James took a hand. 'Indeed the marquess is. But he believes the bridge, when once it is finished, will increase the business of Westminster greatly to no detriment of the City.'

'Aye, once it is finished! And when will that be, eh? There's not a City merchant that would venture on its opening this decade nor yet next. You take too much upon yourself, boy!' Truculence imbued every line of Balthasar More's body.

James's fingers tightened on the document he held. 'I understand you have but recently returned from the Indies,' he said smoothly. 'We hear startling tales of the wealth to be seen there.'

'The riches of the Indies are beyond imagining.' Balthasar's eyes lit up. 'I have seen Maharajahs' palaces studded with jewels, princes weighted down with precious stones.'

'Dancing girls with rubies in their navels – and elsewhere?' suggested Richard with lewd emphasis.

Balthasar More's face took on an expression of distaste. 'The noble marquess, your father, assures me you will provide my daughter with a healthy and sober husband. I trust he is not mistaken?'

Lord Richard stared at the merchant and stifled a giggle. The two lawyers kept their heads down over their documents but their ears were almost visibly twitching. James dropped the marriage contract and advanced towards the merchant. 'Sir, I have had the pleasure of conducting Lord Richard in a cultural trip through Europe and can assure you no young man could have proved more industrious in the pursuit of the classical arts.'

There was little response from Balthasar's suspicious

glance and James hurried on. 'Lord Richard bought many treasures to add to those displayed both here and at my lord's Gloucestershire seat.' He waved a hand at the statuary placed around the room, the paintings hung between the heavy bookcases with their burden of rich leather bindings gleaming behind brass latticework, the figurines decking the marble mantelshelf.

Then he cursed himself as the merchant pressed hard on his cane, rose and advanced towards a picture blazing with the brilliant colours of a festive Venetian canal scene. Backed by the Piazza San Marco, gorgeous barges sparkled on rippling water. Sunlight gilded the stonework and set in relief the dark detail of scimitar-shaped gondolas. Though small, the picture dominated its surroundings.

'Canaletto, hmmm?' he said in a knowing voice.

James glanced towards Richard but the viscount was playing again with the model of the bridge. 'Indeed, sir, you have truly recognized the great master's touch. But may I draw your attention to this urn the viscount found in Rome. It is from ancient times.' Richard had insisted upon buying the battered stone relic though the greasy eagerness of the salesman suggested it was of dubious authenticity.

Balthasar threw it a suspicious glance but before he could comment, the library door was flung back and the Marquess of Brecon entered, followed by three dogs. All were huge. The marquess's well-cut coat of tobacco-brown velvet, liberally embroidered with gold and worn over a brocade waistcoat, could not disguise his barrel chest any more than the snuff-coloured silk breeches could hide the trunk-like girth of his legs. The massive head was blessed with godlike features; strong facial bones, flashing dark blue eyes, a straight nose and a classically shaped mouth only slightly marred by an excess of flesh. A wig powdered brilliant white offered a cascade of curls that fell to just below his powerful shoulders.

The marquess surveyed the room, his gaze pausing for a moment on the figure of Lord Purbeck in a way that suggested he was not pleased with his son and heir. The young man hastily swept his father a graceful bow.

'Mr More, a great day for us both!' The marquess rubbed his hands together.

Balthasar bowed deeply. 'My lord, a pleasure.'

'Well, Richard, you are to be made very happy.' The marquess looked around. 'Have we nothing to drink?' his mouth tightened in disapproval.

'Wine will be here immediately, my lord,' James interposed hastily.

'Fine, fine.' One of the dogs advanced and thrust a nose into a hand. 'Lie, sir!' snapped his master and pointed imperiously to a corner of the library where the other two had settled. But the dog ambled over to sniff at the small spaniel hovering beside the viscount. She whirled and snapped at the hound, who sprang back, then bared his teeth and growled low in his throat.

'God damn it, Hector, I told you lie!' roared the marquess. He gave him a hefty kick that sent the animal yelping across the room to join his brothers.

The wine arrived and was dispensed by the lackey, gorgeous in the Brecon livery of dark green and gold.

'We shall drink to the union of my son and your daughter,' the marquess said in ringing tones, his eyes firmly fixed on the merchant. 'Come, Richard, raise your glass.'

Richard hurriedly picked up the glass of Madeira held out to him on a silver salver. Only James saw the wink that the tall footman gave him.

'Time for signing, I think.' The marquess approached the table with glass in hand. 'But where is your daughter? I know Richard can hardly wait for another sight of his lovely bride.' In a seemingly unconscious gesture, the marquess's hand fell over a large leather money pouch that rested on the table beside the contract document.

On cue, the door opened and Mrs More and her daughter entered.

It was James's first sight of the future Viscountess of Brecon. She looked a sweet little figure, richly arrayed in blue satin embroidered in a gold that emphasized the unpowdered curls peeking below a matching cap, the blue giving depth to the rather pale shade of her eyes. Her nose was perhaps a mite too long and her mouth rather small but it was prettily curved and could no doubt smile attractively should the occasion call for delight. At the moment, however, the girl looked worried.

The object of her concern leant heavily on her daughter's arm.

Mrs More was an ample figure tightly laced into scarlet satin. Her ashen face was slippery with sweat and the hand that wasn't pressing on her daughter dabbed at her forehead and mouth with a lace handkerchief.

'Sit, Mama.' Charlotte tenderly guided her mother to a chair.

The roomful of men stared in consternation as the woman sank her limp body down on to the polished leather with a long sigh, laid her head against the carved wooden back and closed her eyes.

Balthasar hurried forward and took hold of the nerveless hand from which the handkerchief had fallen. 'Abigail, my dear!' There was no response and he turned to his daughter. 'Charlotte, how comes your mother to be in this state? She cannot, surely, have been this unwell at the start of your journey?' His voice was curt and the girl flushed.

James Bennett brought forward another chair and placed it beside that occupied by Mrs More. Charlotte hardly noticed the courtesy. 'Oh, no, Papa. She professed to be so much better. It was as we neared Brecon House that she seemed to suffer some sort of fit. I was all for returning home but she insisted she would recover, that you expected us.'

James tore a strip off the margin of one of the documents and, ignoring the lawyers' protestations, lit it from the candle burning ready to melt wax for sealing the contract. Quickly blowing out the flame, he held the smouldering paper under Mrs More's nose.

The eyelids fluttered then opened. A groan issued from the slack mouth.

'Oh, Mama,' cried Charlotte. Then to James, 'Thank you, sir, for your thoughtfulness.' The pale eyes regarded him gratefully before the girl returned her attention to Abigail More.

The marquess came forward, his face a picture of distaste. 'Madam, you are, I fear, most unwell. I will send for a doctor and my housekeeper will convey you to a room where you may rest.'

A moment later the sombrely dressed figure of Mrs Jones appeared. With brisk efficiency she conjured up footmen to convey the fainting woman from the library, and followed, muttering about loosening stays and providing purges. Charlotte More and her father completed the procession.

Just before Balthasar More's tall figure disappeared from the room, the marquess cried, 'But, sir, the contract!'

The merchant turned. 'The devil take your contract! I cannot think of such things now.'

'But, when?' pressed the now agitated nobleman.

Balthasar raised a despairing hand, shook his head dolefully and left the library.

'What the hell!' the marquess burst forth, his fingers tightening about the leather pouch.

The merchant's lawyer carefully moved it to his side of the table. 'So, we shall need another meeting for the signing of the contract,' he said, his greasy face doleful.

No doubt the fellow had looked for some benefit from the morning's work, thought James. But so did we all. And who could say when the contract would now be signed? Or what would happen if it wasn't?

Chapter Ten

Fanny wrenched her arm from her brother's grasp. The imprint of his fingers still burned into her flesh as she stumbled down the stairs in Canaletto's wake and rushed out on to the street.

For a moment, caught in the press of people thronging Fleet Street and small as she was, Fanny thought she had no chance of seeing which way the Italian had gone. She tried leaping into the air, then found herself caught up in a strong pair of hands. 'You need a stepladder, lass, or springs in your heels,' laughed a deep voice, 'but I'll do what I can.' Sam Wood, the master carpenter who had grown up with her and Ned, lifted her up and at last she could see over the crowds. And there, in the distance, was Canaletto disappearing into a carriage.

'Thanks, Sam,' she cried as she was lowered to the ground again. Heedless of his detaining cry, she pursued the cab.

Fanny didn't consider what she was going to do if she managed to catch up with Canaletto. All her energies went into running as fast as she could, ignoring the stares, the shouts and the jeers that followed her. 'Don't fancy you then?' 'Come to me, love, I'll treat you right.' 'Chasing your fortune, lass?'

Hustled by a large woman carrying a bundle of laundry on her head, Fanny lost sight of the cab. It was only for a moment but the next instant she looked, it had disappeared.

It must have turned off. But what business could Canaletto have in the villainous stews that lay down the only alley his conveyance could have taken?

She came level with its entrance and, sure enough, there was the cab. It had stopped and the door was open, but so narrow was the lane she could see nothing else.

Fanny set off down the alley, only to be pulled up with a sickening jerk as a large arm grabbed her.

'You'll never be going down there!' Sam roared.

'I must, you don't understand.' Fanny tried to pull away but Sam was too strong for her. 'It's my future,' she shouted furiously: 'Look, there goes Signor Canal's cab.'

Even as Sam stared, the cabby whipped his horse and the vehicle slowly trundled further into the stews of London, leaving one elegant leg sticking oddly out from a side alley.

'Signor Canal!' screamed Fanny. With a surge of energy, she pulled herself away from Sam's restraining grip and set off through the reeking mud of the alley. As she ran, a window opened above her head and without even a cry of 'Gardez l'eau!' a chamber pot was emptied just behind her flying skirts.

Behind her pounded Sam, not quite as fast but reassuringly powerful.

'Dear God,' moaned Fanny as she reached the alleyway and saw the slumped figure. Canaletto's wig had once again tumbled off the stubbly scalp and the ruined coat skirts were bunched beneath his awkwardly collapsed body. His seemingly lifeless head rested beside a rough and bloodied piece of stone. Heedless of the mud and filth, Fanny dropped to her knees.

A groan reassured her that he still lived. 'Hush, signor, you are safe now,' she said and inspected his head.

'Good God!' said Sam, arriving breathless. 'Who's this piece of fashionable jetsam?'

Fanny gazed in horror at a nasty scalp wound. 'Sam, fetch your cart, we must carry him home. And send your lad for a physician.'

'I cannot leave you in this place.' Sam glanced anxiously about them. There was no one else in the dark and dim alley, half the buildings appeared deserted but distant scratchings and squeakings suggested otherwise. 'Rat-infested, that's what these places are and I'm not referring to the four-legged rodents either.'

'Sam, go!' protested Fanny furiously; her impatience with his inability to see what had to be done almost throttled her. 'While you're being a worry-guts, Signor Canal will die!' Still he stayed, his open face contorted in a battle between his instinct to do her bidding and his understanding that she would be in extreme danger if he left.

'Sam, I'll never speak to you again if you don't go and get that cart now!' As so often in their relationship, Fanny found herself infuriated beyond belief by his slow and careful ways.

Sam stared at her for a moment longer then drew a heavy hammer from his belt loop. 'Swing this at any rat that appears,' he said in a loud voice.

'Yes, yes,' Fanny took the tool. 'Now go!'

As she heard Sam's footsteps fading, Fanny's heart pounded painfully. She felt very alone with this unconscious man. This was a place for the dregs of humanity, thieving scoundrels who would stop at nothing to scavenge a mean living.

There was another groan. 'Signor Canal, Signor Canal,' she implored, rubbing his hand between her own. His face was so pale, so twisted in pain. 'Help is coming, you're safe, I'll look after you.'

For the second time that day she was rescuing this man from death. Surely some fate was at work here. Surely it meant that her destiny was tied to his?

A spasm of pain went through Canaletto. The front of his coat fell slightly away and Fanny drew a sharp breath as she saw the knife sticking from his waistcoat.

Her hands fluttered as for once in her life she hesitated over the right course of action. Would pulling the knife out risk unplugging Canaletto's life force? Or would it ease his obvious pain?

There came an eldritch shriek. Fanny whirled around, the hammer held aloft in both hands. Only to see a huge cat leap on another, his claws sinking into the scraggy coat. There was a flurry of maddened feline, slashing feet and teeth and then a bloodied cat raced into the depths of the alley pursued by his vengeful attacker.

Fanny's arms sagged and she lowered the hammer.

Canaletto gave another groan. She sank into the mire and grasped one of his hands. His face was so pale, his breathing so ragged and there was that knife sticking out of his side! Again Fanny reached towards it, then her courage failed her. Instead she ripped off the fichu from around her neck and gently wiped the sweat from his forehead.

Her eye was caught by the flash of a gold chain hanging from a waistcoat pocket. Why hadn't his attacker removed this rich prize?

Perhaps this hadn't been a random act of violence, perhaps it was tied in with the incident at the docks. Could someone have followed their journey from the wharf to Fleet Street?

It was all too much for Fanny. Life in London could be violent all right, but this sort of incident was beyond her experience.

Canaletto moved more restlessly. 'Signor, signor,' she pleaded, 'help is coming.'

He gave no sign of hearing. Fanny wished she could speak Italian; good as his command of English was, in his present state he would be much more likely to understand his mother tongue.

She looked around for Sam and his cart. Another time she would have registered the way the dark shadows emphasized the sinister quality of the wretched buildings, how sagging rooflines, broken windows, crumbling plaster and rotting timbers, jam-packed so tightly upon one another that no daylight could penetrate this foul alley, all built up a dread impression of somewhere that belonged to the gateway to hell. But she was too worried about Canaletto to wish she'd brought pen and paper with her.

Long, long minutes later, Fanny at last heard the creak of cart wheels. She had never been so pleased to see Sam's powerful figure. 'Oh,' she cried, 'I've been so frightened.'

Sam's breathing was laboured, his huge chest rising

and falling as he gulped for air. Fanny could not resist burying her head in his jerkin. The scent of his honest sweat at that moment seemed sweeter than any rose or lavender water.

'I knew I shouldn't have left you,' he patted her back awkwardly. 'We'll soon have your friend on the cart and be taking him home.'

Holding her with an arm around her shoulders he went to the corner of the lane. 'Ah, here's Tom. Come on, lad, what kept you?'

'You set such a pace, Sam, as though the hounds o' hell were after you, I was afeard of losing the way. Right puffed I am, give us a chance to catch our breath.' A corpulent young man, with a shock of dark hair and a round face flushed red and shiny after his efforts, leaned panting against the corner building.

'Young chap like you don't need rest! Grab this chap's legs and help me lift him on to the cart.'

'Careful, Sam. He's been knifed as well as hit his head. Slip your hands right under his shoulders, don't clutch at his coat in that way.'

'Fanny, girl,' said Sam good naturedly, 'You stand over there and let us men get on with the job, we'll see him right.'

Fanny watched agonizedly as they settled a grunting and groaning Canaletto in the cart, his head on a bundle of sacking, his legs in their stained and torn stockings hanging limply over the end.

'Right, Tom, you take the left shaft and I'll take the right.'

The little procession set off back for Fleet Street. 'Have you sent for a physician?' Fanny kept an anxious eye on Canaletto's pale face.

'My lad has gone for the apothecary. He should await us,' Sam puffed, his large strides trying to accommodate themselves to Tom's shorter gait.

Once out of that awful alley, Fanny felt that everything must now improve. But Canaletto twitched and jerked as the cart jolted over the ill-made street. Fanny called to Sam to go more slowly.

'I thought you wanted him back as soon as possible,' Sam puffed over his shoulder.

'But not shaken into a syllabub!' Fanny protested, trying to prevent Canaletto's head being knocked against the side of the cart.

His eyes opened and looked straight into hers, their grey puzzled and clouded. '*Dio mio*,' he said. Then, 'My bag!'

How could she have forgotten the heavy leather satchel he'd guarded so carefully?

'It's gone, signor!' It must have done, otherwise she would have seen it.

Canaletto gave a groan that had nothing to do with physical pain. 'All is lost!' he hissed as his eyes closed and the restless twitching resumed.

Fanny glanced nervously around them. Had the thief got what he wanted with the satchel? Or would he be back to make sure he'd finished the painter off?

Chapter Eleven

The apothecary arrived as soon as Canaletto had been carried up to Fanny's room.

As he took hold of the knife, Fanny braced herself for the rush of blood.

There was none. The apothecary frowned, unbuttoned waistcoat and shirt, then exclaimed in surprise.

'Why, 'tis a money belt,' said Fanny as she registered the fat roll of canvas around the painter's waist supported with straps over the shoulders. It looked weighty.

'He may be thankful he was wearing it. It would seem to have saved his life.'

Blunted by the stout canvas, the point of the knife had only just penetrated the ribs and the wound was slight.

Together they stripped Canaletto of his shirt and the heavy belt. Then the apothecary staunched the blood seeping from the wound and wound a bandage around the ribs. The patient groaned during his ministrations but remained unconscious.

''Tis the injury to the head that's knocked the gentleman out,' the apothecary observed, carefully washing the nasty gash with the warm water Fanny had brought. He added a salve then wrapped the head in a bonnet of linen strips. 'If he regains consciousness, he should do well enough with rest. I'll leave some laudanum to ease his discomfort.'

Fanny paid him with a silver coin from Canaletto's pocket and he left.

Fanny knew she should be going through the laborious business of preparing copper plates for Ned. She felt no compunction in staying with her patient. The process of polishing, burnishing and finally cleaning each plate before the delicate business of adding the varnish was tedious and boring.

Standing by the foot of the bed, her legs beginning to feel a little wobbly after all her exertions, she watched the fine-featured face on the pillow and worried over the restless way it worked itself.

Then, suddenly, the brilliant grey eyes were open, surveying her and the room with a puzzled frown.

'How do you, signor?'

'Ah, Signorina Fanny,' Canaletto said jerkily. 'Shall I ever manage to free myself of you?'

How dare he say so? Fanny was furious.

'Ah,' he said painfully, closing his eyes. 'That was not kind of me. But I am not very kind, everyone tells me.' He looked at her again, 'How came I here?'

As Fanny described how they'd rescued and brought him back, Canaletto winced. He put up a hand to his head. 'A picture I must be, yes?'

'And, I'm right sorry sir, but when we found you, there was no satchel. Was,' Fanny hesitated for a moment, 'was its contents very valuable?'

Canaletto groaned. 'Most of my fortune. I was advised to bring it to England, the markets on the continent, with the war, you know, being so volatile. At least I still have,' Canaletto's hand moved to his waist, then felt furiously beneath his shirt. Panic filled his face. 'No, that has gone as well.' He looked at her with an ugly despair. 'I am ruined!'

'No, sir, no!' Fanny felt her antagonism melt away. She picked up the canvas belt and laid it beside the painter. 'It is quite safe, as you can see. More, it has saved your life. Look, this is where the point of the knife entered.' She showed him the slit in the canvas. 'It could have killed you.'

Canaletto painfully pulled himself up in the bed and took the belt. He carefully inspected it then laid it down again with a profound sigh of relief. 'All is not quite lost.' He closed his eyes and lay back against the pillows.

'The apothecary has left you a draught of laudanum. Take it now and rest. We'll bring you sustenance later.'

Downstairs in the reeking atmosphere of the workshop an angry Ned faced her. 'Fanny, what is this Sam tells me about Signor Canal being attacked? Why didn't you send for me?'

Fanny eyed him carefully. There was little trace now of the alcohol he had so recently drunk. A copper plate resting on the sand-filled leather cushion showed he had returned to work.

Sam leant his massive frame against the wall, his head almost brushing the low ceiling. 'Ned, 'twas no fault of your sister's. I collected the cart and Tom, I never thought to come for you as well.'

'And then brought Signor Canal back here? After his insults to us?' Ned flung down his graver, his normally good-tempered face contorted with rage.

Fanny wearily removed her mob cap and sat down abruptly on a stool. Too much had happened that morning.

'Let the lass alone, Ned,' Sam said roughly. 'She needs spirits, not lecturing.'

Fanny felt the steady pressure of his hand on her shoulder with gratitude. At this moment she could forget his infuriating slowness and consider nothing but the comfort his presence could bring.

She looked up at him. 'Thanks, Sam, but I am fine. Go home now, Mary and your child wait for you.' Once Sam had begged her to marry him but she'd known she was not the wife for him any more than he was the husband for her. Now, as he left the shop with one last, troubled glance at her, she almost regretted that decision.

'Canaletto is nothing but trouble,' Ned fumed. 'I cannot believe you didn't just let him go nor throw his boxes after him.'

'Oh, Ned!' Fanny said despairingly. 'You cannot mean that.'

Lucy appeared, her hair newly coiffed, her best apron in place, her face sulky as ever. 'For once my husband is right. The man is nothing but trouble. And who is to look after him, may I ask? You, Fanny, hardly have time and you cannot expect me in my condition to dance attendance on a sick man. Someone should be looking after me.' Lucy placed both hands in the small of her back, arched her swollen body then sagged dramatically against the door of the workroom.

Fanny lost her temper. 'No, Lucy, I do not expect you to help. You haven't helped since you arrived in this house. You are vain, selfish, lazy and stupid. I don't know which is the worse fault. You are ruining my brother's life and do nothing for your own. I dread what sort of life your child will have.'

Lucy lost her air of martyrdom. Her eyes narrowed, her mouth compressed and little areas of white appeared around her flared nostrils. 'Ned,' she said shrilly, imperiously. 'You cannot allow your wife to be talked to in this way.'

Ned looked helplessly from Lucy to Fanny, picked up his graver and turned his back on them, sitting on his stool and hunching his shoulders over his work in an attitude of aggressive defiance.

Lucy tightened her lips into thin lines. 'You cannot speak to me like that in my house,' she said with a venom that shook Fanny.

'*Your* house? This is the Rooker house and has been so since before our father's time.' Fanny was not far from tears. 'You have done nothing to make it yours. You neither cook nor wash nor clean. You don't deal with customers nor assist Ned in any way.' Her voice shook with the accumulated distress of ten months of Lucy's sullen presence.

Lucy looked at her contemptuously. 'He hasn't told you?' Her eyes flicked towards her husband. 'Ned, I am bidden to my brother's table for dinner. By the time I return, I expect that Signor Canal,' she gave his name a contemptuous twist, 'to have been removed from under this roof.' She walked steadily through the workshop to the street door, opened it and passed out.

'Ned?'

His back was still towards Fanny but the defiance had gone out of it.

'Ned!' repeated Fanny.

He turned slowly round, his expression depressed and defeated. 'Lucy's brother, Alderman Fowler, gave me a mortgage on the property. Don't look at me like that,' he shouted at his sister. 'I had to have the money.'

'Why?' Fanny demanded baldly. But she knew. It was the gambling. No use to ask which wager or lottery purchase had place him so perilously within Alderman Fowler's debt. 'You know how ruthless Lucy's brother is in such matters.'

Ned's gaze fell. 'John Fowler assured me he was happy to make the loan. Lucy and I were to be married, what better man to go to? I meant to redeem it within the twelvemonth.'

'And now you're in default?' Of course, he would be. Lucy's extravagance, her insistence on hiring a maid of all work, had increased the pressures on Ned while the rapidity with which she had lost her charm after marriage had driven him to seek comfort in the tavern and gin shop, neglecting his business.

'Lucy wants you to leave,' Ned muttered, unable to meet his sister's eyes. 'She says you undermine her authority.'

'What authority?' exploded the sorely tried Fanny. 'She doesn't know how to control poor Harriet. I'm the one who gives her cooking lessons and tries to ensure she cleans properly!'

Ned slumped on his stool. 'I know, Fanny, I know. But her brother now holds the purse strings. Until I can rebuild my business, I have to do as she says.'

'Which means turning your sister out of her home?' Fanny was in despair. Never had she thought her brother could be so weak.

What was she to do? And how was she to throw a wounded man out on to the street?

Chapter Twelve

James Bennett arranged the papers on the library desk with jerky movements. It was two days since the collapse of Mrs More had destroyed the signing of the marriage contract and this was the first summons he had received from his employer.

He stiffened at the sound of frenzied barking in the hall. There was a yelp of pain. A moment later the door was flung open and the marquess entered, followed by a hound with head hung low and tail between his legs.

The dog crept underneath the desk and the marquess strode across to the model of Westminster Bridge and stood regarding it with brooding eyes. 'Never thought the damn thing would get this far! It should have sunk years ago.'

James waited.

'And at the Commissioners' meeting this morning I shall have to sit through news of further delays and insufficiency of stone and accusations at the Portland quarries of gross incompetence. Why I ever got involved, I'll never know.'

James said nothing.

'Well? Don't you have papers for me?' The tone was impatient.

'They are here, my lord.'

'Bring them to me, damn you!'

James picked up the letters he had prepared and took them over. 'This contains your instructions regarding the redesign of the formal garden at Amberley.' He laid it on the edge of the table that held the model. 'And this is to the tutor of Lord William and Lord Robert outlining their future instruction. You remember it was decided their instruction in the classics should be increased?'

'You mean you suggested they were damnably behind,' grated the marquess, flicking a contemptuous finger at the correspondence. His slightly protuberant blue eyes, so like his son and heir's, suddenly levelled themselves at the secretary's. 'Fire the tutor, go down to Amberley and take over their education yourself.'

'But, my lord, I am your secretary.'

The marquess lashed out and caught James's mouth with the back of his hand. The seal ring grazed his lip, drawing blood. 'You will not answer back, boy!'

For a moment master and servant locked gazes.

'What else have you for me?'

Wordlessly James licked the salt blood from his lip and handed over a sheaf of bills.

The marquess gave them a contemptuous look. 'Burn them.'

'But, my lord, there are several two years overdue,' James said automatically. 'The traders are hard-pressed and have spoken most eloquently to me of the need for settlement. They say, that is, I fear you will receive no more services from them until at least part has been paid.'

'Nonsense, they know the worth of my custom. And if they are so foolish as to withdraw their trade, there will be others to supply what they will not.' Once more the eyes bore into his. 'Your duty, Bennett, is to turn off such nuisances, not press them on me. You do yourself no service.'

The burning pit of resentment in James's stomach stoked its fires and it was with relish that he said, 'It will not be so easy to turn off the collection of certain short-term loans you arranged in the expectation of Miss More's bridal jointure and Mr More taking over the mortgage on Brecon House.' He offered several more documents.

The marquess snatched them from him and tore the papers across with one powerful movement of his hands. The two halves fluttered to the floor. James said nothing. The action could make little difference.

The marquess strode across to the desk, snatched up a pen, dipped it in the porcelain inkwell. 'Bring me the letters.'

James obeyed.

A signature was scribbled at the bottom of each.

James sanded them.

The marquess turned restlessly to the window, jamming his hands in his pockets. 'Damnable that we haven't heard from More.' He turned suddenly towards James. 'Go down there this morning and enquire regarding the health of Mrs More.'

'Early apricots arrived from the Amberley hothouse yesterday, my lord. Perhaps a basket?'

'Yes, yes, anything you think. Just press upon the Mores the necessity of an early signing of the contract.' The marquess strode impatiently around the library, his dog's eyes following every move. He stopped abruptly in front of the Canaletto and gazed at the incandescent scene. 'No reason why the merchant should hesitate over the contract other than the indisposition of Mrs More?'

James followed his thought processes perfectly. 'I am confident there cannot be, my lord.'

The marquess suddenly turned away from the picture. 'You handled that affair well, Bennett. I can no doubt find some sort of reward for you when the contract is signed.'

Now, James knew, was the time to broach the matter that had been burning within him for the last two days. 'My lord, forgive me but do I understand from the viscount I can wish you happy?'

The heavy-jowled face of the marquess froze. 'You presume too much, Bennett.'

It was impossible to decide what this meant and equally impossible to pursue the matter further.

'I expect news when I return this afternoon.' The marquess clicked his fingers at the dog beneath the desk. Both left the room.

James bent to pick up the torn fragments of the demands. At least moneylenders could not be put off as easily as tailors or provision merchants. He glanced at the long-case clock. The location he was desperate to visit was not on his way to the City but with a horse from the marquess's stables there should be time enough for all to be completed before his employer returned from his meeting.

It was a little after eleven o'clock when James arrived in Downing Street. Without checking that the basket of apricots for Mrs More was still properly stowed in the saddle bag, he tied his horse to the railings and commanded a street urchin to look to it. Then he bounded up the steps and banged impatiently on the door.

A few minutes later he was being shown into the parlour of the first-floor lodgings.

Arranged on an upholstered chair, amongst the usual sweet disorder, reading a novel and dressed in a loose wrap-over gown of sprigged muslin, was Anne Montesqui.

'James, how delightful!' she said but the look in her sea-green eyes suggested the visit was far from welcome.

James stared at her, his thoughts tumbling over themselves in the usual confusion her beauty always brought to him.

'Nothing to say?' she murmured with a hint of a smile.

It was enough to bring him to her side. 'I thought you were still to be in the country.'

The smile deepened. 'Then why visit?'

'I had to know. Is it true?'

The book was laid aside. 'You talk in riddles, James. Is what true?'

'Why, that you and my lord, the Marquess of Brecon . . .' he stumbled to a stop.

'That I and the Marquess of Brecon, what?' The smile still hovered on her luscious mouth but the eyes were watchful.

'Richard said,' James hesitated then rushed into, 'Oh, Anne, it can't be true! Not after all we have shared!' All his heart was in his eyes as he looked at her.

She returned his gaze with a cool stare. 'You presume, James.'

This echo of the marquess told him all he needed to know. But still he couldn't quite believe. 'But you told me, you said . . .' once again he stumbled.

Her smile became warm but her eyes remained watchful. 'James, you are a charming young man. I enjoyed our times together, first in Venice and then here in London. And you are intelligent. You must see there could never be more than the occasional hour of pleasure between us.'

A groan burst from his lips. 'How can you say so?'

Anne rose, a graceful movement that swayed the soft material of her gown and fleetingly revealed the ripe outline of her body beneath. She briefly rested a hand on James's shoulder as she passed over towards the window, a butterfly touch that burned his skin. 'Be realistic,' she murmured. 'You have neither fortune nor position. How could there ever have been more?'

James said nothing. The truth of her words was so blindingly obvious he could only wonder he had deluded himself for so long. He gazed at the soft curves so invitingly displayed as the light from the window made transparent her flimsy garment, and tried to ignore the ache that spread through him.

It was impossible. He rose, grasped her in his arms and kissed her passionately.

For several sweet seconds he felt her body respond, then she pushed him away.

'You are too free, sir!' she gasped.

'You say that to me?' he glared at her, a mixture of anger, wretchedness and desire filling his confused soul.

Her expression became hard. 'Our dalliance gives you no rights.'

He continued to gaze at her, his breathing fast and

ragged. He wanted to ravish her or to hit her, he didn't know which desire was the greater, found it impossible to do either and cursed his inability to act.

She stood still and implacable by the window, almost as though she dared him to touch her again, but the coldness in her face kept him immobile. 'No one yet knows, James, but, yes, I am to become the Marchioness of Brecon as soon as Viscount Purbeck is wed to Miss More.'

'You scheming hussy,' he burst out.

Her eyes narrowed. 'Temper your language.'

'Anne, forgive me, but the marquess! The man is an animal!'

'Sir, you go beyond the bounds!'

'No, but you and he! You must see—'

'I see that it will be impossible for you to remain with my lord after our union.'

It was too much. James gave an incoherent exclamation of disgust and left the room, slamming the door behind him.

The urchin who'd watched over his mount received a too large coin, flung in too great a haste. The horse was untied and mounted with awkward speed and in a moment James had spurred him into Whitehall. There the traffic forced him into a slower pace. He rode, jumbled and jostled amongst the carriages and carts, unable to work out where it was he was supposed to be going. He only knew he wanted to fling himself into the Thames.

Chapter Thirteen

As the door slammed behind James, Anne resumed her seat, picked up her novel and soon lost herself once again in the story of a serving girl who rose to gentility through marriage to a rake whose advances she had spurned until the ring was on her finger.

But a few minutes later her maid announced that Mr Granville sought admittance.

Anne received him with delight. 'Patrick! I have looked for you ever since my return from the Wiltons.'

He made her a brief bow, scowling. 'I go to the continent for a brief trip and arrive back to find my sister has lost her wits and buried herself in the country, leaving my lord the Marquess of Brecon to find other charmers to entertain him. I am not pleased with you, Anne.'

'So you stayed away to punish me?' she gave him a slow, luxurious smile but he failed to respond. 'Come, Patrick, allow me some skill with men. Brecon writ me every day. The longer he was without my company, the hotter he grew. We are now engaged.' She stretched out languorous arms.

He came swiftly to kneel at her side, taking one of her hands in his. 'You have brought him to the point! Oh, Anne, I knew you could succeed.'

She looked down at his long face. His quicksilver temperament could turn a chilling severity into dancing charm through nothing more than a smile that transformed not only his too-thin mouth but also his eyes, set like a Tartar's slightly on the slant and sea green like her own.

He was smiling now. 'My lord has engaged me to ride with him tomorrow. I shall congratulate him.'

She placed a finger on his lips. 'Say nothing. All is to remain secret until the contract between Richard and Miss More is signed.' Then she cocked her head on one side. 'Still, Alexander must, I think, understand I would tell my brother.'

'Your half-brother.' His smile was both intimate and bold.

'My half-brother.'

He kissed each of her fingers in turn. 'Did I not say all you had to do was to keep him dangling and he must offer?'

Anne shivered and pulled away her hand. 'But, Patrick, what if this proposed marriage for Richard fails? He tells me without it there will be no money.'

Her brother rose in a single, supple movement. His tall body loomed over her. 'Money to the Brecons is very different from money to you and me. Tell him you will be happy to live in penury amongst the treasures of Brecon House.' He twirled suddenly on one heel. 'Oh, Anne, as long as you can move within society as marchioness, what matters money? We have managed for so long, you and I, on so little. But now, with your help, I will charm myself an heiress.'

Anne smiled indulgently at him. Five years older than herself, so much of the time he seemed younger.

Their mother had been wooed from Patrick's father, an impoverished Irish gentleman, by a French count. Widowed by the resultant duel, she had fled with her lover to France, leaving Patrick to be brought up by aunts among the mists of Ireland. At seventeen he'd gone in search of his mother. After two years of racketing around the continent, he'd found her, widowed a second time and living with his beautiful half-sister on the remnants of the count's fortune. The countess, gradually losing her battle with a wasting disease, had succumbed to his charm and on her deathbed made him Anne's guardian.

How many years was it now they'd eked out a precarious existence, always seeking the marriage for her that would bring them security? Too many. And for too long now every glance in her mirror reminded that her dazzling looks were but lent. The lovely oval of her face remained unchanged, as did the profusion of her dark hair, but close inspection could now detect the first flaws in the soft perfection of her skin, particularly around the eyes and mouth. Time was indeed a-flying and it was essential she gathered this rose of social respectability that was at last offered. She could not afford to be too nice over the character of the man who offered it.

'Come, sit by me, I have seen too little of you these last few weeks.'

Patrick flung himself into the chair beside her own, his eyes still gleaming with delight. 'Sweet sis, amuse me.'

'Oh, I have to tell you of life with the Wiltons. That would amuse you, though not above half an hour.'

'I trust you have behaved yourself?'

The blue-green eyes opened wide in hurt surprise. 'How can you doubt it!' Then she brought a finger to her mouth and lifted an eyebrow in thought. 'I should confess, however. Ignorance brought me near disaster at one point.' The eyes peeked at him in sly amusement.

'I trust whatever it was hasn't completely ruined your reputation.'

Patrick's tone was suddenly harsh. Anne clasped her hands tightly together in the lap of her loose gown and assumed her most seductive manner.

'Why, I had with me the most delicious of *bergère* hats. I wore it for the first time with a delightful sack dress and my hair dressed *à la mouton de tête*. Rosie has quite mastered all those little sausage rolls and with their darkness powdered, the style is charming.'

'To the point, Anne,' ground out her brother, rising and moving across to the window, where he stood, tapping at the glass.

Her hands tightened until the knuckles were white but her voice was lighter than ever. 'Well, the dress was yellow silk with ribbons and bows of white, you will swoon with desire when you see it. So what more natural than that I should trim the hat with white ribbons to match.' She paused as Patrick Granville groaned.

'Lud, Anne, must you always be such an idiot? Here we are, establishing ourselves as respectable *ton* with no small difficulty, devoid as we are of family or friends, and you have to proclaim yourself a *Jacobite*! Not more than a month after the rebellion has been put down.'

Anne laughed, a rippling sound of teasing amusement that never failed to enrapture listeners. 'We are but newly arrived from the continent. Had you explained to your innocent sister the implication of white ribbons for one's hat?'

He gave a shrug that said it was impossible to guard against every contingency of life. 'And the consequences of the thoughtless ornamentation of your headgear?'

'Oh, my lady takes me aside, praises my courage but advises against such flaunting of my political sympathies at this time. Rosie changes the ribbons to yellow and my friendship with the Wiltons deepens with every moment,' she concluded triumphantly. 'The second George would seem as unpopular with certain sections of society as ever his papa was.'

'You were fortunate,' Patrick said sarcastically. 'The Bonnie Prince found how thin on the ground Jacobite supporters actually are in this country.'

'Ah, Patrick, how careful you are always, cannot you sometimes just plunge into life? You remind me of my Lord Wilton. Never have you seen such earnestness! Such philosophizing over higher moral values. Would you believe that the historical painting is to rate higher than the portrait or landscape?' She paused, laughing, and he laughed with her.

Encouraged, she continued, 'You must own I was sorely tried. And when my host showed me a dull and drear encounter between some gods that he proclaimed a masterpiece, I had to point out a divine Venetian view by Canaletto hung almost next door to it and say I held that to be far superior.'

Patrick's smile died from his eyes and they narrowed. 'Canaletto! I have told you, I will not hear that man's name upon your lips.'

Anne placed a hand upon his cheek. 'Patrick, as I

have assured you before, 'twas nothing, a pleasurable dalliance, nothing more.'

He snatched her hand away. 'I trust such dalliances are now at an end! The marquess will not stand for any but the most circumspect of behaviour.' He strode to the other side of the small room. 'I was a fool to let you talk me into pretending in Venice that we knew not each other. I should have been there, at your side, protecting you.'

'What, and scare away my suitors as you did so often before? It is bad enough that you have foisted that ancient fool, Madame Fournier, on me. I tire of inventing ploys that take her from my side.'

'She lends you respectability.' He paused, his head flung back, his eyes regarding her. 'You have heard Canaletto plans to visit England?'

Anne sat very still. She nodded, her eyes on her brother.

''Tis impossible you should meet, you will not meet.' Patrick came and sat beside her again. He took her hands in his. 'Do not even think it.'

Anne hoped he could not see how her pulse was racing. There was so much Patrick did not know. So much he must never know.

Chapter Fourteen

James Bennett did not throw himself into the Thames. He went instead on his errand to the More household in the City.

All his life, James had submitted to whatever rigours were necessary to advance himself. He had early decided that the life of a provincial lawyer was too circumscribed. He wanted, he needed, to have wealth and position.

At university he had worked as hard at forming connections as he had at his studies, his aim being a recommendation to a person of influence. An interview with the Marquess of Brecon had seen him become tutor to the viscount for the Grand Tour.

And afterwards he had secured the position of secretary to the marquess. He had seen it as the first step on the ladder to advancement. Today secretary, tomorrow some well-paid sinecure the marquess or some connection of his had in his bestowal. One that would offer him the possibilities of riches as well as position. After all, he had intelligence, education, languages and it wasn't only Lord Richard who'd had his manners polished by the tour. It might take a few years but James had been confident that at some stage he would be able to offer Anne Montesqui a life worthy of her beauty.

Now he saw what a fool he'd been.

Gradually as James rode towards the City, the tumult in his heart and body settled. By the time he reached the quiet road off Cheapside where was Balthasar More's handsome four-storey brick house with its wealth of decorative stonework, built after the great Fire of London, his mind was working coolly.

A servant who answered the door took charge of the basket of apricots and said he would ascertain if Miss More was at home.

James was shown into a room on the ground floor, sparsely furnished with a few good pieces. Hardly had he had time to study the one painting on the wall, a gloomy river scene with ruins, than the door opened again and two men were shown in. 'I will enquire if Mr More is available,' the same servant said.

The florid face of one of the men darkened. 'I have an appointment and am expected,' he said abruptly. 'Alderman John Fowler, as if you didn't know, the number of times I have been to this house. Your master would be better served by someone who could note his regular visitors.'

'I regret I have not been with Mr More for long,' murmured the man as he eased himself swiftly out of the room.

'Impossible to get good servants these days.' Alderman Fowler plumped himself down in one of the chairs with a nod towards James.

He was a well-set-up man of some thirty years with a pugnacious jaw and eyebrows that beetled over small, deep-set eyes. He was almost as tall as James and as he turned to his companion, James was startled by the breadth of shoulder in the well-cut dark brown coat, its skirts long with large outside pockets. By his dress, the man looked as though he could well be another city merchant doing business with Balthasar More.

His companion, though, appeared thoroughly out of place. Not only was his dress that of a fellow of the lower sort, it had seen much wear, his shoes were battered, their ties scarcely holding together, whilst his breeches were secured around his waist with rough twine.

He seemed ill at ease, glancing around the room nervously.

'Sit, Scallion,' said the alderman, rather as he might have spoken to a dog. 'I'll warrant that fellow will be back quick enough once he has spoken to Mr More. He'll not keep us waiting, not if he knows what's good for him. Then you can tell him your story.'

''Tis the stone, you see,' the man's tone was ingratiating. 'That's the key.'

'Yes, well,' said the alderman and James thought the glance he sent him held a warning for the other man. 'Keep all for our meeting.'

The servant reappeared. 'Miss More will receive you,' he said to James.

'And Mr More?' asked the alderman petulantly.

'Will be available shortly,' the man replied imperturbably and led the way out of the room.

James followed him into the lavishly panelled hall, up a handsome oak staircase to the first floor and into an airy parlour lit by three large windows. Like the room downstairs, the few pieces with which it was furnished were of excellent quality.

Charlotte More stood in the centre of the room dressed in grey silk, her eyes deeply shadowed with weariness. 'Mr Bennett, it is good of you to call and the apricots are deeply appreciated.'

She spoke so sweetly and looked so brave, James found himself coming quickly forward and bowing low over her hand. It felt icy and very small. 'I trust that Mrs More is recovering from her indisposition?' he asked gently, lightly holding that cold and fragile hand.

'The doctor is hopeful she has passed the crisis and that she will gradually recover something of herself.'

'I am truly glad to hear it,' he said. Instinctively, he picked up her other hand and warmed them both with his, rubbing them gently. 'You must have given her the best of nursing.'

A delicate flush coloured her pale cheeks. 'You are kind sir. I feel her suffering so.' She gently pulled away her hand but continued to stand with innate dignity, her blue eyes translucently bright as though tears might spill over any minute. 'Sir, I have to thank you for your help that day we came to Brecon House. Your behaviour was – was everything I required.' The large eyes blinked briefly.

'It was nothing. I wish I could have done more.'

'You will take a cup of tea? We have a new consignment of Bohea – 'tis excellent, most refreshing.'

James chose a chair and watched her pull the bell. 'I trust Mr More is in good health?'

'Excellent, I thank you,' Charlotte said, a little dryly.

'He operates from these premises?' James's interest had been piqued by the other two visitors he'd left downstairs.

Charlotte settled herself in a chair not far from his, her skirts billowing prettily as she sat. She smoothed them down with a gentle gesture. 'He has an office downstairs but his main business is with the East India Company elsewhere in the City.'

'He is here today?'

She nodded. 'Did you wish to see him? You have a message from the marquess, perhaps? I can enquire whether he is free.' Her eyes looked worried and for the first time James wondered just how willing she was to enter into this marriage with Lord Richard.

He knew, none better, that the young man had only his background and position to recommend him. But James had assumed that the glory of joining the aristocracy, of gaining an unassailable position in society, would be overwhelmingly attractive to one such as Charlotte More.

Now, faced with this girl, recognizing her straightforward honesty, sensing courage allied to acute sensibility, he felt that this estimation could have been overhasty.

She had given him a perfect opportunity to press the question of the contract but he shook his head. 'Nay, I just wondered.'

A servant entered, a woman past her first youth, neatly dressed with a white cap and apron. Charlotte requested tea be brought.

'I thought you might like some,' the servant said, glancing at James in an open and friendly way. 'I have everything ready.'

Charlotte smiled at her, 'I can always rely on you Molly, can't I?'

'That you can, Miss Charlotte, and always have been able to, since you were in your cradle. It'll be a sad day for us when you leave this house and go to what could be foreign parts, so different as it'll be.' She sneaked a glance towards James as she stalked from the room.

'You must not mind Molly, she has been my friend since ever I can remember,' Charlotte said.

'She is just as my mother's Jenny,' James said quickly. 'None of us is allowed to retain a shred of character in the eyes of our friends when Jenny is around. She always speaks her mind.'

Charlotte laughed and James congratulated himself.

She regarded James with frank eyes. 'Can I ask you, Mr Bennett, to tell me more of Viscount Purbeck? When I tried to question my father, he said such matters were not my concern. But I think they are of great concern to me.'

'Indeed, I have to agree. What would you know?'

'Why, what sort of man he is. You must know, looks matter to me not, be the soul pure and honourable.' Then she flushed again, deeper, as though she feared she had insulted the viscount's looks, which, indeed, James thought, by inference she had.

Now how, in heaven's name, was he to answer her? Loyalty to his employer demanded he declare Richard someone she could respect and admire as a husband through life. But, thought James suddenly, did the Brecons deserve his loyalty? He remembered his meeting with the marquess that very morning.

'Miss More, you know what young men are like,' James offered.

She smiled at him, looking very young. 'Alas, sir, I do not.'

'Of course, you have no brother,' he said. No, nor sister either. It was her position as only heir to Balthasar More that made her so attractive to the marquess.

'Alas, my mother bore many children but none apart from myself survived the first few years of life.'

'I am more fortunate than you. I have three sisters and two brothers. They live in Bristol with my parents, being as yet not out of the schoolroom, but I dearly love them all.' It was an exaggeration. The girls were spoilt and the boys boisterous. None had James's intelligence, all seemed happy to consider their lives centred on the city in which they were growing up. Yet he did enjoy their prattle on his infrequent visits home. James glanced at Charlotte More and decided honesty would get him further here than any other approach. 'Of course, they are much younger than I, two babies died between myself and Lydia, the nearest to me. They all try my patience at times and I cannot pretend any of them offers me the companionship I would value from a sister or brother nearer to me in age.'

Charlotte learned forward earnestly. 'Oh, I understand, Mr Bennett. I, too, long for such a companionship. If I could find it in marriage, I would value it above everything.' She paused and smoothed her gown again. 'I understand you spent two years with Lord Richard on the continent. You must have grown close. Please, will you not tell me what you mean by saying, "you know what young men are"?'

James gazed at her eyes, their soft blue serious. An outrageous thought entered his mind. So outrageous it was irresistibly attractive.

As he wondered if he should succumb to its seductiveness, Molly reappeared, followed by a younger maid.

Molly placed a silver kettle and spirit lamp beside Charlotte More and lit the lamp. The other servant set alongside it a tray bearing a small silver teapot, two small flowered porcelain bowls with matching saucers, a silver ewer that held cream and a bowl of sugar. Then Molly brought over a polished wooden box from a side table. Charlotte removed a key from a chatelaine hung at her waist and unlocked the caddy.

James watched the elegant deftness of her movements as she used a wide-bowled spoon to add tea leaves to the silver pot, then carefully tipped in hot water from the elegant kettle. All the grandeur of Brecon House could not conjure up such grace as he saw here.

James refused the offer of cream and was handed a cup of the fragrant tea by a beaming Molly, whose smile seemed to say, 'There, can't my Miss More do things in the proper style?' As the door closed behind Molly and the other maid he made up his mind.

'Miss More, I had charge of Lord Purbeck; I was his tutor, responsible for his well-being. He was, is, far above me in social standing. It was not a relationship of equals. There were,' he hesitated as though doubtful of how to put what he had to say, then continued in an earnest voice. 'Let me say this, if there were failings on Richard's part, I am sure they were but the faults of youth and that, married to one such as yourself, with intelligence, character and moral strength, he cannot but prove a worthy partner.' He injected as much admiration into his eyes as he could and held her gaze for a long moment.

Again came that pretty flush as she dropped her eyelids, veiling her expression. When she raised them, James knew that he had struck exactly the note he'd hoped.

'Sir, I appreciate your loyalty and trust Lord Richard honours it truly.' She replaced her tea bowl and saucer carefully on the table by her elbow and James admired the graceful turn of her head and neck.

He was wondering how to take the conversation in the direction he wanted when an elderly woman bustled into the room. 'My dear Charlotte, you should have sent Molly to wake me! What would your father say if he knew you were entertaining a young man all on your own!'

'Dear aunt, you were so tired from helping to nurse Mama I did not like to disturb your rest. Nor was it necessary; this is Mr Bennett, from Viscount Purbeck and the Marquess of Brecon. He brought Mama apricots from Amberley, the Brecon seat. Mr Bennett, may I present Mrs Tallent, my aunt.'

Mrs Tallent's face had the appearance of deeply lined dough, with currants for eyes. Her mouth was loose-lipped, her figure amply filling the voluminous black silk dress with fine lawn apron and fichu. She surveyed James with lively curiosity. 'My, you're a pretty fellow. I trust your master is as handsome,' she said jovially, pulling the bell then seating herself.

James found himself catching a glance from Charlotte that was full of amusement. 'Aunt,' she said severely, 'pray do not let my father hear you talk so. It was Mr Bennett who was so kind when Mama collapsed at Brecon House. You remember my description of that sad event?'

Mrs Tallent clapped her hands together. 'Indeed! I blame myself, Mr Bennett. If I had but realized what a sad state my poor sister was in, I would have insisted on accompanying Charlotte. As it is, we now wait on her recovery before Mr More will think of rearranging the signing of the contract. It is a matter of some concern to my sister and, of course, to myself. We so look forward to dear Charlotte's elevation.'

Here was someone James had no compunctions about quizzing. 'I trust Mrs More will soon have recovered sufficiently to allow the contract to go forward?' he suggested with studied politeness, carefully avoiding Charlotte's glance whilst watching the sudden stillness of her expression.

'Alas, my poor sister is so very unwell. The doctor has declared complete quiet essential for her recovery.'

'So Lord Purbeck must await with patience the sealing of his engagement to Miss More?' James suggested smoothly. He noted the downcast eyes and hands that clasped each other tightly in the grey silk lap and decided the prospect of delay did not displease Miss More.

Molly came in with an additional tea bowl and saucer. 'Ah,' said Mrs Tallent in delight, 'you forestall all my wishes.'

The servant said nothing but smiled easily as she waited for the bowl to be filled, then handed it to Mrs Tallent.

'Mr Bennett, more tea?' asked Charlotte while Molly hovered at his elbow.

He rose. 'Alas, I have errands to perform and the marquess, and Lord Purbeck, will be eager to hear how Mrs More does. Perhaps I may call again?'

Charlotte rose with that particular grace that was her own. 'Indeed, we shall be most happy to see you, Mr Bennett. Perhaps Papa will be available when next you call.'

'Lud, indeed, my brother-in-law will be most happy to talk to an emissary from the marquess.' Mrs Tallent's hands were all of a flutter and she gave James a beaming smile as he bowed low.

As James had hoped, Molly showed him down the stairs. 'I trust the apricots were received with favour?' he asked as they neared the top of the long flight.

'They are the finest quality, sir,' she said, a trifle stiffly.

'I expect your nearest market is Smithfield? Does that not offer splendid fruit?'

'Indeed, sir, it does. As fine as any great estate.'

'Miss More is fortunate to have someone of such discernment in her household. Tell me, do you attend the market for her?'

'I does. Often with Miss Charlotte herself.' This was said with a speaking look that suggested Molly had accurately gauged his interest in the More household shopping. 'I suppose in his lordship's house she will not perform such errands?' she continued in a disapproving tone.

'She will have a life of leisure with Lord Richard, all pleasure and entertainment,' James said cheerfully.

'Hmmpf!' Molly snorted. ''Tis not the life she's been brought up for.' Then added hastily, 'Begging your pardon, sir.'

'You probably attend the market early for the best choice?' James offered. They were near the bottom of the stairs and the front door loomed.

'Nine is our usual hour, sir,' Molly said, and her brown eyes twinkled at him.

He pressed a silver coin into her hand and took his leave well satisfied with his visit.

Outside James rescued his horse from the attentions of the lad he'd pressed into service on his arrival.

'I walked him, mister,' the urchin said. 'I was not feared.'

'Good, that's good,' murmured James without listening, his thoughts still busy with the scene he'd just left.

He found a suitable coin and tossed it to the lad, who immediately bit it to prove it, then he walked the horse a little down the street to check the legs had not stiffened during the wait.

It seemed the urchin had spoken true, the horse's gait was easy. James turned him a little beyond the More house and was about to mount when he saw the door open. Alderman Fowler and Scallion, his disreputable companion, came out.

'I told you how it would be,' Scallion whined.

'Tush, leave Balthasar More to me. We have found the key to the man; I shall turn it as and when I see fit.'

A carriage rumbled past and drowned their conversation. James mounted his horse. As he overtook the alderman and his companion he heard Scallion say, 'I told you, I need the money. I did the job and I've not been treated right. It's not fair.'

James sensed rather than saw the alderman silence his companion as he passed.

Had he recognized James as the man who had shared the More front parlour? If so, what had they been talking about that the alderman was concerned should not be overheard?

Chapter Fifteen

Canaletto's head ached and his insides protested. Two days after his near escape from death, his body still announced it needed rest.

When he'd woken the morning after the attack, for a moment he'd thought he was at home in Venice. But the light had been all wrong. It had none of the wavery incandescence of sun reflected off water. And why did he feel so dreadful?

Then it had all come back. The loss of McSwiney's address, the first attempt on his life, his kidnapping by Fanny Rooker, the brush with death in that awful alleyway. He saw again Scallion's mean, malevolent face and the flash of his curiously wrought gold earring as the knife was raised.

Despair hit him as he remembered that he'd lost the major part of his fortune. The fruit of so many years' painstaking hard work – what had been left, that is, after the presents he had lavished on the woman he had hoped would share his life. All had gone.

At least, though, he was still alive.

Canaletto lay in the bed and tried to feel grateful for that fact but gratitude was hard to summon. His ageing limbs hurt too much. The thought of how hard he would have to work if he was to build up his fortune again made him feel so tired he couldn't even think of getting out of bed. All those years he'd toiled away, imbuing architectural detail with his vision of Venice, its colour, drama and magic. Then insisting on prices that valued his views as the masterpieces they were.

Now the money that he had intended to invest in this booming English market to provide for his old age had gone.

If only he were younger and had his old energy. If only he could feel this situation was a challenge and not a disaster.

After all, there was enough gold coin in his money belt to keep him until his first commission could bring in more funds. That is, if only he could find McSwiney.

And if only he could have a bowl of Maria's fish soup, subtly spicy, comforting, familiar, then he really would begin to feel better.

The door opened and little Miss Fanny entered bearing a steaming bowl and for a moment Canaletto thought his wish had been answered.

'A dish of hot milk and bread,' Fanny said cheerfully, placing her tray on the bedside commode. 'The milk seller called not an hour past and the bread is yesterday's baking. Come, let me help you.' She grasped his shoulders, really for one so small she had astonishing strength, and gently pulled him up the bed, rearranging the pillows more comfortably.

Canaletto looked down at a nightshirt he failed to recognize.

''Tis Ned's,' Fanny said calmly, giving him the bowl. 'I fear your garments are beyond repair. If you will give me a key to your box, I will find you something else to wear.'

Canaletto carefully unpicked some of the stitches that held the canvas body belt together, and extracted a key.

'But I'll not retrieve them today. You need to nurse your wounds.'

Canaletto raised a spoon of the milk sops. They mightn't be fish soup but they were surprisingly good. In a remarkably short time the bowl was empty and Fanny looked satisfied.

It struck Canaletto then that she had lost something of the cheerfulness that had been such a part of her character. And surely her eyes looked as though she had been crying?

It was too exhausting to ask her what had happened. No doubt that harpy of a sister-in-law was at the bottom of whatever it was. And no doubt Miss Fanny would find a way to deal with her. Canaletto found he had limitless confidence in the girl's ability to handle whatever life threw at her.

And already his eyes were closing. He was asleep before Fanny had left the room.

Sharp voices woke him. Canaletto could tell from the light that several hours had passed. Already he felt more alive. His intestines had settled, his aching had lessened. He lay and listened to the sound of bitter argument. The slam of a door produced an abrupt silence and shortly afterwards Fanny brought him mutton broth with barley. Her eyes were red but her manner determinedly cheerful.

'Eat it all, it will give you strength.'

She had skimmed the fat from the surface and the rising steam smelled appetizingly nutritious. Canaletto fell upon the soup eagerly. Almost he felt up to questioning her as to what the trouble was. Except she whisked out of the room before he could summon up the strength.

Once again his sleep was disturbed by shouting and Lucy's whine razored incomprehensibly up the stairs. Then he thought he heard his name. Was it his presence that was causing all this unpleasantness? Was Fanny's pleading, the hurt in her voice, on his behalf?

It was many years since Canaletto had felt beholden to anyone and never towards a woman. Now it made him uneasy. For too many years he had been alone, emotionally as well as physically.

Apart from his mother, the only comfortable relationship he had known with a woman was his sister. To have had her son as his apprentice had been a delight that had gone beyond the excitement and anticipation of the lad's enormous talents as a painter. Bernardo and he had enjoyed a comradeship that had reached its peak with a tour of northern Italy. Now the boy was making his own way and Canaletto still missed his companionship. He had no expectation that such a relationship would be repeated.

Once in his distant youth he had thought he had found a great love. After two months of intense delight had come bitter disillusionment. All the more bitter for destroying his trust in his father as well as his love.

That had pushed him into making the break from painting scenery. How scornful his father had been about his prospects. Looking back now, though, Canaletto wondered for the first time whether his father's scorn had not hidden jealousy of a talent so very much greater than his own.

Canaletto refused to think about his much more

recent disappointment. Instead he returned to considering his present position.

Would Scallion be satisfied with the fortune in his satchel? Or had he intended to rob Canaletto of life as well as money?

But why should a painter such as he be in peril of his life?

What was it Miss Fanny had said, that the English painters would have to look to their laurels now Canaletto was amongst them? Could jealousy or fear for their livelihoods have put his life in danger?

Canaletto's vanity knew no bounds but even he found it difficult to believe a report of his arrival in London could stimulate such an extreme response.

No, there must be something else.

Canaletto smoothed his bedsheet and decided he had to treat it as a puzzle. After all, he was no stranger to sorting out puzzles.

It had started years ago with a request from Joseph Smith.

Joseph entertained visiting Englishmen lavishly, gave them advice, told them where to visit, introduced them to ex-patriots and to Venetian noblemen. And he showed them his collection of paintings by Canaletto then took their orders. For it soon seemed a Venetian view by the topographical master was an essential memento of their visit, even at the prices Canaletto insisted on charging.

Now, Joseph said, one of the aristocratic young sprigs was in trouble. Canaletto told Joseph he wasn't interested. Venice was lovely but amoral and young men in search of adventure should expect trouble. All these youngsters were accompanied by bear-leaders and

sufficiently supplied with money to extricate themselves from any peccadillo.

But Joseph had pleaded. 'Tonio,' he'd said, using that
coaxing voice with its English accent that Canaletto
found so different, charming in its unmusicality. 'You
see everything that happens in Venice. Please, help my
young friend. A valuable watch given him by his father
has disappeared and he is so worried.

Canaletto had shrugged his shoulders, 'What can I
do?'

'You know Venice as no one else, Tonio. There is
nothing that goes on that your eyes miss. Is there not
something you can do to recover the item? After all, his
father has ordered two of your views.'

'Go to the officials,' Canaletto had suggested. 'Let
them instigate enquiries.'

Joseph had shrugged. 'Milord is reluctant to bring
himself to the notice of the authorities. He desires a
less formal approach.'

Then he'd described the time-piece, its jewels,
enamelling and gold chasing, and Canaletto had been
intrigued. Such a piece should not be impossible to
trace.

But, 'You ask me to produce my paintings without
delay. Always you drive me to finish commissions for
your friends,' Canaletto had waved a hand at the
painting of St Mark's Square he'd been engaged upon
that day. 'I've no time to search for lost watches.'

'Ah, Tonio, for me!' Joseph had pleaded. He had a
way that got under your skin and in the end Canaletto
had agreed to see what he could do.

Traversing the city as he did so often, dressed incon-
spicuously, studying every angle offered by buildings,

canals and inhabitants intent on their daily lives, Canaletto was as well acquainted with the con merchants, the pickpockets and other petty criminals as he was with the senators, priests and first citizens. He'd chosen carefully who he approached with news of the reward and it hadn't taken long for word to travel to the right quarter.

Milord had received back his property.

Over the years there had been other incidents, lost and stolen property, unfortunate involvements with one or another of the amazingly high number of personable women, both respectable and professional, who inhabited the pearl of the Adriatic, together with some more sinister entanglements. Yes, he had had great practice in solving puzzles.

Well, then, if this Scallion had been set upon him by someone, that someone had to have known he was coming. Moreover, he had to know the boat by which he was arriving. Who did that include?

The Rookers had known through an Italian engraver, a friend of Jacopo Amigoni's. There were many Italian artists in London, did they all know Canaletto's details?

McSwiney knew, of course. Would he have told others?

Who had Joseph told? It was he who had written to McSwiney. Had there been anybody else?

Canaletto gave up, the list was too long.

He flung back the bedclothes, slipped his thin legs off the bed and tried to stand up.

At first he swayed uncertainly and had to clutch at the night table but then he found his balance and managed to stagger around the narrow bed, panting slightly at the effort it called for.

As he stood triumphant, in came Mistress Lucy, her swollen stomach preceding her, her face sour and aggressive.

'You have been here long enough, Mr Canal,' she said abruptly. 'Two days ago I allowed myself to be persuaded you needed time to recover. That time is now expired.'

'I did not ask to be brought to this house,' Canaletto said curtly, conscious of her supercilious eyes on his bare legs beneath the nightshirt and the thick stubble on his face.

'Indeed, we are both sufferers under my sister-in-law's interfering ways. Well, she has come to the end of her reign in this house. She, too, must now find somewhere else to live.'

Canaletto could hardly believe his ears. Edward Rooker's sister to be turned out of her home? For a moment he forgot his own quandary, how in his weakened state he was to find somewhere else to lodge. 'Why?' he asked simply.

Lucy merely gave him a cold glance and turned to go. 'By this evening,' she said as she left.

Almost immediately Fanny entered, her arms filled with clothes, her manner urgent.

'Signor, you must go, now!'

'Mistress Lucy said by evening.'

'Oh, Lucy! 'Tis not her! You are in danger, signor. Not five minutes ago, watching this house, I saw the man who tried to push you in the water and steal your fortune.'

'Jack Scallion!' Canaletto sat abruptly on to the bed, panic flooding through him. 'Where?'

She dumped a suit of clothes on the bed, her breath

coming quickly, and straightened out coat and breeches while she talked. 'I slipped down the road to get more ink for Ned. I saw Alderman Fowler across the street, Lucy's brother.' A delicate shudder ran through her. 'I cannot abide that man! His eyes dart and dive like a rat's.' She added a shirt and a cravat to the bed. 'I thought he was coming here, to worry Ned, so I watched, to see if I should come back and help.'

Yes, Fanny would. She was more protective of her brother than a cat with her kittens.

'Instead I saw him accost a man leaning against a building, as though idling away time. There was just something about the alderman's attitude, it was as if he wanted to speak to the man yet feared to be seen, the set of his shoulders was so shifty.'

The girl certainly was an observer!

'He pushed the man into a small alley and it was then I saw that the other was the villain who tried to escape with your satchel at the dock. So I forgot about the ink and came straight back. You must leave now, signor.' She sagged against the door frame, momentarily out of breath.

Canaletto's thoughts scurried around his tired brain. 'This fellow, he wait for me?'

'What else could he have been doing? Why else would he stand at just that point?' Fanny said impatiently. 'He had a hat pulled down over his eyes, as though he didn't want to be recognized.'

'Could you be sure, then, that it was he?' For a moment Canaletto's confidence in Fanny's powers of observation faltered.

'Forget the sharpness of that nose, the way his chin juts or the way his mouth sneaks up at one corner? I remember his legs, too, thin and bandy. No, signor, doubt me not.' Fanny pushed herself away from the door and grasped the handle. 'You must dress and go.'

'But how does he know I am here? When he left me for dead?'

Fanny shrugged exasperatedly. 'How do I know?'

'But he has my fortune, what more does he want with me?' Canaletto still found it hard to accept his life was at stake.

'Signor, you ask questions and I have no answers. Why do you not find somewhere else to stay? Somewhere safer?'

'But where?'

Fanny clapped a hand to her forehead. 'Fool that I am, I forgot. I spoke this morning to a painter I know; he specializes in draperies for many of the major portraitists. He did not know your friend, McSwiney, but told me those interested in the world of art frequent Slaughter's Coffee House. I am sure you may find him there or, if not, someone will know of his direction. Now, quickly, dress. I will bring you water and a razor to shave then command you a carriage. And ensure that rogue does not follow you.' Fanny slipped from the room.

Canaletto stripped off Ned's nightshirt, too voluminous by far for his slight frame, and started to dress, noting with some relief that Fanny had had the wit not to offer him his best wear. Canaletto mourned the loss of his second-best coat and breeches. What an idiot he had been to don such fine clothes before he'd landed. Such vanity!

His ribs ached as he secured the body belt over his wound and then drew on his shirt and work-a-day breeches. By the end all his limbs were trembling with the effort. Even as his fingers worked as quickly as they could, his mind was in a turmoil.

Fanny reappeared with hot water and razor and removed his stubble, working in concentrated silence while Canaletto worried about trusting himself to a coffee house. How could he be certain to find McSwiney there?

But Miss Fanny seemed confident and what other course was there open to him?

'There, you look fine enough to visit the king,' she said, wiping soap from the corner of his mouth. 'I will arrange a carriage for you.'

She disappeared with the bowl of soapy water. Canaletto wiped the sweat from his forehead with the corner of the sheet and picked up his wig. Then stuffed it in a pocket. Mud clung to the hairs and, anyway, his head ached too much to put it on. Then he saw that the soft bonnet he wore whilst painting had also been brought. That girl was thoughtful! He arranged it carefully over the bandages. He must look a fright but it would have to do.

He swept up the small pile of silver coins someone, no doubt Fanny, had placed on the night table, then, his legs hardly carrying him, Canaletto left the room and staggered down the stairs.

In the workshop Ned Rooker was bent over a copper plate resting on a cushion. How could he work so calmly when his women folk seemed intent on raising drama around him? And how could his hand seem so steady today?

It was no work of art he was intent on etching, though, just a crude drawing furnished with scurrilous verses. No doubt a satiric broadsheet to be sold in the streets. A waste of the lad's talents; no wonder his sister had been so keen to improve his chances.

Ned leapt to his feet. 'You are recovered, signor?' he asked with what seemed genuine concern. 'Fanny says you are to leave us. She has procured you a carriage and it awaits you at the door.'

Canaletto thought of the evil look in the assassin's eye as he had raised his knife in that dark and dreadful alleyway. He thought of bright and resourceful Fanny who, despite his incivility, had twice rescued him from death.

'Signorina Fanny, your sister, is feared for my safety. She says there is man outside who attacks me.'

Ned shrugged his shoulders and his sullen look returned. 'Fanny has an active imagination.'

'She seeks to protect those she is loyal to,' Canaletto said sternly.

Ned shifted his feet uneasily.

'Signorina Fanny says she will prevent this – this fellow from seeing my carriage – , no, that is not it, from following after my carriage. I think she does this, she is in danger.'

Ned's head rose at that and his eyes sparked. 'You suggest, signor, I do not protect my sister? God's blood, but I would never let her suffer!' His eyes bored into Canaletto's. 'Especially for one such as you!'

Canaletto allowed the insult to pass. 'I look to you, signor, that Signorina Fanny comes not into danger.'

Outside waited a carriage drawn by a sturdy-looking horse. The driver raised a finger to his tricorne hat and nodded at Canaletto. 'You the gent I'm awaiting, then, sir?'

A little way down the street Canaletto could see Fanny chatting to a comfortably sized matron holding a wriggling chicken by its feet. His keen glance raked the press of people in the street. He could not see Scallion. With a sigh of relief he climbed into the carriage, let down the window and looked out at Ned. 'Tell Signorina Fanny I send for my boxes as soon as I have a direction.'

Ned nodded but said nothing.

'Where to, squire?' asked the driver.

'Drive on west,' Canaletto ordered, he was taking no chances on ears listening for a direction. Time enough to give the address of Slaughter's Coffee House when they were out of range.

The carriage started and he settled back with a distinct lessening of tension. Miss Fanny had been wrong, Scallion hadn't been waiting for him.

Then, faintly but distinctly, from behind came the sound of a fracas.

Canaletto let down the window and leaned out.

'Careful, sir,' warned the footman. 'Like as not you'll get your head whipped off, there's little enough room in this road.'

Canaletto hardly heard him, his every muscle was strained to distinguish what was going on in the road behind. All he could see was a crowd gathering, all he could hear was shouting and unseemly cries.

He almost asked the carriage to be stopped. But what could he do? He was too frail to fight. He'd be no help to Signorina Fanny. And whatever was happening back there, she had organized it so he could escape.

Canaletto collapsed on to the hard seat of the carriage, closed his eyes and sent up a prayer to the lord in heaven for the safety of little Miss Fanny.

Chapter Sixteen

William Pitt, Paymaster General to His Majesty King George II, stood gazing out of the window of his office.

Across Whitehall he could see the Privy Gardens where walked fashionable men and women, a few officers and a child chasing a dog. Beyond that was the Thames. Just out of sight, behind Richmond House, was the almost completed Westminster Bridge.

It was the 'almost' that irked Pitt.

There was a knock at the door to his office and his secretary entered carrying a small sheaf of papers. 'Sir, we have news!'

Pitt turned eagerly. 'Fairbrass is returned?'

Erasmus Fortune shook his head sadly, 'Alas, no, nor never will be.'

Pitt sat heavily at his desk. 'Tell me the worst.'

The secretary took a seat opposite his master, placed the papers on the desk and leant forward. He was a svelte young man, his wig fashionably small, his dark clothes of exceedingly fine cloth. 'He had been missing some days. The foreman suspected he had abandoned his job – he was reckoned too old for quarrying, a man down on his luck.'

The muscles beside Pitt's mouth worked, he leapt up and walked agitatedly around the room, banging his right fist into the palm of his left hand. 'God damn it, Fairbrass was a good man once. We should have sent someone younger. I blame myself.'

'There was no one else, sir, if you remember.'

Pitt looked down his eagle's beak of a nose at the secretary. 'Well, what happened?'

'Some lads playing in a copse beside the quarry found a body and reported it to the constables. The foreman identified it as being that of Fairbrass. His throat had been slit from ear to ear.'

Pitt sighed deeply and flung himself back into his chair. 'So how came we to hear?'

Erasmus Fortune smoothed the deep cuff of his coat and pulled out the lawn ruffle of his shirt sleeve to greater effect. 'His room was searched. Amongst his effects was the start of a letter to you, sir.'

'Bloody fool,' Pitt grated. He pulled at the long lobe of his ear.

'Had he not written, sir, it could have been weeks before we knew.'

'True. So what was in the letter?'

Erasmus picked up the small sheaf of papers he had brought in and handed over the one on top.

Pitt laid it on the desk, smoothed out the creases and read: ' "To William Pitt, Paymaster General." Bloody fool,' he repeated. 'He proclaims his mission to any who can read.'

Erasmus maintained a diplomatic silence.

Pitt continued with the letter: ' "Dear Sir, It is time I write you a report although, alas, I have little to communicate that will gladden your eyes. Your fears may indeed be well founded and I anticipate some news in that regard shortly. Tonight I—" '

Pitt turned the piece of paper over but there was nothing else. 'What of the night he disappeared?'

'Apparently he drank cheerfully in a local tavern with another quarry worker, one Jack Scott. He has also disappeared. It was assumed they had left Portland together. Scott had been there not above seven days. Word is he struck up a friendship with Fairbrass almost immediately.'

'Having no doubt identified him for the agent he was!' Pitt said bitterly. 'Undoubtedly with help from someone in authority at the quarry. What is known of this Scott?'

Erasmus shook his head. 'Nothing, sir. He came from nowhere then went back there.'

Pitt banged the desk in frustration, 'Damn it, there must be something else! That letter suggests Fairbrass was near the heart of things. What of his effects?'

The secretary removed a small canvas bag from the bottom of his papers. 'This contains all, apart from the odd garment.'

Pitt took the bag, assessed its lightness, opened it and shook the contents on to the desk. A small shower of low denomination coins, a battered comb, a razor and strop, a pen and some blank sheets of paper were all that came forth. He spread out the coins, studied them absentmindedly, then with greater attention. He picked out three or four, 'These are not of the realm, Fortune.'

The secretary took one. 'Tokens, sir, from the quarry, in lieu of coinage. They could no doubt be used for local tender.'

'Of course, of course.' Pitt tapped irritably on the desk with one of the tokens but he had already lost interest in them, his mind had moved on to other matters. 'Someone knew why Fairbrass was there, or at least suspected.'

'I fear so, sir.'

'Damn fool,' he said again.

'He's paid for his foolishness, sir.'

'Quite!' Once again the restless paymaster general rose, went to the window and looked in the direction of the bridge. 'At least we can say there are grounds for more than mere suspicion on the matter of the stone. But we must know more, I cannot proceed without some evidence.' He turned towards his secretary. 'Who else do we have that we can put on the case?'

'A remarkable paucity of candidates, sir. You remember Mr Fairbrass was a last choice.'

'Quite!' Pitt said with a curtness that silenced the secretary. 'That will be all, Fortune.'

Erasmus rose, 'These are for your attention, sir,' he said, placing the small pile of papers in the centre of the desk, then he gave a small bow and left with studied grace.

Pitt returned to his desk. He ignored the documents brought by his secretary and sat with steepled fingers, thinking. After a little while he sighed deeply and opened a drawer in the desk. Cursing under his breath, he rifled swiftly through the papers with which it was generously furnished and eventually unearthed a letter.

Opening it out, he reacquainted himself with its contents. Then he gave the bell on his desk an impatient jangle.

Erasmus Fortune reappeared. 'Sir?'

'Find out if the *San Marco* from Venice has arrived in London. Oh, and Fortune, ascertain if a Mr Owen

McSwiney still resides at this address.' He scribbled on a piece of paper and handed it to the secretary.

After Erasmus had left, Pitt picked up the token from his desk and gazed ruminatively at it. 'Can an ageing painter help where a skilled agent has failed?' he murmured to himself.

Chapter Seventeen

It had not taken Fanny long to find a likely looking cab and persuade the sturdy driver to wait outside the Rooker establishment. 'Signor Canal will be here presently,' she told him. 'He will be most grateful to be conveyed to his destination.'

Scenting a goodly tip, the driver quietened his horse and took up his position.

Fanny slipped across the street, dodging between carriages and pedestrians, making her way to the opposite side of the street, a little way down from the waiting man she had marked earlier.

In the interim he'd moved from one doorway to another and obtained a news sheet to hide behind as he leant against the shop front.

A little further down the road waited another cab, the driver slouched in his seat and seemingly asleep, his bony nag resting a leg, its head in a bag of hay.

Sudden despair spread through Fanny. She had been so confident she could prevent Scallion from following Canaletto, now she wondered how she was to keep her promise.

She stopped in front of a window filled with hats and pretended she was enamoured of a huge poke bonnet while she watched the reflection of her brother's door and waited for Canaletto to emerge and enter the waiting cab.

Once again she had rushed into a situation without properly considering its outcome. Ned used to tell her that one of these days she would land herself in a dung heap and now it looked as though this could be it.

What was it about the Italian painter that had got her embroiled this deep when she ought to be worrying about her own future? Canaletto had made it clear there was no hope of his taking her on as a non-paying apprentice and she could never afford a tenth of the fee he was asking.

Did she see him as another Ned – older, more sophisticated but still a dreamer? No, there was nothing of the dreamer about Canaletto, yet there was something vulnerable. An air, perhaps, of someone lost.

What a ridiculous thought. Canaletto was a famous painter who had come to England to conquer a new market, he must have reserves of confidence far beyond anything Fanny could comprehend.

His air of vulnerability must be due to his injuries.

This thought brought Fanny back to Scallion. Who was he and why was he still following Canaletto? He had his fortune, why did he need his life as well?

Fear ran through Fanny and threatened to overcome her resolve. She sneaked another look at the figure lounging in the doorway nearby. How much longer could she maintain her interest in the shop window without him noticing her? She pulled her cap further over her betraying copper hair. All she needed now was for Scallion to identify her as the one who'd pushed Canaletto out of the way of the swinging hook on the dockside and then felled him with her loaded reticule.

'Why, 'tis Fanny! Where have you been, child? It must be near a sennight since we've seen you. I declare 'twas only yesterday John asked me what had become of you. He has a new consignment of drawing paper he longs to show you.'

It was Sarah Stannard. Normally Fanny would be delighted to chat with Sarah, today she wished her anywhere but here.

Then she realized that this woman could serve her purposes much better than a window full of hats. 'Dear Sarah,' she said, unobtrusively placing herself so she had a direct line of vision to Ned's shopfront, 'I shall visit you both tomorrow without fail. I regret exceedingly having so neglected you.' There was a movement by the shop and she peeked over Sarah's substantial shoulder, but it wasn't Canaletto. 'What with Lucy being so near her confinement and Ned's affairs to organize, I find it difficult to take time for my own pleasures.'

'Huh, that Mistress Lucy! She gives herself such airs. As though her brother being alderman allows her licence to consider herself above such simple mortals as ourselves. I know not how you can deal so well with her.'

Fanny would have given a lot to have told Sarah Stannard her own opinion of her sister-in-law but loyalty to Ned kept her silent. She shrugged a shoulder, 'Her condition, you know,' she said vaguely. Then she saw Canaletto emerge from the shop. And saw Jack Scallion lower slightly the news sheet he was reading.

Canaletto entered the cab.

The paper was thrown to one side and Scallion moved swiftly towards the second waiting cab standing beyond Fanny.

'Sarah,' Fanny said with a die-away note to her voice, 'forgive me, I feel far from well.' She gave a convincing stagger right into Scallion's path. 'Ah, I faint,' she cried and, throwing out her arms, clutched at the front of his cloak and gripped one of his arms, clinging on to him like a monkey.

With a foul oath, Scallion tried to cast her off. In his effort to reach the waiting cab, he almost dragged her along the road.

'Why, Fanny, lass, whatever be the matter?' Sarah tried to assist Scallion in his attempt to remove Fanny.

Fanny allowed herself to be disentangled, but just as Scallion was about to board his cab, she cried, 'Why, he has stolen my reticule! Stop him! Stop thief!' With a speed unusual for one so near to fainting, she ran forward and grasped the end of his cloak. Others came to her assistance, shouting and cursing.

None cursed louder than Scallion. Kicking out, he grabbed at the cab's door, opened it and managed to climb inside before any could stop him and cried, 'Off with us, man!' The cabbie whipped his horse.

But the nag was more interested in finding the last of the hay at the bottom of his bag. The cabbie cursed and whipped harder. Brought back to his duties, the horse attempted to pull away but now Ned had arrived and grabbed at his reins. Hauling on them, he brought the horse to a standstill while the crowd dragged Scallion from the cab.

In vain the villain protested he'd stolen no reticule, that the girl had flung herself at him, that he had urgent business that must be undertaken.

His audience was scornful. While Fanny threw a convincing fit of hysterics and was comforted by Sarah, hands ransacked Scallion's cloak and pockets, the outcry growing more intense as no reticule was found. 'What hast thou done with it, then, thou whoreson devil?' 'Where's Miss Fanny's purse, you rogue?' 'Who's your confederate?'

Fanny sobbed louder and louder. ''Twas my sainted mother's and had my market money. Ned will never forgive me! Did I not see another villain run off in the direction of the Temple? It'll be him that has it, I'll warrant. This rogue threw it to him!'

'You scheming baggage,' Scallion screamed in outrage. 'You had no purse!'

'Oh, sir!' cried Fanny. 'How can you say such a wicked thing!' Looking beyond Scallion's contorted face, she could see Canaletto's cab had long since cleared Fleet Street. He was away and safe!

Not having found a stolen purse, many of the crowd now began to return to their business. Several, though, felt there was more entertainment to be gained from this confrontation and they were rewarded by the appearance of a large man dressed in a capacious coat and carrying a sturdy stick.

'Here's the fellow will take you into custody,' somebody shouted to Scallion.

'Ay, he'll bring you afore the magistrates,' agreed another.

But Thomas Black, hunter of malefactors for the profit it brought him, ignored Scallion and addressed himself to Fanny. 'I have information you are a thief, Fanny Rooker. It is my duty to take you afore the magistrates that you may be justly punished.'

Fanny stared at him, truly stunned. Those still

interested in what was happening looked at her with changed eyes. Only Sarah dared accost Thomas Black.

'What, accusing young Fanny of theft! That's a scandal! Fanny Rooker would pass by an unguarded pile of sovereigns and never think of taking a one. You should be ashamed of yourself.'

Ned let go of the cabbie's horse and came forward, his expression angry. 'You'll never prove such a charge against my sister. She is innocent!'

Warmth ran through Fanny at his unhesitating support. Dear Ned, he was her brother and together they would stand against the world.

Thomas Black remained unmoved. 'There is evidence, mistress, no doubt about it!' He pulled roughly at Fanny's arm and Sarah had no choice but to let her go.

At that Fanny found her tongue. 'You have no right!' She tried to pull herself free but the thief-taker had her firmly. 'I have stolen nothing. Who says I have? What is the charge?'

'A petticoat, a silk petticoat.' A small gasp ran round those who still stood near.

'Lucy!' exploded Fanny. 'This is Lucy's doing!'

'Lucy?' repeated Ned. 'Nay, that cannot be.' He looked at Fanny with new eyes. 'She said something of the sort this morning. Did you take it, Fanny? I know you have little love for her.'

Fanny stared at him. How could he suppose for one moment she would touch any of Lucy's possessions? Or anyone else's come to that!

Then, just as he had at the dock, she saw Scallion take advantage of a change of mood in those holding him. Quietly he freed his arms and if his erstwhile warders noticed, they had ceased to care.

Stealthily he climbed aboard the cab. The driver whipped the horse, this time with more effect. No one tried to stop him escaping, all eyes were on Fanny and she made no outcry.

There was no point and Scallion had no chance now of catching Canaletto. The painter had escaped.

Some small part of Fanny's mind rejoiced. The major part, though, wrestled with the unpleasant facts of her arrest.

She knew who was to blame. Not silly, stupid, malevolent Lucy; she wouldn't have an idea how to set this brute on her sister-in-law. No, the brains behind this ploy belonged to Alderman Fowler. Not content with gaining control of the Rooker house, he appeared determined to remove Fanny from her family home.

The fear that ran through Fanny now was ten times stronger than that raised by Scallion. If Alderman Fowler was behind this, she had no hope of proving her innocence. She was doomed for prison!

Chapter Eighteen

Once the cab had cleared Fleet Street, Canaletto gave the direction of Slaughter's Coffee House.

He sat back with his heart still racing.

He was certain he had escaped without being followed, but what, though, was happening to Fanny Rooker?

Fanny was the most organizing female Canaletto had had the misfortune to encounter, but she was also resourceful and brave and had shown him astonishing kindness. He hoped the commotion he had heard did not mean she had come to any harm. Whatever it had meant, though, she had obviously found some way to stop that villain following him.

Canaletto pulled up the cab window and tried to convince himself that the quick wits he had seen Fanny display would take care of her whatever the situation. Then, unpleasantly jolted along the rough roads, he found himself yearning for the smooth travel of a gondola on the canals of his beloved Venice. This trip to England was turning into disaster. Why, oh why, had he come?

Because there was nothing left for him in Venice, Canaletto told himself sternly. This was where he had to make a new career for himself. This was almost certainly his only chance to rediscover success. He mustn't throw everything away.

Taking some deep, calming breaths, Canaletto let down the window again and saw with a delight that revived him that they were passing through a market. A huge open rectangle was edged with a small picket fence and filled with stalls and busy shoppers. Through the cab window came the tang of fresh vegetables mingled with a clean, earthy aroma. The cab's progress round the edge of the market was made frustratingly difficult by a throng of carts and chairs. 'This is where?' he shouted up to the driver.

'Why, Covent Garden, sir. 'Tis the quickest way to St Martin's Lane!' The chap sounded aggrieved, as though his route was being questioned. For a moment Canaletto toyed with the idea of telling him he wouldn't know if he was being taken around three sides of a square, then thought how foolish to put such an idea into his head. Instead he contained his impatience and studied the scene around him. Housewives, servants, street vendors, people from every section of life were here searching for the best bargains amongst this rich offering of fresh food.

Then depression descended. Once he could have painted such a scene and made the human element as telling as the topographical detail. Once he'd cared as much about the people in his pictures as the bricks and mortar. Vividly came the realization that for many years now he had added figures to his paintings as gracefully and as automatically as chimneys on a roof, a few quick brush strokes completing a character sketch that offered less than a reflection in water. After all, as Joseph had once said as he tried to persuade Canaletto

131

to complete a commission, his patrons didn't want human life, to them figures were merely accessories to the main point of a Canaletto: the view, the *veduta*.

Was that another reason why orders for his paintings had dried up? Had he allowed success and the pressures put upon him to complete more commissions than he could comfortably handle to drive out part of his genius?

The cab jerked to a halt behind a cart laden with barrels that appeared to have a wheel stuck in a particularly large rut. The cabbie cursed and shouted. The driver of the cart called for help, various fellows detached themselves from their business, sauntered over and placed their shoulders behind the halted vehicle, straining and pushing as the pair of horses gamely pulled, the wheel rocking back and forth between each attempt to dislodge it from the rut.

What a waste of time! Canaletto dragged himself out of his introspection and fumed at the delay. What if Scallion should have escaped from whatever wiles Miss Fanny had practised upon him and, by some mischance, chosen to come this way? What if he saw him?

The painter shrank back in the cab, his heart thudding. The wound in his head began to ache and his legs felt weak.

He should have stayed in Italy. Even though the commissions had all but dried up, he could have tried his hand again at etching. His first attempt, a set of views published a couple of years ago, had been extremely successful. But it was whilst he had been working on these that he had fallen in love. Now every movement of the burin brought back the feelings that had engraved themselves so deeply on his heart.

No, life in Venice had become too depressing, it was

time he made a new start. While his health was good he needed to earn money to replace his stolen savings, otherwise his old age would be spent in poverty.

Canaletto took a peek out of the cab window. In front of the cab was a view of straining backs. Standing and watching the attempts to move the loaded cart were prosperous-looking citizens, shouting their encouragement. Through the whole scene, heaving men, shouting onlookers, busy shoppers, surged an energy that was immensely invigorating. He had been right to come to England.

Then Canaletto caught a glimpse of a red silk skirt and a head of dark, powdered curls under a starched white cap. His heart started to pound.

It couldn't be, could it? Heedless of the possibility that Scallion might be in the vicinity, Canaletto leant out of the cab window and gazed across the market. There, there was that flash of red again. He strained to see better.

Even at fifty Canaletto's sight was as keen as ever it had been in his youth. And his visual memory was exceptional. He could rebuild the most intricate building detail from a rough sketch. And he didn't even need sketches to enable him to people his paintings. Already he had memorized several useful vignettes amongst the market inhabitants. Although he had only caught a glimpse of the woman, surely he could not be mistaken? For this was no ordinary woman, this was she whose every curve and feature he knew as well as the Doge's Palace or St Mark's Cathedral.

And she was about to vanish. He opened the cab door, he had to catch her.

But then there came a cheer as the cart with the

barrels was finally pushed free of the rut and traffic began to move again. Canaletto hesitated. The red skirt had disappeared. Had it indeed been she? Could she be in London?

Canaletto's heart thudded painfully as he closed the cab door. His thoughts tumbled over themselves like water over rough stones. He felt the excitment of youth, he physically ached to be with her, to hear her laugh, have her listen, have her throw him her particular, laughing look that combined interest with teasing and a certain ironic detachment, as though part of herself was always held back.

Canaletto straightened. His imagination was over-active, a result of his injury and uncertainty over this move to London. It couldn't have been her in the red dress but, even if it had been, she had no part to play in his life now. Never again would he lay himself open to the hurt he had suffered after her disappearance from Venice without a word.

'Slaughter's Coffee House, sir,' sang out the driver as the cab stopped. 'And even wiv that 'old up, no one could have managed it more speedily than myself, if I say so as shouldn't.'

Canaletto descended, his legs stiff after sitting still for the ride. 'Careful, sir,' sang out the cabbie as he staggered and put out a hand to prevent himself falling. 'Don't want a mishap, do we?'

What an idiot the man was!

Irritated and once again depressed, certain of only one thing, that McSwiney wouldn't be here, Canaletto paid the driver and entered the coffee house.

It was an obviously popular location, the smoke-filled rooms were crowded with a selection of prosperous-looking men reading newspapers, drinking coffee and engaging in lively discussion. A number looked up as Canaletto entered, regarded him with a moment's interest, then returned to their pursuits.

'Yes, sir, can I help you? Coffee for sure.' Slaughter or one of his staff, dressed in shirt sleeves and a long white apron, offered the way to an empty place at one of the tables.

'I seek one Owen McSwiney,' Canaletto explained carefully. 'He may be found here from time to time?'

The fellow's round face beamed. 'Oh, ay, he's here so often he gives this place as his direction! Henry!' he shouted at another apron-clad waiter. 'Has Mr McSwiney come in today yet?'

'I think he's in the back, sir,' came the answer.

Dio mio, were things at last to go right with him? His heart beating, Canaletto followed his guide through to the back of the coffee shop where the air was smokier and the smell of roasted coffee even stronger.

There, seated at a table reading a newspaper, was a large, dramatic figure dressed in a dark green coat with a yellow velvet waistcoat over a voluminous shirt and wearing his own grey hair, its wildness matched by an exuberant beard.

· He looked up as they approached and his sleepy eyes beamed in happy astonishment.

'Tonio!' he said and launched into Italian. 'The winds must have blown fair, I hardly expected you to reach these shores so soon!' He rose and embraced the painter. 'Can you forgive me for not being on the dock to meet you?'

The sound of his native tongue made Canaletto conscious of just how much of a strain it had been to speak the harsh English tongue. Relief flooded through him, he collapsed on to the bench and placed his aching head in his hands. Faintly he heard a concerned voice asking if he was ill. It mattered not that his wits could no longer control his body. Now Canaletto had found McSwiney, surely all his problems would be solved!

Chapter Nineteen

Soon Canaletto felt a new man.

After a reviving cup of coffee, McSwiney took him off to his lodgings, a couple of small rooms in a shabby brick house not far from St Martin's Lane. 'Here we are,' the Irishman said jovially. 'Two chairs, you see, and there's a table. And through here,' he led the way into the second room, 'you'll see a truckle bed.' He drew it out from beneath his own. 'Old Jackson brings me hot water night and morning and attends to the necessities. You'll be as comfortable here as anywhere.'

Drawing out the truckle had swallowed up the small amount of floor left free by the bed. Nor did the first room offer sufficient space to set up an easel or enough light to paint by. Canaletto set down the canvas bag Fanny had loaned him to hold a few belongings. The next step had to be to find somewhere of his own with a studio.

But not before he'd discussed commissions with McSwiney.

They talked over a meal at a nearby tavern. 'You can trust the beef here,' said Owen, as eagerly he attacked a well-loaded plate and waved an encouraging knife at Canaletto.

The painter found little appetite for the thick slices

of meat, greasy gravy and overcooked vegetables. He remembered Fanny's mutton broth with nostalgia.

'Now, what of business?' he asked, pushing aside the plate after a couple of mouthfuls.

'Ah, well now, patrons and commissions, is it?' McSwiney caught the eye of a serving lad and waved an empty tankard at him. Canaletto had hardly touched his beer; he'd found it thin and sour. 'There's no rush about such things.'

Canaletto found his ready impatience rising within him. 'I need to establish myself,' he insisted, leaning forward on the uncomfortable wooden bench, so that his face was close to McSwiney's. The Irishman had aged considerably since he'd last seen him. His healthy flush had now deepened to something more hectic. Lines were cut deeply down the side of his mouth and the skin sagged wearily below his bloodshot eyes. Close to, the elegance of the coat was tarnished by wear and stains.

Canaletto tried not to feel worried. The Irishman had always swung between good fortune and disaster. The fact he was now at a down needn't mean he couldn't swing up again – and take Canaletto with him. 'All your connections,' he said persuasively. 'There must be someone you know who wants a London *veduta* from Canaletto?'

'Well now,' McSwiney dabbed at his mouth with the large white napkin. 'It'll depend.'

'Depend? Depend? On what?' Canaletto felt panic. McSwiney had been the first to sell his paintings to the English, it had been the Irishman who had established his reputation.

Then McSwiney had returned to London. He'd made

138

trips back to Venice and for some time they had remained in contact but it had been a long time since McSwiney had given him a commission. Not since Joseph Smith had begun promoting his work to the English. When Canaletto had noticed the fact, he'd decided, without discussing the matter, that McSwiney had deferred to Smith's interest; after all, he owed him for board and lodging over a long period, not to mention other favours that had no doubt assisted him to mend the shattered fortunes that had driven him into Italian exile.

McSwiney gave a discreet belch, his world-weary eyes fixed on Canaletto. 'Well, old friend, it hurts me to say this but we had better have matters straight between us right from the start.'

Canaletto sat very still.

'You know Joseph is my very good friend, even as you are, but I have to say he has no real understanding of art.'

'He has amassed a considerable collection, including many of my best works,' Canaletto said stiffly.

'Oh, aye, he has! Cunning fellow that he is. He kept, as you say, your best work and pressed you with a plenitude of commissions into working too fast. Pot-boilers, that's what you produced for him on too many occasions.'

Canaletto's eyes narrowed. 'You have seen how much of my work?'

McSwiney reached across the table and patted his hand. 'Now don't use that haughty, citizen-of-Venice tone with me. We all know your worth.'

But his eyes were sharp and Canaletto remembered the perception of McSwiney's remarks when he had first viewed his paintings and how silent he had been the last few times he had visited his studio.

'Your great genius is not lost, I know that. When not under pressure to dash off another pretty piece of trivia for yet another of old Joseph's contacts, you have shown flashes of it.'

Canaletto waved the remark away like a buzzing fly.

'All that is necessary, Tonio,' McSwiney's voice was creamy with bonhomie, 'is a recapturing of your old freshness. Indeed, you are probably saying to yourself now how different are the views you are seeing in London, don't I have the right of it? How that none of your stock Venetian figures will fit into an English *veduta*? You'll be getting out that notebook of yours and your eyes will be excited by all the new possibilities you see around you, isn't that the truth?'

Canaletto said nothing. Bitter bile was flooding into his throat. All his uneasiness over the past months clarified into a moment of searing truth. McSwiney was right. He hadn't lost his market because of war or because too many English had pictures of Venice. He'd lost it because he'd sacrificed his vision for easy money. He couldn't blame Joseph Smith, not entirely. He'd been too anxious for financial security.

And where had it got him? Lost in a strange land, pursued for no good reason he could think of, his savings stolen, his life threatened and the one anchor he had believed in suddenly shifting. He forgot about eagerness for large fees, all he could think of was what McSwiney had said about his painting during those years he'd worked so hard at all Joseph's lucrative commissions.

He reached for his tankard and swallowed the thin,

sour liquid, almost relishing the churning of his stomach as it hit still tender gastric juices protesting against the greasy beef he'd forced down.

'Tonio.' Again that creamy voice. 'Don't despair, man. I believe in your genius. I know you're going to produce great paintings in London. And you're right to come to me, I have the contacts, I'll arrange commissions, sure I will.'

Canaletto sat still and stiff, his eyes refusing to meet McSwiney's. This was not what he expected.

'Now, why don't we consider your first work, eh?' McSwiney continued. He paused, an eyebrow lifted encouragingly.

After a long moment, Canaletto said slowly, 'The new bridge? I'd heard many are interested in a view.'

'Westminster Bridge, is it? Oh, that's a subject worthy of your palate, no doubt on it. And you've arrived in time. It's still not completed. By heaven, but the thing must be eating money!' He wiped up the gravy from his plate with a piece of bread. Several front teeth were missing but the rest had made short work of the meat and vegetables.

'Aye, I have seen the bridge, it's quite a sight.' He had no intention of letting Owen know he had reservations about the view. What was important was to get the commission; he knew, despite the slurs McSwiney had cast on his work, that he could make something of the river. He forgot McSwiney's comments about his capacity for genius. All that reverberated in his mind were the insults: potboilers, dashed-off pieces of trivia.

'Well, now, let's see.' McSwiney leant back with a hearty belch. 'Why don't you prepare some sketches while I go forth and sweeten the market?' Then he seemed to recollect the state in which Canaletto had arrived at the coffee house, for he said, 'But not for a day or so, not until you have recovered from your journey. Now, let's order some brandy while you tell me of your adventures between Venice and here. I'll warrant you have many an incident to relate, eh?'

Canaletto was grateful for the brandy, a surprisingly good one, but found himself reluctant to relate just what had happened to him since he'd landed at the London docks. McSwiney should have been the perfect audience but Canaletto found he now did not want to risk an incredulous raise of that left eyebrow or a smooth comment that that was what you had to expect in London.

McSwiney hardly seemed to notice his reticence. He poured glass after glass from the bottle that had been left on the table and talked of what he would do to assist the painter. 'For the usual fee, you understand,' he added at one point. 'No more than the usual.'

Canaletto's head started to ache again and his attention wandered. It was a relief when McSwiney called for the bill and said they would go back. Then he found he was expected to pay for the meal. All his doubts about the Irishman rushed back. McSwiney was hardly an advertisement for success. Could he really secure a useful commission?

Chapter Twenty

Alderman John Fowler lived in a narrow house just within the City. Burned down in the Great Fire, it had been hastily and badly rebuilt.

John's grandfather had told him all about the fire. 'I was only a lad but something like that you don't forget. The flames, the crackle, the noise of collapsing buildings, the shrieks of poor women who saw their homes devoured before their eyes. They blew up houses, too, lad. That was the king's doing. Saved the rest that way, they did. Ah, it was terrible.' Each time he told the tale, which was often in his last years, the old man would sigh heavily. 'Just remember, young John, don't tie your heart up in houses. Don't do no good.'

What John came to see as the moral of that tale was, don't invest large sums in building solid houses when they could be lost as easily as those erected for a tenth the price. Build cheap and sell on, that was the way to make money.

John rose early each morning, before the sun was up. By rush light (so much cheaper than tallow and after twenty years his eyes seemed as sharp as ever) he would go over the accounts for his workshops. The Fowlers had been goldsmiths for more than six generations and John had successfully passed his apprenticeship and become a member of the powerful Guild of Goldsmiths. He very soon found, though, that it was more valuable to employ others to work for him, producing the gold and silver plate there was such a ready market for these days, not to mention items of jewellery, whilst he devoted himself to the more practical pursuit of turning his receipts into yet more money.

There were so many opportunities these days, many of them connected with land. It was, of course, necessary to hide certain of your activities, no use to lay oneself open to retaliation from those who felt themselves hard-done-by in his dealings with them. And a knowledge of who could be hired to take care of various matters without concerning themselves too much with the propriety of their actions was valuable as well.

John Fowler had laid the foundations of his fortune through marriage. Margaret Fowler was a capable woman who had never had any pretensions to good looks. Her advantage had lain in a handsome jointure, provided by her successful goldsmith father.

No sooner had Margaret seen John Fowler entering her father's house for an informal guild meeting, than her heart became set on him. John had never grudged the time he'd taken to ensure she'd first noticed and then encouraged his suit. He'd made sure her father was happy with the situation, that he felt he'd at last found a worthy husband for his eldest daughter. The other two girls were beauties, no trouble marrying them off well.

It had not been difficult to prise a handsome jointure out of Margaret's father or to enlist his backing in his attempt to become one of the youngest aldermen in the

City. Once his position of power was assured, with his wife's money safely in his hands, John Fowler had embarked on his carefully worked-out plan to become one of the wealthiest men in the City of London.

After checking his workshop returns, John broke his fast with his large but well-controlled family. None so far had been reckless enough to challenge their father's authority and John Fowler wondered sometimes why that should cause him a niggling dissatisfaction. Then he retired again to the small front room he used as an office.

A few minutes later his sister was announced. She was breathing fast and looked distraught, her hair not properly dressed beneath her stylish bonnet, a shawl carelessly thrown over a dress that looked too hastily assumed. From the awkward way the fichu sat on her neck and one shoulder of the gown rucked up, John would have bet the back would prove to be done up all wrong.

John rose immediately and drew forward the only other chair in the room. 'Come, sit down, sister. You should not be stirring yourself in this way. Could you not have sent a servant and asked me to call?'

Lucy sat herself heavily in the chair and wiped her brow with a none-too-steady hand. 'I couldn't remain at home, not without Ned.'

'Ned? What has he done?'

'John, what has happened to Fanny?' Lucy's eyes were huge in her face, her hands wrapped themselves nervously round each other. 'A neighbour arrived last night with some story she had been placed under arrest. Ned was beside himself!' She burst into tears.

John opened the door and roared for a servant, then

directed him to bring brandy. He produced a large square of fine linen and thrust it at Lucy. 'What's that dolt of a husband of yours done?' he repeated angrily.

'Oh, don't,' Lucy moaned into the handkerchief. 'I can't bear it if you are unkind with me as well.'

' "As well, as well"! Who else is unkind to you? Ned? Wait until I get hold of him.'

Lucy moaned louder. 'John, don't. Ned isn't unkind, not really. He's just worried about Fanny. And so am I.'

'You?' John shot the word out in startled surprise. 'You resent Fanny, you told me so. Pleaded with me to do something so you could be – what were your words – "I want to be mistress in my own house", wasn't that it?' There were times his sister exasperated him. Never happy, always reaching for something, never able to grab hold of events and twist them to her purposes. But he'd always been her protector, from the time their mother had died in childbirth when Lucy was two and he fifteen, already started on his apprenticeship. There'd been two children between him and her but they'd died as well; his father had retreated into a world of work, producing pieces that increased his reputation and whipping his son every time he felt the boy wasn't working as hard or as effectively as he should.

Lucy had adored her older brother and somehow she had made life something more than hard work and harder knocks.

But the pretty, self-willed child had grown up into a woman who had no talent for making the most of life and John felt a familiar exasperation take hold as Lucy gasped on a sob, which turned into a hiccup. 'A constable came this morning afore I was up and demanded access to Fanny's room. Then he produced my silk petticoat which he said he'd found hidden beneath her mattress. Proof of Fanny's guilt, he said.' Lucy gave a huge gulp and her eyes widened even further as she gazed at her brother with something like horror, 'But even though it looked like it, I knew it wasn't mine.'

'Of course it was yours,' he said roughly. 'Don't you remember, when I asked you why you weren't wearing it the other day you said you'd lost it and suspected Fanny had stolen it? I trust that is what you told the constable?'

Lucy's gaze dropped to her lap, her hands wrestled with the handkerchief. 'I screamed for Ned and when he came and heard, he called me a bitch and ran out to the court in Bow Street saying he'd see she was freed. But the constable laughed and said he might as well stay for all the good it would do.'

'Ned always was a fool,' John said laconically.

His servant brought in the brandy. John poured a glass and insisted Lucy drink it. In a neat, practised way, she downed the spirit and closed her eyes for a brief moment as it took its effect. He wondered how much gin she commonly drank during the day.

'Now, look, Lucy,' he said grimly, 'that was your petticoat Fanny had in her room, you must have no doubt about that. When Ned realizes what a little thief he has for a sister, she can go sing for her home and work. You will be free of her and can arrange for Ned to take a paying apprentice. And you can take charge of your house like a wife and soon-to-be mother should. As Margaret does here,' he added in a more kindly tone.

Lucy stuffed the handkerchief in her mouth, stifling a squeak such as a dying mouse might make.

Perhaps he shouldn't have added that bit about

Margaret – the two women had never got on – but something needed to be said. John had severe doubts about Lucy's ability to manage any household, let alone one that encompassed what should be a lucrative engraving business. John gave an impatient sigh. No doubt he'd end up paying some mature woman good money to do the job for her.

'But what of Fanny?' Lucy insisted. She'd stopped wringing the handkerchief and seemed a little calmer.

'Hell's bells, why keep on about that misbegotten whore? She'll get no more than she deserves!' John burst out. He immediately regretted losing control in that way for Lucy suddenly sat up straight and regarded him with alert eyes full of cunning.

'You tried to bed her and she would have none of you, that is it. Oh, John, how could you?'

'What nonsense you do talk, Lucy.'

'Nay, you'll not slide out of it like that, John. I know you too well.' Then Lucy's triumphant expression changed back to one of aggrieved woe. 'But what will happen to Fanny? I know I said I wanted her out of the house but not like this!'

John gave another impatient sigh. 'Just how do you think you'll be rid of her, then, eh? Don't imagine that Ned, however tired he gets of the bickering between the two of you, will consent to losing his assistant. Fanny is too useful to him. Nor think that Fanny has any choice in the matter. For where could she go? This way, with her in gaol, you'll be able to assert yourself.'

'Gaol!' Lucy screeched. 'John, you cannot mean it! I would never wish gaol on Fanny!'

John downed a glass of brandy in one gulp. Dealing with Lucy was more difficult than handling half a dozen mean-minded customers. 'Lucy, do you or do you not wish Ned to assume the respectability of a painter? To cast off the craftman's image he now wears as an engraver? So that you can live in a house without customers constantly calling, to get rid of the dirt and hazard of his present calling?'

'John, you know that 'tis my dearest wish.'

'Know then that I have given him a commission as a painter and anticipate I can arrange further commissions. But not if little Fanny is always at his elbow pressing him to keep his engraving business going. So I am about to foreclose on his Fleet Street premises.'

Lucy let out a cry of distress.

'Don't upset yourself, sister. Think I will see you homeless? No, I have chosen a house for you in a respectable part of town.' He glanced at her before adding, 'I will take a loss on the Fleet Street property but for your sake I shall be happy to see you settled somewhere that is worthy of your beauty.' He sat beside her and laid a hand on her arm. 'Won't you like to be a lady with servants to do your work? Meeting those who have sufficient fortune and aesthetic appreciation to commission your Ned to paint . . .' he hesitated for a moment, uncertain exactly what such people might want his brother-in-law to capture with his brush, then hurried on, 'perhaps their estates.'

'Why, like Signor Canal,' Lucy said brightly. 'All say what sums he commands for his views.'

'Signor Canal?' For a moment John was thrown. 'I thought he no longer played a part in the Rooker household.'

'You say true, brother. I despatched him myself yesterday. We'll see no more of him, I promise you.' Lucy spoke with satisfaction, smoothing the fine cloth of her gown over her bulging stomach. 'Would you believe that Fanny, Fanny of all people, wished him to take her as apprentice? I am glad you have removed her from our lives, John. I could not have borne to see her become a painter.'

John looked carefully at his sister. She had lost all sign of distress over Fanny's fate. So that was all right. What with the expenses incurred in hiring the thief-taker and suborning the constable, he was going to need to turn a tidy profit on the Fleet Street property to come out ahead on this operation. Still, it was worth it if he could see his sister properly settled. It would suit his social ambitions to have a painter for brother-in-law rather than a humble engraver.

'Now, Lucy, I shall ask Michael to procure a chair to take you home. You should be resting so near your time.' John opened the door and bellowed again for his manservant.

He turned back after commanding the chair to find his sister already rising from her seat. 'Now, when Ned gets back from the court, be ready with a glass of spirits and a sympathetic smile. Ask him to tell you of his commission from me, remind him how near he is to becoming a father, remove from his mind his sister's misfortune. He will soon be amenable to your every wish and whim.'

'Dear John, did ever sister have a better brother?' Lucy settled her shawl around her shoulders. 'I suppose I should send my respects to Margaret. You don't, I hope, expect me to speak to her today?'

He guided her to the door with an arm around her

shoulders. 'No, indeed, I will say all that is necessary for you.'

Michael had the sedan chair already waiting. John helped Lucy in, deposited a quick kiss on her cheek, then shut the door, told the chairmen where to go and gave a last wave as they set off in the direction of Fleet Street.

With a sigh of relief, John turned back to the house, then stiffened as he saw who waited for him by the front door. 'I told you never to come here,' he said to Jack Scallion.

'You told me a great many things but few words have you kept,' Scallion snarled at him.

The man looked even meaner than usual and there was a look in his eye that made John say abruptly, 'Come in, then, we'll speak in my office.' As he held open the door for the villain, John cast a quick glance up and down the street, but could see no one he recognized. There was the possibility that his sister had glimpsed the fellow, but Lucy would not remember him.

Once in the office, John firmly shut the door, sat himself down in the chair behind his desk and said curtly, 'Well, then, speak.'

Scallion ran a finger across the polished wood of the desk, let his gaze linger on the silver inkwell and knife that lay on the mahogany surface and the calf bindings of several books on law arranged on a shelf. His dress looked even worse than usual; there was a tear in one sleeve, mud bespattered his breeches and he hadn't shaved for several days.

'Guvnor, it ain't right! I been cheated out of my rightful gains. I was the one what despatched that dago and what I got out of it, tell me that, eh?'

'Canaletto is an Italian, not a dago, Scallion, and you did not despatch him. Was it not my sister who informed me of this?'

'But his fortune, didn't I get his fortune?' whined the other man.

John Fowler leaned back in his chair, rested elbows on the arms and looked at him with such cold regard, Scallion took an involuntary step backwards. 'You have bungled every stage of this affair. What should have been a simple matter has been strung out beyond all conscience. I cannot imagine where your reputation for efficiency in these matters was won. How dare you demand payment for despatching a body that was no more a body than I am?'

'But, guvnor,' whined Scallion, 'didn't you promise you'd look after me when that warm 'un in Cheapside came across?'

Fowler slammed his hand down on the desk. 'The paucity of your information in that regard has allowed him to prevaricate. I am by no means sure we have achieved what should have been cast iron.'

A look of cunning crossed Scallion's face. 'There's them as would pay good money for what you calls a "paucity of information". Straight up!'

John let out a slow breath, holding the other man's shifty gaze with his own. 'You breathe a word of this to any other man and it will be the worse for you,' he hissed.

Scallion leant his hands on the desk and shoved his face towards John Fowler's, the gold earring in his left ear trembling. 'You just give me some of what I'm owed, that's all I'm asking. Man can't live on air.'

For a long moment John sat with Scallion's foul

odour filling his nostrils, the man's anger pulsating the air around them. Then he made himself relax. 'Come, man, I'll not let you starve. A labourer is worthy of his hire, I'll not deny that. Tell you what I'll do, I'll send word to the Golden Lion when the matter's done and your money awaits. In the meantime,' he stared the other man in the eye, 'you would do better to finish the job you've left undone.'

Scallion never flinched. 'That's all you've got to say, is it?'

'Remember my words,' warned Fowler. 'Never think you can move without my knowing.'

Scallion made a rude gesture with two forefingers then snatched up the silver knife from the desk. 'I'll keep this until I receive what's owed me,' he snarled and made rapidly for the door.

Not rapidly enough.

With astonishing speed, John Fowler was up and round the desk and had caught Scallion round the neck before his hand could reach the doorknob. He brought Scallion's arm up behind his back in a cruelly hard lock. An inch further and the arm would break. Holding it there, he removed the knife from the man's breeches' pocket.

Scallion sank to his knees, whimpering. 'Lord love us, guvnor, I was only holding it against what you owes me. I didn't mean no 'arm.'

John Fowler released the arm then kicked the villain so hard that he lay sprawled on the floor, whimpering with the pain. Then he kicked him again, in the ribs, and thought he heard one break. Scallion shouted in anguish.

Finally John hauled him to his feet, opened the door,

propelled him out of the office and along the hallway. 'Just remember,' he spat in the man's ear as they reached the front door, 'I tell you what to do, you don't tell me. I hear you've breathed one word of this to another and your life will be at an end.' He opened the front door and flung Scallion into the road.

Chapter Twenty-One

'I think I may have your first commission organized,' McSwiney said.

It was mid-morning the day after their meeting in the coffee house. McSwiney had gone out early, telling the painter to rest up. He'd arranged for Jackson to send up a mug of ale and some bread and cheese for breakfast.

Then, as the painter was gingerly shaving himself, he'd returned, cock-a-hoop. 'I'm bidden for supper and cards tonight. And there will be Thomas Hill, the Duke of Richmond's old tutor. You remember, the first commission I ever obtained for you was those two views you painted on copper for Richmond? I know he values them well. Hill and I are old friends and we dine next door to Richmond House. If I haven't organized him into persuading his grace of the value of commissioning you to paint a view of the place, you can send my bones to the bottom of the river.'

He sounded so confident, Canaletto felt a lightening of his spirits. 'McSwiney, you are a true friend.' He gave the tall Irishman a quick embrace, then had to wipe soap off the man's coat. 'Now I must find lodgings; here I have not room nor light to paint.'

McSwiney glanced round the tiny bedchamber. 'I know a man,' he said instantly.

'Good,' said Canaletto, wiping his face and picking up his own coat. 'Let us go.'

His friend looked at him keenly. 'I think not. You need more rest. You must be strong to paint the masterpieces you are capable of. I will go and see what is available then return.'

Canaletto did not object. Some quiet hours sitting in McSwiney's not unpleasant parlour would be of enormous benefit.

After the Irishman had left again, Canaletto did indeed sit quietly and thought about his life's work. Gradually a desire to paint that he had not had in many years grew in him. During the time he had wandered around the north of Italy with his nephew, Bernadetto, he had rediscovered the joy of drawing. Drawing not for making essential notes for yet another painting, but for its own sake, capturing a landscape in strokes of a pen.

That had led to his venture into etchings, an enterprise that had proved wholly satisfactory, not the least because he had been able, through the title page, to pay due homage to Joseph Smith for all the help he had been given by him. By a delightful coincidence, Joseph had at last been made the English Consul in Venice just before the etchings were published and could be so addressed.

Yet Canaletto had had no urge to continue in this new medium. Nor had he wanted to translate either drawings or etchings into paintings. Now McSwiney had reawakened the joyous itch he had had as a young man to capture in paint what he saw around him.

He longed for his palette, his pigments, his brushes. But all he had brought with him from his baggage was a small workbox with sketching implements.

He would send for his boxes.

Canaletto went downstairs and found McSwiney's landlord, a dour man who had a business collecting and selling second-hand clothes (the piles of garments sent a curious odour floating up the stairs). Jackson was obliging enough and produced a youngster willing to take a message to Fleet Street for a small coin.

'You will only speak to Signorina Fanny,' instructed Canaletto. 'She is small with red hair. Do not say anything to her brother, Mr Ned, or his wife, a woman with dark hair who is,' his hand traced a massive stomach over his own lean one.

The boy grinned in understanding and was gone in a flash, running down the street as though the faster he earned his coin, the larger it would be.

Canaletto went back upstairs to wait for his boxes.

Not more than five minutes had passed, however, before Jackson wheezed his way up the stairs followed by a slim young man of immaculate appearance. ''E asked for Mr McSwiney, sir, and when I told 'im 'e wasn't 'ere but you was, 'e asked to see you.'

The elegant young man gave the astonished Canaletto a small bow. 'Erasmus Fortune, at your service, Signor. I am sorry to be the means of disturbing your peace, but my master, Mr Pitt, the paymaster general, would be immensely gratified if you could find it within your power to visit him at his office in Whitehall. I have a carriage waiting outside.'

It was a most unexpected development and Canaletto was suspicious. How did this unknown but obviously important personage know of his presence here?

When he learned that it was through Joseph Smith, Canaletto thought he understood all. This Signor Pitt wished to commission a painting. Excitement flushed through his veins. He found his wig, removed most of the mud and replaced his velvet bonnet, ignoring the tightness of the fit over his bandages and the way they peeked below the line of the hair. 'I am most happy to follow you, signor,' he told the young man. 'To meet your Signor Pitt.'

Downstairs Canaletto told Jackson the boy was to be asked to return later for his payment and that the boxes, when they arrived, were to be taken upstairs and piled in McSwiney's parlour. He ignored the fact that they would take up much of the available floor space.

The journey did not seem overlong and Canaletto thought they might easily have walked the distance. This Signor Pitt must be very anxious to discuss the view he wanted. Any last vestiges of the depression prompted by McSwiney's adverse comments vanished. This would be something to tell him! Pray heaven he had found suitable lodgings so that Canaletto could get all his things properly settled and begin work without delay.

The painter commented favourably on the appearance of London as they travelled. Erasmus Fortune proved adept at making pleasant conversation that contained nothing of substance and it was in an excellent mood that Canaletto was finally brought into the paymaster general's handsome office.

Sitting behind a large desk Canaletto saw a man with an extraordinarily large nose and an air of great hauteur.

'Signor Canal, I am most honoured to make your acquaintance.' Pitt came forward and offered his hand.

Canaletto stuck out his right leg and dipped him a neatly elegant bow that acknowledged the other man's importance. 'Signor, Canaletto is most happy to make *your* acquaintance. Canaletto will supply most assuredly what your lordship requires.'

Pitt's eyes narrowed. 'You will, will you? What do you know about the business, then?' Before Canaletto could respond, Pitt wheeled on Fortune. 'What have you been telling him?'

'Nothing, sir, nothing at all.' Canaletto realized the young man was not nearly as self-assured as he'd thought.

'I have number of subjects you might like to consider,' he interposed eagerly. 'The new bridge, perhaps, Westminster Bridge?'

'Devil take you, man, you have been talking!' Pitt roared at Fortune, who blanched and took a step back.

'Sir!' he protested.

Canaletto could not understand what was happening. 'Signor, please. Signor Fortune and I, we do not discuss painting subjects. I just suggest this myself, I, Canaletto.' Nervousness was making it difficult for him to remember his English.

The big-nosed man looked startled. 'Painting subjects? What the devil do you mean, painting?'

Canaletto began to wonder if somehow he had missed some vital phrase. 'You send for Canaletto, it seems *importante*. I am painter, I suggest subject.'

Pitt's face suddenly relaxed, he threw back his head with a shout of laughter. 'God, man, I apologize! Of course! Nay, Signor Canal, I regret to inform you I am not in the market for one of your *vedute* – much as I admire your work,' he added hurriedly. But, please, sit down. Fortune, a glass of wine for us both.'

Thoroughly bewildered, Canaletto sat and Erasmus Fortune disappeared from the room looking decidedly relieved.

'Now, my dear signor, let me explain.' Pitt sat behind the desk and drew forward a piece of paper. 'Some few days ago I received this letter from my old friend, Joseph Smith. He tells me you have rendered various of my fellow countrymen considerable service during visits to Venice.'

Canaletto's heart sank. He waved a deprecating hand. 'Nothing, it was nothing, signor. I know Venice, I know Venetians.'

'Well, my friend Joseph speaks glowingly of your powers of observation and deduction.' The paymaster general paused as a servant brought in a silver tray bearing a decanter of wine and two glasses and placed it on the desk. Pitt rose. 'You will partake, my dear sir?' he asked with a charming smile.

Canaletto inclined his head but refused to allow himself to respond to the charm. 'Thank you, signor, I like very much.'

Pitt handed him a filled glass and took one himself. 'I have this claret imported direct from Bordeaux then bottled here for my own cellars. I trust it meets with your approval?'

Canaletto had seldom tasted a better wine. He smiled briefly and said nothing.

Pitt resumed his seat. 'Well, now, signor. I have need, His Majesty has need, of a man with acute observation and skilled powers of deduction.' He threw a rueful grin across the table, man to man. The control he'd lost so badly earlier had been skilfully recovered. 'In fact, I confess, we are in the devil of a mess and you, my dear sir, could be our saving.'

Chapter Twenty-Two

Canaletto sipped his wine and still said nothing.

William Pitt turned the wine glass stem thoughtfully for a moment then he looked up at Canaletto with another of his frank smiles. 'Let me speak plainly. You mentioned Westminster Bridge earlier. You have seen it?'

'When I arrive, I look a little.'

'And you saw it seems nearly complete, yes?'

'Yes.'

'I have to tell you, sir, that this damned bridge is so far behind its due date of completion I am in despair. Initially it was to have been funded by the public through a series of sweepstakes. For reasons I know not, none of the sweepstakes raised near enough. But even if they had, the expenses of building the bridge have constantly run ahead of the estimated amounts. For some years now, the government has been providing the costs.' He rose and walked over to the window and stood gazing out in silence for several minutes.

Then he turned to Canaletto. 'Be good enough to step over here, my dear sir.'

The painter joined him at the window and looked across a wide and busy highway to a pleasant, large and walled public garden. Pitt waved a hand to the scene to his right. 'There, beyond where you can see, is where the bridge is and where a whole new city is developing. There are our Houses of Parliament, our great Abbey of Westminster. New houses are being built, new roads constructed. When the bridge is open, there will be a constant flow of communication between this area and the south of England. Commerce will be served, the public will be served, trade will increase, London will benefit, must benefit.' Pitt's manner became increasingly agitated. 'The bridge must open as soon as maybe, but what happens? Every meeting of the commissioners we hear of more delays, more expenses. There was another meeting but yesterday and it was exactly the same story.'

Pitt swung round, half sat himself on the sill of the window and contemplated his feet, neatly shod in highly polished leather with silver buckles. 'Of course, not everyone is enamoured of the idea. City merchants believe their business will suffer. For many years they fought all suggestions for a second bridge.'

Canaletto found this hard to credit. True, there was only one bridge across the Grand Canal in Venice but Venice was a city built on water and it was as natural to step into a boat as walk across a piazza. For such a huge city as London to have but one crossing for a river the size and power of the Thames seemed incredible. He remembered how undeveloped the southern bank had seemed during his voyage up from the docks the day of his arrival.

Pitt started walking restlessly around the office. Canaletto leaned against the window frame and watched him.

'A major problem with the bridge has been the

supply of stone. For some time now I have suspected something more than incompetence or misfortune. I sent a man down to the Portland Bill quarry in the south-west of England, one Harry Fairbrass. He disappeared, then his body was discovered with its throat cut.'

Canaletto did not like the sound of that at all.

'The start of a letter was discovered in his room, which suggests he was about to uncover some information of value to me.' Pitt stood still, his hands held out in supplication. 'You see my problem? I believe in that quarry there is proof of nefarious activity.'

'And you need some other agent to go down?' suggested Canaletto quietly.

Pitt looked relieved. 'Precisely. I congratulate you on your acumen, signor.'

It had hardly taken genius to work that out! Canaletto, though, failed to see how he could help, even if he was willing to go, which he wasn't. 'You need man skilled in these matters.'

'Precisely! And someone with good reason for wanting to be there.'

Pitt approached his desk and picked up the letter again. 'I was grappling with this problem when I remembered this letter from your good friend and mine, Joseph Smith, suggesting I might find a use for your investigative talents. It seemed an obvious solution.'

If Canaletto had properly understood this man, he was being asked to undertake a commission of the most dangerous sort. In a land he knew nothing of, amongst people whose language he spoke imperfectly.

'Sir, please, I cannot do this, you know? My English, it is not good.'

Pitt glanced back at the letter he held. 'Joseph writes, "Tonio's command of the language has become excellent, he is able to converse on any subject,"' he read expressionlessly. He tossed the letter back on the desk. 'My dear sir, there is no danger! Who would suspect a world-renowned painter who has come to capture the beautiful scenery round the isle of Portland?'

Even the mention of 'world renowned' lacked power to sway Canaletto. 'Sir, I am city topographical artist. What business would I have in quarry?'

Pitt walked over to a table at the side of the room and Canaletto saw that it bore a folder tied with silk. Pitt undid the bow, opened the heavy leather cover, flipped over several loose-leaf pages and picked out one which he brought across. Canaletto saw with dismay that it was one of his etchings. No one knew better than he that many of the views were of the countryside. 'And have I not heard that one of your masterpieces is of a stone-cutter's yard?' asked the paymaster general.

'Not a yard – a building with repairs, merely,' Canaletto said despairingly. He knew the picture. It was indeed one of his major works, one that he had painted with deep commitment.

'No one at the quarry will either know or care anything about your works. It will be enough that you are a painter and Italian. That will be sufficient to remove you from any suspicion.'

Canaletto could not have the same confidence.

He was caught in a dreadful quandary. This William Pitt must be a powerful man. How was he going to turn him down without ruining his chances of commissions from the very men the paymaster general must mix with every day?

Canaletto had no illusions about the nature of any ruling élite. London might be ten times larger than Venice but the rich and the powerful would still move in a small, charmed circle. Word that a particular painter just over from Italy was not a good prospect for commissions would pass through it like fire through a dry cornfield.

'Sir,' Canaletto said desperately, then drew a deep breath and started again in a calmer voice. 'Sir, this is deep honour you pay me. Alas, Signor Joseph is too, what is the word?' he paused for the briefest of seconds, 'Yes, generous, that is it, too generous. My English, it is not so good as he say. If I say little, look like I capisco, then people think I speak – how you say – like a native?' He could see from Pitt's expression that this attempt was not going down well. 'The small ways I 'elped some few peoples in Venice. It was nothing. As I tell you, I know the place, the peoples. Here, I know nothing. This place you speak of, Portland?' he spoke the word with careful emphasis, dragging out the two syllables, 'I can maybe visit there but I cannot find out things for you.'

He saw immediately that he'd made a serious error even to suggest he might be prepared to go.

'You would have no trouble,' Pitt said quickly. 'The whole place is given over to the quarry and preparing the stone. You cannot talk to anyone without the subject coming up. You, with your painter's eye that sees everything, your sharp brain that sifts what it sees, and your English that, as you say, so obviously announces you to be a foreigner, you will be perfectly placed to find out what is happening to that damned stone!'

'But, signor,' Canaletto was struck with a happy thought, 'I do not have my tools; my brushes, my pigments, all are with my baggage and I do not know 'ow to find it.'

'You've lost your baggage, man? This is something we can help with. Tell me the circumstances and I will arrange that it is located.'

For a fleeting moment Canaletto wondered if he shouldn't tell this powerful man everything that had happened to him since he'd arrived in London. But a lifetime of instinctive secrecy held him back. You never knew what use other people would make of the knowledge you gave them. Knowledge was power and it was safest to keep yourself as private as you might.

'Sir, it's that I do not have studio. When I find that, my boxes come.' He made a graceful gesture with his arm. 'Had you so kindly offered me to help you in two, maybe three weeks, then I might be able. But now, so soon after I arrive, before I have my work in hand, oof, it is impossible.'

The eyes of the man facing him narrowed. Canaletto braced himself for another loss of temper.

Abruptly Pitt turned away. 'I am disappointed, Signor Canal. I believed you could have rendered His Majesty signal service. Service that could command considerable reward.' The words hung in the air between them.

Canaletto almost reconsidered. He thought of the stolen fortune that so badly needed replacing. But then he remembered the shocks and traumas of the last few days. They would be as nothing if he did as this man suggested and was discovered in the act. He valued his life. And McSwiney was confident he had his first commission. From the Duke of Richmond, no less, a man who knew Canaletto's worth. There was, surely, no way this William Pitt could interfere in this matter. Still, it behoved him to be careful.

'Signor, I regret I cannot help you but you have many men more worthy than I for this commission. Some English painter, perhaps?' Inspiration struck, 'Mr Hogarth?'

The paymaster general burst into laughter. 'Oh, signor, you know nothing of the art world of London. Mr Hogarth is an enemy of the establishment, he would seek to pervert the course of justice before aiding it.' He smiled winningly at Canaletto. 'But I can see you need time to arrange your affairs here. Let us help you and then, perhaps, you can aid us.'

Canaletto took a step towards the door. This was a man more dangerous when charming than when out of temper. 'Please, no. I do well with Mr McSwiney, he helps me.'

'Ah, yes,' Pitt said reflectively, 'Owen McSwiney. Of course.' He seemed to capitulate. 'Well, you know where to find me if there is anything I can do for you.'

Erasmus Fortune showed Canaletto out of the building with graceful words that wished him well in London.

Canaletto walked back to the lodgings off St Martin's Lane hoping without much confidence that McSwiney was not about to be subjected to pressure to make Canaletto change his mind.

Chapter Twenty-Three

By the time Canaletto returned to the lodgings, McSwiney was there. He looked worried. 'Where have you been, man? I arrive back to find you gone and Jackson trying to send packing some young ruffian who declares you owe him money. When I ask where you are, Jackson tells me a "right nob" came for you. What in heaven's name is up?'

'My baggage? It is come?' Canaletto asked eagerly, though a single glance as he'd entered the parlour had been enough to see there were no leather boxes stacked waiting for him.

'Baggage? I know nothing about baggage.'

Canaletto didn't know whether to be relieved or worried. 'Any minute it could arrive. The young ruffian, he returns?' He didn't seem able to get out of the mangled English speech he had assumed in Pitt's office.

'What? Oh, yes, I believe he does. Don't you wish to know what I have been up to?'

'Ah, you have found me studio, lodgings?'

McSwiney threw himself down into the large, upholstered chair that was the main piece of seating in the room, shook his head mournfully and switched to Italian. 'Saw several lodging places. Nothing any better than this for space or light.'

Canaletto thought he understood. McSwiney wanted him under his eye. He wanted to be able to monitor his painting.

At every turn people were trying to manipulate him. 'I thank you for your efforts, Owen,' he said with heavy sarcasm and left the room. As he descended the narrow stairs he found he was shaking with anger.

Canaletto paused outside Jackson's parlour. This was no time to lose his temper. He needed to maintain a cool head. When he felt he was once more in charge of himself, he knocked at the door.

Jackson reported that young Matt would return very shortly to give his report and take his wages. 'For I told him, sir, you was not a man to go back on your word,' he finished.

'Indeed, no,' murmured Canaletto. 'My boxes, they arrive?'

'He told me nothing,' Jackson said austerely. 'Only that he would return. Ah, there's the scamp now,' he added as a shadow went by the window. There came a heavy knocking at the front door.

Canaletto answered it and found himself pulled out on to the front step by Matt.

'Don't want no one to hear,' the youngster said in a loud whisper, 'being as you said it was all confidential, like.'

'You saw Signorina Fanny?' demanded the painter. Looking back, she seemed the only person since his arrival in England who had genuinely cared about his fate.

Matt, a skinny youth who looked half starved but had bright, knowing eyes, shook his head. 'She's gone, sir.'

'Gone? To market, perhaps?'

Matt shook his head more vigorously. 'Nay, sir, gone. Lives there no more.'

Canaletto wondered if his command of English had indeed deserted him. 'You went to the right place?'

'To the sign of the copper plate in Fleet Street, to Mr Rooker, sir.' Matt looked injured. 'I knows my way about, sir.'

Canaletto took a deep breath. 'Tell me everything. Who did you speak to?'

Matt jammed his hands into the pockets of a disgraceful pair of ragged breeches and stuck out his lower lip. 'I enters the shop and there's a man bent over some work. He tells me to be off and I asks for Miss Fanny Rooker. 'E sighs deeply.' Matt acted this out, his thin shoulders heaving in a way that Canaletto would normally have found comical. 'Throws down 'is tool and bawls "Lucy", then disappears out the back.'

'The sister-in-law,' murmured Canaletto.

'So into the shop comes this woman wiv, like what you said,' the filthy small hands described a large arc in front of his shrunken stomach. The thin mouth split into a broad smile. 'Reckon she could 'ave dropped it then and there.'

'You asked her for Signorina Fanny?' urged Canaletto.

Matt nodded vigorously. 'Aye, sir, I did, and she told me to be off. So I said I couldn't, not afore I'd spoken to Miss Fanny. That I 'ad an important message.'

'And she said?'

'Why she looked me up and down as though I be some dog turd,' Matt managed somehow to convey Lucy's haughty demeanour, 'and said in that case I need

171

not linger because Fanny Rooker,' he mimicked a tone of contempt for the name, 'was there no more.'

So the harpy had got rid of her sister-in-law, had she? Canaletto felt his anger rise again. How dare she turn Fanny out and how in heaven's name could Ned Rooker have allowed it? He grabbed Matt by his bony shoulder, 'You ask where Signorina Fanny go?'

Matt shook himself free with an injured expression. 'O' course, sir. But she said as 'ow it was none o' my business and to tell whoever 'ad sent me 'e wouldn't get no joy out of 'er.'

'What did that mean?' asked Canaletto of the world in general, frustrated beyond imagining.

'Why, sir, it's plain as plain. Your Miss Fanny 'as run off with some other man,' Matt said contemptuously. Then seemed to realize he could be placing his wages in jeopardy. 'O' course, it might be something else. In any case, Mistress Lucy was a right piss pot. So, seeing as you'd told me not to ask for your baggage from anyone but this Miss Fanny, I comes back. To find you gone!' he added in injured tones.

Canaletto paid him what he'd promised and went back upstairs thinking deeply. What was he to do now? He didn't believe Fanny had gone off with another man but how was he to find her? And could her disappearance have had something to do with the commotion he'd heard behind him as his cab left Fleet Street?

Canaletto tried to persuade McSwiney to go and see Ned Rooker.

But the Irishman refused. 'Nay, Tonio, I am off to cards on your behalf. We have to eat first and I mustn't be late. 'Tis all in your interests,' he added as Canaletto's face darkened. 'Come, the girl has gone off to some

relation. Tomorrow I will go and see what I can find out
and organize your baggage. That, after all, is your main
concern, isn't it?'

But Canaletto wondered if it was.

Chapter Twenty-Four

Canaletto woke early next morning, as was his habit. For a moment he wondered where he was. Beside him rose another bed like a cliff from a beach and drifting down came powerful snores.

It all came back to him and he left his bed without reluctance. He sorted out the clothes he'd discarded the night before and wondered how soon he could get hold of the rest of his clothes and clean linen.

He felt again uneasy about Miss Fanny. He thought of her cheerful face, astonishing resourcefulness and the way she had rescued him from certain death not once but twice. He owed her his life. Later today he would find out exactly where she was, it should surely not be beyond his ingenuity to manage this without alerting that rogue Scallion.

Then Canaletto stopped thinking about Fanny as irritation at the loss of his second-best coat and breeches flooded through him. All he had now were his working clothes, worn all during the voyage, and his very best wear. Until his finances improved, he would not be able to afford more.

He wondered how McSwiney had fared the previous night. He looked down on the sleeping figure and wondered if he could wake and ask him. But the half-open mouth with breath stinking of stale spirits told him he'd not get sense out of him until much later in the day.

Before McSwiney had gone off to his friends, Canaletto had mentioned the name of Pitt to him, putting it forward as a contact of Joseph Smith's.

McSwiney had stared at him, 'Never get involved in politics, Tonio, especially not in England. They're a rotten, corrupt lot. You can't trust any of them further than that chair.' He'd re-tied his cravat in a more fashionable style.

'Especially, I suppose, Mr Pitt?' Canaletto had asked disingenuously.

McSwiney had shrugged his coat back on. 'As to that, they say he's more honest than most. One of the few not lining his pockets. Which is all most of them do. Getting rich, that's the name of the game in England these days. If you don't have a lucrative position, you pester any relation or acquaintance with influence.'

'What if you don't have any such relation or acquaintance?' murmured Canaletto.

'Why then, life is hard. I have no sympathy for any such, I have made my way myself.'

'How did you meet Joseph?'

McSwiney waved an airy hand. 'I had an introduction to him on my first visit to Venice.'

Canaletto permitted himself a small smile. But he did not pursue the matter.

He did wonder now, though, how McSwiney had fared with his friend, the Duke of Richmond's erstwhile tutor. Had there, perhaps, already been a commission arranged?

Whether it had or no, it was important that Canaletto

should survey the new bridge, make a sketch and assess the possibilities for a *veduta*. Work on it should commence as quickly as possible.

Canaletto disentangled his workbox from the canvas bag Fanny had loaned him and found his way downstairs.

Outside, dawn was breaking. But the sun, instead of flushing the sky pearl, filtered its light reluctantly through a smoky haze that hung over the city like a pall of grey muslin.

It was a depressing atmosphere and Canaletto sighed as he set out for the river. At least the trip to Whitehall yesterday had taught him the way to the bridge. Judging from what the paymaster general had said, Canaletto had only to continue past his office in the direction of the Abbey, and he would come across it.

Much of the city was already waking up. A nightwatchman trudged home with tired steps, his lantern now out. Carts rattled by laden with produce. Canaletto wondered if they were off to Covent Garden Market. A milkmaid urged on a cow, a stool under her arm. 'Fresh milk?' she asked Canaletto. 'Fresh as day, sweet as hay.' He shook his head, she bestowed a saucy smile on him and gave the slowly moving animal a prod.

Night revellers proceeded noisily home. A couple, laughing loudly, supporting each other with arms around their necks, were led by a now redundant links boy, his torch flaring uselessly in the rapidly brightening light. Behind them stepped another figure, a broad hat shading his face, a cloak swept around his shoulders in a way that reminded Canaletto of Venice at Carnival time.

Then a rowdy group of young men dressed in richly

brocaded coats over silk embroidered waistcoats, their neat wigs topped by fashionable tricorne hats, swept by, laughing and drunkenly joking.

Canaletto felt a wave of nostalgia for the days of his youth and the camaraderie he'd found with the stage folk he'd mixed with before he'd broken with his father.

One of the youngsters staggered, hiccuped and turned away to spew his guts into the drainage channel down the centre of the road.

The fleeting sense of nostalgia vanished. Grateful for his clear head and what was at present a well-behaved stomach, Canaletto walked more briskly. His plan was to reach the river before the day really started.

He passed the walled Privy garden he'd seen from Pitt's window. Ahead of him he could see the great towers of the imposing Abbey. He was almost there.

Sure enough, a few minutes later, Canaletto came upon what at first glance seemed a massive building site. Houses had been pulled down to make a broad road up to the bridge and now fine new brick ones were being erected on either side.

And there, at the end of the new road, was the river and Westminster Bridge.

A rough gate was set across the bridge entrance. Canaletto walked down to it. A small watchman's hut was empty, no workman was in sight. Beyond a litter of building materials the massive stone flashed white in the ever-increasing light of early morning. The bridge seemed to be nearing completion, already the balustrades had been started. Could there really be concern over delays in its construction?

Impatiently, Canaletto turned away from any such considerations and gave his attention to the view downriver. There was the City of London, the spires of its churches piercing the polluted grey sky, the river curving round so that the dome of the great cathedral looked almost as though it was built on the south and not the north bank.

Slowly Canaletto took in the skyline and prospect offered by each bank, and the boats on the river itself, already in motion, early though the day was. And gradually his slim store of confidence began to evaporate. Once he would have enjoyed the challenge, now all he could feel was doubt. It wasn't the lack of lambent light or a sun-filled sky, he could fake that. It wasn't the width of the river, that was no more than the Basin of St Mark's which he had painted several times. One of those views had produced a masterpiece, the water filled with boats delineated with the superb confidence he'd owned at that time. He still had the technique but he feared the vision had gone.

No, the main problem that faced him was that nothing in the waterfront panorama commanded attention. Where, oh where were majestic buildings to provide a focus?

And how to feature the bridge itself?

Canaletto found the steps that led down to the water. Here from a long causeway ferrymen plied for trade. From one boat were climbing out a party dressed for festivities. They had obviously spent the night carousing somewhere. Perhaps the Vauxhall Gardens McSwiney had mentioned as another subject worthy of his brush. From other boats traders unloaded baskets of produce. The quality seemed excellent, almost as good as the fruit and vegetables grown around Venice. Canaletto bought a couple of carrots and started to nibble one as he sorted out a likely boatman from the scores that shouted for his business.

'The fee is set,' McSwiney had warned. 'All you have to do is choose man and boat.'

Canaletto selected a small but wiry boatman who seemed bursting with energy. He settled his passenger in the small boat then asked, 'Straight across will it be, sir?' Canaletto, munching on his carrot, set his workbox between his feet and nodded. The ferryman leapt in and started pulling hard on his oars.

From the river the new bridge loomed up with massive importance. The stone looked even whiter against the grey of the river and the darker grey of the sky. 'Is it always like this?' asked Canaletto, throwing the end of his carrot into the water.

'Like what, sir?' puffed the oarsman.

'No sun,' Canaletto waved a hand at the sky.

'Indeed, sir. 'Tis the sea coal as what everyone burns. See all them chimneys?'

Canaletto examined the Westminster skyline as they moved further away from the shore and saw smoke rising from building after building, little trails of darkness that built up until the sun was almost obliterated.

'Wind sometimes blows away the smoke. But most days it's like this,' offered the boatman. 'Course, when it's raining, which is often, it's worse.'

The news didn't encourage Canaletto. He turned his attention back to the view and forgot he wasn't in a gondola on a slow-moving canal. 'I wish to look at bridge, please. Perhaps you stay still?'

There was a quick sucking in of breath from the ferryman. 'Tricky, that, sir, what with the tide. Takes all my time to cut across it. 'Tisn't helped by that bridge you thinks so much of, increased the current it 'as. Danged construction, it'll do for all us watermen. Soon as it's opened, that's our living gone, see, sir? No need for the likes of us, then. Me, me father, 'is father afore 'im and 'is father afore 'im, we've all bin watermen. Right liberty it is, take an honest fellow's living away like that. And what good's it going to do? That's what I ask.' His face grew red with the effort of pulling on his oars and the bitterness of his complaint. ''Tis a ruddy crime, that's what it is.' He glanced at Canaletto, cunning in his dark eyes. 'Foreign gentleman, aren't you? 'Eard about the bridge, 'ave you?'

Canaletto nodded, 'Italian. If you can manage somehow to, how you say, linger, so I can see, I pay you price.'

Avarice gleamed in the boatman's eyes. 'Tell you what, sir, I'll take you upstream a-ways then we can come down on the current. I'll back on the oars and you'll have the view you want.' Without waiting for agreement, the boatman changed direction, glancing over his shoulder as he skilfully moved the craft in the direction he wanted across the major path of the river's crafts.

For a while Canaletto's view was upstream. 'What is that building, there, on the other bank, some palace, perhaps?' It was built of red brick or stone, was fair sized and undoubtedly picturesque.

'Oh, aye, that's Lambeth Palace. Archbishop of Canterbury lives there.'

'Canterbury?'

'Place down south, in Kent.'

'So, Kent? Is there a bigger palace for Archbishop,' Canaletto stumbled over the word, 'of London?'

The ferryman shook his head. 'Nah, not as important, 'e ain't.'

Canaletto filed away the fact for later cogitation. The ways of England were undoubtedly strange. Still, that building could offer possibilities. He started chewing on his second carrot.

The ferryman worked his boat round and rested on his oars for a moment. 'There, sir, there's your view of the danged bridge.'

The full length of the bridge could now be seen and the surge of interest Canaletto had felt on his first viewing came surging back. This was indeed a subject worthy of his brush.

He looked again at what could be seen of London through the arches and found the view subtly altered. The frame of the arch gave it additional interest. The church spires fretted the skyline, the buildings crowding the waterfront on both sides offered such variety. Maybe he could, after all, make something of this.

They were now in the pull of the tide and the bridge was coming up rapidly. Canaletto could see in some detail the massive interlacing of the wooden scaffolding that supported the first five arches from the southern bank.

'Take me there,' he ordered the ferryman, pointing excitedly towards the latticework.

'Bit o' courtesy wouldn't come amiss,' muttered the ferryman, bending his shoulders into the task. 'Ask the world, some people do, then not a word o' thanks.'

Canaletto hardly heard him. He'd jettisoned the last of his carrot and opened his workbox. Carefully he unstoppered the bottle of ink, checked the point of his quill pen, then with rapid strokes, using his left hand to steady the notebook and hold the ink, he started to capture the bridge and an outline of the buildings beyond.

As they approached the bridge, his eye was caught by a bucket hanging down from the largest latticed arch. It reminded him of a lantern he'd used a few years ago to direct the eye to a particular point in one of his engravings and add interest to the composition.

The arch with its latticework of scaffolding and the hanging bucket drew closer. 'Want to go under, guv?' asked the ferryman. 'I'll have to pull for the shore else.'

'Yes, under,' commanded Canaletto. Rapidly he sketched in the outline of the arch. He ignored the bucket and concentrated on capturing the skyline for both banks as the boat moved ever more swiftly through the surging waters under the arch, its passage bringing the boat directly beneath the hanging bucket.

Canaletto gave an anguished cry as a large drop spattered on his sketchbook, ruining his work. Another dropped on the sleeve of his coat.

At first Canaletto thought they were drops of dirty water from the bucket. Then he looked more closely and realized the dark blotches were not water, they were blood.

Chapter Twenty-Five

It was several minutes before Canaletto could feel anything but anger at his ruined sketch and the damage to his coat.

With bile rising in his throat, he looked upwards as they cleared the bridge. There had been no workmen there when he'd stood at the approach and there was nary a sign of one there now.

He spat into the water and tried to think. The drops had to have come from the bucket and that must have been left hanging from the previous day. From this side he could see that it was secured to a tall derrick, a wooden lifting frame that rose straight up from the side of the bridge.

'Where to now, sir?' sang out the ferryman.

Canaletto saw they were well clear of the bridge and still continuing downriver. 'To the steps,' he said.

With a resigned air, the ferryman began the laborious business of bringing the boat round and rowing back against the tide.

Canaletto stoppered his ink bottle, found a rag in his workbox and blotted the drop of blood from his sketchbook. He was left with a rust-coloured stain on the drawing. A much larger, darker stain adorned the sleeve of his jacket. He leaned over the side of the boat, dipped the rag in the water then rubbed at the sleeve. It improved a little but not much. What devilish misfortune was dogging his clothes? And why should blood drip from a bucket?

Some of Canaletto's anger died down as he considered.

The boat was about to pass under the arch once again. He looked up and thought he could just see more drips, heavy and viscous, forming round the bottom of the wooden container.

Canaletto kept his eyes on the bucket as his ferryman, grunting with the effort of dragging the boat back underneath the bridge, pulled with powerful strokes through the eddying waters, then altered course for the causeway leading into the water beside the Surrey end of the bridge.

Canaletto picked up his workbox, offered the boatman some coins, saw the man's face, took them back before he could object and gave him a piece of silver. Too much, no doubt, but he wasn't prepared to haggle at this moment. There were more important matters occupying him. He scrambled from the boat and found his way up the steps to the start of the bridge.

As on the Westminster side, there was a rough gate and more building rubble. The gate was locked but with a little effort it was possible to scramble over. Breathing hard, Canaletto picked his way through piles of dressed stone towards the derrick. It was the simplest of contraptions, no doubt erected to aid lifting stone from barges below the bridge, for piles of masonry lay about.

Canaletto approached the derrick with care, it was erected on the edge of the bridge, where there was no protection against falling into the water. He edged nervously forward and glanced down at the river waters swirling below. It seemed a very long way down and his head swam with vertigo. Hastily he drew back and looked instead at the hauling rope, wound round a large cleat on the frame. He put down his workbox beside a pile of the stone and started to unwind the rope.

'Hey!' shouted a voice. 'What do you think you're doing?'

Running along the bridge towards him, dressed in workman's clothes, was a large young man with a shock of fair hair.

Canaletto continued to unwind the rope and felt it take the drag of the bucket's weight. It was heavier than he'd thought it would be.

'What the devil are you up to?' demanded the young man as he came up, his face flushed.

'This bucket, it must rise.' Canaletto puffed, pulling once more on the rope. '*Dio mio*, such a task.'

'Why, 'tis the Italian gentleman! The one Miss Fanny rescued t'other day!'

Canaletto almost let the bucket rope go in astonishment. He could remember little of that agonizing cart ride back to the Rooker establishment. Had this young man been there? There seemed no good reason for him to say so if he hadn't. He looked an honest soul and certainly bore no resemblance to Scallion. Given everything that had happened to Canaletto since he had arrived in London, the coincidence of meeting him here seemed nothing. If Fanny Rooker herself had appeared walking along the balustrade, Canaletto would not have been surprised.

'I regret, your name, I know not.'

'Sam Wood. What be you doing, sir?'

'You must help. This bucket, it must rise, now!' ordered Canaletto. Such was the authority in his voice that, after one startled glance, the young man obeyed. He caught hold of the rope from Canaletto and with a few strong pulls brought the bucket above the level of the bridge.

As the bucket rose into sight, Canaletto steadied its swaying, manoeuvred it on to the stonework and looked inside.

Shock paralysed his brain and he swayed on the edge of the bridge. If the young man hadn't grabbed his shoulders, he would have fallen down, down, down into the water beneath. 'Careful, sir,' Sam said and helped Canaletto to sit on the rough surface of the bridge, pushing his head between his legs.

As the singing in Canaletto's brain lessened and the mists cleared from his mind, he saw his rescuer visibly whiten as he looked into the bucket. 'Christ's blood!' Sam ejaculated.

Canaletto forced himself to take another look. In the bucket, glaring up at them with open-eyed outrage, was a severed head.

This much Canaletto had seen before. Now, as the mists cleared from his mind, he noticed that in one ear was a curiously wrought gold earring in the shape of a snake. He looked more closely at the features. Yes, there could be no doubt, this was the head of Jack Scallion, the mean-featured man who had attacked him on two separate occasions and stolen his precious satchel. How on earth had he ended up like this? And where was the rest of his body?

Canaletto gave one quick glance over the edge of

the bridge at the swiftly running river and reckoned that that question at least had an easy answer.

Canaletto looked up at the young man again. 'What is your business here?'

'I work on the bridge, every now and then,' Sam added hastily. ''Tis mostly stonemasons now and I be carpenter. But now the balustrade is being erected, platforms is needed to finish off the finials that will carry lights.' He glanced uneasily towards the bucket, 'What'll you be wishing to do with that?'

What indeed?

''Tis just, well, workmen will be along any minute. Does 'e want to take it to the justices? Or shall it be tipped into river?' Then Sam scratched at his abundant hair with a large hand. 'It be a puzzle, though, what should have happened to Ben.'

'Ben?'

'The nightwatchman.'

Of course! Canaletto had wondered why no one had challenged his entry on to the bridge. No doubt there were materials here that could be of value to any number of rogues. Even, possibly, those who would wish the bridge ill. He remembered the bitterness in the ferryman's voice as he'd rowed him across the river.

Canaletto looked across at both banks. There were far more little boats now clustered around the causeways. *Dio mio*, how many men earned their livelihood this way? All of them would no doubt like to see the bridge vanish into the depths of the river.

'I'd best be looking for Ben,' Sam's broad forehead creased in worry. 'If he's fallen asleep, it'll be the end of his job for sure. Look sir, will you come with me or be you all right if I leave you here?'

Canaletto didn't much want to stay with the bucket and its grisly contents but found his legs were reluctant to rise. 'You go, come back and tell me what, what you find.'

Sam set off along the bridge without another word.

Canaletto arranged himself so that he sat with his back against a large piece of stone and looked out over the Thames. However, the bucket, sitting beside him, blood very slowly oozing out round its bottom, intruded on any contemplation of the view. How could you consider a skyline when a decapitated head sat beside you?

Canaletto shut his eyes. He couldn't, though, shut his mind to the questions that buzzed around like bees in a hive of honey.

How had the dead man come to his end? What had he been doing on this bridge in the middle of the night? He couldn't, surely, have expected Canaletto to be there? Who had he found instead? And why had he been killed?

Canaletto struggled to his feet and began to study the area around the base of the derrick. Almost at once he saw that a large, dark stain had soaked into the rough surface of the bridge. He knelt and examined it, then dabbed a cautious finger into the part where the stain seemed thickest. The tip of his finger was coloured a rusty, viscous red. It had to be blood.

The stain must have been made some time after work had finished for the day, otherwise it would have been overlaid with dust raised by workmen.

Canaletto continued searching and was rewarded by finding a silver coin almost hidden beneath one of the stones not far from the patch of blood. Carefully he drew it out. Quite soon after he found another coin, similarly half hidden. He didn't find any more and after a little while he gave up the search, sat down on one of the stones and tried to imagine what had happened there the previous night.

He soon put together a vision of Scallion on all fours in the dust, trying to pick up fallen coins by the light of the moon. It had been quite bright, he remembered. And as Scallion scrabbled in the dust for more coins, Canaletto saw, as vividly as if it was taking place in front of his eyes, a figure raise a sword and bring it down like an executioner on the man's outstretched neck.

Canaletto shuddered as he imagined the strength needed for the weapon to have been brought down with sufficient force to sever head from shoulders.

The murderer must then have hauled both pieces of the body over the edge of the bridge and dropped them into the water. Had he realized the head had been caught in the bucket? Had he cared?

Before dropping Scallion into the water, though, he must surely have retrieved those coins the villain had picked up from the bridge and then, no doubt, he'd rescued as many of the rest as he could find.

Who was he?

Any number of people could have had cause to exterminate the sort of vermin Scallion had obviously been. Canaletto knew many such in Venice. They scavenged amongst the low life, stealing whatever they could, available for hire by anyone with desperate needs.

No doubt Canaletto had been but one of many victims.

And he could now rest safe. The man who had

dogged his footsteps ever since he had set foot in England was dead.

But how was he to find out what had happened to his money?

There was a shout and Canaletto turned to see Sam Wood running along the bridge.

'Nightwatchman's dead too,' he announced. 'Hit on the head. I found his body behind some stone. We must tell the constables.'

Both of them set off back across the bridge. After a few minutes Canaletto asked Sam if he knew anything of Fanny Rooker's whereabouts.

'Fanny?' Sam turned an anguished face to him. 'You didn't know?'

Canaletto halted in the middle of the rubble-strewn bridge. 'Know?' he demanded.

'Why, she was arrested for stealing.'

'Stealing?' Canaletto clutched at the man's arm. 'Fanny wouldn't steal!' He was quite convinced of this.

'It was Mistress Lucy's petticoat,' said Sam disconsolately. 'Everyone knows how she and Mistress Lucy are at enmity.'

'You don't believe this, this lie?' exploded Canaletto.

Sam stopped, strong emotion breaking out on features that normally looked carved out of a particularly hard piece of wood and raised a hand. 'I could never believe ought against Fanny, sir, and I'll knock the block off any man who suggests it!'

Canaletto took a swift step back, 'Softly, man, softly. Tell me, Signorina Fanny, where she is now?'

Sam's huge shoulders sagged, he turned away and passed a hand across his eyes.

Canaletto grabbed at his coat front and forced him round again. 'Tell me! Where she is?'

'She's in gaol.'

'In gaol?' Canaletto was appalled.

'Even worse, sir, she's about to be transported – to the Americas!'

Chapter Twenty-Six

The smell was indescribable.

Certain elements could be identified: there was the reek of cold, damp stone from the walls of this miserable cellar, the rank odour of so many unwashed bodies, the sharp stench of urine and faeces, all mingled with the pungency of gin. Yet above all these smells was another Fanny could put no name to. It was an aroma peculiar to the prison and seemed compounded equally of misery and high spirits.

The misery was immediately obvious from the vast numbers of men and women who either sat in dull despair or wailed, pulled their hair, beat themselves or weaved around the place with a demented aspect accosting others. Every now and then a fight broke out between two or more inmates. Few seemed to care what the outcome might be.

But not everyone seemed devastated to be incarcerated in this huge, bleak cellar. There were men in fetters playing cards with so abandoned an air, Fanny was convinced they had been imbibing spirits, a fact soon proved by the arrival of a warder with a bottle which he gave to one of them in return for some money.

In another corner a young girl of comely appearance but wearing clothes of a sorry condition, appeared to be in merry conversation with a young man as poorly dressed as she.

But poor Fanny couldn't take heart from any suggestion it might be possible to pass days in this place with a semblance of equanimity. Indeed, she found any mood other than that of deepest despair to be extraordinary.

From the moment the thief-taker had laid hands on her in Fleet Street, things had gone from bad to very much worse.

There had been the terrible place she had been held overnight, filled with women Fanny feared were no better than they ought to be, despite the well-dressed appearance of some.

Before that, though, she had been questioned by one it was announced was a justice. He was a man of commanding presence, apart from the bend in his nose that proclaimed a break at some stage of his career, and was dressed in fine velvet, with his lawn of the best.

He had taken her apart, into a very small room with hardly space for the both of them. There she had been thrust so close to him her face had been continually presented with the glittering embroidery and golden buttons of his waistcoat.

His silky smooth voice had elicited every detail of her arrest and she had almost begun to hope that he believed her story when his hand wandered down her fichu and his fingers toyed with her nipple.

'Why, here's a pretty maiden,' he said in a quickened voice. 'Not as pretty as some, maybe, but comely, yes, comely indeed.'

Fanny grabbed at his hand and tried to pull it from her breast. She might as well have tried to lift a cart from the street. His other hand went round her waist and pulled her even closer. 'Where is it you live, eh? Is there a back door where a man could come calling?' The fumes of his heavy breathing were noxious, his teeth, such as there were, for most of them had been lost, yellow and rotting. Then he brought that mouth down on hers and his hard body drove her against the wall.

Fanny was outraged beyond all sense of her own best interests. A swift jerk of her knee rendered the justice incapable for several minutes. Spluttering and gasping, he leant against the opposite wall, his watering eyes hot and malevolent.

'I am innocent,' she spat at him. 'Any who dares say otherwise is a blackguard.'

'Say you so?' The silk had disappeared from the justice's voice, it rasped now with unpleasant force. 'We shall judge of it in my court tomorrow morning.'

That night, among the whores and petty thieves, Fanny learned by listening that the justice was well known for taking his pleasures with females brought before him and that a more accommodating attitude on her part might have gained her a sympathetic hearing.

But next morning the man sitting on the carved chair on its dais, his face stern, seemed a different person from the lecher she'd met the previous day. Fanny was handled roughly and made to stand at a bar opposite the clerk who sat at a table below the justice. On that table were arranged the luscious folds of a silk petticoat.

On each side of the room were rows of seats occupied by curious faces.

Bruised by the rough handling she'd received since her arrest, furious at the situation she was in and unable to credit that justice would not prevail, Fanny attempted to speak stoutly in answer to the charge.

But her words were cut short by the magistrate, everything she said was denied. And when presented with the petticoat, she had to admit that it did indeed look like the one given to Lucy by her brother.

'But, sir,' protested Fanny, 'I never . . .'

'Quiet!' came the thundering reply. 'Let us hear how and where this garment was discovered.'

Oh, Lucy, Fanny thought as she listened to the story of the finding of the petticoat beneath her mattress, how could you have done this to me?

Then one of the faces in the small gallery above the court room caught her eye. It was Ned.

Immediately hope arose. He would help her. He would testify that she must be, that she was innocent.

But Ned did not speak.

His expression was that of a man tormented beyond understanding but still he didn't speak.

Fanny listened to her sentence without comprehension. The magistrate's voice was rich with satisfaction as he proclaimed the seven years' transportation but all she could take in was the despair on Ned's face and all she could understand was that he had not uttered one word in her defence.

Once in the gaol, however, with the heavy gates slammed behind her, she stood in the malodorous and dreadful place and realized that the evidence had been too damning and nothing could have saved her. Fanny's soul raged against her sister-in-law as, exhausted and in failing spirits, she sank down on to the dank and filthy stone floor.

'Well, my dear, and are you to provide drinks for us all?'

It seemed the imperious but cheerful voice was addressed to her. Fanny looked up.

It was doubtful if she had ever seen a more unpleasant sight than the woman who stood in front of her. A long, puckering scar ran from one eye down to the side of the mouth, drawing up mottled skin so that the cheek resembled a cobbled street slashed by a drain. The eye itself was clouded and vacant. Its fellow was an evil-looking slime green set in a white that was nearer yellow and laced with red veins. Nor was the unscarred half of the face more pleasant than the scarred, disfigured as it was by more mottling. One ear was torn, the other sported an enormous gold ring. The hair was a tangle of greasy curls, the dress an assemblage of rags that somehow managed to cover most of her voluminous person, only a heavy breast sagged into sight as she stuck her arms akimbo and her one eye fixed Fanny with a stare that seemed almost friendly. 'Well?' she demanded again. 'Lorst our tongue, 'ave we?'

Fanny scrambled to her feet. This was no woman to have towering over one. 'I'm sorry, I didn't understand you spoke to me. I, I have no drink.'

'No, but you'll 'ave coin, a well-dressed maid like you.' The slime-coloured eye assessed Fanny's frock, badly stained now and far from fresh but still a world away from that which most of the other inmates wore. 'Well, it's the practice of new 'uns to stand liquor to the inmates of what's known as Bartholomew Fair.' She flung an arm out to encompass the terrible cellar, her one good eye glittering in expectation.

Fanny shook her head. 'Alas, I have nothing.'

It was a fact she'd already had cause to regret. It seemed that money could buy your way out of this noisome place and into superior accommodation.

The woman spat, the spittle just missing the hem of Fanny's dress. It lay gleaming on the dark stone. 'And I took you for a right old buttock and twang mort what could be relied on to fix us up.'

Fanny had no idea what she was talking about but from the way those around were eyeing her, it seemed plain she commanded respect.

'I'm hoping my brother will bring me some coin.' Surely Ned was even now on his way to her?

The woman bellowed with laughter, throwing back her head, her whole body shaking. 'Oho, brother is it? We all knows about brothers!'

'Cut it, Scarface, let the girl alone.' The newcomer was a self-possessed woman of some forty summers with a plain face and skimpy hair who had somehow managed to keep herself neat, though her clothing's threadbare and stained condition bore eloquent testimony to the length of time she had been in the gaol. She threw an arm around Fanny's shoulders.

'Scarface *Nell*, if you please,' came with another great laugh from the other. 'I'll have my full name from such as you, Mother Comfort.'

More women and some men came up, comments were thrown at each of the two women, inciting them: 'Let 'er 'av it, Nell, you know what she's like', 'Don't you let 'er get away with it, Dot'.

Dot, also known as Mother Comfort, withdrew her arm from Fanny and stuck her hands on her hips. She gave a small toss to her head, 'Outface me, would you!'

she shot at Nell, who started to roll up her sleeves in a most meaningful way.

A small hand pulled Fanny away. 'You don't want to get involved in their fight,' said a quiet voice.

She was a slight girl not much older than Fanny, her face white and pinched, her feet bare on the foul stone floor, her dress torn and tattered. Her features were dainty, or would have been if she'd been clean and her tangled hair washed and tidied. 'Scarface Nell is always after the new ones, she's a devil for the drink.'

Fanny allowed herself to be led to a little distance from the confrontation, still, it seemed, confined to words.

'I'm Amelia, in for debt. You're in for theft, due for transportation,' the girl said, ignoring the whirl of insults that were being thrown in the middle of the throng of prisoners.

'How did you know?' Since she'd arrived, Fanny had not been given an opportunity to tell anyone her history.

'Everyone knows everyone's business here,' Amelia gave her a sweet smile. 'You'll soon get the hang of things. Like, stand up to Scarface and she'll be no trouble to you, in fact, you can trust her, which is more than can be said for Mother Comfort, she's one to watch.'

'Why, she seemed a friendly soul.'

'That she does. She's in here for whoring and running a bagnio.'

'A bagnio?'

'A whorehouse. Mother Comfort's always looking for new talent, meets all the stages from the country, takes under her wing any young miss seeking her fortune in

London.' Amelia cast down her eyes. 'I know, I was one of them.'

'You were?' Fanny couldn't take it in. Everything seemed upside down in here. This sweet looking girl a whore? Scarface Nell to be trusted? And Mother Comfort a seducer of young women?

The girl gave a small, bitter laugh. ''Tis easy enough now to say I shouldn't have gone with her. She made it all so easy and, truth to tell, a life as a rich man's fancy can be delightful. Dot arranged I lost my virtue to an old man who set me up in style. I had clothes and jewels, a maid and everything I could wish for.'

'What happened?' Fanny eyed the girl in fascination.

Amelia sighed deeply. 'He caught me with a young man from the mercer's next door. Then it was out on my ear and the young man wanted nought to do with me. But once again Mother Comfort was there. She'd been paid handsomely for my virtue and now that it was gone, she gave me a roof over my head in return for the use of my body.'

Amelia didn't sound too downcast by the memory.

'But what brought you here?'

'I fastened the affections of another gentleman who was lavish with his favours. He set me up, encouraged me to order fine clothes, to run up bills with tradesmen, milliners and others. Then one day a letter came that said goodbye, he'd had to leave the country but he hoped he'd see me again some day. And when the news got around, bills flew in upon me like pigeons on corn. I drowned in them.'

'Did Mother Comfort provide no help?'

'Nay,' Amelia said scornfully. 'I'd left her without a *douceur*. She laughed in my face, said I'd have to fend for myself. So my creditors sent me afore the magistrates and here I am and here I stay 'till I can repay my debt.'

'And when will that be?' cried Fanny, thinking the tale a sorry one. Amelia seemed such a gentle soul, one who had as little place in this terrible gaol as Fanny herself.

'Why, I cannot think I will ever be released,' said Amelia plaintively. 'For I have no relatives or friends to provide my debts. Have you any will help you? For if you have coin, you need not remain here, you know?'

Fanny nodded, 'I was told on entrance better accommodation could be provided could I but pay for it. Alas, I have nothing until my brother arrives with funds.'

'A brother! Oh, Fanny, I'm so pleased for you,' Amelia gave her another of her sweet smiles.

There came a great cry from the prisoners clustered around Mother Comfort and Scarface Nell. It seemed a blow had been struck, quickly followed by another, but which of the two women had instigated the fight was impossible to tell.

It was all over in a matter of moments, with Mother Comfort on the ground and Scarface Nell grinding a triumphant shoe into her chest. 'Don't ee be messin with the likes of I!' she said triumphantly then swaggered off to another part of the gaol.

Fanny was awestruck. 'Was it brawling brought her here?' she asked Amelia.

'Oh, she's always in and out. Sometimes licentious behaviour but usually for whoring.'

'Whoring?'

'Well may you look surprised! I cannot imagine a

man mounting such but I assure you 'tis true. Men are animals that just seek gratification of their desires.'

Fanny looked after the retreating figure of Scarface Nell then thought of her brother, Ned. And of Sam. And then of Signor Canaletto. She could not imagine any of them, particularly Signor Canaletto, going anywhere near Scarface Nell.

'You would no doubt be equally amazed were I to tell you of some of the men I have allowed to be taken in the fact with me,' Amelia continued, her eyes wide and laughing. 'One or two of them would make Scarface Nell seem pretty! And you will ask me why? And I will tell you, 'tis for money. A craftsman has the skill of his hands by which to make a living. Does he insist his customers are pretty fellows who wash their hands? The only skill I have is that of my body. I cannot be too nice in the choice of my customers either.'

Fanny's head whirled and she began to feel a little faint. Abruptly she sat down on one of the straw mattresses that lay on the floor and fought to hold on to consciousness.

Chapter Twenty-Seven

'Why, Fanny, how's this?' cried Amelia, sitting down beside her and reaching for her hand.

'I'm sorry,' Fanny murmured. 'I think it's hunger, I've not eaten since yesterday.'

'Oh my dear Fanny, life is hard for you! Here, I think I have a piece of pie somewhere.' Amelia felt about her person and brought out from some pocket a fragment of pastry which she offered to Fanny, who eyed it doubtfully. 'I assure you 'tis fresh!'

Fanny's pangs of hunger and a desire not to offend the helpful girl drove her to accept the morsel and she had to admit that it tasted among the best food she had ever eaten. 'Is this what we get fed?' she asked, licking the last crumb from her fingers.

Amelia laughed, a genuinely amused sound. 'A penny loaf that's none too fresh, that's what's handed out to such as us. Nay, that pie was purchased by another prisoner, one generous enough to give me a part. For, alas, I have no funds for such delicacies.'

'And you shared it with me!' Fanny was touched. This girl might be a whore but she had true feelings. A tiny spot of warmth was lit in her breast.

A raffish looking fellow with long legs and a surprisingly handsome face swaggered over. 'Come, adorable

Amelia, 'tis time for our game,' he said, reaching a hand to pull the girl up. Then he gave a start as though he saw Fanny for the first time. 'Why, beauty is come amongst us. Perhaps,' he said, raking her with hot brown eyes in a way that made her feel uncomfortable, 'you will honour us by taking a hand?'

'Nay, Ben, she has no coin,' Amelia said shortly.

'Ah, so.' Ben sounded regretful. 'Never mind, lass, we'll pass an hour or so together later.' The two went off to a further part of the gaol, the fellow produced cards and an animated game commenced. Fanny wondered briefly what Amelia used for a stake but the awfulness of her own position soon drove out any other consideration.

The gloomy light from the high barred windows gradually faded as night came. A flare outside the huge iron gate hardly illuminated the scene. The noise, the confusion, the terrible atmosphere, together with the press of people, many of whom seemed diseased or mad, all combined to make poor Fanny feel transportation could not be worse and might even offer an improvement. If, that is, she could survive until then.

Amelia had not again approached her. Others did, some curious, some malevolent. She found herself losing her inborn instinct for courtesy and choking off those who would discourse with her.

Eventually, worn out by all she had endured, Fanny found herself slipping into a fitful sleep. Only to be dragged back into heart-beating consciousness by the urgent pressing of a body upon hers.

Ben, the man who'd taken Amelia off for cards, was exploring her body with avid hands, his lips slobbering kisses on her mouth and neck. 'You're a pretty one,' his voice gasped into her ear. 'Treat me right and I'll see you right. Nothing I can't do in this place.' A tongue insinuated itself into her ear while one long leg divided hers, making it impossible to move away. Fanny fought and screamed but her strength was nothing to his and no one seemed interested in her struggle, her cries were but one strand in the cacophony that even in the dead of night filled this miserable cellar.

'Be still, you bitch,' the man grunted as his hand attempted to lift up Fanny's skirts. She threw her head from side to side and managed to bite the hand that tried to anchor her upper part to the floor. He cursed freely, 'You whore, you bawd, don't you know what's good for you?'

One large hand held her throat while the other whipped up the folds of her skirt, tearing it in the process. Fanny, half choking, felt again the terror that had seized her when the magistrate had attempted her virtue and this time she knew she could not win.

Then, as suddenly as it had started, the attack ceased. Her throat was released, the man gave a strangled grunt and rolled off the straw matress.

'Miserable cur, ain't you got no common feelings?' demanded Scarface Nell, wielding a chunk of wood. In the dim, flickering light, Fanny saw her drag the recumbent body further away. 'Keep yer 'ands to yerself in future, Barnacle Ben, an' everything else as well.' There came a rustle of straw as the large woman plumped herself down beside Fanny. ''Ow far'd 'e got, then?'

Fanny stammered that, apart from some tears in her dress, she seemed to be intact.

'You need a knife in 'ere. No respecter of persons

most is. What's the matter, doll? 'E damaged you after all?'

'No, it's just, just I can't find my locket.' Fanny tried to discover if it had fallen down her bodice. 'The chain must have broken in the struggle,' she mourned. 'I'll have to look for it when day comes.'

Scarface Nell gave a shout of coarse laughter. 'You'll be lucky! Locket, you say? That will have gone soon as you came in! Thieves the lot of 'em in 'ere. Can lift anything easier than a washerwoman a 'andkerchief.'

Fanny remembered the way Mother Comfort had flung an arm around her neck. Was that how it had been done?

'Course you can check the straw, but you won't find a thing, unless it's a rat, an' I don't mean the two-legged sort. That cursed whorseson over there,' a jab of her toe indicated Fanny's attacker, beginning to recover consciousness, ''e's one of your whoreson conmen. We calls 'im barnacle cos that's what 'e is. The one what takes advantage of a con 'is partner's set up. Barnacle Ben, that's 'im. 'E'll con 'is mother out of 'er wedding ring.'

'The locket was my mother's,' mourned Fanny, 'the only thing I have left of hers.' Bitter anger filled her. Come the morning she was going over to Mother Comfort and claim it back.

'Best thing you can do is say it's lorst and offer a reward. Silver coin is all they value in 'ere.'

Fanny remembered the way the two women had fought, she had no desire for that sort of confrontation. 'Ned is bound to come tomorrow with funds.'

'Ned, that'll be your brother, Ned Rooker.'

'How do you know?'

'Oh, I knows everything wot goes on round Fleet

Street. I knows that thieftaker wot arrested you, 'e'll 'ave 'ad 'is orders from that Alderman Fowler.' Scarface Nell spat on the floor. 'Nasty bit o' work 'e is.'

'How do you know?' Fanny repeated.

'Told you, knows everything I does. Makes it my business. It was 'e got me sent down last. Didn't like me decoratin' 'is front door!' The woman chuckled unpleasantly. 'Nasty temper 'e's got. But I'll see to 'im afore too long.'

Barnacle Ben staggered to his feet. 'Bawds, jades, the lot of you,' he threw over at Fanny and Scarface Nell. 'It'll be worse for you, see if it don't.' All attempt at courtesy had gone.

Scarface Nell made a rude gesture with two fingers in his direction.

'Aren't you afraid what he'll do?'

'Nah,' Scarface Nell said scornfully. 'I knows more'n what 'e does. 'E 'as to watch 'imself round me, I can tell you. 'Course,' she added thoughtfully, 'things is better for any girl 'e takes a fancy to. Always manages to fleece the newcomers, does Barnacle Bill, and 'e's willing to share 'is good fortune with them as is good to 'im. 'E's a pretty fellow, too.' Lasciviousness laced her voice.

Fanny shuddered. She felt naïve and stupid. She thought she knew her way around Fleet Street and its environs, now she would never walk there again without wondering if that man could be a barnacle, or that woman a whore.

Then desolation swept over her as she realized that she would never walk down Fleet Street again.

'You cry, pet, tears never 'urt. Feel better afterwards.' Scarface Nell gave Fanny an awkward pat. 'Remember, I'm on your side.'

It was a measure of how much in Fanny's life had changed that a woman such as Scarface Nell could seem the best friend a girl could have.

The following morning, as Fanny was struggling not to collapse under the full horror of her situation, a warder came to her. 'You 'as a visitor,' he said.

Ned! Fanny's heart rose joyfully. But the figure following the warder was not her brother.

'Signor Canaletto!' she exclaimed in astonishment. If the king himself had appeared, she could not have been more surprised.

The painter was dressed in the working garments she had taken out of his baggage before he left Fleet Street, but he wore them as though they were made of silk rather than kersey. He had swapped his bonnet for his wig and looked a very gentleman.

He struggled to maintain his composure as he took in the surroundings. 'Signorina Fanny, I'm . . . that is to say . . . I don't know . . . first . . . and now this,' he was incoherent and Fanny for the first time forgot something of her misery at the sight of his deep shock.

She clasped his hands tightly. Their warmth was wonderful. 'Signor, don't distress yourself, it is nothing to do with you.'

'But you, in this place,' he threw a horrified glance around the dank cellar known as Bartholomew Fair and at its noisome inhabitants. 'Tell me everything, how you came to be here.'

'Oh, signor, Lucy says I stole her petticoat and I didn't. But the constable found it beneath my mattress!

How it came there I know not.' Under questioning from Canaletto she gave him all the details.

Canaletto was under no doubts about the truth of the matter, 'Mistress Lucy organized it so, 'tis obvious!'

'Oh, I cannot believe it, signor.' Even now, Fanny could not bring herself to accept Lucy hated her so much. Much more troubling was the possibility her brother might believe her guilty.

Fanny tightened her grip on the painter's hands. 'Signor, can you send a message to Ned? Ask him if he will come and see me?'

'I will talk to your brother myself.'

'No!' cried Fanny. 'You will put yourself in danger, I cannot have that.'

'Oh, Signorina Fanny, you should not think of anything but yourself now!' He lifted one of Fanny's hands and kissed its dirty back. Then he drew her into a darker part of the cellar, away from curious ears, and dropped his voice. 'But not to worry. Scallion is dead, he cannot follow me more.'

'Dead!' Fanny gasped. More of her fellow prisoners gathered around them, drawn by anything that brought something of the outside world into their miserable surroundings, their eyes curious, their ears straining to catch anything said. She dropped her voice and whispered to Canaletto, 'Oh, do not say he found you and you had to kill him!'

'No, no,' he soothed her. 'He was despatched by I know not who.' And in a low voice he told some tale of Westminster Bridge, a bucket and Sam.

'Sam?' Fanny was by now completely bewildered. 'Sam Wood? Oh, of course, he builds the platforms for the masons to work from.'

'Sam is good man,' Canaletto said firmly. 'When I ask where you have gone, for I sent a messenger to you but yesterday, he tells me of this terrible thing. He goes to magistrate to report the bodies, or one body and one head, and I, I come here.' He looked fiercely round and Scarface Nell stepped back, sweeping out an arm and taking several others with her, leaving a small clear area around Fanny and Canaletto. 'So, you see, I can visit your brother and ask why he does not visit you here.'

The relief of having contact established between Ned and herself was too much. Fanny slid to the ground, searching for a handkerchief to wipe away her tears. The edge of her torn gown had to do.

Canaletto crouched down beside her. 'Signorina Fanny, please, I make all right. I can do this, you shall not suffer more.'

'Oh, sir,' Fanny gave a big sniff and tried to smile, though the light was so bad she could hardly see the expression on Canaletto's face and he could surely not discern hers. 'It's just, you see Ned and I, we have been all to each other ever since the rest of our family died. That is, we were until he married Lucy,' she gulped in her effort not to give way to the desperate distress she felt. 'He swore to me marriage would not change our love for each other. That I would always be his dear sister, that he loved Lucy, but in a different way.' The tears were rolling down her cheeks now. 'But everything has changed. He is not the same person. Lucy has changed everything.'

Canaletto settled himself beside her on the cold, dank ground, seemingly heedless of its dirt. 'I know how you feel, believe me.' He seemed to consider for a moment then carried on. 'Many, many year ago, I'm very young, perhaps as you now, I work with my father in Rome. We paint scenery, it is before I become view painter.'

This unexpected piece of information cut through Fanny's misery. 'Painted scenery?'

'Is very important in Italia. We create fantastic worlds.'

'Fantasy,' murmured Fanny.

'Yes, fantastic. Everyone come to see our scenery – and the show, of course.'

'Of course,' Fanny murmured as the lilt of his voice managed somehow to lift a part of the misery that filled her soul.

'The actors and singers love our work. We create such special world for them the public cannot help but admire their performance.'

Even through her despair Fanny could be amused at how for Canaletto his work had to be the most important part of the performance.

'There is beautiful young singer.' Canaletto's voice altered, nostalgia and something more deepening its light, detached tone. 'Maria her name. She, well, I think she love me.' Now it was as though he had to struggle to tell a difficult tale.

'I'm sure she did, signor,' Fanny said gently.

Canaletto laid a hand on her arm. 'Please, can you not call me Tonio? I should so like that.'

Fanny was touched beyond measure. That this eminent man, so much older, so much beyond her in every way, should ask for her to use his Christian name was such an honour it took her breath away. Almost it made her awful surroundings fade away. But not quite.

'Signor . . ., Tonio, please, what happened?'

Through the gloom she could see a tight smile twist Canaletto's lips. 'For several weeks I am happy. Happy as never before. I think perhaps we marry, have children. Then I find out,' he looked away from her, out into the gloom-filled gaol thronged with the mad, the bad, the curious, the desperate. 'My father, she go with him too.'

The hopeless despair in his voice took Fanny out of her own misery. 'Oh, Tonio, no!'

'I could not believe, but it was proved to me beyond all doubt. My father and Maria!'

'That is too terrible. To have your faith in both your father and your love destroyed.' Fanny could hardly bear to think about the awfulness of it.

'I work with my father since I am boy. I think perhaps he value me. I cannot understand how he do this to me.' The words came jerkily and Fanny knew for certain that this was something he had kept within himself for a very, very long time. 'I ask him, beg him, why he hurt me like this.'

'And what did he say?'

'He say I too young, do not understand life. Maria like man with experience.'

'That's dreadful!'

'Now I think I understand. He feel old, want to know he better than his son. I better painter than him but not better lover. But then I hate him. We have big argument. I tell him I no paint scenery, I paint views. He have to find other assistant.'

'What did he say?'

'He is very, very angry. Tell me I no have success. That I will be failure, come back to him begging for job again, but then he not need me.' Canaletto looked at

Fanny, 'I no see my father many, many years. He hurt me but I hurt myself. I love my father. More than Maria. She was nothing!' But beneath the contempt in his voice, Fanny thought she heard, even after all these years, a defiant rejection of what had been real passion.

'So you're saying I shouldn't let Lucy come between Ned and me?'

'My father and I say bad things to each other. We each lose each other. That is bad; families, blood, it means so much.'

Fanny thought of her brother, the patience with which he had begun to teach her the techniques of engraving, the jokes they'd shared, the dreams. 'It's too late, signor.'

'Tonio,' he said quietly.

'Tonio,' she repeated. 'I'm in here and doomed for transportation. For seven years. Shall I ever see Ned again?' Tears spilled over.

Canaletto became agitated. 'You will, Fanny, you will. I promise. Now, I must go, things I do, you see. But, here.' She felt coins pressed into her hand. 'Order food, be calm, of good spirit. I come back soon and Ned will come, I assure you Ned will come.' Canaletto patted her hand, then, with astonishing agility for one of his age, he rose and, without looking back, threaded his way through the crowd of prisoners towards the entrance gate of the gaol.

Fanny watched him go, numbed and bemused.

'Your fancy man, eh?' Scarface Nell was back, her ghastly face contorted into a semblance of a smile. 'You're a sly one!'

'No, no!' protested Fanny. 'He is but a friend.'

'Nice friend, to give you coin,' Scarface Nell winked

with her good eye, a slow, lascivious wink that said she knew all about good friends.

Fanny looked down at her hand, now filled with silver. She was amazed and touched by the amount. She picked out one of the larger coins and showed it to Nell. 'This to the person who can bring me my locket,' she told her. 'And here,' she pressed some of the other coins into her hand, 'this for alcohol.'

'You leave it to me, duck,' the one good eye gleamed with an avaricious light. 'I'll see you get your piece back.'

Sure enough, it wasn't long before one of the prisoners brought a small, gilt locket to Fanny. 'I found it yesterday but knew not whose it was. How fortunate I can return it to you.'

Fanny handed over the silver coin with relief, resentment and disappointment mixed in equal measure. 'My thanks, Amelia,' she said.

Chapter Twenty-Eight

Canaletto left the prison and went straight to Fleet Street.

Though the door was open, no one was in the shop. A copper plate, a few lines etched into its surface, rested on the work cushion. Noise filtered down from the upstairs region.

Canaletto followed his ears.

In the front room, Mistress Lucy was in hysterics.

'You mustn't leave me alone, Ned. I vow I am unable to contain myself.' Her bloated figure sat in the chair by the window, her head was flung back, her features distorted in passion. A lace handkerchief was clasped tightly in one hand, her neck fichu was all awry.

Standing in front of her, a glass of some liquor in his hand, was Ned, his open face distressed and anxious. 'Lucy, drink some of this, it will do you good, help calm you.' A violently outflung hand caught the glass, it fell and shattered on the floor, the liquid splashed all ways. Ned's already strained voice tightened several notches. 'Lucy, you will only do yourself and the child mischief.'

'The child, that's all you think about. No thought for me, your wife!'

'Lucy, I must see Fanny, surely you understand that?'

The hysterics wound themselves into demented shrieks. 'Fanny, Fanny! You care nothing for me!' Lucy flung herself from side to side against the wooden arms of the chair. Ned attempted to hold her but the violence of her fit was such his arms were pushed away.

To one side stood a slight girl of fifteen or sixteen wearing a simple cotton dress covered with a large apron. She wrung her hands helplessly, her eyes huge in her round face.

Canaletto strode in, shoved Ned aside and slapped the hysterical woman across the face.

Lucy stopped screaming and hiccuped in surprise. Red-rimmed eyes, flicking like a frantic stoat's, gazed at him in horrified amazement.

'Mistress Lucy, you will answer my questions,' Canaletto said sternly.

'What right have you—,' started a furious Ned. Canaletto silenced him immediately.

'Your sister is in gaol, suffering the most vile conditions, and what have you done?'

Ned flushed a brilliant scarlet and said nothing.

But the little maid piped up. ''Tis her,' she said, pointing an accusing finger at the still astonished Lucy. 'Every time 'e said 'e 'ad to go to Miss Fanny, she threw another fit. Ever since 'e came back from the courthouse it's been bedlam 'ere.' Her voice was contemptuous.

Canaletto returned his attention to Lucy. 'So, mistress, what say you about this affair?'

Lucy gave another hiccup, choking back her sobbing, her eyes frightened.

'You accused Signorina Fanny, did you not? While knowing she was innocent.'

'Lucy!' gasped poor Ned, the colour now draining away from his face. 'Tell me you did not.'

'You, young man, are idiot,' Canaletto told him, his voice full of scorn. 'Do you not know your sister? Or your wife?'

Ned dropped his head in a shamefaced way. 'I couldn't believe Lucy would do such a thing,' he muttered.

'You preferred to believe Fanny could steal?' thundered Canaletto.

'I thought there'd been some mistake,' Ned sounded utterly bewildered and as though his world had turned over.

'The mistake was yours!' Canaletto returned his attention to Lucy. 'You have sinned, going to magistrate, telling lies about Fanny,' his voice roared.

At that Lucy broke into a loud wail. 'I didn't! I wouldn't! I just wanted Fanny out of my house.'

'Aha, now we have it! Why, what has poor Signorina Fanny done that you should want her, as you put it, out of your house? The house she thinks is hers?'

Lucy had lost her aggression. Her expression looked mutinous but defeated. 'Fanny is always telling me what to do. She makes Ned see me as nothing, as someone without a brain in her head.'

Dio mio, thought Canaletto. What a spineless creature we have here. No wonder poor Fanny has been run off her feet. But even as he said this to himself, he felt a moment's sympathy for Lucy. It would not be easy to fit into a tight brother-and-sister duo. Especially when the sister was as managing as Fanny.

'So what did you do?' Canaletto asked again even

more sternly. He had no intention of letting the initiative slip from him.

Lucy brought out a handkerchief as tears started to pour down her face. 'Can I speak to you alone, sir?' She shot a sideways glance at Ned that was compounded of entreaty and fear.

'Oh, for heaven's sake!' he exploded. 'What can you have to say to Signor Canal that you can't say to me? Who am your husband?'

'Please,' entreated Canaletto. 'Leave us together. Go and see your sister.'

Ned looked at Lucy but apparently the prospect of being able to unburden herself to a comparative stranger was sufficiently attractive for her not to complain at a visit to Fanny.

'Please, take food and some coin to the signorina,' Canaletto urged. 'She has great need. Also a fresh gown. If you sweeten the warders with largesse, it will be simple to give them to her.'

Ned's mobile face reflected a great sense of guilt. 'Lucy, I'll be back shortly.' Still he hesitated for a moment, looking at his distraught wife, then he turned on his heel and left the room.

'I'll wait within call,' the maid said in an excited whisper before she, too, went outside.

Canaletto brought up one of the other two chairs in the room so he could sit near the pregnant woman.

'Now, madam, we are alone.' He picked up one of the hands that was pulling nervously at the fine lawn of her handkerchief. 'Please, I not intend distress you but Signorina Fanny is in terrible place. I try to release her.'

Lucy sat up a little. 'You think there is a way Fanny

can be set free? Oh, sir, I would like that more than anything. Except to have Ned look at me as once he did.'

'But I must know. How was it Fanny was arrested? What was the evidence?'

Lucy looked at him out of her red-rimmed, swollen eyes. At last she gave a great sigh. 'Why, sir, it was only that my brother, the alderman, he kept asking me why I didn't wear the petticoat he gave me. 'Twas very pretty, yellow silk embroidered with green leaves. Even Mistress Hayles, the attorney's wife who lives three doors away and is always looking down her nose at me, even she had none so pretty.'

Canaletto sighed. This was going to be a long business but he needed the facts. 'So, why had you not worn it for your brother to see his pretty sister in the so grand petticoat he had given her?'

Lucy slanted a look at him through her eyelashes, well pleased with the compliment. Already she seemed more composed. ''Twas some few months back. I wanted to help Ned in his workshop.' She raised her eyes full to Canaletto's, earnest and pleading. 'Fanny is his help-meet in his business as she is in his house. I have no place.' Her voice was sad but without self-pity. 'I thought if I could perhaps prepare his plates, then I could be a proper wife.'

Poor, silly little woman. Had she any idea of the skill needed to prepare plates for engraving?

'I had just come in from visiting and wore my best petticoat.' Lucy's voice was hushed as though what she had to say was so horrific it had to be whispered. 'There was a pan heating on the stove. The smell was terrible,' her nose wrinkled in remembered disgust. 'I called for

Ned or Fanny to say the ink was overheating but no one came. So I picked a cloth and lifted the pan. At just that moment the cat chased a mouse across the floor and tripped my feet. I staggered, the pan tipped and black ink went all down my petticoat.' Lucy gave a high-pitched wail. 'It was ruined! I couldn't wait to find Fanny and tell her all was her fault. If she hadn't left the pan on the stove, my petticoat would have been safe!'

'Did you not tell her, then, what had happened?'

Lucy gave a great sniff. 'After a moment I thought how angry my brother would be when he knew. The silk cost him so much!'

'But an accident! When you were trying so much to help your husband, your brother must forgive?'

Lucy's eyes grew wide, 'Sir, you do not know what my brother is when he is angry. I did not dare! No, I went upstairs, changed my dress and buried the petticoat beneath other clothes. Later I smuggled it out and gave it to the sattan hawker, well,' Lucy dropped her gaze and pulled at the sodden handkerchief, 'she gave me sixpence for it, there was a deal of unmarked silk, you see.'

'And so when your brother asked where his fine gift to you was, you said, what?'

'Why, sir, that it had been stole!' Lucy's gaze was once again wide eyed and straight. 'And I knew not who the thief was. What else should I say?'

What indeed!

'But that day I arrive, you said then about your petticoat, that it was stole. You suggest Fanny take it.'

'Tush! 'Twas nothing. By then I'd told myself so often it had been stole, it seemed the truth. And Fanny might just as well have taken it. I'm sure she would if it had been there for her!'

Canaletto found this hard to tolerate but all was not told yet. 'Your brother, of course, knew what your petticoat was like. He could bring forth another, so it seemed to come from Signorina Fanny's mattress?'

Lucy returned to pulling at the handkerchief. 'I only told him how much it wore at me having Fanny ordering everything in the house. Even after it was no longer hers since my brother made Ned a loan. John told me he would give me a house. It would be protection for the interests of my child.' Lucy laid a gentle hand on her swelling stomach.

'So, you tell your brother you are unhappy with Signorina Fanny who organize too much your house. When you tell him this?'

Lucy shrugged her shoulders. 'Lud, how am I to remember? Perhaps three, four days ago? I was bidden for dinner with him and his wife. Not that I care for Margaret, a plain, managing sort of woman. But she asks how things are and I was out of sorts that day.' She suddenly looked at Canaletto. ''Twas the day Fanny brought you back injured. Without a word of a request or would I mind, or any such courtesy. No, takes over, orders everything so you can be accommodated.'

Canaletto murmured some sort of an apology.

Lucy paid no heed. 'So I told them just how things were and how intolerable life was with Fanny in the house.'

'And so your brother decide to make things better for his sister. And arrange Signorina Fanny is arrested for theft of petticoat what was never stole!'

Lucy's face crumpled once again. 'I never meant

Fanny to go to prison! As soon as the constable came and found that petticoat beneath her mattress, I went to my brother.'

'But to no good?'

'Oh, sir, he told me not to be an idiot. Everyone thinks I have no mind of my own! And if I'd told him I knew Fanny could not have stole the garment, well, it would all have come out, about the ink and selling it and all, wouldn't it?' Lucy looked at him ingenuously. Then her eyes narrowed and she added viciously, 'Well, I can tell you, my brother consorts with thieves and vagabonds.'

Canaletto was taken aback. 'How say you? Thieves? They wear a sign for you to recognize?'

Lucy shrugged. 'I know a rogue when I see one.'

'And you see one with your brother?'

'The day Fanny is arrested, he was talking with one such in the street not far from here.'

Canaletto remembered Fanny telling him how she had seen Alderman Fowler with Scallion, setting him on to watch the house. But Fanny hadn't mentioned seeing Lucy in the street as well. 'You did not talk to your brother?'

'Indeed I did not! He would not have thanked me interrupting his business with such a one as that. No, I went into the baker's and bought a loaf so he should not see me.'

'Ah, so.'

'And yesterday, when I was leaving my brother's, why, there was that same man again!'

'Scallion?' This was news.

'Was that his name? How is it you know him?' Lucy looked both piqued and surprised.

'It may be a man I have met,' Canaletto admitted. 'You say he came to see your brother?'

'Well, he went into the house as I entered the chair my brother had called for me.'

Canaletto thought about this briefly then put the matter on one side for deeper cogitation later. 'So, now you can say Fanny could not have stolen your petticoat?'

Lucy looked suddenly scared again. 'Why, as to that, how do I know she did not steal the other off someone else? That is what would be said!'

She appeared terrified of her brother. And maybe with reason. What good would it do to drag her before the justices? A powerful city man such as Alderman Fowler would undoubtedly swear any such tale was a farrago, a nonsense. The thief-taker would not implicate such a one as he, not for a mint of money, for his future would then be of no account. No, it needed someone more powerful than Signor Alderman Fowler to aid Miss Fanny.

'You do not deserve such a husband as Signor Ned, nor such a sister as Signorina Fanny,' Canaletto ground out.

Lucy collapsed in wails of tears again.

Canaletto went and opened the door. Hovering just outside, as promised, was the maid. 'See to your mistress,' he commanded her and ran down the stairs.

In the workshop he found Sam Wood.

'I be finished at the magistrate's,' he said the moment he saw Canaletto. 'But no good will come. They know not the dead man nor his business. Such as he cannot engage their time. Even for the death of the watchman they say they are unlikely to bring anyone to justice.

They only say they will send word if our story is needed at any time. We know what that means!'

Well, Canaletto had not hoped for more.

'Has 'ee seen Fanny, sir?' Sam asked eagerly.

'Aye, and she's in health, but, Sam, that place! No maid should suffer so.'

Sam's face fell. 'I should go to her but my wife is that jealous, it's more than my life is worth.' He coloured slightly. 'There was a time I hoped— Well, it was not to be and Mary is a good wife to me and the little one is everything.'

Canaletto comprehended all he had not said.

'Is there not something you can do for her, sir?' Sam looked at him with hopeful eyes.

Canaletto opened his hands, 'Maybe. But,' he added quickly as Sam's face lit up, 'it depends not on I. But, if I can, what is to happen to Signorina Fanny? She cannot come back here, not with such as her,' he jerked his head at the ceiling. 'You and your wife could not?' He left the question open.

Sam shook his head vigorously. 'Nay, sir, Mary would never agree.'

'Perhaps Signorina Fanny has other friends, or relations?'

'Well, she's always been popular round Fleet Street, but after this, well, I dunno!'

Canaletto thought for a moment. 'Sam, I need studio. I lodge with friend but I have no light or room to work. Perhaps you know of somewhere?'

The young giant thought deeply then his face suddenly lit up. 'Aye, that I do! A cabinetmaker was round at my master's t'other day, saying he has this house in Silver Street, with his workshop and everything. He has a studio and lodgings to let. Not long built and, says he, with lots of light.' Sam took a deep breath as though unused to saying so much. 'Shall I show you, sir?'

'Later,' said Canaletto. 'If you will give me your direction, I will send word. Now I have to visit someone of importance.'

Chapter Thirty

Canaletto had not thought there would be a problem in gaining access to William Pitt.

However, on his presenting himself at the paymaster general's offices, the egregious secretary, Erasmus Fortune, had been most courteous but regretful. Mr Pitt would not be available until that afternoon. Canaletto agreed to return at four o'clock, after dinner.

He had had plenty to occupy himself in the meantime.

But when he again presented himself at the Whitehall office, it was to hear that Mr Pitt had been called for an urgent meeting with other leading politicians. If he cared to wait, the secretary suggested, the paymaster general was not expected to be long.

So Canaletto took a seat and kicked his heels, carefully rehearsing the phrases he had assembled for this interview, muttering under his breath, oblivious to the amusement he was causing Erasmus Fortune.

At length Canaletto felt as fluent as was possible and still Pitt had not arrived. He withdrew his sketchbook from the back pocket of his jacket and started studying the damaged sketch he'd made that morning.

Eventually he requested and received the use of ink and a pen. After much trimming with the secretary's knife, he produced a nib he felt able to make use of to copy the sketch on to another page of his sketchbook.

Then Canaletto started to add more details. One stroke of the pen sketched in the rope, another set of rapid passes added the bucket. He studied the result. He wanted to add more to the background but instead of the smooth and meticulous recall he usually enjoyed, Canaletto found that all he could concentrate on was the terrible contents of that bucket.

Finally he abandoned the attempt to sort out viewpoints, skylines and sight lines, turned to a clean page in his sketchbook and drew Scallion's face. Not the drawn, lifeless countenance that had stared up at him from the bucket that morning, but the mean and cunning visage that had dogged his footsteps from the moment his boat had set sail from Le Havre.

Canaletto would never call himself a portraitist but he was used to adding quick and telling vignettes to his canvases. Unlike many artists, he had never found it necessary to make preliminary sketches for these. Now Scallion's face appeared on the paper as mean and unpleasant-looking as he'd been in life. Canaletto added the snake earring then studied the sketch. All it needed was the addition of a grey wash to create shadows and highlights and the man would be instantly recognizable to any who knew him.

He blinked and realized that the light was fading. Erasmus lit candles and apologized for the lengthening delay. Canaletto began to be afraid that Fanny would have to spend yet another night in that terrible place.

Then Pitt entered the office.

'Signor, my apologies for keeping you waiting in this way. I must have a moment with Fortune, here, then we shall talk. Have you been offered refreshment? Fortune, wine for Signor Canal!' The paymaster general disappeared into the room beyond.

A servant was sent for and more excellent red wine produced. Canaletto returned his sketchbook to his pocket and sipped gratefully at his glass while he waited until Erasmus emerged weighed down with papers.

'Mr Pitt will see you now,' the secretary said cheerfully.

'Well, Signor Canal, so you have changed your mind? My deepest thanks,' said the paymaster general, offering his hand, a beaming smile on his face.

Canaletto bowed and launched into his prepared speech. 'Sir, there is a little matter which has arisen in which it has occurred to me that perhaps each of us is in position to give other some help.'

'Ah!' Pitt's expression became blank. He sat behind his desk. 'Proceed, Signor Canal.'

It was not exactly an encouraging response. With increasing trepidation but managing to keep his English more or less as practised, Canaletto launched into an account of Fanny Rooker's arrest and imprisonment.

Long before he had finished, Pitt's face had cleared. 'So, you are suggesting I may be able to organize a release for this young lady?'

'She has been most shamefully wrongly imprisoned,' Canaletto burst out.

'If that is so, we should be able to rectify the situation,' Pitt said smoothly. 'I have to inform you, however, that it is not my signature that is needed on any release.'

Canaletto felt despair. Surely this man could not refuse to help?

'However, I see no reason why a note to my colleague should not produce the desired result.' Pitt rang the bell on his desk and Erasmus entered.

The curve of his mouth as he took the dictation infuriated Canaletto. The man obviously had only one idea of what his interest in this girl could be. There was no point in trying to explain; the more he were to protest, the more convinced the man would be that he'd got at the truth.

'If you are swift, Fortune, you will catch my colleague with the Minister. I left them in his office discussing a possible peace with France.'

Erasmus left and Canaletto tried to refuse to discuss the matter of Westminster Bridge until the secretary returned with the precious piece of signed paper, but Pitt would none of further delay.

'I suggest before travelling west to the Portland quarry, you talk with the Marquess of Brecon.'

Canaletto raised an enquiring eyebrow.

'The marquess is one of the bridge commissioners and thoroughly acquainted with all matters concerning its construction.'

'Perhaps you think him, as you say, in the know of the delays?' Canaletto contributed eagerly, determined now to play his part and solve this mystery as soon as maybe.

Pitt threw back his head and laughed heartily. 'Brecon? Nay, man, you have it all to wrong. The man lacks the brain for deviousness. And his position is unassailable.' It was as though the last circumstance was the more important. Pitt picked up a coin from the inkstand on his desk and began to play with it. 'We suspect, however, that he is being used by a City merchant, one Balthasar More, who is implacably opposed to the bridge and has a financial interest in the Portland quarry. More is to marry his daughter to Brecon's son and heir, the Viscount Purbeck.'

'A merchant's daughter?' Canaletto stared at Pitt. Things in London were certainly different to those in Venice. There the aristocracy only married within their own, closed circle.

Pitt smiled, 'Money, my dear signor, endears itself to even the highest in the land. You see how delicate is the situation? I have no wish to endanger this match should there be no hint of suspicion to attach itself to More. On the other hand, if he is involved in what amounts to little less than treason and Brecon's son should be affianced to his daughter, well . . !' It was unnecessary to spell the matter out.

'So, you want me to talk to this marquess to see if he has idea there is nefarious,' Canaletto was exceedingly pleased at being able to produce this word and repeated it, 'nefarious reason for delay?'

Pitt nodded, never taking his eyes from the painter.

Canaletto thought about this dubious suggestion. It sounded as though Pitt was using him. 'I think he not happy to discuss bridge with me. I think it is better you do this.'

'We have already talked with all the commissioners,' Pitt said smoothly. 'They, of course, insist everything goes smoothly. The delays in the stone are, they say, merely little local difficulties. Brecon would be insulted if I approached him direct. But you, signor, you can talk to him about the bridge on the grounds that he may wish to commission a painting.'

But McSwiney was supposed to handle commissions! Canaletto's eyes narrowed. 'You expect I call on this marquess? With no introduction?' For it was obvious Pitt wished to be kept out of this confrontation. He sat straighter in his chair. 'I no tradesman! And he no talk to tradesmen!'

Pitt held up the hand with the coin. 'Hush, man, no such thing! The day after tomorrow the Earl of Martock holds an open day at the new house he has had built at Wimbledon.'

'Wimbledon?'

'A small village outside of London. Several gentlemen have bought properties around there – the proximity to London, you understand. Brecon will be there, Martock is married to his sister.' Pitt started to spin the coin on the desk, slapping it down before it lost momentum, then setting it once again to spinning.

'The earl will be delighted to welcome you, he is a well-known patron with a renowned art collection. Indeed, you probably recollect he has one of your paintings?'

Canaletto nodded pleasantly, trying to recall the name. But Joseph had commissioned so many paintings and often he had not taken down who exactly had ordered them.

'I have already sent the earl a note suggesting that he will enjoy meeting you. You will not find it difficult to encounter Brecon there.'

Canaletto did not relish the fact that Pitt had felt so confident of his change of heart after hearing of his visit that morning but the prospect of viewing not only a notable architectural building but also a number of fine pieces of modern art was immensely attractive.

Pitt started flipping the coin up in the air, catching it, placing it on the back of his hand then examining which side down it had come. Canaletto found himself watching it, fascinated.

'This More who is connected with stone, you have talked with him?'

Pitt slapped the coin on the desk irritably. 'Of course. He was damnably offensive! Swore the bridge to perdition, forecast the demise of the City's trading pre-eminence and professed himself grossly insulted at the suggestion the quarry was in any way to blame for any difficulties.'

'I wonder he supply stone if he fears bridge so much.'

'Money, man, money!' Pitt spun the coin with both hands, it danced across the surface of the desk. 'More's not one to pass up a fat contract. Particularly if he can gain the money and still confound the construction! But we have no proof! It was to gain that that Fairbrass was sent to Portland.'

The spinning coin tumbled on to the floor. Canaletto picked it up and placed it back on the desk.

Pitt ignored his toy, rose and strode over to the window where he stood playing with the cord of the blind and surveying the rapidly darkening outlook. 'The national debt increases month by month. This war over the Austrian succession is draining our budgets and raising tax demands to dangerous limits. Westminster Bridge looks like costing over four hundred thousand pounds instead of the ninety thousand originally quoted. We cannot afford to continue paying out thirty thousand pounds every time the commissioners demand it.' He turned back to Canaletto. 'And we need the bridge in operation, increasing trade and development in the west of London by opening up this route to the south.'

The painter followed no more than the gist of all this. He found himself picking up the coin he'd placed upon the desk and idly examining both its sides while he listened.

'That was found amongst Fairbrass's effects, it's a token,' Pitt said abruptly. 'Issued by the quarry that supplies stone for the bridge. Good alternative to coin, keeps the workers spending their wages locally.'

He came and sat down again. 'I have to find out who is behind these damnable delaying tactics. And I can promise you, if you help solve this, you will not be the worse for it.'

Canaletto replaced the token on the desk. He would have preferred something more definite but somehow he felt he could trust this tall, volatile man with the big nose. Slowly he nodded.

'Good man!' Pitt opened a drawer and took out a heavy, gilt-edged card. 'The invitation. If Brecon isn't there, it'll be a wasted journey and we'll have to think again, but I am confident he will be.'

Then Erasmus Fortune returned. 'Alas, sir, I just missed him. I sent a messenger with the letter to his home with a request it be signed immediately. I have now learned your colleague went instead to a ridotto. We cannot obtain a signature now before morning.'

'Signor, I am sorry.' Pitt spread his hands in regret at his ineffectiveness. 'But already it is late. Come tomorrow morning, I will have the letter then.'

Canaletto was left with no alternative.

He returned early the following morning and had to wait no more than an hour before the document was delivered.

Erasmus Fortune handed it over with a smirk. Canaletto snatched it from him and ran down the stairs, hiring the first carriage he could find.

The prison governor read the letter with a resigned air. 'There are, of course, expenses connected with the release of a prisoner,' he said to Canaletto.

It was no more than he had expected and he handed over a small amount of his precious store of money.

The governor looked at the silver coins with contempt but Canaletto stared defiantly at him and finally the man shrugged his shoulders and sent for the prisoner.

There was a defeated slump to Fanny's shoulders when she entered the office but the torn dress had gone. It seemed Ned had indeed brought her a replacement.

Then she saw him and was overcome with delight. 'Oh, signor!'

He took her hand and bowed over it with a courtly gesture.

'Yes, yes,' said the governor testily. 'Well, Mr Canal, all seems to be in order. Take the prisoner, the warder will open up for you.'

Fanny appeared quite unable to take in the fact that she was free to go. Canaletto slipped a hand under her arm and gently steered her through the door and along what seemed a never-ending corridor. Until eventually they both stood outside the prison.

The sun hardly cut through the smoke above the buildings but Fanny screwed up her eyes as though it was blinding. She stood blinking, smelling the air with its odours of horse dung, dead dog, urine and other delightful by-products of life in a big city.

'Oh, sir, it's so wonderful! It all smells, oh, it smells of freedom!'

She looked at the people who passed, intent on their business. 'I can hardly believe that they do not see me branded as a common criminal!' she marvelled. 'Or do not smell upon me the stench of the gaol.' She gave a small gasp and brought a hand to her mouth. 'Scarface Nell!'

'Who?'

'A fellow prisoner, signor. She's a whore and a fighter but she was kind to me. And I've left without a word to her.'

It didn't seem to Canaletto that this was a matter that should concern Fanny for a moment. Filled with devils, that prison was. 'Come,' Canaletto pulled at her sleeve. 'Is there not a market near? I would buy some fruit and cheese and bread.'

'You are in lodgings, then?' Fanny turned to him with quick interest. 'I am a selfish creature, I have been so concerned with my own troubles, I have completely forgot to ask if you were able to seek out your friend, Mr McSwiney.'

'I found him, yes. Your direction was right, Owen spends much time at the coffee house.'

'And now you stay with him?'

'He is very hospitable but with little room. Now I have found place my own, with studio.'

'That's wonderful!' Fanny hugged his arm. Canaletto was touched at her excitement. For here was someone who had lost the home that had been hers since childhood and must now be wondering where she could go.

'Yes, it is good.' Canaletto left it there. 'But can we not find a market?' They had been walking briskly and had now cleared the prison walls. But he failed to see a shop selling comestibles nor yet a street trader.

'Why, Smithfield is in that direction.' Fanny indicated north. 'Please, you have to tell me, how did you persuade the justices a mistake had been made?'

'Ah, I enrolled the help of Mr Pitt, who is the paymaster general, is he not?'

'My!' she said wonderingly, with obviously little idea who Mr Pitt or what a paymaster general was.

'He is man of power,' Canaletto added as he linked her arm with his.

They were much of a height, which made it comfortable to walk together, except that soon they found themselves in a stream of people all going in the same direction.

'So many persons,' Canaletto said in wonder. 'Many must attend the markets in England.'

'No, indeed, I cannot imagine why so many go to Smithfield. Unless, unless,' Fanny spoke jerkily, 'I think at Smithfield as well as traders' stalls there are stocks and the pillory. Oh, say not today they are to put some poor soul on display there!'

Chapter Thirty-One

The next minute they were in the market and there, at the far end, set upon a platform, were two pillories manned by warders.

Fanny shrank against Canaletto. 'We will leave this place,' he said firmly.

But it was too late, too many people were pressing around them. They were carried forward locked into reluctant fellowship with the excited crowd travelling in but one direction, through the stalls of the market towards that open stage.

Till they could go no further.

Shouting and whistling was in Canaletto's ears, hard bodies pressed about him and Fanny. Then there came a roar as a cart worked its way through the crowd. Two men, their hands secured behind them, were led up on to the platform.

The first man was brought to stand behind one of the pillories. He was well made, muscles bulging under the thin shirt as his arms were roughly raised, cords of sinew standing out on the neck that was forced down over the bar so that the top of the close-cropped head was presented to the crowd. But not before terror could be seen upon his pleasant features. Fanny clutched at Canaletto's arm and buried her head against his shoulder.

Then excited jeers brought her head up again.

The second man was shorter than the first. As his hands were unfastened, one went out in supplication to his fellow prisoner. Then warders had to lift him up so they could fit his neck and wrists into the semicircles that waited for them. The upper bar with its matching semicircles was slammed down and the warders released their hold on the man's body so that the tips of his toes in their shabby leather shoes strained to support his weight without success. His red-rimmed brown eyes bulged under sandy brows and his tongue forced itself out of his mouth, its generous lips giving forth strangled gasps, spittle gathering round its sides.

'He'll choke to death,' screamed Fanny. Canaletto drew her to him and held her so that her head was buried in his shoulder as missiles began to fly past them.

Cabbages, potatoes, turnips, swedes, most dirty and rotting, were hurled with a force that bruised and battered. Then came rotten eggs. The odour of decay was everywhere and the air was thick with insults. Venom and hate swirled all around.

'I can't bear it,' Fanny moaned.

Elbows jabbed into them as arms were drawn back to throw yet more missiles.

Fanny shuddered and tears poured from her eyes. Canaletto was now holding her with both arms, his head pressed close to hers. He could feel her heart fluttering and jumping. What, he wondered, had these men done to incur this terrible punishment?

'Whoreson buggers!' screamed a woman standing next to them. 'A pox on your unnatural practices!' There was the sound of a stone hitting the wood of one of the pillories. It was followed by another. Then above the cries of the mob could be heard a long scream from one of the prisoners. Something like a collective sigh of satisfaction ran through the crowd.

There were more jeers, more shouts, more throwing of vegetables and stones. Then wild cries of satisfaction that made Fanny bury her head still further into Canaletto's shoulder. The short man's face was dark, swollen and still, its upraised features bespattered with bits of rotting leaf and smeared with egg. His bulging eyes were filled with the terror that had preceded death. The other man still lived, his body reacting against every hit, squirming with the effort to avoid what was being thrown, blood streaming from his head and hands.

'Come,' Canaletto said to Fanny, 'I think we move now.' Carefully he pulled her back, easing their way through crowds so drunk with excitement they took no account of the two removing themselves from the scene. Yet more people were arriving, drawn by the noise and word of what was happening.

Tears spilling heedlessly down her face, Fanny stumbled along. Canaletto knew that without his arm, she would sink to the ground, a helpless heap to be trampled by the uncaring crowds.

On the edge of the market, he found a carriage, the driver enjoying an unimpeded view of the show. Trembling himself now, Canaletto assisted Fanny inside and shouted up to take them to Silver Street. Fanny huddled against his side. Canaletto tried to warm her cold hands and gradually her shudders stilled.

'Oh, how dreadful, dreadful,' Fanny said at last.

Canaletto wanted to ask her what crimes the men

had committed but feared to bring the scene back into her mind.

The cabbie drew up outside a small terrace of smart, four-storey yellow brick buildings. 'Here is my studio,' said Canaletto. 'And home.'

He led Fanny through a small passage that ran through two almost identical buildings, past a cabinet-maker's workshop on the ground floor.

The door to the workshop was open in the mild weather and Daniel Spragg could be seen planing down a piece of wood, his prematurely white hair caught back from his broad face with a black string. The moment he saw Canaletto he hurried forward. 'Betty says to bring Miss Rooker through to the back, she has water heating in the kitchen.'

Fanny's face lit up. Daniel took her through then returned to his workshop. 'It went all right then, sir?'

Canaletto nodded. He couldn't quite remember how the subject of Fanny had come up the previous day as he viewed and agreed to take the space for rent. Perhaps it was while Daniel was explaining where he could pur-chase certain of the items he needed. The man had such a sympathetic air, Canaletto had found himself opening up in a way that was rare.

'Yes, thank you,' he said now, then his attention was caught by the splendour of the secretaire the man was working on.

'Your skill, signor, is remarkable,' he told Daniel. 'Craftsmanship I admire above everything.'

Daniel lovingly rubbed one of the sides he was pol-ishing. 'Indeed, sir, but craftsmanship, I am afeared, is dying. Too many men seek nothing but riches. Take this house.' He gestured at the walls surrounding them. 'We searched long and hard before we found one sufficiently well built to satisfy me. So many these days seek easy fortunes by erecting a building that collapses before the term of its lease is out (and you will not believe the shortness of some leases). They use shoddy materials and skimp on every detail.'

'Indeed,' murmured Canaletto. He was not particularly interested, he had no intention of acquiring a property in London, but his capacious memory stored the information nonetheless.

Daniel warmed to his theme. Rubbing harder and harder at the deep shine of the wood, he continued, 'Many there are who make tidy fortunes by cheating honest men. Whatever you buy these days and from whomever, it pays to be wary. Honesty is out the window, my dear sir. There is none too high nor too low they will not take the advantage if they see it.'

'I thank you for the warning,' Canaletto said gracefully. 'And I see one who is honest man!' He swept a small bow.

Daniel was embarrassed. 'Please, sir, I do not ask for compliments. I speak from the heart. You are most welcome here and I know Mistress Spragg is taking good care of the young maid.'

Canaletto turned the conversation back to the secretaire and the two men discussed the finer points of cabinet-making until Fanny emerged, shining clean, her copper curls damp from washing.

'Oh, signor, at last I have lost the smell of that dreadful place.'

Canaletto thanked Daniel and they left the workshop.

Behind the main house was a space that could once

have been a garden. Now most of the area was occupied by a handsome wooden building. Canaletto found the key in the pocket of his jacket and opened up the door.

'Is my studio,' he said proudly. There were windows but the main source of the ample light that flooded the room came from skylights in the roof. 'North,' he said, waving at the light.

Canaletto watched Fanny anxiously as she surveyed the area.

She turned slowly in the large room. He hoped she was appreciating the space, the light, the long trestle table that ran down one of the walls and the small bed that sat in a corner. 'There is water pump just outside,' he informed her eagerly. Such a convenient source of supply was a lucky chance.

She stirred at last into speech. 'You will live here as well as paint?' she said, nodding towards the bed and it was obvious she didn't approve of this accommodation for him.

Canaletto smiled, at last she seemed to be coming back to life. 'No, come see my rooms.' He bounded out of the studio and into the house, using a back door. Fanny followed him as he led the way up the narrow stairs that wound round a square, wood-panelled well. As they passed the tiny landing on the first floor, Canaletto explained that was where Dick and Betty Spragg lived.

'This my parlour,' he said, opening one of the doors on the second floor. The room faced south with three deep windows that let in generous amounts of light. Two simple chairs and a round table were all the furniture. 'My room there,' He indicated, but did not open, a door in the back wall.

Fanny's bright eyes took in everything. 'My, you can be comfortable here,' she said. 'And it's a good area, lots of new buildings.'

'Is Golden Piazza over there.' He went over to the window and stood looking down the small road opposite. He'd walked along it when he'd visited the place the previous day. It led into an elegant square lined with houses that obviously belonged to gentlemen. He'd known then that this place would suit him exactly.

Canaletto looked at Fanny. She was standing by one of the chairs, running a hand along its polished back. For the first time since the plan had occurred to him, he felt less than certain about its acceptability. 'At moment on next floor is lawyer and wife. But they look for lodgings with more room. Till then, perhaps you willing to sleep in studio?'

He saw immediately that the suggestion had stunned her. 'You want to be apprentice,' he said in a rush. 'I soon have commission. I have studio. I need assistant. You work with me?' His voice rose hopefully.

It had all seemed so simple to him once he'd appreciated the situation. Fanny Rooker, the girl who had twice saved his life, had been sentenced for transportation for a crime she could not possibly have committed.

Canaletto had known immediately he had to do whatever was in his power to rescue her. The only question had been, where could she go after he'd secured her release?

He had to find her a new life.

And, after all, the matter was easily solved. She had asked him to take her as his apprentice. Well, he would.

Between his first and second visits to Mr Pitt's office in Whitehall the previous day, he had visited Silver

Street with Sam and arranged to rent the studio and the second-floor rooms.

Everything had gone so smoothly. Now Canaletto realized he had taken too much for granted. For Fanny shook her head.

'Sir, I cannot.' She sat down heavily on one of the chairs. 'You are very kind, signor, but I see it will not do.'

Canaletto drew the other chair near to hers, sat down and took her cold hand in his. It shook. 'Signorina Fanny, why will it not do?'

She wouldn't look him in the eye but pulled away her hand and clasped it with her other. 'I am a criminal,' she whispered. 'You cannot have such a one as your assistant.'

'You are not criminal,' Canaletto spat out the words. 'Never think that!'

Fanny paid no attention. 'I have no money for a premium and you yourself said your assistant should be fully conversant with preparing canvases, grinding and mixing your pigments, skilled in painting.'

All this was true.

'Fanny,' Canaletto said gently and laid a hand on the interlaced fingers that held each other so tightly the knuckles were as white as picked bones. 'You have skill as artist, you draw, prepare plates for engraving and etching. You keep your brother tidy in his business, no? You can do same for me. There will be no queston of payment of premiums. As for preparing canvases and pigments, pouf!' he snapped his fingers in the air. 'Is nothing. I teach you how in three minutes. And you organize my supplies, my business, everything. So I do nothing but paint. And soon you help with that too.'

Fanny remained sitting with her head bent and Canaletto found that he was holding his breath. It was ridiculous for him to be so concerned that this plain little miss should come and join him here. But he was Antonio Canal, citizen of Venice, a man of standing and position who knew the niceties of conduct. He owed Fanny Rooker his life and he had to pay his debt.

Then she raised her eyes to his and he knew he had understated his reasons. The misery and distress there was shocking. He remembered the bright and resourceful girl with the delightful gurgle of laughter. He caught her hands again in his, raising them to his narrow chest. 'My dear Signorina Fanny, I want very much for you to come and help me. I need you,' he added simply and knew it for the truth. Her courage and light spirit could help him through the bad days, her zest for life and desire to become an artist would surely enable him to recapture the vision of his youth. If he was to succeed in London, Fanny Rooker was vital to him.

She smiled and though the smile vanished again almost immediately, for a moment she had looked almost as she had that first day on the docks. 'Signor—'

'Tonio,' he said with gentle sternness.

'No, signor, if you are to be my master, I your apprentice, I should call you signor.'

He beamed at her. She could call him what she wanted. 'That is good, very good. And you do not mind to sleep in the studio? Perhaps,' he fought with himself for a moment then decided he had to make the offer. 'Perhaps I sleep there and you in the bedroom?' he waved a negligent hand at the back room.

He need not have worried.

'That, signor, is the nicest offer you could have made but I am happy with the studio. Indeed, to have all that room for my own, even if only at night-time, will be luxury.' She gave him another, slightly stronger, smile.

Canaletto bounded up. 'Then let us get my boxes and your things.' He wanted everything organized as soon as possible. Tomorrow was to be a busy day.

Then he added, 'We show Mistress Lucy the Americas will not enjoy your presence.'

Fanny clapped her hands together. 'Let her tell her brother so, let Alderman Fowler know his plans have come to naught!'

Chapter Thirty-Two

At the sign of the copper plate Ned was in his shop. He looked up as the door opened and then stared in disbelief at Fanny. 'By all that's holy,' he gasped. The gasp turned into a cry of pain as the copper plate he was working on slipped off the cushion and hit his foot.

'Signor Canaletto convinced the courts that I was innocent,' Fanny said, her back ramrod straight. 'And now I am to be his apprentice.'

Ned placed the plate on the work bench and came forward, 'Oh my dear Fanny, I never thought to see you again outside that prison!' He swept her into his arms and for a moment Fanny breathed in his gin-laden breath. Then she gently withdrew.

'We have come for Signor Canaletto's boxes and my things,' she said and looked up at the stairs. 'Be Lucy up above?'

Ned shook his head. 'Nay, her brother sent a chair for her not an hour ago. She is to spend the day with him and his family. I was bidden too but pleaded work.' There was a hint of a slur in his speech and he swayed slightly as he stood.

'Oh, Ned, don't say you've been drinking again!'

He flushed. 'I won't then! Devil take you, Fanny, I'm no boy to be scolded.'

It was as if he had plunged a knife into Fanny's heart. Something inside her went icy cold and she finally realized their long, loving relationship was no more.

In a shaking voice she directed Daniel's apprentice, who had come with them, towards where Canaletto's boxes had been stowed.

After a moment Ned lumbered over to help and Fanny left both of them being ordered by Canaletto about the stowing of his baggage on the cart they'd borrowed from Daniel and went upstairs to stuff her few belongings into a cotton bag.

For a moment she stood with the bag in her hand and looked at the narrow little room where she had slept most of her life. Her heart was heavy. She had desired above all things to be taken on as an apprentice and now she had her wish. But at what a cost! Her good name ruined, her relationship with her brother destroyed.

She gently closed the door of her room and went downstairs.

When all was packed on the cart, Fanny said goodbye to her brother with distant formality.

As she and Canaletto took one of the long handles of the cart and the apprentice the other, a wave of nostalgia overcame her. She wanted to rush back and fling herself on her brother, beg him to give up the spirits and take Lucy in hand.

'You are in order, Signorina Fanny?' asked Canaletto, looking at her anxiously.

Fanny took a tighter grip on the handle and nodded. The first move must come from Ned. She had done all she could for him.

Together they hauled the cart through the crowded streets. Several times it proved impossible to avoid freshly dropped dung and Fanny knew their shoes would require considerable cleaning after they got back to Silver Street. Somehow this gave her a strange comfort.

Canaletto's large box was unloaded into the studio with Fanny's bag. His smaller one was taken upstairs. He sorted out coins to the apprentice and Fanny gave the lad generous thanks. He blushed and said it had been no trouble.

Fanny liked him and felt herself comfortable with Betty and Daniel Spragg. Perhaps, in time, she would begin to feel that this was home.

Canaletto wanted his small box unpacked first.

Out came a dark blue velvet coat with gold braid frogging down the front, breeches in heavy grey silk, lawn shirts, cravats and some linen small clothes.

Fanny helped Canaletto hang the coat and breeches over the chair backs, stroking the fine material with a gentle hand to try and remove some of the creases.

'Is important they look good tomorrow,' Canaletto said, his expression worried.

Fanny took in the full glory of the outfit. 'You attend some grand function, signor?'

'There is to be open house tomorrow in village called Wimbledon, the new home of milord Martock. Has much fine architecture, ornaments and paintings. I am bidden.' Canaletto spoke with simple pride.

'My,' Fanny said, greatly impressed. 'You are acquainted with my lord Martock? Have sold him paintings in Venice, perchance?'

'I have not met the noble lord,' Canaletto confessed.

'Though my friend Joseph Smith arranged he commission me for painting many years ago.'

'And he has invited you to see it in its new setting?' Fanny suggested.

Canaletto said nothing.

She picked up one of the cravats. 'Perchance Mistress Spragg may allow me to make use of her smoothing iron.'

'Later,' said Canaletto. 'First, the studio.'

This took rather longer to organize than his clothes.

There were lumpy bags of precious pigments to be laid out on the trestle table. As each bag was produced, Canaletto checked and itemized its contents.

'Prussian Blue. I am one of first to use this, Fanny. It is so intense soon I found no need for ultra marine. This is green earth; it is called earth but it comes from the sea, is a clay, *terre verte* we call it.' He placed another bag beside the first. 'And this Naples yellow, it can sing, Fanny, so clear. And here vermilion, not natural colour, made by alchemy. Never buy vermilion powdered – traders so, so unscrupulous – add red brick or red lead. This is red lake, gum from tree, is good with other pigments for pinks, purples, delicate shades. Now these are earths, various: red, yellow, browns and umbers, much subtlety here.' Gradually the line of pigments lengthened.

'So many, signor!'

'Not so many. Some painters work with more but I mix and I tone. So important you explore harmony and pattern of shades, of colours, like you contrast and play up design of lines and shapes.'

How Canaletto's English improved when he got carried away with his subject matter!

'We must buy linseed and walnut oil, for the medium, you understand, and turpentine and varnish. Too dangerous to bring, if bottle break, mess terrible! But preparation needed for the oil, heating, refining, we have much work to do before even we prepare pigments.'

These were matters Fanny had heard talked of by painters of her acquaintance but the processes had remained mysterious. Even as those of preparing plates and inks for engraving and etching had once been mysterious to her. Now, it seemed, all was to be made plain.

Packed at the side of the box was Canaletto's palette, together with a rich collection of brushes.

Canaletto checked anxiously for damage. 'Miniver hairs,' he said, taking out a selection of various-sized brushes, their spindle handles long and smooth.

Fanny looked at the caked tops of the brushes and wondered how he painted with them.

'Oh, these in chalk now,' Canaletto smiled at her and she blushed at his quick understanding. 'By this means the moths are prevented. Before I use, I clean in water.' He laid out brushes of different sizes. 'You must check quills always for damage.' His long fingers gently caressed the little holders that kept the hairs together and held the handles. He paused on the largest, 'Here we have quill from vulture, here from goose, this from chicken and this,' his finger touched on the smallest, 'this from dove.'

He selected other brushes, 'Here hog hairs, white of course, they are finer but still must be worked hard, whitewash on walls good, before using for painting picture. Here squirrel hairs.' The brushes were laid out on the table. 'Buy pots so they upright,' said Canaletto. 'Is better.'

At the very bottom of the box Fanny found a heavy marble slab about a foot square. She hauled it up.

'Porphyry,' said Canaletto. 'Not marble. For grinding. Marble too soft. There is pestle as well.' He rootled around in the bottom of the box and brought up a large glass pestle with a flat bottom which he laid beside the slab.

Fanny looked at a sizeable box that had been taken out early on and placed at one side of the table without explanation. It had a lens at one side. 'Signor, please, what is that?'

'That is *camera obscura*.'

Fanny was not much wiser. She looked it over curiously then found out how to open the box.

'It is an aid for taking outlines of buildings, I show you some day,' Canaletto said as he placed on the table a pile of sketchbooks.

'These my drawings of Venice, every aspect. Most valuable. Soon I add drawings of London. Already I start with the bridge.'

'Oh, signor, you are going to paint Westminster Bridge? That will be a view indeed!' Fanny wanted to know how he was going to approach this painting, which viewpoint he was going to take and what the background would be, but something about the way Canaletto had turned to fiddle with the equipment on the table suggested he did not wish to talk about this project.

So she started to put together the lengths of wood that made up into Canaletto's easel, slotting in the pegs without instruction. By now her hands were filthy.

Fanny finished and looked around the studio. 'We need a bowl,' she said.

'And food,' said Canaletto.

Fanny suddenly realized it was long past the dinner hour and she was extremely hungry.

Canaletto took out some coins. 'Pie shop near here, Daniel say. Perhaps we eat one – with meat?'

Fanny's face lit up. 'That would be excellent.'

'And some ale,' Canaletto added.

Fanny used the pump outside the studio to wash her hands then went off shopping. By the time she returned, Canaletto had sorted out pens, ink and charcoal and was standing back looking at the equipment on the trestle table with an air of satisfaction.

Fanny lifted a large wicker basket on to a clear space. 'I bought this as well, signor, since we shall have need of it.' She looked anxiously at him but he didn't question the purchase. From the basket she produced a tin bowl and a generously sized meat pie that gave off appetizing smells. Still in the basket was a flagon of ale.

Canaletto cleared a portion of the table. From a small cupboard in a corner of the studio he fetched two pewter plates with two steel knives and forks, a larger plate for the pie and two pewter mugs.

Fanny was touched when she saw how much he had managed to arrange the previous day.

'What a feast!' She arranged the pie then pulled out one of the two stools set underneath the table.

Canaletto cut into the pie and put a slice on each plate.

As Fanny started hers, she said, 'Signor, please, tell me how you arranged for my release, for I am much puzzled how it can have been effected.'

He studied her for a moment, as though deciding what to tell her.

'It is long story,' he started.

Fanny listened, her eyes growing rounder and rounder as he described his visit to the paymaster general and the delays in the building of the bridge.

''Tis certain it has been some six or seven years since construction began,' she said as he finished. 'But such perfidy is hard to believe!'

Canaletto said nothing.

'And you are to discover the truth of the matter! Signor, I am truly honoured to be assistant to a man of such worth.'

He made a deprecating gesture but she could see that her words were sweet to him.

She finished her piece of pie then looked round the studio and said, 'There is a good fireplace over there, signor. If we obtained wood, I could cook for us.'

Canaletto wiped his mouth fastidiously on a handkerchief. 'Your mutton broth, signorina, was . . .' he bunched his fingers, put them to his lips then exploded them in a smacking kiss. 'I ask Daniel about wood.'

There was a small silence while Fanny thought of the utensils she would need to cook with.

Then, 'What business has this Alderman Fowler?' Canaletto pronounced the unfamiliar words with care.

'He is, or was, a goldsmith, a member of one of the most powerful of the city guilds.'

'Was?'

'He has told me he now employs craftsmen to produce the work. He says there are better things for him to be involved in.' Fanny spoke with scorn.

'This better work, it is . . . what?'

Fanny put her elbows on the table, rested her chin on her hands and looked thoughtfully at Canaletto. 'Merchanting – he travels much – and property.'

'Property?' Canaletto carefully dislodged a sinewy piece of meat from his back teeth.

'He explained it to me one time,' Fanny flushed as she remembered how the alderman had tried to take liberties with her at Ned and Lucy's nuptials. 'He said he stood to make a pretty sum from a parcel of land he bought at Westminster, adjacent to the new bridge.'

'This alderman must be a man of foresight. And of substance.'

'Oh, indeed,' Fanny said with a touch of bitterness. 'But there was little enough marriage portion for Lucy. The alderman was not pleased with her choice for husband. He would have preferred a city merchant, someone who could have assisted him in his plans. But Lucy admired Ned's artistic calling.'

'And this so far-sighted man of substance, why should he have doings with any such as Scallion?'

Fanny shrugged, 'He is not nice in his habits, John Fowler. I believe he was none too gentle in the way he disposed of the occupants in many of the properties he bought. One such as Scallion could be of use in many ways.'

'Ah, maybe I understand.' Canaletto mused in silence for a little and Fanny cleared away the plates, brought water from the pump in the tin bowl and washed them. She had no linen for drying so left them draining on the table.

'You know,' Canaletto said, 'is very strange this Scallion killed on Westminster Bridge. Why there?'

'Perhaps it was a private place for meeting,' suggested Fanny, looking around to see what else she could busy herself with. 'At night-time, no one would be there and no passers-by could disturb them.'

'There must be other places most suitable for a meeting. But, yes, it was private, once the watchman is removed. But is it not curious, Scallion seem to wish me ill, then he himself is killed?' Another pause for contemplation. Fanny didn't know what to say so she started to straighten the items on the table.

'Mistress Lucy knew all my details, how I was to arrive?' enquired Canaletto.

'Why, I suppose she was present when Ned and I discussed our plans. But Lucy never listens, signor.'

'Even those who do not listen hear sometimes.'

Did he mean Lucy had told her brother about Canaletto? It seemed too unlikely and Fanny said so.

Canaletto rose. 'I go visit the alderman. You have his direction?' he asked Fanny.

'Why, yes. But signor, be careful. He may no longer have that rogue to set on you but he is dangerous.'

Canaletto set a hand on Fanny's shoulder. 'Disturb yourself not, signorina. I surprise him and he will not attack Canaletto in his own house.'

Chapter Thirty-Three

The manservant who answered the door told Canaletto that the alderman was with his family in his parlour. The implication was that he was not receiving.

'I think he will see me,' the painter said smoothly, wishing he'd had something better to wear than his shabby working clothes. But the wig was good, his bandages were gone and he'd applied more powder after removing the last of the mud.

The servant showed Canaletto into a small room off the narrow hall and the painter hadn't had time to go through more than once the phrases he had rehearsed on his way before the alderman himself arrived, curiosity written all over the narrow face that did, indeed, look like the rat's to which Fanny had once likened it.

'Mr Canaletto, an honour to meet you.' He held out his hand. 'I have heard much spoken of your excellent paintings of Venice. I wish I had commissioned one myself for I was once there, a most excellent city. My wife will be delighted to meet you and we have my sister, Lucy, with us as well. You will come and join us in the front parlour?' It sounded a generous invitation but Canaletto recognized something forced about the alderman's geniality.

'Forgive me, I have certain business I would discuss with you in private.'

Interest replaced suspicion. Fowler looked at Canaletto as a merchant would a promising bolt of silk or a consignment of unpolished gems. 'Indeed? But you will take some refreshment? Michael some canary and two glasses. Quick, man!'

The servant was gone in a blink of an eye.

Now, Mr Canaletto, how can I help you? I daresn't imagine you wish to paint my humble home?' He gave a hearty laugh that rang false. 'But perhaps you feel a view of the Goldsmith's Hall would make a pretty subject? Well, I am willing to put the matter to my guild but I have to warn you they are not likely to agree to your charges . . !' He stopped in mid-flight as Canaletto held up a hand.

'Alderman, that is not why I come.'

John Fowler looked surprised, sat himself down and moved his shoulders beneath the rich stuff of his jacket in a way that suggested he had no idea what this could be about but was willing to listen.

Canaletto arranged his legs elegantly and leaned slightly forward, his slender fingers poised above the carved arm of his chair. 'Signor, since my arrival in London some seven days ago, I have been attacked twice, and left for dead.'

Surprise gave way to puzzlement on the alderman's face.

'The second time I was robbed of considerable sum of money.'

The puzzlement deepened. 'Sir, this is distressing news but I fail to see what connection it can have with me.' And Canaletto couldn't fault the smoothness with which he said this. He seemed genuinely bewildered.

'It appears that the rogue who attacked me is seen in your company. I am anxious for his direction so I can recover my property.'

John Fowler flushed angrily. 'Sir, you insult me to suggest I have had aught to do with attacks upon your person or robbery of anybody.'

Canaletto held up his hand again, 'Nay, signor, I do not accuse you. But you know Jack Scallion, do you not?'

He watched carefully while he spoke the name and was rewarded by a flash of some unpleasant emotion in the alderman's eyes. It was gone in a moment.

'Scallion?' murmured the alderman. 'A name such as that I should remember.'

'Your sister, Mistress Lucy, saw a man of his description entering your house as she left your property three days ago.'

'Lucy!' The word burst from the man's lips but he had himself under control again in a moment. 'Ah, now I think I remember the man. Yes, indeed, one of that name did come to see me.'

'You can furnish me with his direction?' asked Canaletto pleasantly.

The alderman furrowed his brow. 'Alack-a-day, I know it not. The man wanted, oh, some small service which I was unable to fulfil.'

Now the man was definitely lying. Interesting.

'As I say, I am anxious to recover my property, you can understand this?' Canaletto pressed the man. 'Perchance you suggest where I might apply to find this man?'

John Fowler shrugged. 'I wish I could assist you, my dear sir, I do indeed, but I would have no idea how to find this man you speak of. Our acquaintance can scarcely be defined as that. We spoke no more than several words together.'

Canaletto would be prepared to swear that the man had no idea that Scallion was dead.

Which suggested that the alderman had not been responsible for that death.

The servant brought in wine and poured it. Canaletto drank, found it excellent and wondered how to proceed from this point. Then he remembered something Fowler had said on his arrival. 'You say you have visited Venice, sir?' he asked courteously.

'Oh, aye. Some two year ago, it'd be.' The alderman relaxed a little with the change of subject. 'Spreading my wings a bit, I was. My wife's father is a merchant and he introduced me to Balthasar More, of the East India Company. I'm a warm man, sir, money to invest. Merchanting offers excellent returns, people are so hot for goods these days. Mr More was off to Venice and suggested I accompany him. We were to explore opportunities, as you might say.'

Now Fowler seemed completely relaxed, quaffing his wine with evident enjoyment, seeming to find pleasure in describing the advancement of his business.

'And you found opportunities, signor?' Canaletto asked courteously.

'Not in Venice, no. We stayed there overlong for my taste. Merchantmen from Italy these days are so harried by French privateers the returns are too perilous for such a cautious businessman as I.'

Cautious was not a word Canaletto would have

applied to the alderman. Knowing but venturesome was how he summed the man up. Still, Canaletto knew well the dangers of the privateers.

'I came by merchantman from Italy,' he said. 'The risks at sea I reckoned less than those overland.' Certainly for one carrying large sums of money. But there had been the odd frisson of fear as sails appeared on the horizon and the captain made every effort to outsail any possible privateer. 'And we encountered no alien forces.'

'You had the luck, then.'

'But it vanished when I came to land,' mourned Canaletto.

'Ah, yes, your property as was stolen.'

'And practically my life.'

'Indeed? Yes, you mentioned an attack, did you not?'

'But your sister-in-law, Signorina Fanny, she save me.'

The man's eyes shifted uneasily. 'Miss Fanny is a girl of some resource.'

'It's to be thankful she has been released from her unfortunate imprisonment,' Canaletto said smoothly.

'Released?' Fowler's voice came out in a squawk. 'On what grounds?' He didn't sound at all pleased.

'Why, that the charge was patently false.'

'False?' Again that squawk.

'Oh, it was proved the petticoat could not be Mistress Rooker's,' Canaletto said mischievously.

Fowler glanced towards the ceiling. No doubt his sister-in-law would be in for an interrogation once the alderman rejoined his family.

'And Miss Fanny, she has returned home?' The

alderman now had his voice under control but it was thick with menace.

'Nay, I have taken her as apprentice.'

'Indeed? You be a brave man.'

Anger surged through Canaletto. 'Fortunate, rather. Signorina Fanny is skilled artist, she works hard and is, as you say, resourceful. What more could I need?'

The alderman's eyes practically popped from his head and he was lost for words.

Canaletto rose. 'I thank you for your time. My apologies to your lady wife.' He deliberately omitted any mention of Lucy.

Fanny's face lit up as Canaletto entered the studio. 'Oh, signor, you are safe!' she exclaimed.

For the first time since he'd left Italy, Canaletto felt someone actually cared whether he lived or died. It was a good feeling.

'I ran no danger with the alderman,' he said, inspecting the way she had sorted out all the equipment on the trestle table.

'What did John Fowler say?' she pressed him.

Pleased with what he saw, Canaletto pulled out a stool, and gave Fanny a full account of his conversation. 'I was foolish,' he said after he'd finished, 'but I hoped I could get this Scallion's direction. Now I know not what to do!'

'Scarface Nell!' said Fanny with an air of inspiration. 'She told me she knew everyone and everything around the Fleet. Perhaps if you were to visit her, she would be able to tell you something of Jack Scallion.'

'Signorina Fanny, it is idea most excellent but,' he

looked up at the sky. Twilight was stealing over London. 'It is too late now and tomorrow I go to Wimbledon.' He looked across at Fanny, 'You know this Nell, perchance she talk to you better than to me.'

She stiffened on her stool and became agitated, 'Oh, signor, return to that place? Indeed, I cannot.'

Canaletto realized how insensitive he had been. 'Do not worry, Fanny, I should not ask. I go day after the morrow.'

Fanny's anxious eyes looked into his, she sighed deeply and gazed at her hands, the fingers locked painfully tight together. 'Perhaps you could leave me a small sum of money tomorrow, signor?' She glanced up at him. 'Then, if I find I can bring myself to visit that place, I can take her some small comfort. I told myself this morning that I should take my leave of her in some way.'

Canaletto was inexpressibly touched that she should even consider the matter. 'Here,' he handed over a coin. 'If you go, you have deepest thanks from me. But not if you become distressed. I want not that.' He looked at her anxious eyes, then added, 'No danger you will be locked up once more, please, I assure you.'

Fanny still looked worried. Then suddenly she jumped up and went over to the small bed. 'See, signor, I have ironed your cravats. Now you will be properly smart tomorrow amongst all those gentlemen and women.'

Canaletto went and inspected his neckwear and was gladdened by the care she had taken.

'And Mistress Spragg says that to heat a kettle of water till it steams, then to hold the velvet of your coat in the steam, will rid the material of its creases. Oh, signor, shall we not try this?'

Fanny was halfway to the door. Canaletto, wondering how they were to light a fire when he had no fuel and was in any case not supplied with a kettle, was about to follow when the studio door opened without so much as a knock.

'So this is where you have hidden yourself, is it, Tonio?'

Large, blocking out the light, beaming with goodwill, his grey hair even more artistically dishevelled than usual, and followed by another man, was Owen McSwiney. 'I take it very ill that you should disappear like that with only a note to say you were still alive.'

He didn't look upset.

'Here, Patrick, come and meet the great Antonio Canal.' McSwiney gestured to his companion. Perhaps as a concession to him he spoke in English. 'Tonio, I present Patrick Granville, a fellow Irishman, another of life's adventurers.'

Patrick Granville swept a graceful bow. 'I hope you forgive this intrusion. When Owen said he was off to visit you, I could not forbear to plead I might accompany him. I am, signor, one of your most profound admirers.' Another bow.

Certainly an Irishman, with that open charm that enfolded you like a warm wrap. An adventurer? Looking at the twinkling, sea-green eyes and long, mobile face, Canaletto could believe it.

He gave a small bow of acknowledgement. 'A friend of Owen McSwiney's is welcome. You see us settled in splendid accommodation. This place, you applaud choice, yes?' Canaletto waved an expansive hand around the space. 'And I introduce my new apprentice, Fanny Rooker.'

Owen McSwiney sketched a neat bow in Fanny's direction. 'Rooker, eh? A member of the engraving family?'

Fanny looked inordinately pleased at this. 'You know my brother, Ned, sir?'

'I have seen several of his prints. And you are Tonio's apprentice?' He looked inquisitively at her. 'This is very sudden.'

'Signorina Fanny shows much talent,' Canaletto said repressively. He had no wish for the matter to be discussed further.

'Glad to hear it because we could soon have your first commission, Tonio.'

'From the duke?' Canaletto realized he had been so busy the last couple of days he had completely forgotten to ask McSwiney how things had gone with Thomas Hill.

Granville was wandering down the length of the trestle table, picking up odd pieces of equipment, looking at and then replacing them. Infuriatingly, not quite in the same place.

McSwiney perched himself on one of the stools. 'A note came today. Hill has written to the duke. It's the damndest nuisance but he has retired from Richmond House to his country place at Goodwood. Hill cannot understand his love for what he calls the most insignificant of houses, but he is confident word will soon come from there for Richmond holds you in the highest estimation.'

Canaletto's initial excitement dissipated. This meant nothing.

Granville reached the end of the table and leant against the wall, hands in the pockets of his breeches, his slanted eyes surveying them all in the manner of a man being entertained.

McSwiney reached for the plate with the remains of the meat pie and absentmindedly picked at the pieces of pastry and gobbets of steak. 'Glad to see you have your easel already erected. Early start tomorrow, eh, Tonio? Canvas already prepared, Miss Fanny?'

Canaletto slammed the top of his box down on the canvases that lay rolled up in its bottom. 'I have invitation for tomorrow. To meet the Lord Martock, perhaps he likes view of his new palazzo,' he said provocatively. McSwiney would not like the suggestion Canaletto could make connections without him.

'Martock's at home? *You* are going there?' Patrick Granville sounded astonished.

'Indeed, yes. I am invite,' Canaletto said coolly.

'Capital, that's capital,' McSwiney exclaimed hastily. 'So are we! Why, we shall all go together.'

Chapter Thirty-Four

Canaletto had the distinct impression Patrick Granville was not at all happy at McSwiney's suggestion but he said nothing and quickly seemed to forget his displeasure, if indeed displeasure it had been. Nor did he probe into how it was the painter, newly arrived in London, had received an invitation to an occasion the whole of London society had been angling for cards to.

The other two men had shown no inclination to leave the studio. As the twilight deepened, Granville had sent for wine and Canaletto realized an evening of drinking and gossip lay before him.

He took the two of them up to his parlour so that Fanny, hardly able to hold her head up through exhaustion, could collapse into her bed in the studio. He lit candles and hoped the session would not last beyond this set.

Many were the winks from McSwiney over Canaletto's choice of apprentice. Canaletto finally burst out with, '*Dio mio*, man, you think that plain girl is to my taste?' only immediately to feel guilty. Fanny had virtues of character and intelligence that meant more than physical beauty. That they were not the sort he considered could tempt a man into bed was not her fault.

'Indeed, Owen, I think we can assume Signor Canal is a man with the most elegant of tastes in women,' Patrick Granville said, lounging in a chair borrowed from Daniel Spragg, quaffing from one of the pewter mugs they'd brought up with them from the studio. 'Eh, Tonio?'

'You have known McSwiney long?' Canaletto enquired, anything to turn the conversation.

'Oh, aye. Several years, now, ain't it, Patrick? Was it not that theatrical venture of mine in Paris, before this present war? When you brought me such a delicious little dancer. What she could do with her body!' McSwiney sighed. 'Alas, the show failed, as all my shows seem to.'

'You should stick to the art world.' Canaletto felt very tired. 'There your taste is unassailable.' He turned to his other visitor, 'You are theatrical entrepreneur too?'

Patrick laughed easily. 'By heaven, no. That was my one and only venture into the business. Now I merely enjoy the performances – and the performers.' No suggestion as to any other activity. The cut of his dark green coat and cream breeches, the richness of his brocaded waistcoat, the fine quality of the lawn at his wrists and neck, all suggested gentleman, one of means. Yet there was something about him, an air of, what? Opportunism? He exuded energy and an attractive exuberance for life.

Canaletto yawned, it had been a long day and he needed to have all his wits about him for the morrow. He suggested he call with a carriage to take McSwiney and Granville with him the following day, Pitt or, rather, Erasmus having supplied him with funds to 'cover expenses'.

'Nay, I am taking you in my carriage,' Patrick Granville announced with grand generosity. It did not take long to arrange that Canaletto would walk over to McSwiney's lodgings and they would then both of them repair to Granville's lodgings.

The day dawned fine with a balmy warmth that promised summer would soon be here.

At Granville's Downing Street address a large carriage awaited with an elaborate coat of arms on the door. Canaletto examined this with interest. Granville appeared to have some illustrious ancestry if the quartering could be trusted. Arms were important. It was a matter of great pride for Canaletto that the Canal family had a coat that announced they were only just below the rank of aristocracy. He enjoyed incorporating the arms into a painting or engraving from time to time but to be able to display them on a carriage like this would be very satisfactory.

Patrick Granville ran down the steps of the house. He welcomed the two men and tossed a word of greeting to the servants equipping the carriage.

The footman opened the door, unfolded the steps and stood back. Patrick and his guests entered.

The two bench seats, front and back, facing each other and upholstered in button leather, well padded and comfortable, offered ample room.

McSwiney immediately settled himself in one of the corners facing front, leaving Canaletto little option but to take the seat opposite – you could hardly allow your host to travel with his back to the direction they were travelling in. 'Won some lottery, Patrick?'

'A wager only,' Granville paused in the doorway of the carriage. 'Nay, Signor Canal, please sit beside McSwiney, you will be much more comfortable.' Canaletto changed his seat with alacrity. 'My opponent announced his pockets were to let and I suggested a loan of this barouche be the stake for a final turn of the cards.' He spread out his arms along the seat's rich padding. 'So now we ride in comfort.'

Soon the coach was rattling along through the country west of London, through the village of Chelsea, towards Fulham and its bridge across the Thames. The countryside was green and gentle and Canaletto appreciated looking at the expanses of market gardening on offer, half-listening to McSwiney and Granville discussing Lord Martock's new seat.

'Not a penny spared, Patrick. James Gibbs as architect, the best stone, the finest marble. And the man's collection of art and furniture is unsurpassed. All London will be there today.'

Canaletto wondered how he was to find the Marquess of Brecon if there was to be such a crush. Perhaps his host could effect an introduction?

'You know milord the Earl of Martock well?' Canaletto asked McSwiney.

'I have been of some assistance to him in acquiring various works of art, yes. But with the expense of this new house, well, his lordship will not be in the market for new commissions, I'm thinking.'

Patrick chuckled as Canaletto gave a brief sigh. 'Believe it not, those keen on the arts are always in the market, no matter how empty their coffers. 'Tis a different matter to extract payment, however.'

'How they expect starving artist survive?' enquired

Canaletto sourly. Then decided on a venture. 'Know you milord of Brecon, Owen?'

McSwiney gave a shout of laughter and slapped his thigh. 'Brecon, is it? You'll be even more pushed for a commission there. The man's on his uppers. Like Martock, he's overshot himself building. But what a palace he's created in Piccadilly! William Kent no less engaged for the designs.' Granville frowned, his good humour disappearing. McSwiney rattled on. 'I had the honour to visit the marquess shortly after the place was finished. Had a scheme for him to commission a series of statues, gods and goddesses for the terraces. From Rysbrack. Would have been the perfect finish, emphasized the classical purity of the building. The man tried to pretend it would not be in keeping with the architectural intentions. Poppycock, he couldn't afford it! Nor recognize the importance of the scheme. Man's a philistine. Only interested in his aggrandizement.'

Patrick intervened, his tone tart. 'McSwiney, you're a gossip and worse. A man who believed everything he heard from you would soon be lost. 'Tis true his Piccadilly residence has been constructed with no care for expense but Brecon is more than solvent.'

'Is it not the case he's touting his son in return for merchant's gold?' McSwiney sat back in his corner of the carriage with the air of a man who has just proved his point.

Granville's tone became even more austere. 'I believe the Viscount Purbeck is to contract a marriage with the daughter of one of London's leading merchants, a most respectable man.'

'Tush, tush, Patrick, no need to sound as though a lemon is in your mouth.' Then McSwiney suddenly clapped a hand to his forehead. 'Lord, is it not the fool I am? Is it not the fact that it's your sister who's to marry the marquess?'

A thin smile split Granville's mouth. 'Nothing is arranged and one should not speak of these things. But, unless the marquess risks his honour, I believe a match may be imminent.'

'Take no notice of my rantings,' McSwiney laid a pleading hand on the other man's upper arm. 'Haven't I just the most god-awful way of saying the wrong thing at the wrong time?'

'It matters not,' Granville said indifferently. 'I am glad to have been able to put you to rights on the marquess and his state.'

McSwiney turned to Canaletto. 'Saw there was one of your views in the library. One of those potboilers you turn out for Joseph.'

So, the marquess had one of his paintings already, that made his interest in another, of Westminster Bridge, all the more likely. This was a lucky circumstance. But the talk of the noble lord having – what was the phrase Granville had used – his pockets to let? Well, that was interesting. Pitt had mentioned nothing about it.

Their progress became hampered by other carriages. Soon they were in a procession of vehicles. Wild flowers blossomed in the hedgerows, birds were singing, the terrible pall of smoke that seemed to hang continually over London had disappeared and Canaletto should have been feeling light and expectant. Instead he found he was feeling depressed; was it because of McSwiney's mention of potboilers?

In company with many other vehicles, their carriage arrived at the entrance to Wedmore Park. The elaborate, wrought-iron gates were held back by a smiling, constantly bobbing woman, behind her a white-painted, classically designed lodge. 'Palladian even to the entrance,' murmured McSwiney. 'Oh, for a touch of the gothic, some moment of romanticism to ginger up this excess of good taste.'

'You're a poseur, McSwiney,' Patrick Granville said with a smile that removed any sting from his words. 'At one moment you're all admiration and the next you're denigrating the very thing you previously admired!'

'Tonio, defend my reputation!' pleaded McSwiney in mock outrage.

'No man has a keener appreciation of artistic values,' Canaletto offered austerely.

The procession of carriages wound its way along what would one day be an impressive avenue of beeches. The young trees had been carefully planted and there was not a weed to be seen in the circles of soil around each. On either side stretched parkland.

'I see he's imported several mature specimens. I wouldn't like to hazard what that will have cost the noble earl,' commented McSwiney, admiring a strategically placed Cedar of Lebanon that spread its elegant branches over a small herd of very hirsute cattle grazing on lush grass.

Rounding a nascent shrubbery, the avenue suddenly offered a clear view of the new house.

'Is that not a pleasant sight!' exclaimed Granville, shading his eyes from the glare of the sun, now nearing its high point in the sky.

Canaletto found the house was, indeed, imposing. The building was all symmetrical splendour, from the steps that winged down either side from the columned portico at *piano nobile* level, to the pavilions flanking the main building.

'If you will keep with me,' said Granville, 'I will ensure you see everything. It was the last thing Canaletto wanted. With the marquess to quiz, he needed to be on his own. Muttering some apology, he darted down from the carriage and fought his way round to the other side both to try and get away from the two Irishmen and to obtain a better view of this palace. At last he was being presented with a building worthy of his brush. And all the tender greenery around would surely make a graceful frame for the soaring splendour of the architecture. But how to find a proper viewpoint.

It was too difficult. All over the drive carriages were rolling up to deposit their passengers at the massive main entrance before a servant directed the drivers where to go.

But at least McSwiney and Granville appeared to have given up waiting for him.

Canaletto settled the shoulders of his velvet coat, smoothed the front of his embroidered waistcoat and joined the fashionable throng that chattered eagerly as they mounted the steps towards the pillared portico of Wedmore Park.

Memories of fashionable occasions in Venice crowded in on Canaletto. How long had it been since he was among high society? For a moment he forgot his mission and entered the house with a pleasant sense of anticipation.

The earl and his countess stood in the hall receiving their guests informally. Canaletto murmured his name and mentioned that of William Pitt. But no flicker of understanding crossed the noble countenance, heavy with rolls of fat. The eyes of the couple were glazed, as though they had long lost any sense of time or even the identity of friends and he doubted either had heard anything he'd said.

Pressed by the multitude following, Canaletto sighed and moved on. How was he ever to find the Marquess of Brecon amongst this ever-increasing mob of brilliantly dressed and superbly confident members of society?

Chapter Thirty-Five

James Bennett followed Charlotte More up the steps of Wedmore Park and inhaled sweet perfume from the folds of creamy silk skirt that swished so near his nose. The nearness of those folds was captivating. He shut his eyes and imagined away everyone else but the two of them. Then someone bumped into him and he was forced to concentrate on the ascent. His hand still retained the feel of hers as he'd helped her down from the carriage. Her eyes had been modestly lowered, not a glimpse of their delicate blue to be seen. But her hand had trembled as he clasped it in courteous care. Balthasar More, following closely behind his daughter, might well have noticed anything more overt.

The campaign James had launched that day he'd first visited the More household had been almost too successful.

The carefully contrived 'accidental' meeting in Smithfield market had been a delight. Charlotte had seemed enchanted at his unexpected appearance, on his way, he'd explained, to the City for the marquess. He'd expressed interest in the produce on offer, professed his ignorance of cauliflowers and cardoons. Had allowed himself to be led from stall to stall, instructed in the judging of quality and freshness, the recipient of advice on varieties, admiring the charming directness of her conversation. No flirtatious glances, no teasing inflections of the voice or ambiguities in the speech. She was, he thought, all purity and honesty and he admired her exceedingly for it.

He had no compunctions over his plan. Indeed, he felt that to save Miss Charlotte More from the Viscount Purbeck had to be a worthy aim. He told himself that it was impossible he should speak to her father on the matter of the viscount's character. There were too many factors against it, not least the possibility he would garner Mr More's opprobrium to himself as well as the viscount. For should not he have taken more care of his charge in Venice? Should not he have taken closer note of who Richard had consorted with, instead of pleasuring himself with Anne Montesqui?

No, a word to Balthasar More would not be wise. Instead, James spoke frankly and well to Charlotte, on food and its value to life and to pleasure, on life in general with particular reference to various passages of the Bible. He then let slip the fact he had yet to make the acquaintance of Sir Christopher Wren's masterpiece, the new St Paul's Cathedral.

In no time she had offered the services of her aunt and herself as guides to its glories. What of Mrs More, he'd asked. Was she now well enough to be deprived of both her nurses?

Charlotte had smiled in appreciation of his concern but Mrs More, she said, perhaps through the beneficent effect of the apricots had greatly improved the previous evening and was now insisting both her daughter and her sister take the air as frequently as possible, to make up for days of incarceration in the sickroom.

Why then, James had suggested, perhaps he could tell his master, the marquess, that the marriage contract might soon be signed?

She'd dipped her head and allowed that her father had indicated that if her mother continued to improve, there would be no reason for further delay.

'Richard, Viscount Purbeck, will be overjoyed,' he had assured her solemnly. Then they'd both fallen silent until he'd insisted on accompanying her and Molly home, taking the heavy basket from the housekeeper, who'd smiled at him in a way that showed her perfect understanding of the situation.

The following day James had organized matters so he'd been free to meet the More ladies on the steps of St Paul's. The cavernous interior of the cathedral with its sepulchral solemnity then proved conducive to a deepening understanding between Charlotte and himself.

So intent was James on presenting himself in the most advantageous light to Miss More, on watching her reactions and assessing which development of conversation and subject would prove most fruitful, he was at first blind to the fascination she quickly began to have for him.

The directness of her character, the softness of her voice and manner, the way she had of smiling that seemed to suggest no one had ever pleased her quite so much, he found all enchanting. He began to wait for the little smile that lifted just one corner of her sweet mouth, the crinkle of her eyelids that said she was amused at something he'd said. It was all quite, quite different from the way Anne Montesqui had bewitched him but it was equally intoxicating and much, much more *comfortable*.

The order from the marquess that he accompany the More party to his brother-in-law's open house aroused conflicting emotions in James. There was delight at the thought of spending so many hours in Charlotte's company, and dismay at the evident nearness of the marriage contract, plus anxiety at the possibility others would discern the rapport between them.

Balthasar More, his mouth puckered in disapproval, turned to James as they neared the top of the steps. 'How are we to find Viscount Purbeck in this mob?'

'Fear not, sir, the viscount is to await us in the Blue Salon,' James said cheerfully and noted the increased tension in Charlotte's shoulders.

Soaring marble walls, veined columns and a triumphantly coffered ceiling that floated high above the admiring crowd, all underlined the pretensions of the earl and his countess to be leaders of society.

James had met both in London at the house of the marquess and introduced the Mores with aplomb. The countess scrutinized the prospective bride with insulting care. The earl offered the tips of his fingers to the merchant. Balthasar More, unexpectedly intimidated by his surroundings, gabbled some words of appreciation of the honour of being present that day at such a magnificent abode.

James received no more than the very briefest nods of acknowledgement. It was no more than he should have expected but he felt the slight deeply. More than anything, he longed to be on a footing of equality with these august beings.

The paying of respects over, the small party moved on.

'Magnificent, magnificent,' Balthasar More kept muttering as they made their way with others towards the back of the hall where a short flight of stairs led towards the reception rooms. His eyes flicked from statue to statue, from the marble pillars to the huge gilded side tables supporting vast urns, from the frieze at the back of the hall, a splendid romp amongst gods and goddesses, to the paintings arranged along the corridor that led from the hall to the salons.

Charlotte stared straight ahead, her spine rigid. As they negotiated the steps, James caught a glimpse of her little feet, shod in cream kid adorned with a silk rosette, appearing and disappearing from her skirts like sugar mice.

Following the instructions given by the earl's steward when he'd met him earlier in the week for this precise purpose, James led the way into the first of a series of magnificent reception rooms.

Gilt flashed from furniture and mouldings. Two mighty chandeliers coruscated down from the elaborately plastered ceiling. The flashing of their drops was reflected in mirrors set between the long windows. The walls were hung with red damask, an admirable background for the display of a part of the earl's superb collection of paintings. Ancestors, arrogantly surveying those circling the room, were interspersed and topped and tailed with classical scenes, Italian Renaissance religious subjects and just a few darker pieces from northern Europe. Ranged round the walls were ornate side tables and massive chairs upholstered in damask – red, of course. Also red were the curtains billowing down from the windows. It was, James had been informed, to be known as the Red Salon.

'Sir,' James said to Balthasar More, 'the Blue Salon is the next.' He gestured towards the tall polished mahogany double doors that were drawn back, their brass door furniture glittering against the polished wood.

Only to stop in dismay as a small man turned from the contemplation of a large landscape by Claude.

Canaletto!

James could hardly think. How had Canaletto managed to materialize here? And with Richard in the next room!

'Signor Bennett! Surely, it is?' The modulated voice with its Italian lilt carried clearly over the background chatter. There was no hope the Mores had not heard.

'Signor Canal, what a surprise! You are in England?' What a fatuous remark! James was furious with himself.

'You have abandoned your clerical garb?' the painter asked

'I am no longer a tutor,' James said, struggling to make the best of the situation. 'I am now secretary to my lord the Marquess of Brecon. Miss More, Mr More, may I present Signor Antonio Canal, the great Venetian topographical artist?'

Charlotte offered her hand with a graceful gesture, more than matched by the way Canaletto bowed over the fingers, his lips not quite touching them, in the best of social etiquette. 'Signorina, my pleasure,' he murmured.

'The painter, eh? Seen one of your works at the Marquess of Brecon's house,' Balthasar More said in the throwaway voice of the best name droppers.

'Indeed?'

'My daughter is affianced to the Viscount Purbeck, heir to the marquess.' More's voice was full of self-satisfaction.

'Signorina, I wish you happiness.' Then he addressed himself to James again. 'Sir, this is a most happy meeting. I wish most greatly to meet the marquess.'

James prepared himself to explain the impossibility of leaving Miss More, then inspiration presented him with a perfect opportunity to remove the man from these rooms. He took Canaletto a little apart.

'You can see how I am placed at the moment, but I am most anxious to talk with you, sir. I understand that in the grounds there is a small temple to Apollo, a pillared, classical edifice. Ask one of the lackeys how it can be reached. I will meet you there shortly.'

'And you will introduce me to the marquess?' insisted the painter.

'Indeed,' James recklessly promised. Anything to get rid of the man. It was essential to prevent Richard encountering him.

Chapter Thirty-Six

Fanny knocked on the prison door with her heart in her mouth.

It was as though the blood of prisoners seeped from cracks in the mortar securing the dark stone. She seemed to hear soundless screams drifting out of the small, barred windows; to her the miasma of despair cloaked the closed architecture of the prison's walls. Her terror of finding herself once again incarcerated was so strong she could taste its acrid flavour in her mouth. Her fist against her lips, she ran from the gate before it could be opened to her.

Then she stopped, clutching the soft rolls she had brought with her to her bosom. She owed her release to Canaletto. Without him she would still be in there with nothing but wretchedness and servitude in an alien land to look forward to. This was something he wanted, the least she could do was carry out his wishes. With enormous determination, she turned round and marched back to the gate.

The warder did not appear surprised to see her again, or perhaps he did not recognize her, washed and tidied as she was.

A small payment sufficed to have her taken into the general cell where she had been incarcerated.

The first person she recognized was Amelia. The girl was lolling against the man known as Barnacle Bill. His hand was down her bodice and she seemed not all displeased by the fact. Before she could notice Fanny, prisoners moved between them.

Then Fanny saw Scarface Nell. The huge woman was screaming with laughter at some no doubt bawdy joke made by a small, slippery man Fanny hadn't noticed during her imprisonment.

Fanny advanced towards them. Scarface Nell saw her, dismissed the small man and beckoned the girl over.

'Never thought to see you again, doll!' The scarred eye crinkled into disappearance. 'What's the matter, missing us all?' She screamed with laughter at her sally and there were guffaws from some around her.

Fanny offered the rolls. 'I thought these might be welcome,' she said and the words came out in a whisper.

Scarface Nell looked at the soft, sweet bread with an expression that was first cousin to nostalgia. 'Doll, they're my favourite.' She grabbed one and bit into it, the three front teeth that were all she had chomping into the roll with eager bites. A little crowd of prisoners gathered to watch her, their eyes following the fall of crumbs; disappointment greeted the sight of Nell's fat fingers, wet from a large lick of her massive tongue, greedily picking up the last of them. No droppings from Nell's table for any of them.

Nell eyed the other two rolls, then she extracted a piece of cotton, grey with use, from some portion of her tattered dress, carefully wrapped the bread in it and secreted it somewhere in her skirts. 'Kind of you, doll,' she said and patted the dank stone ground. 'Got time to sit and pass the day with old Nell?'

Fanny sank to the ground. Now that she'd made herself come here, her mission seemed bizarre. Even, perhaps, dangerous? She looked at the curious and avid faces of the prisoners clustered around them. Who were they, what were their contacts? What word would be sent out to the world of ruffians and villains?

'Gert-orf!' Nell shouted at her hangers-on. 'Can't yer see, her and me is visiting?'

Who knew by what means the woman managed to impose her will on these people? But her authority was evident, a space appeared around the spot where Fanny and she sat.

'Now, doll, you and me can 'ave a nice little talk, eh?' Nell patted Fanny's hand. 'Gawd, but I'm right glad to see yer! We 'ad a bit of a celebration yesterday, when we knew you weren't coming back. I mean, not often one of us gets away, if yer knows what I mean?'

'I'm sorry I couldn't say goodbye. You were very kind to me.'

'Go on with yer, only did what anyone would.' Nell spoke robustly. 'Yer make life difficult for yerself, doll, yer know that? If yer'd been a little nicer to that whoreson, Barnacle Ben, 'e'd 'ave seen yer right, know what I mean?'

'Oh, but Nell, I couldn't have!' Fanny covered her face with her hands, feeling the blood rush to her cheeks as the memory of that hard, thrusting body against hers swept back over her.

Nell regarded her with a certain interest. 'Never done it, 'ave yer? Well, well, yer better get some pretty feller to show yer what it's all about, then yer can see where it'll get yer. Thirteen I was when I 'ad me first, never looked back. Yer've got something they want, see, and yer can always make 'em pay, one way or another,' she chuckled with an evil relish. 'Life don't wait around for yer, doll, grab it and make it work for yer.'

Fanny was impressed by the indomitable spirit of this woman. Even being confined in these dreadful surroundings didn't seem to inhibit her.

'So, what yer come for, eh? Not just to see old Nell, I knows that.' The pat she gave Fanny's hand was kindly.

Fanny struggled to find a way to begin. 'It's that, well, you see . . .'

'Spit it out, doll, like a sailor do phlegm!'

Fanny plunged. 'You said you knew everyone around the Fleet. And, truly, I believe you must.' Her eyes, large and round, sought Nell's one good one. 'It's that Signor Canal, the gentleman who was able to secure my release, well . . .'

'Your *friend*, eh? I thought we'd come to one afore too long!' Nell guffawed.

'Nothing like that,' Fanny started, then realized that the advent of a protector greatly improved her standing with Nell. 'That is, he's lately come from Italy, from Venice. And has been attacked, not once but twice, and robbed.' The words came more quickly now and Nell's interest had been caught. 'And then Signor Canal found the . . . the,' Fanny couldn't bring herself to say Canaletto had found only the head and fudged the issue. 'He found the man who'd attacked him was dead.'

'And no sign of 'is property, I suppose?' Nell said with gusto.

'Exactly.'

'An' you think I knows 'oo 'e might be, eh, doll?' Nell looked proud of the possibility.

'His name is . . . was Scallion, Jack Scallion,' Fanny said. 'And this is a picture of him.' She pulled out of her reticule a small sketch Canaletto had done that morning. It hadn't the finish of the first drawing he'd made but it accurately captured the man's mean visage and mal-evolent expression.

She handed over the sketch to Nell. As the woman took it, Fanny saw that the name had indeed meant something to her and realized she should have been watching her countenance when she uttered it rather than scrabbling for her reticule.

Scarface Nell looked at the drawing with an unread-able expression.

'You knew him?' Fanny breathed.

'An' 'e's dead, you say?'

'Yes, I'm afraid so.'

Nell's large finger gently traced down the side of Jack Scallion's face. ''E was always a rotter. Lowest scum of society, that one. Stole from 'is own muvver.' She looked up at Fanny, her good eye shining with moisture. 'But we 'ad some good times along the way. Right card 'e could be when the mood or the gin took 'im. Well, that's that, then!' Nell slammed some mental door on her memories. 'Don't know as I can 'elp yer any. 'Aven't seen Jack in an age.'

'You don't know where he lodged, then?'

Nell looked dubious. 'Never 'ad no reglar place. Tried to doss down wiv me one time. Got rid of 'im right quick, I did. Well, you couldn't 'ave the likes of 'im around when you was expecting respectable customers, could yer?'

Fanny found no difficulty in not smiling at the thought of Scarface Nell entertaining gentlemen in her no-doubt mean lodgings.

'Yer could try the Dog and Pullet what's round the corner from Ludgate Church. "E 'ad a room there one time and the landlord was something of a pal.' 'Course, that was afore Jack got taken on by that merchantman.'

'Went for a sailor, you mean?'

'Well, 'e'd always wanted to travel. Me, I like it where I knows it, but Jack always 'ad the urge for ovver places. Grass always greener on some other man's dung 'eap for that one.' Nell laughed coarsely.

'How long was he a sailor?'

Nell scratched her scar. 'Oh, I dunno. Several years? Jack warn't around Fleet Street, that I knows. An' when 'e comes back, 'e's talking foreign. Learnt all these languages, 'e says. Been all over, 'e 'ad, 'e said,' Nell added doubtfully.

'Where?'

'Well,' she thought hard. 'France, 'e'd been there. *Parlayvoo*, 'e was always saying, and *sar var*. An' 'e was always talkin' about the Mediterannee, that's a sea, 'e said. Wiv lots o' sun but right treacherous storms. Comes up out o' nowhere and strips your guts out, 'e said.'

Fanny remembered being shown a globe by the Italian to whom Ned had been apprenticed. Young as she'd been, she could remember his stubby finger tracing the voyage he was to take, from London, round the tip of Spain, through into the Mediterranean, to the boot-shaped piece of land that he said was Italy. 'Not a country, many states,' the engraver had explained. 'I go to Venice, greatest Italian state.' His finger had crept up the leg of Italy on the right-hand side. 'This Adriatic, not Mediterranean. And here, here is Venice. Most beautiful city in world. Built on water.' The engraver had raised his gaze from the globe and looked out of the window to where rain was pouring down. 'And such sun! Light leaps from water to stone, always moving, always liquid. If I could paint that light!' He brought his gaze back to Fanny. 'Only one man paint that light. Canaletto, such genius!'

The name had stayed in Fanny's memory even when the map of the Mediterranean had faded.

But now the map was back also. 'Did Jack visit Venice?'

'Venice? Where'd that be, then?'

'Italy. They call everyone signor and signora, or signorina.' Fanny heard in her mind Canaletto's lilting accent as he called her Signorina Fanny. It made the name sound so much prettier. Everything about the Italian painter was so much more elegant than the roughness of the English.

'Oh, ah! Signor, yeah, 'e said that orl right.'

'And in Venice all the houses float on water; at least, they seem to,' said Fanny, remembering the set of etchings she'd seen of the place.

'Ah, water is it?' Nell looked wise. 'Then that's the place Jack went. Said the only 'orses there was statues. That they 'ad rivers for streets. An' everyone went around in masks.'

'That would be carnival time, I expect.' Fanny produced another snippet of information her mind had stored away and tried to hide her excitement. She didn't know what exactly this information meant but the fact that Scallion had once been in Venice must have some connection with his pursuit of Canaletto.

But there was another connection it would be good to establish.

'Nell, remember telling me it was Alderman Fowler who had got you inside here?'

The good eye regarded her suspiciously. 'Yers, what of it?'

'Well, did Jack Scallion have anything to do with the alderman?'

A slow smile split the scarred face. 'Bless your socks, doll, me and Jack've known John Fowler for years.'

'Did you know John's sister, Lucy?'

'Nah! 'E kept 'er well away from the likes of us. We was the ovver side of 'is life. When I said it was 'e sent me 'ere, should 'ave told you it was 'e wot give me this,' a finger pointed to the livid scar running down her face.

Fanny gasped in shock. 'However did that happen?'

''E catches me going through 'is breeches one night.' A scornful laugh, 'I told 'im 'e was never generous enough wiv me. All 'e said was, 'e wanted value for money. Well, I reckoned I was by my rights.'

'But he caught you!'

Nell nodded. 'Grabbed me by me 'air, dragged back me 'ead, drew a dagger and said all men should know me for a thieving whore.' Nell gave a low, lewd chuckle. ''E wasn't able to service no whore for months afterwards, the kneeing I giv 'im. All wiv my face running red wiv blood.'

Fanny had a sudden vision of rat-faced John Fowler standing over Nell, holding her head back by the hair, slashing at her face. 'I don't know how you can speak of him with such composure.'

Nell wasn't impressed. ''E's scum of the earth but we goes back a long way. It was 'e was the first one as did it to me.' She smiled, a smile that somehow, despite the scarring of her face, managed to be sweet. 'O 'course, soon as 'e started climbing up the slippery pole, it was all different.'

'But he still went with you from time to time?'

Nell nodded. 'Except after this,' her fingers touched the scar lightly. 'Then I told 'im no dice.'

'You mean he still wanted to, even after that?'

'Didn't mean nothing to 'im except 'e thought 'e'd shown me what 'e was made of,' she said contemptuously. Fanny could think of nothing to say to that.

Nell smoothed the scrap of paper she still held. 'Can't say I'm exactly 'mazed Jack's dead. Livin' the life 'e did, well, 'e 'ad to expect a knife in the dark or a pistol, didn't 'e?' She fixed her one bright eye on Fanny. 'Don't know 'ow it 'appened, I suppose?'

Fanny squared her shoulders, it wouldn't be fair not to give Nell all the information she had and this woman was not going to faint in horror at hearing the truth. 'He had his head chopped off.'

There was a tiny instant while Nell looked at her in shock, then the woman gave a great crow of laughter. 'Lorst 'is 'ead at last, eh? Well, bugger me!'

Chapter Thirty-Seven

Anne Montesqui shook out the golden folds of her gown from the constraints of the carriage, smiled graceful thanks at the lackey who had helped her down and waited at the bottom of the Wedmore Park steps for the marquess to join her.

It was the first time he had taken her out into society and she was conscious of looks from those around them. A whisper went through the crowd as his tall, burly figure stepped down beside her. This was as good as a declaration. Surely he could not now fail to make his offer? And surely, then, she would be safe?

Anne smiled at several familiar faces without receiving a response. The thin, scrawny figure of Madame Fournier followed the marquess. Oh, to be able to rid herself of that fool!

She felt the marquess's hand beneath her elbow, burning through the fine silk of her sleeve. All the way there in that jolting carriage, he'd been devouring her with eyes that seemed to dissolve the frail wisp of lawn that veiled the curve of her breasts. If Madame had not been present, he would have taken her, of that Anne was certain.

She'd returned his look from beneath lowered lids,

allowed a small, provocative smile to play around her mouth.

Madame had prudently pretended to fall asleep, resting her head against the padded back of the carriage's seat.

Alexander had leaned forward, 'Anne, I have arranged a surprise for you today. You will be pleased, believe me.'

She gave him another provocative look. 'My lord, you do me too much honour, I can scarce contain my curiosity. Perhaps a little hint?'

For answer he had pulled her hard against him and fixed passionate lips on hers. Briefly she'd responded then had pulled away, breathing hard, sending a warning glance at Madame.

'Anne,' he'd groaned through gritted teeth, 'I'll not let you play with me much longer.'

'My lord,' she had whispered. 'You send me nearly out of my mind. I would lose all decorum if it were not for . . .' her voice had faded, she'd taken out a handkerchief and fanned it in front of her face.

He had drawn back his lips in a snarl. 'Play not the innocent with me!'

She'd tried to look injured. With a sudden movement he had picked up one of her legs, clasping the slim ankle with both his hands and, closing his eyes, placed her foot over his crotch. She could feel him hard and throbbing through the fine barathea of his breeches and the thin leather of her shoe.

She had jerked the foot away. 'My lord, you wrong me!' she'd gasped and turned her face to the window.

He'd given a strangled groan. 'Anne, by God, you send me mad!'

Madame Fournier had stirred and muttered something in her sleep. If sleep it was.

'My lord, I have so looked forward to this day. To spend so much time in your company, to be on your arm in such society,' she had sent him a look from beneath her eyelashes. 'I have hardly slept these last three nights in anticipation.' She opened her mouth in a tiny, tiny yawn, and saw the response on his face.

'Oh, la, did I sleep?' Madame Fournier had come to with a fluster of hands and apologies. The moment was past and soon after that they had joined a procession of other carriages.

Anne had kept her face to the window, ostensibly admiring the view, giving little cries of excitement over the glimpses of the park, making sure the marquess had a fine view of her long neck and lovely profile. And the line of her breast lifted high by the whalebone of her corset.

How much longer, she had wondered as she cooed ecstatically over the charms of the lodge, could she keep this man burning for her, allowing him just so much intimacy and no more?

She could never settle for the life of a kept woman. She needed the freedom as well as the security of marriage. In marriage the marquess would soon dissipate his passion then find another object, leaving her to conduct her own discreet liaison. If James remained in his employ, maybe they could resume their affair?

No, it was too dangerous. For Alexander to discover his secretary had known his wife before himself would be disastrous. Wives could be discarded. Even, her mind retreated from the thought, divorced! James would have to go.

But there'd be other men, other opportunities.

Alexander would be a brutal lover, she was sure of that. Brutality had never attracted her. She knew there were women who welcomed it, longed, even, to be taken by force. Perhaps they were afraid of allowing their feelings to flower slowly, of allowing tenderness to bloom into full-bodied passion until their whole body throbbed with incandescent fire.

As the carriage had slowly ambled up the long drive in the stately procession, Anne drove any such thoughts from her mind. Today was too important. She must be all decorum, all sweet charm and gracious manners. None must fault her demeanour, her suitability for marriage into this society.

Advancing carefully up the steps beside the marquess, Anne allowed herself to pretend they were already married, that she really was an accepted part of this society.

She curtsied prettily to the earl and his countess and ignored the way the earl's hot eyes looked into the cleavage of her gown as she rose.

'Mam'selle Montesqui, I am pleased to make your acquaintance,' the countess said. Her tone could perhaps be called cordial but hardly warm.

Anne was under probation!

Throbbing with resentment, Anne felt the marquess guide her through the hall and into the first of the reception rooms. 'We must be able to tell George we have seen everything,' he murmured.

The room seemed unconscionably hot. Perhaps it was the excess of red everywhere. Or the expanse of flesh offered to her gaze by the paintings on the walls depicting fashionably classical subjects.

It would be nice to be offered something to drink. Somewhere, surely, there must be refreshments? She turned to ask the marquess, then caught sight of James, his graceful length standing beside a girl she could only assume was Charlotte More. Oh, but he was handsome! And everything she desired in a man. Except for lack of wealth or position. Maybe she might have been able to tolerate the absence of one but both was an impossibility.

She turned to place a hand on the marquess's arm to suggest they went and joined the group, then, out of the corner of her eye, saw disappearing back into the hall a figure that shook her to the roots of her soul.

Canaletto!

It was as well Patrick had warned her. 'I will do what I can to ensure you do not meet,' he'd said, 'but it may not be easy. However, you have only to ignore him. You have no reason to do more.'

Simple enough for him to say. But Patrick had never known the full story. Back to Anne rushed memories of heated Venetian afternoons. Oh, the excitement of those days! Even the possibility that she would lose control of the situation and her two lovers encounter each other had merely heightened her sense of adventure.

Then Patrick had grown suspicious and whisked her off first to Paris and then to London. And she had forgot the Venetian painter.

Till now.

If Canaletto should encounter her while she was with the marquess, would he say something to make Alexander suspect the relationship they had enjoyed? If so, she shivered as panic sent an icy tremor down her spine; if so, then she could say goodbye to life as a marchioness.

Anne took a deep breath, pressed her hand on the marquess's arm and said, 'Surely that has to be Miss More and Mr More over there, with your secretary?'

He gave her a calculating glance.

'Why, yes, I will introduce you.' Followed by Madame Fournier, he led the way across the room.

Anne was watching James, afeared he would betray too much gladness at seeing her. Instead she saw his eyes slide away from meeting hers. So, he was being careful at last!

'Balthasar, Miss More, well met! I know Richard awaits your meeting with impatience. My dear Mam'selle Montesqui, this is Miss More who is to be affianced to Richard, and her father. Balthasar, Miss More, may I present Mam'selle Montesqui, daughter of the Comte Montesqui of the Vendée in France.'

Anne smiled winningly at the girl. 'Miss More, I know we are going to be great friends. Shall we not walk a little together and leave these men to discuss the affairs of the world?'

'I should like that, mam'selle, but I believe the viscount awaits us in the next room.' She looked towards the marquess and it seemed to Anne that the girl was in no hurry to go to her future husband.

'Come, Miss More, you will have the rest of your life to spend with Richard. Alexander, you will not object if Miss More and I take a turn round the room?' The marquess was deep in conversation with the merchant. He gave a wave of his hand that Anne took for consent.

Charlotte gave her a sweet smile, 'Why, then, I will be happy to accompany you, mam'selle. And you shall tell me of life in France. I have long had the fancy to visit there.'

Anne linked her arm in Charlotte's and drew her gently down the long, startlingly red room. 'Tell me, do you not think this very fine? How does it compare with Brecon House?'

How Anne longed to be invited to that grand house in Piccadilly. Once that happened, she was sure she would feel secure in her position as Alexander's intended.

Charlotte glanced a trifle nervously at a picture of a crouching lion in dark foliage preparing to leap on unsuspecting peasants. There seemed no guiding principle at work behind the selection of pictures hung on these walls and she wondered if the marquess had an equally eclectic taste in art. 'I have visited Brecon House but once, and then my mama was taken ill and so I had thoughts other than the decor.'

Was there the merest hint that this city miss disapproved of ostentatious display? Anne drew Charlotte's arm a little closer into hers. 'And how is your mama? I was so distressed to hear of her indisposition.'

'Thank you, mam'selle, she does exceedingly well.'

A relief to Alexander, no doubt. A widowed Balthasar More free to find a younger wife who could produce him sons would not suit his purposes at all.

'And you are no doubt anxious that your marriage with dear Richard shall be celebrated as soon as she is completely recovered.' Anne's tone was laughing and confidential.

Charlotte's chilly hand clutched at her arm. 'My father arranges all.'

'Of course. You are so fortunate to have both father and mother still alive.'

'You have neither, mam'selle?' At last Charlotte sounded sympathetic.

'Alas, no. My father died when I was twelve and my mother some three years later. I am alone in the world, apart, that is, from my brother.'

'I envy you, mam'selle, I should like a brother above all things.'

'You will meet mine,' Anne gave Charlotte's arm a little squeeze and looked around the room. There was no sign of Patrick. 'He is supposed to be here today. He comes with a friend.'

'Do you miss life in France, mam'selle?'

'Why, some things. Paris is so sophisticated, so civilized.' Anne nodded pleasantly at a countess she had met at a ridotto; the woman gave her a questioning stare in return.

'You find London not so?' asked Charlotte, surprised.

Anne shrugged her shoulders, a movement expressive of a reluctance to denigrate. 'It has different charms.' A small group passed them going in the other direction, their stares more interested in other guests than the glories around them.

'I find London offers so much of interest. Perhaps you have not had time to visit much?'

Anne gave one of her rippling laughs. It drew masculine attention. 'My dear Miss More, since I have arrived in London, practically every moment has been filled with calls and visits. I have been fortunate, so much of society I know from Paris.'

'Why, then, you have not perhaps visited the Tower

of London or the new cathedral by Sir Christopher Wren?'

'You feel I should enjoy them?' Anne's tone was sceptical.

'My aunt and I showed Mr Bennett St Paul's the other day and he was greatly interested.'

A very slight blush coloured Charlotte's cheek as she said this. Anne noted it with fascination.

'Mr Bennett?' she murmured.

'The secretary to the marquess,' Charlotte glanced over to where the three men were still standing. Anne saw that James Bennett had fallen back, leaving the marquess and Mr More talking on their own. He was gazing at her as she promenaded along the room with Charlotte. But was she the attraction or was it this girl?

'He has called to enquire about Mama with gifts of fruit from the marquess. We talked and . . . and I found he had not visited the Cathedral.'

'And so it was your Christian duty to remedy the situation,' Anne said in a matter of fact way that received a grateful look.

'He . . . he admired very much the nave. It is two hundred and twenty-three feet long, you know. Indeed, the dimensions altogether are most impressive. The nave's width is one hundred and twenty-two feet and the height to the top of the cross is, I believe, nearly four hundred feet.'

'Amazing!' Anne forgot about Canaletto as her mind occupied itself with an appalling possibility. 'As you are so architecturally minded, I would like your opinion of the entrance hall here. I found it . . . overwhelming.'

Gently but inexorably she drew Charlotte More from the Red Salon. Out of the corner of her eye she noted the worried look on James Bennett's face as he watched them go.

Chapter Thirty-Eight

Fanny entered the Rookers' Fleet Street premises nervously.

Ned was working at his bench.

He looked up as the door opened. When he saw who it was, his expression became guarded. He said nothing.

'Is Lucy around?' Fanny asked.

'She's lying down, says she's exhausted and needs rest. She approaches her laying-in you know.' Ned returned his attention to his copper plate, hunching his shoulders.

As if she didn't know about Lucy's laying-in! Fanny drew nearer and automatically began to straighten out the workbench, tidying the tools, wiping away ink smudges, adjusting the tops of the varnish containers. 'Are you very busy?'

He gave a shrug. 'Enough.'

'Would you have time to do me a small service?'

He looked up, his face alight. 'If I can. Oh, Fanny, I'd do anything for us to be as we were.'

A little shaft of joy went through her. 'We shall always be brother and sister, Ned,' she said steadily.

His hand slipped and the burin made an indelible line on the almost completed plate. Ned cursed, flung the plate down and reached behind a bottle of varnish for a mug and took a deep swig of its contents. The liquid looked like water but Fanny knew it was more likely to be gin.

'Oh, Ned!' Fanny didn't know whether to berate or comfort him.

'Don't say anything! You don't know what my life is like.'

Fanny picked up the plate and looked at the mark he'd made. Then she looked at the drawing he was reproducing, a sentimental scene from a second-rate draughtsman, perhaps an illustration for a novel? It was badly drawn, an emotional encounter between a man and a woman. Fanny knew she could have done better herself, except that she would never be interested in turning out such rubbish. She stood studying the plate while Ned sat on his stool and a tear came out of his eye.

''Tis not ruined,' Fanny said brightly. She put the plate back on the cushion, tipped Ned off the stool, took it herself and picked up the burin. 'See, turn it into cross hatching and you have shadow here, with perhaps a small dog?' She skilfully wielded the tool and soon a fluffy animal with long ears looked soulfully up at its mistress, lost to rapture in the arms of her lover.

'But, Fanny, there isn't one in the original!'

'Tush, no one will notice. Who is it who has commissioned this and what are they paying you?'

The printer was one Fanny knew well. 'He'll never look twice at the work, and if he did he wouldn't care. He's paying you nothing, I'd never have let you accept the commission for that!'

Ned looked stubborn. 'We have to eat.'

Fanny said no more, it was no longer her concern.

Ned polished off his gin and leant against the wall, watching her as she put the finishing touches to the plate. 'So what brought you here? It obviously was not to be pleasant to me.'

Fanny put down the plate carefully. She went and slipped her hand around the back of his neck and drew his face down to hers, wrinkling her nose against the smell of gin on his breath. 'Oh Ned, I came because who else would I turn to for help? I love you and always will,' she ended fiercely.

He held her in a brief, hard hug. Then put his hands on her shoulders and asked, 'So, what is it I can do for you?' His face looked almost cheerful.

'I would much appreciate it if you could come with me to the Dog and Pullet,' Fanny said in a breathless rush.

'The Dog and Pullet? What business can you have there?'

Fanny stamped her small foot, 'Oh, don't badger me with questions, just come!'

Ned stretched out his cramped shoulders and looked purposeful. 'All right, Fanny. Heaven only knows what dubious business you've got yourself involved with now, but I'll come. Just let me tell Harriet that I'll be out for a while.'

Fanny waited, torn with anxiety that Lucy might suddenly appear and set all out of sorts again. But Ned was soon back. 'Oh, what a day it is, no need for a jacket,' he said joyously as they went out into what was for once sun and clear skies.

Ned took Fanny by the arm but such was the press of people in the street there was no opportunity to talk as they made their way through the crowds and traffic.

The Dog and Pullet was a low sort of place that looked rickety enough to fall down while you stood wondering if you could bring yourself to enter.

But Ned strode straight in, banging the door back on its hinges.

Inside it was dark and it took a moment for Fanny's eyes to adjust. The benches at the rough tables were almost empty, only a couple of addled sailors sat in silence at one end of the tavern. But there was many a puddle of ale on the surface of the tables and the floor was offensive with litter, the sand churned up and sodden. Two curs snarled in one corner. A large fireplace had the scattered remnants of an old fire.

'Landlord!' shouted Ned.

The sailors hardly looked up.

'Landlord!' he shouted again while Fanny unobtrusively drew her skirts up a little.

'Aye?' rumbled a deep voice.

An unexpectedly small man appeared from the rear of the tavern, wiping the back of his hand first across his mouth and then on the seat of his dirty breeches; a disreputable-looking shirt hung open and displayed an ample supply of wiry grey chest hair. That on his head was grey as well, and greasy, and there were gold rings in his ears. His expression was surly and he had a cast in one eye. He stuck his hand aggressively in the large leather belt that tried to contain a beer belly, belched and waited.

'My sister has a question for you,' Ned said in a lordly way, but underneath the gin courage Fanny recognized nervousness.

Indeed, she was nervous as well. This man might

be small but he looked capable of seeing off any number of larger individuals.

Then a tiny termagant swept out of the back. 'You whoreson cur,' she screamed and beat on his chest with an iron spoon. 'Steal my beef, would you, Bill Fletcher?'

The man fell back. 'Now, my precious, a man's gotta start the day on meat.'

'Only if'n he can pay for it!' the woman shrieked, beating some more at his chest. Then, as suddenly as she had arrived, she'd gone.

Bill Fletcher looked sheepishly after her. ''Ardly worth 'er bed space, that one. But she does own the place. Now, what can I do for you good folks? Drop of ale? Newly brewed an' the best?' he suggested in a voice that said he knew these were not drinking customers.

''Tis about Jack Scallion,' Fanny said decisively. 'We, that is, I believe he lodged with you.'

'That whoreson knave!' All the surliness was back. ''Aven't seen 'im for days an' 'e owes 'is rent. 'Ave you seen 'im?'

'I'm afraid he's dead.' Fanny felt more confident now.

'Dead, you say? Scallion? The devil take 'im! How we going to get 'is rent now?'

Fanny took a deep breath as she embarked on the plan she'd worked out before arriving at the Rooker workshop. 'I reckon we could suit each other there, Mr Fletcher. Jack Scallion had something of mine. If it were still in his room, I'd be willing to pay you what he owes.' It couldn't be more than she had left from the money Canaletto had given her the day before.

Bill Fletcher eyed her suspiciously. 'Little enough 'e's left.'

Fanny's heart sank. If Canaletto's satchel was still in

Scallion's room, this rogue would be bargaining now with her. The leather alone was worth a tidy penny. 'I'll take a look,' she said purposefully.

Fletcher moved between her and the stairs. 'Only after I get my rent,' he said grimly.

Fanny looked him straight in the eye and could see only the production of some coin would procure her access to Scallion's possessions, such as they were. 'How much?'

'Four shillin' that whoreson knave owes,' Fletcher said, an avaricious gleam in his eye.

'Nonsense!' Fanny handed over two shillings. 'And that's too much.'

He stared at her belligerently and she stared back, hoping the quaking in her stomach didn't show on her face. 'You'll not get a penny more,' she warned.

Fletcher flicked the coins against each other then bit them. 'Daylight robbery, that's what it is,' he said gloomily. 'Orl right, then, come with me.'

Fanny climbed the rickety stairs behind Bill and Ned followed close behind. They were led into a tiny slip of a room that contained a narrow bed, no more than a couple of slats with legs. It sported a thin straw mattress in soiled ticking and a roughly cast-aside blanket. It was plain to see that there was nothing under the bed, nor, it seemed, anywhere else in the room. Then Fanny looked behind the door. A hook held a spare shirt and in the corner was a shabby leather bag with a long handle.

Fanny picked the bag up and opened it. There might just be something inside that would give a clue as to where Canaletto's satchel had gone.

Inside was a tinder box, a piece of hollowed-out horn

that could serve as a drinking vessel and a curious-looking white mask. Nothing else. Except— Fanny ran her hand along the bottom of the bag and came up with a coin. Only it wasn't money, it was a token. On one side was a curious device of a mallet crossed with some sort of long, slim tool, on the other the words Parker and Son, Portland.

Fanny could make nothing of this. She slipped it back into the bag and rejoined Bill Fletcher and Ned outside the room.

'Nothing of mine there so I'm taking this instead.' She gave the bag a small heft. 'Little enough to show for a life. He had nothing else in his possession?'

'That one?' Fletcher gave a derisory laugh.

'Who did he consort with?' Fanny asked as they negotiated the stairs again.

'Anyone 'oo was around. Drink with the devil, 'e would. Or anyone 'oo'd pay for his tipple.'

Fanny cast around for some question that would gain her a worthwhile nugget of information. 'Did no one ever call for him here?'

With a swift movement Bill Fletcher swung round on her, pushing her against the wall. 'What's your game? Asking all these questions?'

Ned grabbed him by the shoulder, 'You leave my sister alone!'

The man turned on him with sudden fury in his face and Ned backed up the stairs.

Fanny hastily intervened. 'I told you, Scallion stole something from me. I need to get it back.' She looked at the man with narrowed eyes. 'There could be a reward if you had information that led me to whoever that whoreson gave it to.' She felt odd using the swear word but was sure it would give her more authority in Fletcher's eyes.

He looked at her speculatively. 'Reward, would it be?' He gave a ghastly smile that revealed a straggle of blackened teeth. 'Well, I can tell yer 'e 'ad some dealings with a nob.'

Chapter Thirty-Nine

Canaletto left the crowded Red Salon intent on finding a lackey and the way to the Temple of Apollo.

It had been most fortuitous meeting James Bennett. He had last seen the young man in Venice at carnival time. Joseph Smith had brought him to his studio. Bennett had been distraught and when he had told his story, Canaletto could understand why.

Bennett was tutor to a young nobleman, leading him around Europe. He hoped Canaletto would forgive him if he did not divulge the name of his charge; the matter was of the utmost delicacy. The young man appeared to have been kidnapped and was being held to ransom. A note had been delivered to Bennett demanding a large sum of money for the boy's return.

Apply to the Doge and his secret police, had been Canaletto's immediate response.

Bennett had become increasingly agitated, talked of the need for utmost discretion. Canaletto thought he understood, the tutor feared for his job should it become known that his charge had disappeared.

Still, without knowing the young man's name, the task seemed insuperable and he said so. Then Bennett disclosed he had seen the man who had delivered the note and later recognized him as a trader who sold cheap souvenirs in one of the squares. He had confided in Joseph Smith, who had immediately suggested that Canaletto might be able to discover from him what had happened to the youth.

It had taken Canaletto severals days to extract, through a mixture of bribery and threats, enough information from the man to identify where the youth was being held and to suggest that a rescue might be effected.

Canaletto paused on the marble hall steps as the full story flooded back into his mind. The classical glories of the earl's new home faded and he was back in Venice, watery sun washing the faded and peeling walls of a decrepit mansion, its furniture sparse and rotting. Faintly from outside came the cries of gondoliers mingled with those of traders from a nearby piazza.

With Canaletto was James Bennett and three strong boatmen he had enlisted with the promise of generous payment to help with the rescue.

The locked door had been broken open by a concerted attack by the boatmen, who had then staggered to a stop, riveted by the spectacle before them. Heavy curtains had been drawn over the windows, only flickering candles lit the scene. The air was thick with perfumes, layers of them: sickly sweet scents heavily laden with musk and attar of rose, the sour aromas of wines spilt on floors and furnishings, the heady auras of perfumed candles, and, throbbing through them all, the erotic, suffocating impact of sexual odours.

In the dim, golden, wavering light, young limbs could be seen entwined in maze-like patterns. The bursting open of the door had hardly penetrated the obsession with physical passion that filled the room.

Clothes had been abandoned, young flesh gleamed with sweat, slack mouths nibbled at nipples, hands caressed hips in a surfeited lethargy. Drunk with alcohol, drugged with passion and probably with other, more intoxicating substances, the room's occupants were conscious of nothing beyond the languorous fulfilment of their bodies' needs.

Canaletto felt the power of the room's atmosphere wrap itself around him like the ample body of a fat whore. The tutor gagged, the boatmen let out slow whistles.

Then slowly the fact that they were not alone had percolated through to those in the room.

There had been pandemonium. Canaletto had wanted to hold and question at least one of the other orgiasts but, clutching abandoned clothes, they had vanished through a door hidden behind a tapestry, the last one slamming it in the face of the boatmen and sliding a bolt.

By the time another way round had been found, all had vanished. Only a mask and one slipper sat in desolation on the steps leading down to a canal. It was impossible to tell which of the gondolas being propelled along the water held them and Canaletto knew well the fierce confidentiality of these boatmen. If they were willing to speak, half the scandals in Venice would be revealed but all knew they were safe from gossip spread by gondoliers.

Canaletto had returned to the room to find the young English nobleman unable to take in what had happened. Still naked except for a cloak thrown roughly around his shoulders, with glazed eyes and incoherent speech, he'd grabbed Canaletto and shaken him, sobbing and distraught. Finally, the Italian managed to gather the boy felt happiness had been snatched away from him.

His tutor had castigated the youngster, told him how angry his father would be, shown him the ransom note. This had been torn away from him, crumpled up without perusal and thrown away. Sternly James Bennett had told his charge to pull himself together and had helped him dress.

The last Canaletto had seen of the young man was him clinging to his tutor, sobbing pitifully as he was helped into a gondola.

'Go,' Canaletto had said. 'I will wait for the man behind all this.' For his information had indicated that the organizer of the plot visited each evening at ten.

With the boatmen, he'd waited behind the door at the water steps of the palazzo. At last a gondola had glided along the canal and a burly man had stepped out, hooded and masked, as was the custom at carnival time.

Alas, just as he was about to climb the steps, one of the boatmen had let out a whoop and ran out from behind the door. Immediately their quarry had turned back to his gondola.

Canaletto had run as fast he could down the steps, sword out. He'd almost made it. As the gondolier pushed down on his pole, the point of the painter's sword had caught the man's hood, flipping it up but failing to connect with flesh. In the light thrown by the boat's lantern, Canaletto had seen the flash of a strawberry mark on the nape of the man's neck. Then the gondola had glided away from the steps, leaving Canaletto flailing hopelessly in an attempt to keep his balance.

He had ended in the water and the boatman had had to pull him out.

That had been the end of the story. For some time Canaletto had found himself trying to peer beneath men's wigs for a strawberry mark, he would have dearly loved to have been able to identify the rogue. But the search was, of course, hopeless.

James Bennett had visited Canaletto one last time to express his deepest thanks. A reward had later been handed over by Joseph Smith and Canaletto had told him that was definitely the last time he would help depraved young English aristocrats. He would play the detection game no more.

It was no wonder James Bennett had had to abandon his career as tutor to the young. His noble employer must surely have learned at least something of the Venetian episode, for Canaletto's reward had been too generous to have been supplied by Bennett himself. And the employer would have been unlikely to recommend so careless a tutor to others.

Perhaps when Canaletto met him in the Temple of Apollo, Bennett would disclose how he had managed to arrange the position as secretary to the Marquess of Brecon. But first it was necessary to find where in the grounds the temple lay.

He applied to one of the impressively liveried footmen in the hall. The man's eyes jumped with fright as he apologized for not knowing the location of any temple. 'Interior is what I am, sir. Gardens is not my responsibility.'

Nor did the second footman know. The third footman Canaletto applied to told him, with an air of triumph, the way out to the terrace. From there, he said, Canaletto might well be able to see where the temple was.

Canaletto went in the direction indicated. It led through an ante-room crowded with guests surveying a series of small pictures hung on the three walls that did not contain windows.

It took not more than a few quick glances to identify the story of Cupid and Psyche told with a verve and gusto that matched the house but which Canaletto found indigestible.

A dining-room followed the ante-room. The long table was clothed in white damask and servants were setting out an informal repast. A superb collection of ornate silverware was arranged on a huge giltwood side table with a marble top. It made a fine show. And there, at last, Canaletto found the painting Joseph Smith had commissioned from him for the earl.

He stood in front of it for several minutes, dismay rising in his breast.

How had he failed to see the way he'd squandered his genius? This was a hastily painted work of the Grand Canal, the water a series of squiggled ripples, he could remember exactly which apprentice had been responsible; the buildings painted skilfully but with little to pick the view out from many others he had done, the figures no more than stock characters.

A hand fell on his shoulder. 'Tonio, at last!' There was McSwiney, a glass of red wine in his hand. 'I thought I would never discover you.' There was no sign of Patrick Granville but McSwiney seemed happy enough. 'I met with a splendid fellow who has intimate knowledge of the earl's cellar. He procured us glasses of a fine vintage.' McSwiney took a deep swig of his wine.

'You have seen the Marquess of Brecon?' Canaletto

was proud he could be comfortable speaking the English McSwiney today appeared to prefer to Italian.

'Brecon?' McSwiney gazed around as though the marquess was likely to materialize behind him. 'I saw him some little time ago. In the Red Salon.'

Canaletto gave a sigh that was almost a groan. To have been so near the man! Then his eyes narrowed. Had the marquess been there while he had been talking to James Bennett? Could this talk of finding the Temple of Apollo be a ruse to remove him from the marquess's vicinity?

'Please, you will take me to him?'

McSwiney drank the remaining wine with an appreciative smack of his lips then gave the empty glass to one of the servants. 'Superb! Now, Tonio, let us consider why you are chasing Brecon. To interest him in a view, right?'

Canaletto said nothing.

'And how are you going to do that in this mess of people?' McSwiney threw out his arm in a gesture that nearly brought down a Grecian urn placed on a pedestal perilously close to his shoulder. 'I introduce you here and he'll do no more than give you a glance before dismissing you with the odd politesse.' He looked at the picture on the wall. 'Particularly if he notices this example of your work!'

'I must see him, Owen,' Canaletto insisted. He tried to forget the painting. That was the past. Surely he could produce more masterpieces in this new country that offered fresh views? He was filled with enormous frustration. There could be any number of possible patrons here today but because of this ridiculous business for the paymaster general, he was unable to concentrate on speaking to any of them.

Then he had an excellent idea. 'I go out to the terrace, away from crowds. You bring him there, yes?'

McSwiney sighed. 'It might work. All right, show me where you mean.'

Following the directions given by the footman, Canaletto found the way out on to a generous expanse of almost deserted paved area bounded by a stone balustrade.

Despite his anxiety, Canaletto could not help being captivated by the prospect offered of sweeping green lawns, trees and a lake. The lake had obviously been created by man from some small stream provided by nature, for its banks sustained only vestiges of vegetation in soil newly turned and raw-looking. But already landscaping was creating what in twenty or thirty years would be a verdant outlook.

'Man, what a prospect,' McSwiney sighed, shading his eyes from the sun and gazing into the distance.

Canaletto turned to look at the house, craning his neck to see to the top of the huge façade. Well-proportioned windows marched the length in ordered series; the columns on this side were set into the stonework, which was topped by a long balustrade, not dissimilar from that edging the terrace. Except that the one on the roof bore a number of plinths carrying a series of classical statues. As he looked, an old itch returned to his fingers. How these lines called for his brush!

'I have an idea,' McSwiney said. 'You have your sketchbook, Tonio?'

Canaletto reached automatically into the skirt

pocket of his velvet coat. He drew out the book and a silverpoint pen.

'Now, stand there, sketching.' McSwiney placed Canaletto in the middle of the terrace, facing an enormous stone urn, one of a pair that had been placed on either side of the steps that led to the lawn. 'I will find Brecon and tell him he has the opportunity of a lifetime, the possibility of seeing the world's greatest landscape artist in the process of capturing a view. Bejasus, he will not be able to resist!'

The Irishman vanished back into the house.

Canaletto found himself automatically opening the sketchbook. McSwiney definitely had an eye; that urn, so solid, so ornate in its carving, provided an ideal contrast to nature's lush naturalness. And the green expanse beyond offered interesting sightlines it could be instructive to explore.

Soon Canaletto was sketching in his usual rapid manner. So absorbed had he become in the scene, McSwiney's reappearance was a surprise.

'See, my lord, as I promised you, the great Canaletto actually at work! Marquess, may I present Antonio Canal, topographical artist extraordinary?'

Canaletto turned and was immediately struck by the physical power of the man that stood beside the Irishman.

'My lord,' he said politely.

The marquess offered his hand. 'Delighted to meet the great Canaletto,' he murmured, his dark eyes fixing themselves in an unnerving way on the painter's face.

'I am honoured, my lord.' Canaletto gave a neat bow, holding the sketchbook in the manner of a hat. 'I am just now arrived in London.'

'Ah, yes?' The marquess didn't seem any too interested, he looked as though he was about to leave for more fruitful encounters. Canaletto decided he must plunge in without worrying about the presence of McSwiney. 'I have great desire to paint the new bridge.'

'Westminster Bridge?' The steady gaze never wavered but the voice sounded supremely disinterested.

'I understand you have particular connection,' Canaletto continued smoothly.

'Connection?'

'You are commissioner of bridge, no?'

'Ah, as to that, but one among many.'

'I look at bridge. It has many possibilities for interesting *veduta*.' Canaletto felt he was getting nowhere. 'But bridge is not finished, I am told it is very late.'

'Indeed?' An eyebrow was raised and the voice contained a hint that this was an impertinent suggestion.

'You have problems with stone, no?' Canaletto got to the heart of the matter.

McSwiney hovered on the edges of the conversation looking puzzled. 'Is this a matter to be raised on such an occasion?'

'Is important,' Canaletto insisted. 'Completion means much to a view of bridge.'

'Say you so?' The marquess flicked an invisible speck from the sleeve of his coat.

Canaletto felt he was handling this badly but didn't know how else to proceed. 'You who are at heart of plans, who know intimately progress, you can tell me about finish of bridge, no?'

The marquess's expression darkened. 'You suggest I am some sort of overseer?'

'No, no! Only that you receive reports of what happens. It is great privilege to be able to speak to one so high in authority.'

The flattery had little effect on the marquess, who now looked impatient.

Canaletto remembered his sketchbook. He rapidly leafed through it and found the drawing he'd made of the City of London seen through the arch of the bridge. He opened out the book and proferred it. 'My lord, this is my plan for view with Westminster Bridge.'

The marquess hesitated, then it was as though he couldn't resist seeing the sketch. He took the book.

His eyes narrowed as they looked. 'You have done other sketches? Of views less, what shall I say, less idiosyncratic than with a bucket?' Before Canaletto could answer, he'd flipped over a page and come to the sketch of Scallion.

The marquess looked at it for a long moment, then said, 'You indulge in portraiture as well, I see, Mr Canal.'

At that moment Patrick Granville came out on to the terrace. 'Why, you've found the marquess, Mr Canaletto. Interested him in your bridge project, have you?'

'Ah, Patrick,' the marquess turned with apparent relief, 'I've lost your sister. She has vanished with Miss More.'

'Indeed?' Patrick smiled lazily. 'I expect they are talking secrets the way women do. She will reappear soon enough. Are we being treated to a preview of Mr Canal's next painting? Do you mind?' He reached for the sketchbook.

'But this is no bridge!' he laughed again. 'This chap looks a right scoundrel.'

McSwiney leaned over and flipped back a page. Canaletto began to get anxious for the state of his precious sketches. 'Here is Westminster Bridge, Patrick.'

'Why, so it is. At least, I assume that is the bridge though all we can see is scaffolding! I don't see this as a fitting memorial to your great creation, Alexander.'

'Not mine,' growled the marquess.

'I have been asking my lord when the opening of the bridge will be. I have heard much talk of delays, of problems, perhaps even of deliberate damage with the supplies.' Canaletto was now desperate to get some reaction he could present to the paymaster general.

'What's this?' Patrick looked at the marquess in astonishment. 'What can a painter know of the bridge's construction?'

'Exactly what I am asking.' The marquess sounded as though he was losing patience.

'My lord, I have discovered you at last!' a lilting voice cried from the door on to the terrace.

Canaletto knew that voice and the shock was as icy as a dip in the Grand Canal in winter. Afternoons of lazy delight in a gondola or a lace-hung boudoir surged back into his mind. He moved so that the marquess was no longer between him and the owner of the voice and he could see whether it really was she.

'Anne!' the name was wrenched from him.

'You know Mam'selle Montesqui?' the marquess enquired in a cold voice.

Anne came forward slowly, her eyes wary.

'Why, Alexander,' Patrick said, 'my sister lived for a time in Venice. How could she not meet Signor Canal?'

'My friend, Joseph Smith, introduced us. You remember, that is how I met your son, Richard, as well,' Anne said calmly. Her eyes met Canaletto's in a friendly but distant way. 'How delightful we should meet again, signor.' She placed a hand on Patrick Granville's arm. 'I don't think you've met my brother.'

It was as though they had never spent those honey-laden hours together.

Their association had begun with yet another of those commissions Joseph had involved him in. A matter of lost letters this time, stolen by an absconding maid. Letters, Mam'selle Montesqui had said in that dulcet voice, that were of a very personal nature.

Later, much later, she had confessed to an indiscretion but had never explained who the girl had threatened to show the letters to.

'My half-brother, I should say, and my guardian.'

Now Canaletto looked at Patrick Granville and recognized steel in the man. Could it have been he Anne had been so worried her ex-maid might approach with the letters? Where had he been while Canaletto and his sister had been delighting each other? Back in Ireland? He should not have left his sister alone in that way.

'No need for an introduction, Anne. Mr Canaletto and I know each other – in fact I brought him here in my carriage, with Owen.'

'And you never told me!' Anne turned to the marquess. 'I have had such a happy time talking with little Miss More. What a charming girl she is. Nary a taint of the shop about her. But I grew anxious for your company.' She opened her eyes wide as she looked at him with that soft smile.

The marquess melted. A foolish smirk on his face, he laid his hand over hers. 'You have restored Miss More to her father? They have met with Richard?'

'Your sister, our hostess, begged five minutes with

her. Have you seen Madame Fournier? I seem quite to have lost her.'

'A loss I feel unable to regret,' the marquess said. 'Come, I wish words with you; my surprise has arrived.' He linked Anne's hand possessively through his arm and they moved away without a word to Canaletto.

Patrick Granville handed back the sketchbook with a graceful gesture and followed them.

'Whooh!' ejaculated McSwiney. 'What a beauty! And you knew her in Venice, Tonio? I never realized what a dog you could be!'

Canaletto felt unable to respond. His emotions were in turmoil.

He'd known, of course he'd known, that all was over between them when she'd vanished from Venice without a word of farewell. But somewhere, deep within him, a tiny spark of hope had remained.

That spark had now been extinguished. Worse, he now saw Anne for what she was, a woman who drank deep of life's pleasures but who valued wealth and position more than love.

'I hear there is punch to be served. Coming, Tonio?'

Canaletto shook his head.

Automatically he opened the sketchbook and turned again to the page on which he'd started a view of the prospect from the terrace.

He saw McSwiney shrug his shoulders and leave the terrace.

Canaletto had no idea how long he stood there, gazing at a view he couldn't see, absorbing the bitter reality that he had lost not only love but also the beloved. The woman he thought he'd loved had never existed.

He was finally aroused by the sound of stone scraping on stone from somewhere high above.

Canaletto looked up at the roof just in time to see a statue tip over from its plinth and start hurtling down towards him.

Chapter Forty

For a moment it was as though thistledown was falling from the sky. For a moment Canaletto stared at it, mesmerized. All he seemed able to take in was the fact that the outline of the balustrade against the clear blue sky, where up until a moment before had stood the figure of the earth goddess, Ceres, was as clear as any line in one of his paintings.

Then, just in time, Canaletto flung himself to one side and the statue plummeted on to the stone terrace, missing him by inches and shattering into pieces. A flying fragment caught his cheek and drew blood. Another tore a hole in the velvet skirts of his best coat.

Excited people emerged on to the terrace, their brightly coloured clothes blossoming on the stone like flowers amongst gravel, looking up at the heavens as though another missile might come down at any moment. Someone helped Canaletto to his feet and produced a handkerchief to help stem the blood now pouring from his cheek.

Clutching the linen to his face, Canaletto ignored all their questions. He dashed inside and made for the marble staircase that led from the main hall on to the first floor. Then up the second, slightly smaller flight of stairs that led to the second floor, where the bedrooms lay.

There he stood for a moment, looking around. Seeing a lackey on duty by an ornate cupboard from some Eastern location, he demanded, 'Staircase to the roof, it is where? Quick, quick.'

'Along the corridor, door at the end, sir. The earl has just gone that way, taken a party to see the view from the roof.'

Canaletto sprinted along the rich carpet that stretched between doors furnished with heavy brass plates and walls decorated with paintings from minor artists until he found the door that led to a small, bare, wooden staircase.

Above him he could hear the sound of many voices.

He was too late. By the time he emerged out on to the lead roof, with its generous expanse of walkways and flat areas around the steep pitch of slated roofing, the earl was already there, surrounded by a goodly company of his guests, all exclaiming at the fine view they were afforded. 'You can see three counties,' the earl was saying as Canaletto erupted from the staircase housing beside some fine chimney pots.

All turned to stare at him.

'My dear sir, you have been wounded!' The earl was all concern and several ladies twittered compassionately about him.

'Tonio!' said McSwiney, emerging from the back of the crowd. 'What has happened?'

Canaletto looked at the earl. 'My lord, your statues, one has fallen to the ground.'

There was a joint gasp of horror and then everyone

surged forward to inspect the group of statues that now stood like a row of teeth with one incisor missing.

'How came this, George?' asked the Marquess of Brecon, clamping a heavy hand on his brother-in-law's shoulder. Anne Montesqui was nowhere to be seen.

The earl was pale and furious. 'Someone will pay for this! I shall have their head! I was assured there was no danger. That is, no danger without a wind of some force. They are not to be fixed until next week but they are so fine. I wanted everyone to see how fine they are.' He peered over the balustrade at the shattered remnants of the earth goddess lying on the terrace far below.

One of the crowd put out a hand towards the great god, Zeus, as though to test how secure he was on his plinth, then snatched it away.

Still clutching his handkerchief to his cheek, Canaletto scanned the people clustered round the balustrade. There was Bartholomew More, looking judicial and disapproving. Not far from the marquess was Patrick Granville, a serious expression on his face. The marquess's secretary, James Bennett, was there as well. So much for him seeking the Temple of Apollo!

Any of them could have been on the roof when the earl's party arrived and drifted in amongst the other guests. But why should any of them wish to kill him? Except . . . Canaletto looked again at James Bennett. Suppose he was afraid Canaletto would betray the careless way he'd looked after his charge in Venice? It would undoubtedly lead to the loss of his position and mean he would be most unlikely to get another of any importance.

Canaletto went up to McSwiney, 'Have you been with these people since below, in the hall?'

'A curious question, Tonio.'

'Come, Owen,' Canaletto started to get agitated, the linen he was clutching slipped and blood started to flow again, dropping on to the fine lawn ruffle at his wrist. He cursed and slapped the handkerchief back over his wound. 'Is important. Someone perhaps here now not when you come up, yes? Perhaps that fellow over there?' He pointed to the young secretary.

'Ah, Tonio,' McSwiney sounded regretful. 'I only joined the party just before they gained the roof.'

Canaletto turned to the man standing beside him, a bluff fellow with a country face. 'Sir, you help me?'

The man stirred uncomfortably. 'How, sir?'

'Who join earl as he come on to roof?'

His interrogee looked down at his feet and swung his weight from one to the other. 'Ah, as to that, well, sir, I mean, we were all one party, yes?'

Was it his imperfect command of the language or did the man really not make sense? Canaletto moved on to another, more distinguished-looking gentleman and repeated his question.

'Sir, you are impertinent.' The man turned and moved towards the earl, still inspecting the empty plinth and talking agitatedly with people around him.

'Come, Tonio, this will not do,' said Owen McSwiney. 'You cannot act the Spanish Inquisition with our host's guests.'

Canaletto walked rapidly away from McSwiney, trying to contain his extreme frustration. Why could no one understand that someone had tried to kill him and that patient questioning of everyone who had come up to the roof might help discover who it was? Then he stopped abruptly. In the distance, by another fine set of chimneys, was a staircase housing identical to the one he and the earl's party had used. It seemed there was another entrance to the roof. And, therefore, another exit.

Canaletto's shoulders sagged. Given the symmetry of the house, he should have known. Where did it lead?

The earl's voice floated over to him, 'I shall send men up to remove the statues immediately. Thank heavens no one was seriously hurt.' The party began to descend from the roof.

Canaletto watched them go then made for the other staircase. But before he gained the door, it opened and on to the roof came the countess with Anne Montesqui and Charlotte More. Following them came a slight figure in a pale blue satin coat, his protuberant blue eyes looking bored in a sulky face.

'Signor Canaletto,' exclaimed the countess, moving swiftly towards him. 'What has happened to your face?'

There was a cry of consternation from behind her. The three ladies turned. 'Why, Richard, whatever is the matter?' asked Anne.

She reached out but the young man shrank back, his eyes on Canaletto. He started to shake uncontrollably, wrapping his arms around himself as though he would force his body to be still.

'Lord Purbeck?' Charlotte More exclaimed with an expression of the greatest anxiety.

The countess tried to draw the young man into her arms but he pulled away, his face rigid with horror. 'James promised everything would be all right! He promised!' The words came out in a kind of wail, then his body seemed to collapse and he dissolved into a shivering heap at the foot of the staircase housing, clutched his knees to his chest and buried his face in them.

The countess and Anne tried to bring him to his feet. Charlotte More remained a little apart, her face appalled.

And Canaletto realized that the Marquess of Brecon's son and heir was none other than the young man he had rescued from the house of debauchery in Venice.

Chapter Forty-One

Canaletto tried to help with the hysterical young man but every approach he made produced the same terrified shrinking away.

'Charlotte,' said the countess, 'fetch my brother, the marquess.'

Charlotte More, her face aghast, disappeared with alacrity.

While they waited, the countess knelt and wrapped her arms around the quivering body of her nephew, murmuring soothing phrases in his ears. Anne Montesqui fluttered around the pair of them. Only then did Canaletto realize that since he'd last seen her on the terrace, an accessory had been added to her beauty.

In her lovely ears now hung two huge baroque pearls, their iridescent sheen evidence of their superb quality.

No doubt the earrings were the 'surprise' the marquess had mentioned.

Not once as Canaletto paced up and down the lead roof while they waited did Anne look in his direction.

When the marquess arrived, he had James Bennett with him. 'God's teeth,' said his lordship, surveying his heir. 'Sir, get up!'

The ex-tutor grabbed the viscount's elbow and in a kindly voice said, 'Richard, this will not do.'

'Get him downstairs,' the marquess said curtly to his secretary. 'Louise, send for my carriage.' The countess gave a quick nod and disappeared down the staircase. She was followed by James Bennett supporting a sobbing viscount.

'Anne, come with me,' said the marquess with no softening of his manner. Canaletto watched the lovely figure glide over to her aristocratic suitor and put her slim hand on his arm.

'Of course, Alexander,' she murmured and they, too, left the roof without a glance at Canaletto.

He waited where he was for a moment, then walked across the roof to the far balustrade and leaned over to watch carriages moving like toys in front of the house.

In a little while the viscount and his father emerged, not down the main steps but from some minor door below. A carriage was brought up and the viscount forced to mount the steps by the marquess, who pushed him roughly inside. A lackey closed the door on them.

After them came Charlotte More and her father, escorted by James Bennett, entering another carriage. Then the barouche that had brought Canaletto drew up. It was commandeered by Anne Montesqui, her brother and an elderly female Canaletto did not recognize. He sighed as the carriage rolled away. How were Owen and himself to return home? But more pressing was the question of who could have wanted to kill him.

Four burly workmen arrived on the roof with slings and a quantity of hessian. They began to remove the remaining statues from their plinths.

Canaletto went to find McSwiney.

The incident appeared to have caused little disruption to the party. Guests still thronged the rooms, exclaiming at the treasures. The terrace was deserted, though Canaletto noted the statue fragments had already been removed. He threaded his way through the various rooms looking in vain for McSwiney. No one paid him any attention.

Fruit and pastries were being served together with punch. He took a small almond tart, crimped and glazed with egg, together with a glass, and stood in a window overlooking the front drive, watching guests start to leave, his mind busy with all that had happened.

Then amongst the grand carriages that every now and then pulled up at the front steps, he saw a carriage. Getting into it Canaletto recognized a familiar figure that caused him to drop his pastry in amazement. The stout figure was unmistakably that of Alderman John Fowler.

The likelihood of the alderman having received an invitation from the earl was too remote to be acceptable. What, then, was he doing here? If only he had seen the man sooner, Canaletto could have begged a lift back to London and found out. But it was too late now, the cab was already pulling away from the entrance.

'Hey, Tonio, I've been looking for you!' McSwiney had at last appeared. 'Apparently there's been some upset involving young Purbeck and Granville has had to escort his sister back – he said she was badly upset. I've arranged a ride home for us with an old client of mine.'

The old client turned out to be an aristocrat McSwiney had sold historical pictures to. On being introduced to Canaletto he expressed himself delighted to make his acquaintance but added, 'I view topographical art as on a level with portraits, useful reminders of places or people one has affection for but utterly devoid of artistic purpose.' He peered at Canaletto through myopic eyes, 'I trust I do not offend, dear sir?'

Canaletto murmured something conciliatory and gave up any thought of a commission from this quarter. The journey back was occupied with a heated debate between McSwiney and their host over the relative merits of various historical painters.

Canaletto had no intention of being drawn into the debate and was grateful when he and McSwiney were put down at Tyburn while the client continued towards north London.

The Irishman insisted they take dinner together. 'At my expense, Tonio.' The eating place he chose was busy, full of noise and bustle. People kept coming to their table and chatting to McSwiney, the service was poor and it took an age to complete their meal.

The Irishman was in a strangely ebullient mood, full of the glories of Wedmore and the number of contacts he said he had made there and the possible backer for a play he had a mind to produce. He seemed to have forgotten all his Italian and Canaletto let the English float over his head.

The painter felt bruised by the events of the day. The bitter truth that the woman he'd loved was nothing more than a fortune hunter burned like acid in his stomach and prevented him touching his meal.

Afterwards McSwiney stood in the crowded road and suggested they go drinking together at a club he knew. 'I know a place with cards, rare wine and some lovely women.' He rubbed his hands together.

Canaletto was restless and angry and desired distraction. But he thought of little Fanny courageously going to visit that dreadful prison on his behalf.

'Another time,' he told McSwiney.

By the time he reached Silver Street, twilight had arrived.

Daniel's workshop was all shut up. Canaletto went through the passageway into the garden. There was a light burning in the studio and through a window he could see Fanny sitting on a stool sketching at the trestle table.

She had two rushlights burning, one either side of her; their unsteady light burnished the copper of her hair and picked out green sprigs in the material of her dress. The curve of her neck emerging from the soft muslin of her fichu as she bent over the work looked sweetly vulnerable.

Canaletto entered the studio.

Fanny looked up, her face alive with pleasure. 'Oh, signor, how glad I am to see you. Do tell me, how was your day? Was the house magnificent and did you talk with those you intended?'

Canaletto felt soothed. The traumas of the day dropped away. He pulled out another of the stools, sat beside the girl and reached for her work.

It was a sketch of a man's head, startling in his ugliness. 'Who this?' he asked.

'Oh, 'tis just someone I met today.'

Canaletto studied the drawing. 'I cannot tell the likeness but the draughtsmanship is good. You have used economy and the modelling is very fine.'

She flushed with delight.

He put the sketchbook down and looked round the

334

studio. All was in place. The narrow bed was covered with a cotton spread, his equipment all arranged with care. The easel stood ready.

He had a feeling of deep content. Tomorrow they would start to prepare a canvas for his painting of Westminster Bridge and he would teach Fanny all the skills she needed to assist him.

Then he saw something he did not recognize. 'What is this?' He went and picked up the shabby bag.

'It was Jack Scallion's.'

'You mean you found his lodgings? What of my satchel?'

'Alack-a-day, that was the only thing in his room.'

Canaletto sat heavily on the stool again hit by overwhelming depression. The faint hope that at least part of his lost fortune might be recovered finally vanished.

While Fanny told her story, he automatically went through the contents of the bag, placing each item on the table.

He looked at the Venetian carnival mask for a long time. Then went back to the bag and, at the bottom, found a token. He sat turning it over in his fingers and listened to Fanny's light voice, full of life, describing her visit to the Dog and Pullet.

'So, I am sorry, signor, but I very much fear you will never see your satchel again. But,' her voice became excited, 'Bill Fletcher, the landlord at the Dog and Pullet, said a nob called on Scallion.'

'A nob?'

'Someone in society, a gentleman.'

'He had a name?'

Fanny shook her head. 'Fletcher said he only saw him the once, can't remember exactly when. Said he was all muffled up, went straight upstairs to Scallion's room. Didn't see him leave. But Fletcher said he was tall.'

'Maybe before, maybe after Scallion take my money.' Canaletto shook his head sadly. It was going to take him a long time to accustom himself to this blow. He looked down at the token he had been playing with. 'I have seen one like this before,' he said, laying it on the table. 'At Signor Pitt's office. The man Fairbrass, you remember I told you of agent killed at quarry? Signor Pitt said several found on Fairbrass. He said it is token given to those working there, for payment, you understand? Token only used in Portland.'

'So this means Scallion must have been there also?'

Canaletto was pleased with Fanny's quickness of mind.

'I think he killed this Fairbrass.'

'Just because he had this token?' Fanny gave him back the coin, her expression doubtful.

Canaletto nodded. 'This Scallion rogue of first order. He there for no good purpose.'

Fanny gave this a little consideration then asked, 'But who would have sent him there?'

'That is important question. That is what Signor Pitt wishes know. I spoke today with Marquess of Brecon, man very satisfied with himself, I think. There is story he have need of money. He has spent much on fine house and wishes marry beautiful woman who desires rich husband.' That was not as painful to say as he had imagined it would be.

Fanny regarded him with a thoughtful eye. 'Is it not strange that this man, Scallion, should both rob and attack you and be involved with this matter of Westminster Bridge? Is this not a coincidence truly amazing?'

'My dear Signorina Fanny, you have found heart of matter!' Canaletto jumped up and started to walk around the studio, its corners dim and shadowed, the rushlights throwing patterns on the walls as they flared and wavered.

'Somehow I am threat. It not just my money someone want. Man who employ Scallion to kill Fairbrass use him also to remove me. Except the brave Signorina Fanny prevent him.'

'I am glad he is dead,' Fanny said vehemently.

'But today I am nearly dead again!' Canaletto told how the statue had fallen off the roof and almost crushed him out of existence.

Fanny was appalled. 'Signor, you must have a care!' She looked around the dim corners of the studio as though some assassin could even now be lurking there.

'Perhaps accident, maybe? The statues not fixed.'

'You think it was that?' she asked hopefully.

Canaletto shook his head. 'No wind, nothing to make statue fall. No, it must have been a push.' He used his hands to demonstrate. 'I run up to roof but too late.' As he explained about the earl's party he restlessly roamed around the studio, fingering odd items of equipment. Finally he brought the slab of porphyry from the back of the table to the front together with the glass pestle.

'So you think whoever pushed over the statue joined the earl's party as it came on to the roof?'

Canaletto nodded. 'Maybe. Or maybe he escape down other stairway.' He reached for a bag of pigment. 'You know, Mistress Lucy's brother was at the palazzo?'

Fanny stared. 'You mean Alderman Fowler? But surely he would not have received an invitation?'

'This is what I think. Is very odd, no?' He untied the bag.

'Yes, very odd. Do you think *he* could have pushed the statue on to you?'

'I cannot think of reason but he tell me he visit Venice, perhaps something happen there, something I know but don't understand at moment.' Canaletto gave up the puzzle for the moment. 'Come, I show you grinding of colours.'

Fanny stood beside him and he gave her the glass pestle with its flat bottom. He placed a piece of pigment on the porphyry slab. 'See, press down, it breaks. More press and bits get finer and finer.'

'Just like grinding almonds!' Fanny pressed with determination.

'Must be much, much more fine than almonds.' Canaletto sat on his stool. 'Now I tell you most interesting story. Perhaps it explain why I am threat.' Watching Fanny grind the pigment, Canaletto told her the tale of the last time Joseph Smith had called for his help and the investigation he had carried out on behalf of a young English aristocrat in Venice.

As he spoke, Fanny's grinding grew slower and slower and an expression of horror spread over her face.

'So you see,' Canaletto finished, 'James Bennett would not want me to tell his employer how . . ., how bad he neglect his charge in Venice. So perhaps he wish me removed from life. Perhaps his employer plot together with this merchant over bridge and use Bennett to employ Scallion. But how he know when I arrive? Which boat?'

"'Tis very dreadful,' Fanny muttered into the pigment particles.

'And very strange; the young milord, he . . . he *dissolve* when he see me. Why? I rescue him, why not greet me? I no understand.' Canaletto had puzzled over this all the way back from Wedmore Park.

"'Tis unnatural!' Fanny stopped grinding and straightened her back. 'Chap like that isn't a real man, he's an animal!' Her small face wore an expression of disgust.

Canaletto surveyed her with interest. This was a new aspect of the matter. 'You think so?'

'Why, of course! Just like those men we saw in the pillory. Oh, that was a terrible end but people like that can't be allowed to live with normal folk.'

'You mean those men, that was their crime? That they had enjoyment of each other? Like the young milord and the catamites in Venice? Nothing else?' Canaletto asked in surprise.

"'Tis a crime, signor. A black, black crime.'

He regarded her with interest. 'Not so in Italy.'

'Well, it is in England.' Fanny began again to grind the pigment, jerky movements stressing her words. "'Tis against the law! Law of the land and law of nature.'

Strange! In Italy such things were accepted as a fact of life. But here it was obviously otherwise. This little Fanny was intelligent, had some education and a mind of her own. Yet here she was repeating bigotry like an automaton.

If Fanny with her intelligence and quick wit felt this way, no wonder the crowd had been so vicious. 'So the young milord could end up on the pillory,' he said slowly.

Fanny paused in her work. 'Not him! Aristocracy don't get pilloried like commoners.' She wiped her brow with the back of her hand and left a smear of colour. 'They have friends in high places. Aristocracy always manages to avoid the punishments of lesser folk.'

Was this so? Or was Miss Fanny merely reiterating a prejudice of her class?

It was, though, a possibility. Certainly Canaletto knew that in Venice the tight, closed network of top families whose names were in the Golden Book knew how to protect their members.

Could English milords bribe the judiciary, bring pressure on members of the government to bend justice?

There was much to think about here. Canaletto got up, his joints moving stiffly. 'I go to bed,' he said. 'You too. Tomorrow we start early. Prepare oil for mixing with pigment.' He inspected the results of Fanny's work. 'No grind anymore without oil. Then much, much grinding.'

Fanny gave a little groan. 'It takes so long,' she complained.

'Must be right,' Canaletto insisted. 'Pigment must melt into medium.'

Fanny yawned. 'Well, then, tomorrow I do it till it's so fine it will float through silk.'

'Good,' approved Canaletto. And tomorrow he would pursue several matters that had little to do with painting.

Chapter Forty-Two

Canaletto woke next morning with a clear plan of action. While Fanny prepared breakfast, cold meat, bread and ale, he wrote a letter in Italian to James Bennett.

'Please take this to Brecon House,' he said to Fanny after he'd sealed it. 'You must see Signor Bennett in person, see him read this. He must tell you he will meet me as I request. You must say it is most important. You will do this?'

Fanny beamed at him. 'Of course, signor.'

'Then you will buy linseed oil, also walnut. I will show you how to heat and refine so we can mix with pigment.'

Fanny's expression grew glum. 'Yes, signor.'

'Be happy! Soon I show you how we prepare canvas.'

'Sounds a most delightful occupation.' Fanny sighed as she cleared away the plates.

'All success is based on careful preparation,' Canaletto said sternly. 'No use to think you can rise in world without much hard work.'

'What a sermonizer you are!' Fanny gave him a wide smile as she tidied everything away.

Canaletto began to think that this apprenticeship might work exceedingly well.

'Take the letter round to Brecon House,' were his last

words to her as he took up his workbox and sketchbook and left for the river.

The sky was once again overcast though the weather was fine, the temperature beginning to rise as Canaletto walked towards Westminster Bridge. For the first time he began to wonder how he could live in a place which so seldom allowed the sun to shine.

Then he forgot such matters as he tried to find a good spot at the Westminster end of the bridge for a sketch of the city skyline. He knew that this view was not as successful as the one from the other end but the success of finished paintings depended on marrying together features from different viewpoints so that a wholly satisfactory artistic effect was gained. Only the careful observer of the finished painting noted the liberties taken, the rest received the impression of a scene taken from life.

Canaletto was disappointed to find that it was not possible to get a view of the city from the actual bridge. The balustrade which had already been fixed at this end was so high it wasn't possible to see over and the corbels were so close together you couldn't see through the gaps. He had to station himself at the top of the stairs leading down to the causeway. He told himself he must find a light chair to take around with him for sketching. Perhaps Daniel would make him one. He leant his back against the foundation of the bridge and found this gave him a reasonable support as he worked.

At first he paused every now and then in his work to see if James Bennett approached. As time passed, he began to grow anxious. Perhaps the secretary had told Fanny he would not come. Almost Canaletto regretted not going himself to Brecon House. But after yesterday's events, he could not risk it.

Then, gradually, the lure of his work took hold and he became lost in sketching buildings, towers and steeples and noting the colours and nature of construction materials. By the time James Bennett finally arrived, he had almost finished.

'Signor,' Bennett said courteously.

'Ah,' Canaletto let out a sigh of relief as he saw the young man, dressed in a suit of dark cloth similar to the one he had been wearing the previous day but not so fine. 'You have come.' He put down his pen, stoppered his bottle and held his sketchbook open to allow the ink to dry.

'I was intrigued,' James said in Italian. He stood on the step above Canaletto and his height loomed over the painter. There was an air of suppressed excitement about him. 'However, I have little time so, pray, let us get down to business. It is, I assume, the matter of Viscount Purbeck? I have to tell you, signor, hardly a day passes but I do not blame myself for what happened to him. If I had taken the same care of him in Venice that I had in other cities, he would have been in no danger. But I fear I was,' he paused for a moment then added, 'distracted. For that I shall never forgive myself.'

Canaletto closed his sketchbook and rested it on his workbox. He felt in the skirt pocket of his work-a-day coat for a linen-wrapped packet. In it was a thick chunk of cheese and a piece of bread. 'You will join me, perhaps?' He offered the little repast to James.

'I thank you but I have no need for sustenance.' James stuck both hands in the pockets of his breeches and jingled some change.

'It is indeed the matter of your charge.' Canaletto bit into the sharp cheese, not to be compared with parmesan but by no means to be despised. 'Let us be frank, signor. When we found the young milord in that palazzo it was clear, was it not, that he experienced very great pleasure?'

James Bennett said nothing but his eyes were very wary.

'He had been cunningly seduced by a most clever person. Kept in, what shall we say, *a capriccio*? A fantasy, a land he is very happy to remain in without thought for your concern or anything else. Meanwhile demands are being made for a large sum of money for his safe return.' Canaletto used his teeth to tug free a piece of the bread. 'In Italy if men find pleasure with each other, we do not condemn them. Men are beautiful, women are beautiful, some men find pleasure in one, some the other and some in both.' He ate the bread then another chunk of cheese. James Bennett still said nothing. 'But here in England, I understand things are different. So now I wish to know, when milord came back to England, what happened?'

The young secretary looked at the pinchbeck buckles on shoes that were dusty from the road. 'The marquess made him realize such practices were unacceptable and since he has returned to England his one idea has been to get married.' He gazed defiantly at Canaletto.

'So his father knows what happened in Venice?'

An uncomfortable flush rose in James's face. 'I acquainted him with the facts on our return,' he said stiffly.

'Including my part in the affair?'

James nodded. 'I wished him to send you a suitable reward.'

Canaletto remembered the money he had received. 'And then you became his secretary? When it might be thought you had been at best, perhaps, careless of the young milord you had in charge?' His tone was sardonic.

The flush deepened. 'Are you suggesting I black-mailed him?' James asked angrily, bunched hands pushing out his pockets.

How quick he was to jump to this conclusion! 'Gently, gently. If aristocrats in England are like those in Italy, I am sure the marquess knows how to remove an unwanted servant without such matters coming to light. But maybe renowned painter not quite so easy?'

The secretary quite obviously failed to follow what he was suggesting.

'Since I arrived in London, I am attacked, once and twice, and my fortune is took. I ask myself, who is it who do this?'

James stared belligerently at him, his face puzzled.

'You see, the marquess wishes his son to marry a very rich young girl, no?'

Comprehension began to dawn on James's face. 'And if you inform Mr More what you know about the vis-count, he will stop the marriage, is that what you are saying?'

Canaletto nodded. 'And maybe the young milord is arrested, put in the pillory? As I saw two young men not two days since, stoned to death.'

James burst into a relieved laughter. 'Signor, forget what you are suggesting. Aristocrats do not suffer the penalties of common men.' So, little Miss Fanny had been right! 'If word got out about Richard and his proclivities, the marquess would arrange for him to go abroad. There would be no prosecution.'

'But no marriage, hmm?'

'Mr More might be willing to continue with the match for the sake of allying his wealth with a noble family.'

'I think unlikely,' Canaletto said decisively. 'I have seen what the general citizen of this city thinks of such behaviour. It is called animal, disgusting.'

James winced.

'So I think the marquess would not want me to say what I know.'

A brief inclination of the head showed that James agreed with him, then he looked sharply at Canaletto. 'But you cannot think that the marquess was behind the attacks on you. He would never stoop to such conduct.'

'No?' Canaletto wrapped up the remains of his bread and cheese and replaced it in his pocket. He picked up his sketchbook and found the drawing of Scallion. 'Do you know this man?'

James Bennett took the book as though it might burn his fingers. He looked briefly at the sketch, 'Signor, such people are not part of my acquaintance,' he said disdainfully, then suddenly scanned the drawing more closely. Finally he looked up at Canaletto. 'I have seen him,' he said in a surprised voice, 'but not at Brecon House and never in the company of the marquess. He was waiting to see Balthasar More when I visited the house a little time ago.'

This took Canaletto by surprise. 'Signor More, the father of the viscount's intended?'

James nodded. 'He was with another man, a merchant type, biggish with heavy shoulders. The sort of

man who believes above all in his own self-importance.'
A brief smile of reminiscence crossed his face. 'I was
waiting in an ante-room to see Charlotte, Miss More,
when he and this man you ask about,' his hand waved
towards the sketch of Scallion, 'were shown in. Immediately Fowler – yes, that was his name, Alderman John
Fowler – started cursing the servant and insisting More
should see them immediately. Not a pleasant fellow.'

Canaletto stared at Bennett, his thoughts thrown into
confusion. 'Why were Alderman Fowler and this man,
Scallion, visiting Mr More?'

'I have no idea,' replied James. 'They said very little.
Is it important?'

'Possibly, possibly. Please, tell me anything that was
said, anything at all.'

James scowled in concentration. 'Stone, I think,
came into it. Yes, your chap – Scallion you called him?
– said something like, "It's the stone, you see." ' He
thought a little more while Canaletto tried to contain
his impatience.

'Then he said, "That's the key." ' Canaletto waited to
see if more would come and was rewarded by James
adding, 'Yes and that word "key" was repeated by Fowler
as they came out of the house later. I was preparing to
mount my horse and he said . . . now let me think
exactly what it was.' Again he paused and Canaletto
controlled an urgent need to grab the lad by the coat
and shake the words out of him.

'Scallion was whining something about knowing
how it would be and Fowler said, I'm sure he said,
"Leave Balthasar More to me. We have found the key to
the man, allow me to turn it." '

'The alderman to turn a key,' mused Canaletto,

trying to fit this with everything else into some sort of pattern that made sense.

'Then Scallion, a rogue if ever I saw one, said, "I need the money, I did the job and I've not been treated right." This was as I rode by and it was as though Fowler hushed the man, that he didn't want anything else said I might overhear.'

'Hmm,' murmured Canaletto. 'And you say you are certain you have never seen this fellow near the marquess nor any of his men?'

James Bennett shook his head vigorously.

Canaletto found he believed him. He turned his mind to another matter. 'Did you ever hear from your young milord who seduced him into the palazzo?'

James shook his head. 'He told me he received a message purporting to come from me, asking him to meet me there. When he arrived a young man took him by the hand and said I would come shortly. He took him into a richly furnished room where others were. They supplied him with wine and other, more potent, drinks, and offered him food, playing with him all the while. Richard says he had never seen any of them before but soon,' James Bennett coloured slightly, 'found he was being introduced to practices he found most pleasant. He said he lost all sense of time or place. All he wanted to do was stay there for ever.'

If only Canaletto had been allowed to question the lad immediately after they had found him, perhaps he could have extracted some useful information. But the young man had been whisked away, there had been no opportunity for questions.

'Is this marriage between Miss More and your viscount still in progress?'

James Bennett looked away and scanned the new road leading up to the bridge. On one side were a number of newly built and imposing houses. 'The marquess believes it is.'

Canaletto's attention was caught by the ambiguity of the answer.

'And after what happened on the roof yesterday, Miss More is still willing to proceed?'

James seemed to make up his mind about something. He looked straight at Canaletto. 'No,' he said baldly. 'She is not willing.'

'Ah,' Canaletto breathed softly. 'But Mr More has not indicated this to the marquess?'

James suddenly looked very young. 'Miss More had indicated it to me.'

'Ah, so!' A number of things fell into place for Canaletto.

'In fact . . . in fact, signor, we are to be married at five o'clock today, at a church in the Fleet. There you have no need for a licence. Signor, you would do us great honour if you would be a witness. I had thought to bring in two people from the street but how much better if you could be one of those performing this office.'

Canaletto was taken aback. James smiled at him engagingly.

Canaletto thought of the charming-looking girl he had met the previous day. Then he thought of the viscount as he'd last seen him, hysterical and collapsed at the foot of the staircase housing. Canaletto could only guess at the means used by the marquess to try and erase any deviant desires from the young man but, whatever they had been, they had produced a highly unstable personality. This secretary was intelligent, attractive and undoubtedly ambitious. The only thing he knew against him was the carelessness with which he had watched over the viscount in Venice and that could have provided a lesson he had profited from. With Mr More's backing he could perhaps go far. Wed to this young man, Miss More might not gain the entrée to society that marriage with the viscount would have given her but her chances of happiness must be greater.

Canaletto bowed, "Tis I who shall be honoured,' he said. 'Five o'clock?'

James nodded, took the sketchbook and drew a little map to show the painter how to find the church.

'May I bring my apprentice with me? She is a young girl and perhaps Miss More might welcome a female at the church?'

'Why, that sounds a splendid idea, she can be the second witness.' James now seemed anxious to be on his way. 'I will see you both at five. Now, if you will permit me, I will leave you, I have many tasks to perform before then.'

Canaletto watched James Bennett stride away, his mind turning over what the young man had told him. It changed many of his previous ideas.

Chapter Forty-Three

After a little while, Canaletto picked up his sketchbook and workbox and set off for the City, musing on various possibilities as he walked.

Once again he knocked for admittance at Alderman Fowler's door.

He was shown into the same office as before. The alderman sat looking preoccupied and out of temper, tapping at his desk with a quill pen.

He scowled as the painter was shown in and threw down the pen. 'Well, Mr Canaletto, back again?' He did not rise.

Canaletto sketched a courteous bow then took the unoffered chair in front of the desk, whisking back his coat skirts with as much ceremony as though they belonged to the velvet best he had worn the previous day. He leant his arm along the desk and brought his face confidentially close to the alderman's. 'I come on important mission.'

An expression of interest mixed with a certain apprehension spread over the alderman's face.

'I see the so beautiful earrings you bring to Milord of Brecon yesterday, in Wimbledon, and I think perhaps my friend, Signor Fowler, can provide me with some equally fine pearls.'

Avarice overtook the other expressions. 'Were they not the finest you have ever seen? So perfectly matched. I had the first ten year ago, took me until the end of last to find a pair for it.'

That removed the last question from Canaletto's mind. Not that there had been much doubt; after all, what other reason could have brought the alderman to Wedmore Park?

'It was diverting occasion, was it not?' Canaletto went on conversationally. 'I am so interested to see Mr More there with his so beautiful daughter. I remember, you said last time we meet, you friend of Mr More!' He paused.

The reaction was everything he had hoped. 'The devil take More! I should have known him for what he was when he so nearly sold me those barques in Italy with sweet accounts of their rich merchandise. No hint of the French waiting to pounce on them the moment they sailed. If I hadn't heard elsewhere of the perils, I could have lost a large sum of money. He swore he'd meant no harm and, fool that I was, I believed him. Well, when a man has his reputation, you do. But yesterday ... yesterday—' He seemed unable to continue.

'Yesterday you saw him there?' prompted Canaletto.

Fowler rose in agitation. 'To think in what high esteem I have held that man these many years,' he muttered. 'All I wanted was an introduction to the earl. Chance to see more of the house than that dark room they put me in like any tradesman. Didn't even meet the marquess, had to hand the earrings to his secretary for no more than ten per cent down of their value. The rest to follow. When, is what I ask.'

Fowler pulled hard at an ear lobe. 'So there I was, so near to all that high life and yet so far. I thought I had no choice but to return to the City. Then I saw More.' He flung himself back in his chair. 'It would not have hurt him to have introduced me to his host. Instead he pushes me aside as though I am some worm not worthy of notice. When I . . . when I . .' He ground to a stop.

'When you have the means to ruin him?' suggested Canaletto in a silken voice.

Abruptly Fowler sat up and gave him a straight look. 'What mean you?'

Canaletto got out the sketchbook once again and placed his drawing of Scallion in front of the alderman. ''Tis a matter of the stone for Westminster Bridge, no?'

Fowler's eyes looked scared. 'What mean you?' he blustered. 'You can know nothing of this matter.'

'No?' Canaletto enquired softly. 'Mr More has interests in a quarry in the south, Portland, is that not the name? It supplies stone for Westminster Bridge. The bridge Mr More believes will bring disaster to the city.' He paused.

John Fowler gnawed his lip and said nothing.

'What better than to sell his stone but make certain delivery is delayed? The bridge perchance will fail through lack of capital as government perhaps refuses finance.'

Still the man behind the desk said nothing.

'Government wishes investigate delay. Sends agent to quarry. Mr More learn something. Is worried. Perhaps he ask you if you know man can help?'

The alderman began to look worried himself.

'Perhaps he knows you acquainted with rogues and villains.'

The look of worry deepened.

'You suggest Jack Scallion. He travels to quarry.' Canaletto made a dramatic pause. 'He kill government man!' he ended with a flourish.

'You have no proof of that!'

'Scarface Nell, old friend to you and Scallion both, she have proof,' Canaletto lied.

For a moment Fowler held out, then gradually the belligerence faded from his face and his body sagged, defeated, in his chair.

'Bastard, that's what he is, a bastard.'

It wasn't clear whether he meant Scallion or Balthasar More. Canaletto waited.

'We ran into Scallion in Venice. He tried to pick More's pocket. I caught him, recognized him, talked More out of going to the authorities. Jack said he'd gone for a sailor, been paid off there. Decided to see what Venice could offer. Never lost for a way to turn a dishonest coin, was Jack.' Fowler paused, lost in the past for a moment. 'I gave him something for old time's sake and thought no more about it. Till he turned up again a few months ago, here. Tried to touch me for more. Then Balthasar came, all tentative like, full of scrupulosity, with a tale of some chicanery in the quarry amongst the men. Needed someone who could take them on on their own terms, he said. Jack seemed the obvious choice. Always quick with his wits he was.' Again he paused.

Canaletto waited.

Fowler came to a decision. 'Jack visited me some days ago. He said More had asked him to kill a man at the quarry who was breeding insubordination. Well, Jack's no fool, as I told you. Before doing the job, he got signed on as a quarry worker, a carrier of stone – he had no skills with the cutting or the shaping of the blocks. He quickly sorted out the man More had told him of. Cut above the others, he was, though pretending to be one of them.'

So much for Pitt's belief in the man's professionalism!

'By the time Jack got the man on his own one dark night and despatched him, he'd found out about some delay being made in the delivery of the stone for Westminster Bridge. Well, Jack returns to London, sees More and tells him the job's done. He's paid. But Jack doesn't believe it's enough. He feels he's owed more. Jack's canny, he reckons he knows something as could be valuable but that if he just goes to More and propositions him, like, he can expect a similar fate to that he gave the agent.'

'So he comes to you?'

'Exactly.' Fowler almost beamed. 'Well, I sees it all in a flash. And I sees it was no mistake More tried to palm those barques off on me in Venice that time. He's a tricky bastard and no mistake.'

'But you decide you can better him?'

'I has this property, just beside the bridge. Whole lot of wretched tenements were there. Cleared it and built thirteen substantial properties. Reckoned I'd make a killing, folk'd flock to buy such advantageous sites. But the bridge isn't opened and I've only let two of the houses at ridiculous rents. The ground has lain dead these five years, I'm charged ground rent and I've seen nothing back on all my investment.'

'Your investment, it is much?'

'Nigh on nine thousand pounds.'

An immense sum, Canaletto let out a long whistle. He looked at Fowler with respect. If he could stand the failure of such an outlay, he was indeed a warm man.

'So, you talk to your friend, the merchant Signor More, and suggest if he gives your old companion, Scallion, money and no longer delays stone for bridge, you will not say anything to anyone?' he suggested delicately.

Fowler beamed. 'Got it in one.'

'But More would none of it?'

Fowler scowled. 'Told me not to be impertinent, that I knew nothing of the matter and accused Jack of making up outrageous stories.'

'But you believe this Jack?'

'I know when he's lying. An' he weren't lying to me.'

'And you have spoken with your friend, Signor More, on this matter since?'

Another scowl. 'I mentioned something yesterday. It irked me so. To see him there, behaving like one of the gentry while I'm treated as a tradesman when I come bearing some of the finest pearls in the kingdom.' He brightened suddenly. 'But you say you have need of something similar? My dear Mr Canaletto, let me take you to my premises and show you what is available. Nothing quite to compare, of course, but I have a pair of pink pearls that would grace the loveliest ears the kingdom can produce.' He leered across the desk at the painter.

Canaletto held up a hand. 'Softly, my friend. There is other matter. Was it More who asked Jack Scallion to steal my fortune and my life?'

Fowler stared at him. 'That was the matter you were talking of last time you came, eh?'

Canaletto nodded. He kept his gaze firmly fixed on the other man's.

'Nay, sir, he never mentioned ought of that to me.' The alderman looked Canaletto steadily in the eye and the painter felt sure he was lying. How else would Scallion have known his victim had not died as he'd thought? Except through Mistress Lucy informing her brother that Canaletto had been brought, much against her desires, to her house.

The alderman suddenly clicked his fingers, 'Unless, unless it was the job he'd done for some nob for which, again, he reckoned he'd not been paid his due. He said it'd involved a deal of trouble for him and he was right angry at how he'd been treated. Said he'd claim his rights.' That rang true enough.

'And you know not who gave him such a commission?'

'Nay, he told me not. As I said, Jack was a canny old bugger, he kept things to his chest.' He thought for a moment. 'I'm surprised he told Scarface Nell about the Portland job. Didn't know he'd been seeing her.' A suspicious look entered his eyes. 'Where did you meet with her?'

'In prison,' Canaletto said cheerfully. 'She said she looked for visit from you.'

Chapter Forty-Four

Charlotte fastened the string of pearls her father had given her on her last birthday around her slim throat. Their quiet iridescence gleamed above her creamy skin.

She was dressed in soft gold, the petticoat embroidered with white flowers. It was her third-best gown. Her best, the blue, had been worn to Brecon House the day her marriage contract should have been signed, her second best, in cream, to Wedmore Park the previous day; she would never again be able to bring herself to wear either.

Charlotte took a deep breath and tried to quell her uneasiness.

She was an obedient child. Never in all her life had she gone against either parent's wishes. But never before had so much been at stake.

Love had stolen up on her. That first meeting in the market (she didn't count the time James had called at her house, that had been on behalf of the marquess and the viscount), she had been flattered by his listening to her as though she had as much intelligence and education as he. By their second meeting, a look from his eyes, grey but with a hint of warm hazel in their depths, was enough to send her heart fluttering in her breast. At their third meeting, when he put his hand underneath her elbow to assist her across the road, lightning ran through her arm. And yesterday, ah, yesterday!

She had followed the countess and the charming Mam'selle Montesqui as they helped the quivering viscount down the stairs, horror and distaste rising within her.

Charlotte had had no idea what had reduced him to this state but the very sight repulsed her even as she told herself her duty was at his side.

The viscount had been taken to a bedroom. There his father, his face contorted with anger, had dealt him a stinging blow that sent his head to one side, then given him another that brought it round again.

The viscount had grunted with pain and swayed on his feet. Mam'selle Montesqui had come up to Charlotte. 'Come, this is no place for us.'

Anne had taken her to another bedroom, sat her down in a chair, called for a servant and asked for brandy.

'You see how he needs someone like you,' she'd said. Charlotte sipped the brandy and felt its fire spread through her, quietening the nauseous stirring that had threatened to erupt.

Charlotte had stared at the beautiful woman, her fingers clutching the glass, then she'd drained it, shuddering as the liquid went down. The spirits had made her feel courageous enough to say, 'You surely cannot mean we still should marry?'

Anne had sat and taken Charlotte's hands in both of hers. 'My dear, he is young. It was a momentary disturbance, nothing more. What he needs is to escape from his father.'

'But the marquess wasn't on the roof when, when—'

She didn't know how to describe what had happened. It had been the disintegration of a personality. She shuddered.

'No,' Anne acknowledged quietly. 'But the roots must lie there, in that relationship. Once you have your own house, there will be no repetition, I am sure of that.'

Charlotte gazed into the lovely face so close to hers. 'You are so much older than I,' she said slowly. 'Are you really sure?'

Anne closed her eyes briefly. 'I have experience of the world. I am sure.'

The green eyes were so clear, their honesty so patent, Charlotte felt it a fault in herself she still doubted.

Then her father had knocked at the door to say they were to go home. It was a relief. Even more so to discover that her father had insisted James Bennett accompany them.

It was James who handed Charlotte into the carriage. 'All will be well,' he'd whispered in her ear. 'Trust me.'

Giddy with the effects of the brandy, his touch still tingling her skin, his voice echoing in her ear, she'd tucked herself into a corner of the carriage, neatly crossing her feet in their little satin slippers.

'What happened?' Mr More demanded as the coach drove away from the house.

'The viscount had a shock,' James said calmly. 'He was reminded of a traumatic episode in his past.'

Charlotte listened as he told her father that during the viscount's visit to Venice, he had been kidnapped. The painter, Signor Canaletto, had been instrumental in effecting his release and the shock of seeing him on the roof, so suddenly, had brought everything back to Richard.

'It had been an experience like no other,' James had said, his eyes earnestly gazing into her father's.

Charlotte had studied his profile and remembered their meeting the previous day, another 'accidental' encounter at Smithfield market. Molly had left them talking while she did the shopping without Charlotte's supervision.

Charlotte and James had found a quiet spot by a collection of small box trees trimmed into conical shapes standing proud in their pots. Suddenly he had taken her hands and held them close to his chest. 'I wish, oh I wish,' he'd said, his voice breaking. Then he had clutched her hands more fiercely. 'I wish I had a fortune.'

She had known immediately what he meant. She'd closed her eyes against an incredibly splendid vision of a life spent with this man. 'Honour means more to me than fortune or high places,' she had murmured. 'But honour means you must not say such things.' She'd looked at him and known love was there, plain in her eyes for him to see. And, sick at heart, she'd forced herself to turn away and find Molly.

When the coach reached Cheapside, James assisted her down on to the street. Again his hand had briefly squeezed her elbow and he'd breathed into her ear, 'Send word if I can help.'

Charlotte had not meant to tell her mother what had happened but Mrs More pressed to know what had caused her to look so upset and finally she had blurted out the story. Her father had come in just as she was ending. 'Balthasar,' her mother had said, stretching out a hand, 'we cannot let our darling child go to such a household.'

'The marriage has been arranged,' he had said curtly. 'Nothing has changed.' His face had worn the closed look his womenfolk dreaded.

Charlotte had cried on her mother's shoulder. Mrs More had stroked her hair and told her she must trust her father, but she looked drained and ill.

Charlotte went to her room and found pen and paper. 'I cannot go through with this matter,' she wrote. 'Help me. I will do whatever you suggest.' She read the brief note then added, 'My heart and future happiness are in your hands.' Then she had signed, sanded and sealed the short missive.

Molly had willingly taken it.

She had returned with an answer that had sent Charlotte ecstatically to bed, her heart singing with delight.

Now she checked her appearance in the long, cheval mirror, settled a fetching lawn cap trimmed with gold ribbons upon her blonde curls and added a fine lace scarf over, tucking the ends into her muslin fichu, anchoring them between her breasts. Then she caught up a long cloak, her reticule and a pair of gloves. She was ready.

She gave her room a last look. The note she'd written to her mother was propped up on her writing desk. She had taken her leave of both her parents after dinner, pleading exhaustion after the events of the previous day.

No one should disturb her until morning, when the note would be discovered. In it she had promised that James and herself would call on the morrow hoping for forgiveness. 'James is a fine man,' she had written, 'and your daughter is sublimely happy.'

Molly let her out of the servants' entrance. She had arranged a carriage to take Charlotte to the church. 'Never fear, 'tis a splendid fellow you go to,' she said, squeezing Charlotte's hand.

It was exactly what Charlotte needed to still the butterflies of panic fluttering in her stomach. And when she saw James standing so tall and handsome in his black silk suit outside the church, the last of her tremors vanished.

He helped her down, delight written all over his face. 'You are early, my darling!'

'I couldn't wait and Molly had the cab all ready,' she whispered to him.

'Here are Signor Canaletto and Miss Rooker, who will be witness to our marriage,' James said, drawing her hand through his arm.

Miss Rooker came forward and offered Charlotte a bunch of sweet spring flowers, another hung from her arm. 'I wish you every happiness, Miss More,' she said, enormous hazel eyes gazing at Charlotte out of a small face. 'I am very happy to attend upon you.' She wore a simple sprigged cotton dress, a spotless mob cap upon her copper curls.

'And I to be witness,' said the dapper little Italian painter, giving her a graceful bow. He wore the same splendid velvet coat he'd worn at Wedmore Park and carried an elegant cane. Charlotte gazed around the steps but no one else waited outside the church.

'Come, my darling, the priest awaits us.' James tried to lead her into the church.

Charlotte hung back, 'I expect someone else.'

'Who have you told?' James's voice was sharp and she looked at him in hurt surprise. 'I'm sorry my darling,' he moderated his voice, 'but we said everything was to be secret.'

'You have told Signor Canal and Miss Rooker,' she pointed out. 'I have only told Mam'selle Montesqui.'

'What?'

'Don't look at me like that!' she shrank back, frightened. 'Anne called this morning. She was so sympathetic. She said she knew I was worried about an engagement to the viscount and she wanted me to know that whatever I decided she would support my decision. So, well, I told her we were to be married this afternoon and asked her if she could attend. I did not know then that Miss Rooker was to be here. I thought I would be without a female attendant. She said she was honoured and would if she could.'

'The devil take it, what have you done!' groaned James.

Charlotte was bewildered and shocked by his attitude. Anne had been so charming, so sympathetic, it had seemed so natural to ask her. But now she looked at the panic on James's face and the consternation on Signor Canal's and received an idea of what she might have done.

'Come,' she pulled at James's hand. 'Let the priest marry us immediately.'

They hurried into the gloom of the church, the day obscured by dusty windows so that the only light came from a few candles.

The priest in his white surplice waited in front of the altar, a prayer book in his hands, his wig full, glasses on his nose.

'Sir, you must perform the ceremony with all haste,' James gasped as he pulled Charlotte up the aisle.

She undid her cloak, took off the lace scarf and gave both to Miss Rooker.

The priest looked round, saw all were ready and began the service.

As the well-known words echoed through the church, Charlotte felt so nervous she knew she would not be able to utter her responses.

At the words, 'Charlotte Mary Abigail More, wilt thou take this man to be thy lawful wedded husband?' she heard someone try the handle of the church. It was locked.

'I do,' she whispered.

There was a loud knocking on the door.

The priest faltered.

Charlotte's heart was in her mouth.

'Continue,' demanded James.

'Do you, James Edward Thomas Bennett, take this woman to be your lawful wedded wife, for richer for poorer, in sickness and in health, till death do you part?'

'I do,' said James in a strong voice that gave Charlotte heart.

The knocking grew ever more thunderous.

Once again the priest paused in the service. Loud shouts could now be heard outside. 'Continue,' demanded James again, his voice full and authoritative. 'Only if the service is completed will I pay.'

Quickly the priest gabbled through the rest of the responses. Charlotte spoke hers as quickly as she could. Every blow that hammered on the door seemed to go through her. The shouting grew louder and the door began to shake with the strength of the blows. Any moment now it would give way.

The priest said, 'I now pronounce you man and wife.' James put his arm around Charlotte. 'Is there another way out?' he asked the priest. But a plank in the door shattered, a hand insinuated itself inside the gap and turned the key. The broken door opened.

Charlotte shrank against James as the church seemed to fill with people.

Chapter Forty-Five

It had been Canaletto who had locked the door to the church.

He had no doubt but that Anne Montesqui would tell the marquess of the proposed marriage between James and Charlotte. After all, her future depended on the viscount marrying Miss More.

The party that surged into the church was led by the marquess. He was dressed in riding clothes, a crop carried in his hand. But he had strapped on a sword. Beside him was Patrick Granville, also in riding clothes and also with a sword. The two big men surged towards the altar, their anger throbbing on the air.

'Stop the service!' thundered the marquess.

Behind them came Anne Montesqui. She went to Charlotte. 'Forgive me, my dear,' she said, putting her hand on the girl's arm. 'I have betrayed your secret but it is indeed for your own good.'

Charlotte shrank back against James.

Bringing up the rear came Balthasar More accompanied by two burly men.

'That's the man, arrest him!' he shouted and pointed at James.

'Father!' screamed Charlotte, her hands flying to her cheeks.

'Thought I'd not come to your room, did you?' Balthasar More advanced towards his daughter, his feet ringing heavy on the stone floor, his eyes narrowed in rage. 'You thought to destroy me. Well, this marriage shall never take place, do you hear me?'

''Tis too late,' said the priest, his voice rising calmly and seemingly without effort above the hubbub. 'These two people,' he moved behind James and Charlotte and, standing on the altar steps, placed a hand on a shoulder of each. 'These two are now joined together in the sight of God and no man can put them asunder.'

'By God, then I'll kill him!' The marquess raised his crop and brought it crashing down on James's neck.

Charlotte screamed as James sank to the ground. The constables ranged themselves either side of the marquess and held his arms. 'Now, sir, you can't do that,' said the burlier of the two.

'God rot you in hell,' raged the marquess, attempting to free himself. 'I command you let me go.'

But the constables continued to hold his arms.

'This is your fault,' Balthasar More stood in front of the demented peer. 'If you had had better control of your son, my daughter would never have taken this step.' He paused and looked the marquess in the eye. It was a long, level gaze and whilst it held something in the merchant's face underwent a change, implacability softening into something like resignation. 'Well, perhaps this is for the best.'

The marquess's eyes narrowed. 'You'll pay me her bride price.'

Balthasar drew back, his shoulders straight under his heavy wool coat, its scarlet trimmed with an abundance of gold braid. 'You and your unholy son can go to hell before I'll do that,' he said slowly and clearly.

The marquess's eyes burned more strongly than before. 'You'll regret not doing so when I lay information before the government over the way you have held back stone for the bridge.'

'You cannot blackmail me any longer. I know too much now about your little tricks.' The merchant spoke with venomous vehemence. 'Bribing contractors into providing substandard materials so the bridge will need rebuilding. You think then you'll get it resited and your properties will rise in value. You may be a peer of the realm,' he looked coldly at the marquess, 'but you're a booby.'

The marquess struggled between the two constables who still held his arms.

Patrick Granville stepped between the two men. 'Come, come, sirs! Control yourselves. Let not this unfortunate occurrence destroy all our fortunes.' His voice was easy and authoritative. Anne came and stood beside him. She clutched at his arm, her face lined with worry, her eyes panic-stricken.

Charlotte knelt over her husband, frantically calling his name and rubbing his hands.

Fanny knelt on James's other side, removed his wig, unfastened his cravat and opened his shirt, then called to the priest to bring water.

For Canaletto everything had fallen into place and he was possessed by an anger as deep as that of the marquess or the merchant.

He stepped forward.

'It is time I tell,' he heard his voice with its Italian

accent ring through the church with slight astonishment. This was not his usual style.

'It is time I tell,' he repeated, 'that Mr Pitt, Paymaster General, ask me to discover cause of delays to bridge. The bridge so many wish me to paint,' he added, unable to resist the claim.

He had their attention now, indeed. He hoped desperately that his English would not let him down.

'I have evidence that Mr More hired a rogue to despatch a government agent. Agent discover his plans to delay the bridge, to delay it so much it must be abandoned. Now milord, the Marquess of Brecon, confirms he connived' – Canaletto was proud of that word, dredged up from heaven knew where – 'connived in this plotting, desperate to repair his fortunes.' He was in fine flow now, the words that so often eluded him coming freely. 'Further, he persuaded Mr More to replenish his coffers by giving a fortune with his daughter in marriage to the Viscount Purbeck.'

Canaletto now came to the really difficult bit. He gazed around the company, his grey eyes meeting each of theirs in turn. 'When I come to London, a villain attacks me, not once, twice. Twice I was saved by Signorina Rooker,' he turned and indicated a pink-cheeked Fanny, now bathing James's forehead. 'A third time might have followed but for her. For this she came to prison. I, Antonio Canal, arrange for her to be free!' He felt his chest swell with satisfaction as he said the words. It was one of the few actions in his life he could feel totally proud of. 'But she cannot save my fortune. It goes, pouf!' he snapped his fingers in the air, feeling the weight of the loss suddenly fall away as he spoke. 'First I think this Jack Scallion a – how you say – man on the make? A man who take opportunity. Then I find he is hired as rogue by others. He is the one, that man,' Canaletto pointed a dramatic finger at Balthasar More and Charlotte gasped and clutched at her husband's hand. James groaned and stirred. 'That man,' he repeated, 'hired Scallion to kill the agent of Mr Pitt. Perhaps, think I, Mr More also want to kill me. He was in Venice with Alderman Fowler and nearly perpetrate crime on him. Could he perhaps think that I, who discovered many crimes against citizens of England, that I had discovered that?'

Balthasar More looked uneasily around the church.

'Such a peccadillo, even if I had known, what matter would it be?' Canaletto waved a hand grandly in the air. 'But at that time there had been a matter more serious. The holding of a young milord to ransom that I thwarted.' It was another word that gave him satisfaction and he repeated that one too. 'Thwarted. It was a grave matter and if the truth were to be told of it in England a noble family would be disgraced.' He looked directly at the marquess. 'You had every reason to want I should not be at liberty to tell what I know.'

A look of disdain coloured the marquess's ruddy face. The constables had released his arms but remained standing beside him. 'You place too high a value on your knowledge, signor. Who would believe a mere painter of views against the word of an English aristocrat?'

Canaletto let out a hiss. 'I am citizen of Venice, my standing is not much less than yours.' He controlled himself with an effort.

Then he was distracted for Charlotte gave a small cry as James opened his eyes and flung herself on his chest.

Fanny gently moved her away and helped James to sit.

The others in the church kept all their attention on Canaletto.

The painter decided Miss Fanny could be left to see to James Bennett and continued.

'But there is one matter you, milord, and you, Signor More, do not know. That I bring to England my fortune. A fortune I gather over many years during which my paintings command the highest prices.' Again he let his pride show through his voice. 'Who knows this?' He gave another dramatic pause, then swung round. 'You know,' he said to Anne Montesqui.

Her face paled visibly, she clasped her hands together and brought them to her mouth but said nothing.

'You I told that if I came to England, I would bring money with me to invest in markets safer than the continent. To increase against my old age.' He looked at her sorrowfully. 'I thought maybe we spend it together.' He could bring himself to say this now. His anger against her had finally evaporated.

'You!' she gave a high, unsteady laugh. 'You were no more than an amusement, Tonio.'

'Anne?' The marquess's voice was that of an enraged bull. 'You knew this fellow?'

She had herself under control again. 'It was nothing, Alexander.' She smiled at him as only she could. 'You are my great love.'

He would have been at her but for the constables that grabbed his arms again. 'You whore! You kept me at arm's length, made me beg for your favours, forced me to offer you marriage, and all the time you had enjoyed yourself with this, this Italian worm!'

'Not only him, my lord.' James staggered to his feet. 'I was another poor dupe.'

Charlotte moaned. 'No!' she cried and shrank from him.

He was pale but steady. ''Twas youthful folly,' he said to her. 'If I had only met you before, I would never have fallen under the charms of this witch.' He looked daggers at the still, silent figure of Anne.

'She has the art,' agreed Canaletto. The knowledge he had shared her favours with the Englishman raised no bitterness in him. Her perfidy had destroyed all his feelings for her. He was left with nothing but an empty ache.

'It was when I talked and laughed with you,' James kept his eyes on Charlotte, 'that I knew what true love was.' He looked around the company. 'You are all ruled by greed,' he said. 'Enough is never enough. You scrabble and plot for more, you sacrifice the innocent to your ambitions. I want no more of it. Charlotte and I will find a better way.' He reached for her hand. 'I was always looking for a bridge to take me from my lowly state to one much higher. I was as venal as they. But if I have you, I do not need riches or position. I shall not ask your father for help, we will make our way ourselves.'

'Darling James,' Charlotte breathed and flung herself into his arms. 'I trust you with my life.'

'Damn me, the boy has spirit,' muttered Balthasar More. 'I'll persuade him to join me yet.'

'If you have a business left after Mr Pitt has finished with you,' said Canaletto dryly.

'Oh, as to that, there are accommodations that can be made,' the merchant said suavely. 'A fine here, a contribution there, undertakings to seal it all.'

'And the death of Fairbrass?'

''Twas none of my seeking. I never talked to Scallion. The marquess here,' his disdainful eyes flicked their gaze over the aristocrat, 'suggested his friend Granville could act as messenger between Scallion and myself. The marquess planned to marry Granville's sister, had taken him into his confidence. I merely instructed Granville to arrange that Scallion distract the agent's attention.' A short pause while his gaze locked with Canaletto's. 'None can prove otherwise.'

'It's the truth,' said Patrick Granville, his gaze steady. 'If the rogue killed the man, it was none of our doing.'

They would of course all hang together or they'd hang separately. And More would bribe Fowler. There would be no proof. Frustration filled Canaletto.

Fanny suddenly spoke. 'You hired Scallion to kill Signor Canal?' she demanded of Anne, her voice urgent. 'You stole his money?' She stood with hands on her hips, her head thrown back; she looked ready to tear the woman apart.

Eyes returned to the beautiful figure standing straight and proud in the centre of the church. 'Nay, I'm no murderess, nor yet thief,' her voice rang out.

'Liar,' Fanny said. She turned to Canaletto, 'Tell her she lies.'

'I said she was the only one I told I was bringing my fortune,' he said steadily. 'I believe she told someone else.'

'The marquess!' ejaculated Fanny, swinging round

to confront him. 'So he could have the money as well as protect his son.'

'Tell the marquess?' cried Canaletto. 'And risk him know she not innocent virgin as she said? I think not. No, it was brother she told.' With a swift, unexpected movement, he used his cane to flip Patrick Granville's wig from his close-cropped head. 'There, see, that mark!' Blazing at the nape of his neck was a small, strawberry-shaped birthmark. 'I saw that on man who escaped from palazzo, man who organize seduction and kidnapping of milord Purbeck.'

Chapter Forty-Six

Everyone's attention was now on Patrick Granville. He stood as still as his sister but his eyes frantically searched the church as if for an escape.

'You had many reasons to wish me dead when you hear I arrive London,' Canaletto said. 'I maybe risk marriage between your sister and the marquess. I maybe can identify you as man who arranged seduction and kidnapping of the viscount. And your sister tells you I come with money. From McSwiney you know the boat I arrive on. You arrange with this Scallion that you order to despatch government agent to kill me and steal my satchel. He manage to steal satchel but you mean with payment. So he decide must threaten you, no?'

Granville's lip curled. 'The man was grabbing at me like a mangy cur grabs at food from the table.'

'Did he suggest you meet on bridge? Or did you?'

'He would not have the imagination to fix such a rendezvous,' the Irishman said, with another curl of his lip.

'But you, you think this very clever, no? You hit nightwatchman on head so he no witness so hard you kill him. Then you kill Scallion too so he cannot talk, yes?'

376

The Irishman shrugged. No one in the church moved.

'You tell him he shall have money; drop coins on bridge before him in dark, no light but moon. While he try pick up payment, you raise sword and whoosh,' Canaletto brought down his cane in a vicious stroke through the air. 'You cut off head. Then you toss head over bridge, followed by body, no? You think no trace remains. You do not realize in dark that head in bucket.'

Granville bared his teeth in a smile that would have graced a skull. 'You talk well, signor. But none can prove what you say.'

'But all this nothing to what you do in Venice. There I think viscount not only victim for you. You use your sister to attract young aristos. Then perhaps not all seduced, perhaps some just robbed? Or blackmailed? I do not think you are too nice in your methods.'

'You corrupted my son?' whispered the marquess, his eyes bulging, every ounce of his concentration on Granville. Then, 'No!' he bellowed. With an inhuman effort he dragged his arms free of the constables' restraining grip and drew his sword. 'Have a care,' he swung the blade in a wicked circle. The constables quickly stepped back, expressions of alarm on their faces.

'This is a house of God!' cried the priest. Arms uplifted, he moved towards the marquess, then backed with unexpected speed as the sword slashed through the arm of his surplice. There was a general movement as the others took themselves out of the range of that lethal steel.

Holding the sword level, the marquess shrugged his free arm out of his sleeve, neatly threw his sword into the other hand and released his right arm as well. The riding jacket fell to the floor and was kicked out of the way. The whole process took no more than seconds and nobody dared make a move towards him. Then he extended a foot towards Anne. 'Remove my boot,' he ground out at her.

Moving like an automaton, she came forward, knelt and tugged at the leather. 'Alexander,' she pleaded, grappling with the boot, 'you can't do this.'

'Cease your whining, whore.' He placed his stockinged foot on the grave of a medieval knight and held out the other foot. 'Now this one.'

She bit her lip and obeyed.

He kicked the boots across the church floor, then aimed an even mightier kick at her. But Anne had seen his intention and wriggled out of range, writhing on the stone like some animal, then pulling herself up a pillar, sobbing with a quiet desperation.

The marquess drew himself up, 'Draw your sword, villain!' he made a feint towards Patrick.

The tall Irishman threw off his jacket, 'Why not?' he shouted recklessly. 'What have I to lose?' He held out a booted foot towards his sister. 'My turn now,' he said.

Her face white, tears streaming down her cheeks, Anne sank again to the floor and took hold of first one then the other boot. 'Don't, please, Patrick, don't. For my sake!' She clutched the footwear to her chest.

For a moment he looked down at her and his expression was tender. 'Where's your courage, dear heart?' he said. 'Victory will be mine.'

Then his face grew grim. He stepped towards the marquess and drew his weapon. The sword hissed against the scabbard.

Anne moaned, then, still clutching the boots, levered herself from the floor and sought the support of the pillar again, leaning against it, her eyes wild.

'*En garde!*' cried the marquess and immediately lunged towards Granville. He parried skilfully and gave ground.

Canaletto, his eyes now thoroughly acclimatized to the dim of the church's interior, had no difficulty in following the feint, thrust and parry of the two men that drew all eyes.

But as he watched, a movement in the depths of the church caught his attention for a brief moment. One of the constables was quietly letting himself out of the front door. Canaletto noted the fact and returned his attention to the duel taking place in the centre of the church.

The two men were well matched. The marquess was the heavier; impressive thigh muscles bulged against his breeches as he lunged forward, arm extended. And his skill was the greater, the attacks were all his, Granville could do little but parry, riposte and retreat, parry and retreat. But the Irishman was the more agile. Younger and leaner, he used superior speed to elude the other's blade while watching for his opportunity. Canaletto felt if he could parry for long enough, he must tire the other man out and then would come his chance.

Fanny moved close to Canaletto and he felt her small hand clutch his. His fingers closed round hers comfortingly. 'There is little to choose between them,' he murmured to her and he did not refer to their fencing skills.

'I do not wish blood to be spilled,' she said, moving still closer to his arm.

'I am afeared it will be.'

No sooner were the words out of his mouth, than Granville's blade in a sudden, flashing move so fast the eye could not follow, found the marquess's left arm. Blood spurted out, staining the white sleeve. The marquess leapt back, breathing hard, clutching his wound, his eyes never leaving his opponent. Granville crouched slightly, his blade held at the ready, a smile of pleasure twisting his mouth.

Charlotte buried her face in her husband's shoulder and James's arm came up to hold her tight. Her father took one step towards the pair, then remained where he was, but his eyes were on his daughter rather than the fight.

Anne had loosed her hold on Patrick's boots. Now she stood pressed against the pillar, her hands clasped together and held against her mouth, her eyes following every move.

Suddenly the marquess gave a roar and lunged forward, blade extended to the uttermost. Startled, Granville moved back. He managed to parry and retreat behind a pillar. The marquess gave another roar and rushed forward, around the pillar.

Granville retreated again, back into the centre of the church, stockinged feet moving easily on the stone floor, polished from years of use.

The priest was praying, a monotonous incantation. Balthasar More, his mouth slightly open, had his attention once again fixed on the marquess.

And now the older man was tiring. The blade no longer flashed with the same fire, the lunges came more slowly, the feet moved more sluggishly. Granville moved on to the attack. No longer did he parry and retreat but pushed forward, his blade moving in powerful lunges that pressed the marquess hard.

The candles flared and guttered in the draught from the slightly open door. And from outside Canaletto thought he heard whistles and a rush of feet. But Granville's attention never wavered from his opponent.

For a split second, the marquess's concentration faltered and he lowered his guard. With the speed of a wolf, Granville lunged forward. His sword was within a fraction of the marquess's throat when he slipped on the blood that had dripped from the other's wound. His blade swung wildly as he fought to keep his balance. The marquess gathered the last of his strength and drove his blade into the other man's heart.

For several seconds the Irishman stood, swaying, an expression of startled surprise on his face.

Then the marquess drew back, wrenching out the sword. Blood flowered on the Irishman's shirt, he swayed and fell.

With a scream that cut to the heart, Anne flung herself on her brother's body. Then she pulled his head on to her lap; his blood besmirched the satin of her gown. She pulled the fichu from her neck, wrapped it into a pad, pulled back the shirt and pressed the muslin against his breast. Her eyes frantically searched his face.

Patrick Granville's eyes opened and found his sister's. 'So, the adventure ends,' he murmured.

Anne gave a gulping sob and clutched him closer. 'You cannot leave me, you must not! I cannot manage without you!'

'You will, my darling,' his voice was no more than a breath on the air. Then it expired and another terrible cry rent the church as Anne bent over her brother's body.

'Come, lady, 'tis no use.' Fanny went and tried to detach her from the dead man.

Canaletto looked for the marquess.

The moment Granville had fallen, he must have reached for his boots. Now, his breath coming in sobbing gasps, he scooped up his coat. The flesh wound on his left arm was still bleeding as he held his sword steady in his right hand. Stealthily he backed towards the front door.

'Stop him!' Canaletto cried.

The remaining constable made a brave attempt to apprehend the man – only to receive a wound in the thigh. He fell back with a cry of outrage and the passage to the door was free.

Except, entering was the first constable, followed by the watch, pikes at the ready, whistles blowing.

The marquess fell back. But Canaletto had moved into position behind him; he gave a twist to the head of his cane and drew his sword.

As he placed the sword's point against the man's spine he shouted, 'My lord, all is over.'

Chapter Forty-Seven

Canaletto lifted the mounted and braced canvas on to his easel. 'Now we prepare,' he said to Fanny, rolling up his sleeves to reveal sinewy arms. He wore his round, soft velvet cap on his bald head, now freed from bandages, and the warmth of the day meant no jacket was necessary over the working breeches and shirt.

She moved towards the canvas holding a fat brush.

Oil had been gently heated for several hours until Canaletto pronounced it reduced enough, then mixed with the powdered pigment and the mixture ground again to a consistency that even the Italian admitted was fine enough.

'Now, Signorina Fanny, you may lay on the paint.' Canaletto stood aside, beaming. The ritual of preparing canvas was soothing. Care was needed but no creative skill.

Fanny dipped the brush in the strong red paint and, frowning in concentration, drew it across the canvas, stroking on the colour in even strokes. Her cotton dress was protected by a smock and she hadn't bothered with the mob cap she usually wore so that her copper curls danced in the light that streamed through the windows in the roof.

'Good, good, cover it all.' Canaletto told her, watching

the small hand that moved with increasing confidence. 'A thin layer. No drips, no smears.'

Fanny carefully started to brush the red across the canvas, the paint beginning to even out the variations in the weave.

'But, signor, the colour is so strong,' objected Fanny.

'For long time I cover with beige as undercoat but lately I often paint straight on this priming layer. It works well.'

Canaletto settled himself on a stool to monitor the progress of his apprentice. He felt like a runner at the end of a hard race that was won but at cost. Now he needed the calm of routine to enable him to gather up his forces again.

He sipped at a mug of ale. He was quite beginning to like this thin liquor. Later McSwiney was coming round. Pitt had suggested a name of someone likely to commission a painting of Westminster Bridge and McSwiney was approaching the man.

The paymaster general had been delighted with the successful result of Canaletto's investigation. His financial recognition meant that for the next six months Canaletto had his living expenses. But he needed more security and hoped fervently that the patron Pitt had suggested was not one of those who bargained hard or found it impossible to pay over the full price when the commission had been completed.

'How is this?' Fanny stood back from the blank canvas that now resembled a well-painted piece of wall.

Canaletto came over and scrutinized the finish, took the brush and carefully went over a couple of places where he could see the canvas was imperfectly covered.

Not by more than a pig's hair's breadth but enough to make a difference for Canaletto.

Fanny watched him with an anxious expression. For three days, ever since the marriage and fight in the Fleet church, she had been working hard at grinding pigments and mixing them with medium. Now, hanging from the trestle table were neat pigs' bladders full of paints ready for use.

'Is good,' he said judiciously and she gave a relieved grin.

Someone knocked at the door. When Fanny opened it, there was James Bennett, still wearing a sober suit with his usual neat, small wig, but under his arm he carried a large cocked hat which he placed, somewhat self-consciously, on the work table as though uncertain what else to do with it.

'The marquess has escaped!' he announced without greeting of any sort.

Fanny gasped. 'How did it happen? How could it happen?'

After being taken from the church, the marquess had been placed in gaol to await trial for the murder of Patrick Granville and investigation into the possible abuse of his position as a commissioner of Westminster Bridge.

'Bribery,' Canaletto suggested succinctly. He was not surprised.

'He has left the country with the viscount, it is thought to France.'

'To meet up with Mam'selle Montesqui?' Fanny asked.

Under cover of the arrest of the marquess, Anne

had placed a handkerchief over her dead brother's face and quietly escaped through the vestry door.

By the time her lodgings were applied to, she had left with her maid. Belongings were scattered everywhere, ribbons, gowns, caps, mantles, stockings, shoes, all permeated with that very special scent that provided an aura wherever she went.

Patrick Granville's room on the floor above had also been ransacked; letters, documents and bills lay scattered over bed, chair and desk, and clothes also. There was no sign of Canaletto's satchel. Cynically, he wondered how long his fortune would last in her hands.

James shrugged his shoulders, 'Meet with Anne? I doubt it. I know the marquess, his passion would not survive the knowledge of her true character. Nor is he one to forgive.'

'And your passion, sir?' Canaletto asked with a smile, offering a mug of ale.

'Ah, marriage!' James took the mug and gave a sheepish grin. 'It exceeds all expectations.'

Fanny busied herself with cleaning the brush she had been using, working the spirit down amongst the hairs to remove every trace of pigment. She glanced up from her work with a wide smile, 'And Mistress Bennett? I trust she also does well?'

James stretched out his arms, 'My Charlotte declares she is in seventh heaven. I hope I may keep her in this blissful state.'

'And your papa-in-law?' Canaletto enquired.

James became more sober. 'Ah, the worthy merchant! The man interests me more and more each day. He has apparently convinced Mr Pitt – not, I am sure, without the passing of considerable sums of money –

that all faults lay with the marquess and he will now work to ensure the bridge is completed in the shortest possible time. Meanwhile he appears quite reconciled to our marriage and declares I am to study law, at the same time assisting him in the administration of his business.'

'And his dreams of titled lineage for his grand-children?'

'He declares the aristocracy is rotten to the core and utters republican statements every hour,' grinned James. 'Now I must leave you, Charlotte wishes me to bespeak new clothes. She has expressed a wish to see me in colours,' he arose and twirled himself around. 'Soon we shall invite you to eat with us and then I shall be a peacock!' He picked up his hat, gave Fanny a low bow and departed.

'Well, there's a happy man,' said Fanny, carefully completing the cleaning of the brush with a clean piece of rag. She looked back at the canvas. 'What now, signor?'

'Canvas must dry then we prime again. Prepare my workbox. We will go down to the bridge and make more drawings. There is more angle I wish to capture before arranging my view.'

'But you have decided on the angle, have you not?' Fanny sounded anxious.

Canaletto smiled at her. He was beginning to feel very good about this painting. This was the exciting phase, when anything seemed possible. When putting together the elements of the view gave him a godlike feeling. Or perhaps that of a magician.

'Aye, the view will be through the wooden skeleton

of the Surrey arch.' He had already discussed this with Fanny.

'So that it frames London and the river,' she gave a small sigh of satisfaction. 'It will be a most notable picture, signor. But, please, can you explain why you find it necessary to take all these views. Surely the only one that counts is the one you see through the arch?'

'Signorina Fanny, it is like this investigation. We fit together details in a way slightly different, not as they appear immediately, so the view is – how can I say?—' Canaletto searched for an English word, 'assembled, perhaps that is it. Yes, the view is assembled. And when the public see it, they will say, yes, that is London, that is the Thames. Is it not beautiful? But what they see is chosen by me to provide that beauty. In real life, all is not quite so, so perfect.'

'Nothing was perfect about the way you were attacked, or the loss of your fortune. Nor how Mr Granville was killed in that fight,' Fanny declared roundly. She placed the cleaned brush with the others.

'No, indeed, that is so,' Canaletto acknowledged.

The door opened without knocking and there was McSwiney with a broad smile on his face. 'Me boy, we have the commission,' he announced.

Canaletto stood quite still. Until now he hadn't realized quite how much he had been depending on this.

'He's a prince! Prince Lobkowicz from Bohemia, here in London to buy horseflesh and wanting a memento of his visit.' McSwiney walked over to the canvas and surveyed its rich redness with as much care as if it bore a finished painting.

'Is good price?' Canaletto asked anxiously.

'Aye.' McSwiney said nothing else and Canaletto knew there was something about this commission he wasn't going to like.

'The thing of it is,' the Irishman swung round, 'he don't like the viewpoint.'

'Not like viewpoint?'

'Now, my dear fellow, it's only a small matter but all that scaffolding! And a bucket! Lobkowicz is quite adamant. He wants a broad view, like that of a bird, encompassing river, bridge and city, d'you see?'

Canaletto sat heavily on a stool.

Fanny watched him with concern. McSwiney put his hands in his pockets with a nonchalant air, turned back to the blank canvas and whistled under his breath.

'The palace,' said Canaletto slowly.

'Palace?' queried McSwiney, turning back to him.

'Pink-red, cornered with stone, many angles and battlements, upriver from bridge. Is on right of picture, river run from left across middle, into distance.' He got up, gesticulating with his hands towards the empty canvas. 'Big abbey on left bank, and barge, bright colour, in foreground, perhaps big white sail too.' Then he looked McSwiney sternly in the face. 'And bridge not finished. Lobkowicz to have unfinished bridge.'

McSwiney held his gaze for a moment. 'Quite, bridge unfinished, as now. I will tell him. But you will let me have a sketch to give the man? With description? Then I can obtain a deposit.'

Canaletto nodded. 'Tomorrow, or next day. But, Owen, another patron for view through bridge! Will be fine painting. Not,' he looked straight at him, 'not pot-boiler.'

'My dear fellow, a masterpiece I'm sure. And a

patron will be no problem. Now that we have your first commission, others will follow!'

Canaletto hoped so. For the moment, though, he was going to have to put on one side the view he wanted to paint. And would have to prime a very different sized canvas. 'Come, Fanny, we have much to do!' He rose with determination. 'Owen, you must go.' He pushed the large man towards the door and out of the studio, where both of them were almost knocked over by the young man that rushed in.

'Ned!' screamed Fanny in delight, her curls bobbing as she flung herself into his arms.

'I am a father!' he cried, giving her a hearty buss on the cheek. 'You are an aunt. How like you that?' He released her with a big grin. Then stuck out his hand towards Canaletto. 'Signor, I am happy to see you. I trust my sister keeps you comfortable?'

'Most comfortable, thank you. I congratulate you on your new parentage,' Canaletto said formally. 'And how is Mistress Lucy?'

'Oh, she's fine. Bore the child in two hours with complaints every minute and now declares herself exhausted.'

'And is it a boy or a girl?' Fanny went and got another mug and filled it with ale which she handed to her brother. At this rate, thought Canaletto, he would have to send her out for more any minute. And that jug had been intended to last the day. He was grateful McSwiney had taken himself off without staying for a formal goodbye.

'A boy! Such a handsome little fellow, Fanny, you have never seen a more beautiful baby! Lucy wants to call him John after her brother but I am insisting on Michael. He is to be as great an artist as Michelangelo! I will see to that.'

'You have imposed your will on Lucy?' Fanny said with a doubtful expression. 'I trust your present determination holds.'

'Oh yes,' said Ned. 'You may stake your life on that.' He took a deep draught of the ale. 'And I have renounced the gambling and the spirits. From now all I drink is this,' he waved the mug. 'And I engrave no more farradiddles, I am back to serious work. Fanny, you will be proud of me.' For a moment Canaletto could see the boy he must have been, fair hair flopping over his brow, eyes earnest and anxious for approval. How long would his present resolution last?

'I am truly pleased for you, Signor Ned,' he said pleasantly. 'Now, we send you back to wife and son, your sister and I have a task to do.'

Fanny snatched up the workbox and her sketchbook. 'Signor Canaletto is to show me topographical secrets.' She shrugged herself out of her smock.

Ned looked suitably impressed.

Canaletto picked up his sketchbook. He thought about going upstairs for his wig but discarded the idea, he was more comfortable in his cap.

Outside the sky, for once, was a clear blue. The wind had carried the smoke away from the countless chimneys and allowed the sun to shine down. It was a perfect day. Ahead of Canaletto little Fanny chattered to her brother, her face as she turned to him alive with joy. Her hand swung the workbox, missing passers-by more by luck than judgement.

Around them was all the hustle and bustle of this huge city. Ahead of them was the new bridge that would soon provide an artery out into the Surrey countryside. Growth would follow.

Postscript

Westminster Bridge was opened to the public towards the end of 1747. By the summer of 1748, it was clear that part of the bridge was sinking. By the autumn the bridge had had to be closed and two arches taken down. The bridge did not reopen until 1750. The sinking was never satisfactorily explained.